THE UNBELIEVER

ZACHARY J. KITCHEN

The Unbeliever
by Zachary J. Kitchen

Copyright © 2013 by Zachary J. Kitchen. All rights reserved. No part of this book may be reproduced or transmitted in any form or by any means, electronic or mechanical, or incorporated into any information retrieval system, electronic or mechanical, without the written permission of the copyright owner.

ISBN: 978-1484164679 (Paperback)

Cover design by Joel Ramnaraine
Interior layout and design by Joel Ramnaraine
Typeset in Adobe Garamond Pro

Printed in the United States of America

THE UNBELIEVER

Chapter One

Mad Max Bradley, United States Marine Corps, sweated through his fatigues in the one hundred and ten degree heat on the outskirts of Ramadi, Iraq. He kept still, his back plastered against the wall. Beside him, Lance Corporal "Tornado" Jones held the breaching ram and behind Jones—stacked single file with weapons at the ready—the six man entry team waited.

Sweat beaded on Bradley's forehead. He blinked at the salt sting. He raised a hand, and gave Jones a nod; Jones crashed the solid steel ram through the door. The Marines rushed through without hesitation, a single organism moving in practiced rhythm, each depending on the other.

If you are going to chase after people who make bombs for a living, you better bring a few friends along.

"Right clear!"

"Left clear!"

"Clear up front!"

Nobody on the first floor.

Like most of the homes in this part of town, the stairs to the second floor lay directly across from the front door. Max stared at the doorknob, bent and twisted out of shape.

This is when things really get fun.

Max paused. Smashing in a potentially hostile front door was a wild act of violence meant to surprise and overwhelm the foe. On the other hand, moving up the stairs was a slow, meticulous, and cautious affair. One man kneeled at the base of the stairs, his weapon pointing up its length. A second man climbed the stairs backwards, his weapon aimed on the landing in case some joker leaned over the railing to shoot the guys below.

Now that he was fully covered, number three guy in the stairs dance could walk forward, the regular way people climb the steps, except he kept his weapon straight ahead at the ready. Once he got to the top, all the angles for an ambush would be covered and the rest could pour up and take over the second floor ready to instantly strike out against any threat.

A single, metallic "ping" made all of Max's careful stair ascent plan moot. Falling in a gentle curve from the second story above, like a pop fly coming back to earth, was the olive drab sphere of a fragmentation grenade. Max noticed the almost graceful way the safety spoon detached itself from the side of the explosive and fluttered away.

We are live and in color, gents.

"Grenade!" he shouted as he instinctively threw himself back and flat on the floor, keeping his head as far away from the stairs as he could, with his feet towards the direction of the potential blast. His hands clutched his weapon tight. The shout was echoed by the other men in the room as they also dropped prone. There was a very loud *whump* and Max could feel the concussion against the soles of his boots. Fragments whistled over him to imbed with cracking and popping sounds into the walls all around the room.

Max looked up and caught a glimpse of motion in the gaps between the floorboards above. He pointed his carbine straight up and unloaded the thirty round magazine into the ceiling. The walls of these houses might be made of brick and concrete, but the floors of the upper stories usually were made only of two by fours lined up side by side. Two inches of wood don't do much to stop a rifle bullet, especially a high velocity, 5.56 millimeter NATO spec round. Since the grenade came from the floor above, anyone above was hostile and fair game.

The bursts tore holes in the boards above. Dust and splinters rained down. There was silence for a second, then a thump of metal on wood above him followed by another loud explosion. A hole opened in the ceiling. Shattered boards burst down followed by an unidentifiable chunk of raw meat.

"Looks like he dropped his grenade on himself, the dumbass!" Max shouted as he rolled into a kneeling position. "Tornado" Jones was crouched next to him, still grinning, his teeth shining bright through his grime covered face.

"Should we go up and see what's left, Major?"

"Sure Jones, "Max replied, "by the numbers. Don't get too cocky. Who knows how many more sumbitches are up there." He waved the team forward and pointed at the stairs. The marines took the stairs as they had done a hundred times before—by the numbers, with Max leading the way. The thirty-two year old Naval Academy graduate would never dream of sending his men to do something that he would not do himself. Besides, why let them have all the fun and excitement? The Colonel back at Battalion HQ was usually unhappy when one of his majors went looking for trouble more suited to the more junior officers, but as long as he was not given a direct order to not get his hands dirty, Max intended on doing as much in-close and personal work as he could. There would be time enough to fly a desk later.

At the top of the stairs were the remains of the unfortunate insurgent. It was hard to tell if any of Max's bullets had actually hit the man or if he just got startled and accidentally blew himself up. Jones picked up the AK-47 from where it lay next to the mangled body. The rest of the team cautiously checked the rest of the rooms on the floor. They were clear, but a few of the rooms were a mess: food left out, clothes tossed around, and ammunition pouches scattered across the floor. There had been more men, and that they had left in a hurry. Max reached down and picked up an open soda can. It was still cold. The dead guy's buddies had left recently. Very recently.

"Okay. We got more Hadjis around here somewhere," Max announced to his Marines as he held up the can.

The men began to cautiously inspect the place: checking under the beds, looking for any holes hidden by rugs. Max looked out of the central second floor balcony to check out the walled courtyard tucked in behind. Large, even by the standards of the Ramadi suburbs, extending a better part of the block, the courtyard was a rectangle formed by an eight feet high concrete wall that extended directly from the back of the building. Laundry was drying on wire lines strung across the center of the yard. The bright colors of the clothes swaying in a slight breeze gave the area a slightly festive air. A broken down and partially stripped car squatted to one side of the clothes line.

Could that actually be an old Impala?, thought Max. *Whether they speak Arabic or Creole, a redneck is a redneck the world over.* Then Max noticed that, rather than the usual gate at the opposite end of the yard, there was a squat outbuilding. *Was it a garage? A barn?*

Max waved his hand to get his squad's attention. Corporal Bobby Shea sidled up to him.

"Shea, see that little outhouse back there?"

"Yes sir."

"You think, maybe, our missing dudes are hiding out there? They must have hauled some ass when we started knocking on the door."

"I'd haul ass too if I saw us knocking on my door, sir."

"Since the blocking squad on the street behind us hasn't made any noise at all, I'm thinking that they are probably still in there." Max had made sure that a squad of Marines stood ready to intercept anyone running out the back before he came smashing in the front. They would have caught anyone running, so the remaining insurgents could not have run very far.

"Sounds 'bout right, sir."

"Shea, you are okay for a guy from New Jersey. Let's say we go take a look. Whaddya think?"

"Thank you sir, and can I go first?"

"Yep." Max raised his voice, "Jones. Weber. Rodriguez. You guys come with me and Shea. The rest of you cover our backs and make sure we get no surprises. Oh, and somebody radio the blocking squad and let them know we are moving toward them. Tell them not to shoot unless they can see that it's not a Marine they're shooting at."

They slid back down the stairs. Max grabbed a broom from the back hallway and used it to slowly push open the back door. As he did so, a burst from across the courtyard tore into the partially opened door. Max backed up and discarded the splintered stump of the broom handle. He then dropped to his stomach and slithered toward the door. Since it was still partially opened, he could peek through the crack between the door and the jamb. If he looked under the hinge, it was unlikely that the disgruntled individuals across the way could see him looking out.

From the floor, he saw a young man in a velour tracksuit and white sneakers pop around the door of the outhouse and let rip with his AK-47. All of the rounds went high, impacting well above where Max was lying.

"Shea," Max said calmly, "looks like one of your New Jersey Guido friends wants you to come out and play."

"No way, Sir. I'm a Mick and a right Irish bastard. We don't hang with any Guinea assholes. Besides, Guidos come from Long Island…everybody knows that."

"All the same to me, Shea, all the same to me. Go up and tell the guys upstairs to lay down a base of suppressive fire on that shack and to watch for the death blossom." The "death blossom" is what the insurgents called one of their more stupid war-fighting techniques. An excitable member of their clan would wait for a group of Americans to walk by and then pop up in a window or in a doorway and empty a full thirty-round magazine at once on full auto and then drop back into cover to reload. Then repeat. They rarely hit anything with this technique because, unlike in the movies, any hand held rifle on full auto is hard to control. The barrel tends to climb due to the recoil and the vast majority of the shots go wild and high.

Shea laughed over the next burst. "Whack-a-mole, Sir!"

"Yeah, Whack-a-mole time, Shea." Max learned early that these "death blossom" types kept popping up in the same window or one very near it. All a Marine had to do was get the guy's rhythm, wait for him to blow his wad, and duck down for a reload. Aim at the window and when he popped up again, one shot right in the kisser.

Shea went up stairs and after a moment Max was rewarded with the sounds of gunfire, a lot of it, coming from the second floor. The insurgents were still shooting back, but all of their energy and attention, as well as all of their bullets, were directed at the second floor. Max peered out again, trying to think of the best way to approach this new problem when he saw the kid. There was a young boy, lying prone pretty close to the middle of the clothesline. Max was surprised he hadn't noticed him before; but lying there, in a dishdasha made for an adult, the kid looked like a pile of laundry at first. Growing up in the middle of a war, the kid was smart enough not to make a sound, but his eyes were wide with fear as tracers streaked back and forth above him.

Shit.

Max was always a sucker for little kids and this one could not have been more than five or six, tops. He squirmed into the doorway, glanced up to examine the height of the tracers, and looked back at Jones. He saw shock and fear on the enlisted man's face.

Jones raised his hands. "No fuckin' way, Maj!"

Max ignored him. "When I go, light 'em up. I'm gonna run like a sonofabitch and then jink right. Don't shoot me in the back!"

Without waiting for a reply, Max slung his rifle across his back and leapt into the brightly lit courtyard. In a fraction of a second his legs pushed him to speed. He ran straight for the boy. His hands swung huge arcs from face to thigh, fingers splayed wide. Each stride was as long and as fast as he could muster. He ran with every fiber of his being. It was like doing sprints back on Ingram Field. Except instead of earning a browbeating by the Naval Academy's fitness guru, Heinz Lenz, failure on this run would end abruptly—with a bullet.

Each time his boots struck the ground, the world became crisper and clearer. Every color was bright and every line was precise. The world slowed as he charged into his element. Tracer bullets glided past him, languid bumble bees on a hot July day. This is why Max fought every day to keep from being condemned to a desk. This is why he went out with his boys anytime, day or night. It was a rush to charge into the face of an enemy set on killing you. Like a Viking of old, he felt the most connected with himself and the cosmos in the heat of battle. He only felt truly alive in running headlong into his own death, or the death of the man opposite him.

He reached the boy and with a motion as smooth as the most practiced ballet movement, scooped him up under one arm, and without breaking stride, headed for the derelict car to his right. He slid behind the Impala in a cloud of dust. He lay there for a moment with the kid right in front of him. The kid's eyes were so wide that the irises were just pinpoints in a circle of white. He was trembling, but seemed too stunned to even move or cry. Max had swooped in on him in just a few seconds and he still had no time to process what had just happened. Max grinned at the kid, and, after a second, the boy smiled back. Max then crawled along the car's length to the wall of the courtyard. He waited for a lull in the firing, and then boosted the boy over the wall to the safety of the street beyond. He dropped back just as rounds impacted the concrete wall around him.

With the kid as safe as he was going to be, Max took a second to come up with his next action. He was breathing hard and was still pumped from the run. The outbuilding was now only a few dozen yards ahead of him. His guys were tearing it up from the front, and with a few radio calls, he could get the blocking team to break in from the rear. At that point, all he had to do was lie there behind the rusty Chevy and look up at the blue sky while the boys took care of business.

"Fuck it," he said to himself and vaulted over the car's hood.

He hit the ground at a sprint and headed straight for the door of the outbuilding. Tracer fire whipped by, so close he could feel the heat of their passing. Max thought he could hear someone yelling in the distance for him to get down, but that would have been impossible given all the shooting going on. His rush had begun to ebb during the pause behind the car, but now it was back full force. Feeling lighter than air, he made the door in seconds and jumped up, kicking out with his left foot. His momentum, focused through the sole of a size ten boot, would make him a ram that should pop the door off its hinges.

Max felt the impact of his foot on the door travel up his leg and into his spine. He felt the door begin to give.

And then the world erupted around him.

Chapter Two

Two Years Later

With a bag of groceries under one arm, Max walked up the dock to his boat. She was a forty foot Baltic cruiser with a cutter rig that Max picked up for a song shortly after his medical retirement from the Corps. She had a bright blue fiberglass hull, but the sharp-looking teakwood deck was really what caught his eye. He thought it gave the boat a very classic look and even though it was about five years old, Max thought that she could have popped straight out of an Errol Flynn movie. He had always wanted to live on a sailboat and, with a savings account made pretty sizeable by several tax deferred deployments, he was able to pay for her in cash the day he was released from duty. With a bit of twisted humor he had named her *The Prosthetic Limb*.

The name, of course, honored the titanium and rubber prosthetic that replaced his left foot and shin. Thanks to Doc Stone, he survived that day without much more damage than the leg and the occasional ringing in the ears. After several years in Iraq, the military honed the Medivac system to the extent that he was at the Army hospital in Landstuhl, Germany less than twenty four hours after his injury. From the battlefield, he rode the helicopter to Taqquadam Airfield, where he was quickly stabilized, and then sent on a transport nonstop to Europe. The medical types at Taqquadam called the plane an "Angel Flight." The wounded guys called it "The Meat Wagon". Max was so strung out on pain killers that he remembered nothing from when he passed out in Doc's arms to when he came out of his first surgery in Germany.

First surgery. That's a fucking laugh.

Before the war, Max would see some of the old timers with missing limbs at the Naval Hospital back at Camp Lejeune. He never really gave much thought to what exactly went into being an amputee. It seemed to him that if a guy got his leg blown off in Vietnam or somewhere, the surgeons would stitch up the wound, slap a fake leg on the man, and he'd be good to go. The reality of the matter was much more physically involved and emotionally taxing.

First, the stump of the leg was a tattered mass of bone and rags of tissue. The contaminated and non-viable bits had to be removed...in stages. That involved several surgeries just to get the leg cleaned up and prevent it from getting gangrene.

Then, the doctors collected enough living tissue to cover the bone and make a pad of skin and muscle to protect the stump. That was several more surgeries. Add to that skin grafts—Max's least favorite intervention. Strips of skin were planed off his lower back and buttocks with a very delicate and precise dermatome. A dermatome was simply a scalpel on a roller that slices off the upper half of the skin, saving the lower half to grow back. The thin strip of skin was then sewn on his leg where the skin had been destroyed by the explosion. The pain from that was simply mind numbing, and Max grew to be a fan of the various narcotics that the anesthesiologists, those bartenders in pajamas, so deftly applied every time he went under the knife.

Wound-vac changes were also fun. Some brain-trust somewhere had figured out that wounds would heal much better if they were put under a vacuum. Every other day, the old dressings were peeled off all of Max's open wounds, scrubbed out with an iodine solution to fight infection, and then packed with porous foam rubber. Over that went a covering of thin, clear plastic that was very much like Saran-wrap. A small hose attached to a portable suction device was poked through the wrap and into the foam rubber. Turn it on and voila: vacuum preserved Marine meat.

Once the wounds were closed, the sutures removed, and everything was healed up nicely, Max was relegated to that torture known as "physical rehab." He was fitted for a series of prosthetic limbs, each more sophisticated than the next, and then he went through several months of incredibly hard and painful work to learn to walk again. Max never realized just how much extra energy someone with an artificial foot could expend just walking around a carpeted room. The first few sessions left him dripping in sweat. He thought he never would get back to any semblance of his old shape. Not only was his new leg an issue, but he had been bedridden for so long that all of his body had become de-conditioned. His arms were weaker, his other leg was weaker, and certainly his wind was no where what it had been before the injury.

Max was always in top physical shape. Being laid low and

dependent on others was very annoying to him. Once he "graduated" from physical rehabilitation with a brand new, top of the line, technologically advanced artificial leg, Max started on his own rebuild. Since he had no real duties to speak of, all he had to do was wait around the wounded warrior barracks and wait for the powers to be to process him out. He spent hours every day in the base gym, swimming, lifting weights, and running on the treadmill. He got very good at swimming with only the one whole leg and even got close to beating his old time at the one hundred meter sprint. He hit the road as well, his new prosthetic was well adapted to running. It was his goal to run the Marine Corps Marathon while he was still an active duty Marine and he did so, finishing in three hours forty three minutes eighteen months after he lost his leg and one month before he was finally released from the Corps on a medical retirement.

Put out to pasture.

Fifty percent disability for the leg, another fifteen for a slight hearing loss, and another whopping fifty percent for the PTSD they claimed he had. So what if he woke up in a cold sweat, the sounds of his own yells ringing in his ears? So what if he tended to get nervous around crowds and he insisted on getting a good look around corners before going around them? Those things were simply survival instincts. Not the dreams, perhaps, but the rest just seemed common sense to Max. The dreams were just a little case of the jitters; everybody got them if they were in the suck long enough. He certainly didn't like having some sort of "chairborne ranger" shrink label him with the epithet, "Post Traumatic Stress Disorder." That was for weak sisters: the non-hacker stress cases. Max was tougher than that. He was still the old warrior poet he always knew he was.

New Bern, North Carolina was a good move for Max. He had gotten to know the small town when he was stationed at Camp Lejeune, about a thirty minute drive south down Route 17. It was a quiet, roll-the-streets-up-after-dark sort of place and that suited Max just fine. He could dock his boat just a few minutes' walk from the downtown restaurants and shops (and a few minutes stagger back from the bars later in the evening). He was close enough to the Naval Hospital to get his meds refilled or his leg adjusted if needed, but far enough from base to keep from seeing healthy Marines doing healthy Marine things every day.

The hardest adjustment for Max, more than losing his leg, was losing the Corps. He had lived for the thrill of the fight and the intense challenge of pitting himself against an enemy who wanted him dead every single day he walked out of his hooch. He lived for the competiveness of his unit and the keeping up with the younger men. He took joy in showing them that "the old man" could outrun, out lift, and outfight most of them. Now, he was ashamed, really, to see them or be seen by them. He felt less of a man, or at least less of a man he thought he *should* be. He had become a bit of a hermit, except instead of a cave out in the wilderness he had a boat on the Neuse River. He kept his mind occupied with his books and his body occupied with as much exercise as possible. It served two purposes: firstly, the stronger he was, the less his handicap kept him back and secondly, if he worked out to the point of exhaustion every day, he could get off to sleep without the help of the Ambien he kept in his cabin.

As he walked up the gangplank to the deck of *The Prosthetic Limb*, he glanced up at the condos that towered over the eastern end of the docks. Old Mrs. Pritchett was at her post as usual. Max's paranoia was aroused when he first noticed her and he did a little sleuthing to uncover her story. She was a widow (several times over it was rumored) without much to do and her primary method of entertaining herself was keeping tabs on her neighbors. She purchased a corner condo at the top of the building so that she had great views of both the town and the harbor. With a set of Navy surplus big-eye binoculars on a tripod on her deck, the old lady could keep *very* close tabs on her neighbors. With those things, she probably could read the Sunday paper over somebody's shoulder as he was having a Danish at the coffee shop downtown or figure out who was screwing around on whom from a county away. Every town had at least one little old lady like her: the busy body whose life revolved around the terrible things she thought the neighbors were up to.

Max saw that the binoculars were aimed his way, so he pulled the bread out of the bag and waggled the baguette at her in salute. After months and months of dodging snipers, Max was pretty uneasy with the thought of someone watching him from a high vantage point. He got that old prickly sensation between his shoulder blades every time she was out behind her huge binoculars and he had the strong urge to call in a JDAM strike on her position. Much to his regret, he had a feeling that Cherry Point might balk at being asked to drop a thousand pound, GPS guided, heavy explosive warhead on one of the town's more senior of citizens... even if she was a nosey old thing.

He turned to walk across the deck to the main cabin door and glanced over the bow, noticing a new boat tied up on the far end. How could he not notice it? It was an absolutely beautiful and brand new forty foot SeaSpray cabin cruiser. She had sleek lines that screamed, "one fast motorboat," and a hull that looked straight from the showroom floor. Max had seen one at the boat show in Annapolis a few years back. They were class all the way and had all of the latest gadgets and luxuries. He couldn't quite make out the stern so he could not see the boat's name or home port, but he was pretty sure he had not seen it on the river before. The town was a big destination for boaters from up and down the coast, so, likely, it was someone stopping over before continuing down the inter-coastal waterway.

"Nice boat, ain't it?"

The dock master, a long since retired Navy Chief Petty Officer was sitting on his usual perch, the flat end of a piling, about half way up the dock. He was busy splicing together a section of cut line. Sitting there, his skinny knees pulled up and resting against the side of the wooden piling, he reminded Max of an ancient and wrinkled pelican.

"Pulled in sometime past midnight. I wasn't here, I was havin' a nice nightcap down at Morgan's, but Bob Knightly was pullin' in from giggin' flounder and he seen her pull on up. Said the woman who was pilotin' her in was a sweet sight to see."

"That so?" Max looked the new boat up and down.

"Yep. She left me a nice little surprise slid under my door. Slip fees paid in full, and in advance." Deft from years of experience, his nimble fingers wove the broken strands of the rope together into that intricate cat's cradle of fibers that would make it whole again. He looked at Max meaningfully, "Unlike some people I could mention."

"Yeah, yeah, I get the hint Chief. Good looking woman, huh?"

"Hell yeah. If she is half as pretty as Ol' Bob said, she would be worth taking your sorry ass over to talk to her. I wandered on over this morning to see if she needed anything, but nobody answered when I called. You better move fast if you want to try for a piece, though. I've got half a mind to ask her out for a drink myself. Women love us Navy men."

"Sure they do Chief. It's your looks that'll be the problem."

"Naw, I have forgotten more about how to please a female than you have ever learned your whole sorry life. Leave it to me, I'll get her a singin' and a swingin' from the rafters."

"You have fun; just make sure you don't break a hip."

The dock master just laughed and went back to splicing his rope as Max continued across the deck of his own vessel.

"Cool," Max mumbled to himself.

Entering the boat, he put down his bag of groceries and slid onto one of the couches in the cabin. He pulled a bottle of Laphroaig Twelve Year off the center folding table and pulled the cork with his teeth. He took a swig of the scotch straight from the bottle. The amber liquid burned on its way down his throat and settled in his stomach with a fountain of warmth. He took off his leg and tossed it aside and started to rub his stump. It was pretty sore. Max had gone for a long run that morning and then ran errands the rest of the day. He could do more on it now than he ever could, but it would still ache like blazes if he pushed too hard.

The phantom pain was the worst. Many times he could feel the sensation of a foot that was no longer there. Sometimes it would be a feeling of wholeness, as if it had never been lost; sometimes it would tickle; but at other times the sensation would be pure fire, as if he was dipping the nonexistent foot into a deep fat fryer.

Would I be dark meat, or light meat?

Max popped two oxycontin and chewed them before washing them down with another swig from the bottle. The narcotic on top of the alcohol made him feel much more relaxed. He sighed and picked up the packet of papers for the tenth time since yesterday. One signature and the last connection to his childhood would be gone for good. Since he was an only child, when his mother passed away the family farm passed into his hands. It rested in a formerly rural area of Maryland that was now a suburb of DC. The area had been all farmland when he was a kid, but now the place was full of McMansions, upscale townhouses, and shopping mall after shopping mall. Developers had been after his mother to sell for years after his father died; but, even though she could not work it, she refused to sell. It was where she raised a son and lost a husband. Max's father loved the place and farmed the land every day until he died…literally. When he did not come in one afternoon, she went out to fetch him and she found him on his tractor, leaning back with his hat over his face as if he stopped to take a nap in the shade again. He died doing what he loved best; so Max was glad of that.

When his mother died, the developers came after him, but he refused them just like his mother for the same sentimental reasons. He also thought it funny that a combat Marine would own a farm outside of the District. "I'll never die," he would joke, "because I *already* own the farm."

He didn't get killed, so it must have worked, but he really did not see himself going back to the farm and working the land. Too many memories, and who the hell ever heard of a gimp farmer anyways? He slipped the papers from the envelope, stared at the contract of sale a long time, and then signed it. He chewed another oxycontin, chased it with another swallow of scotch, and lay back on the couch; his foot propped on the table. He was quite a bit dizzy at this point and he closed his eyes and let the room spin. The last pill had gotten him really numb and he felt himself slipping into sleep.

His dreams were really just a fog of mismatched flashes of partial scenes. *Iraq. Afghanistan. Running through a field of poppies, their petals long gone, and their pods swollen and ripe. The opium milk thickly clotted on the cuts the farmers made to bring out the sap. The green stems with bulbous ends swayed as he ran through. The fresh opium covered him, over his uniform, his boots, his gear, and his weapon. The sweet smell of it surrounded him: a mixture of flowers and bubblegum.*

Running through a desert village, an explosion of dust after every step. He comes around the corner and sees insurgents waiting for him, their faces masked by the keffiyah, only their angry eyes showing. He brings up his M4 and pulls the trigger but the trigger feels like an unmoving piece of steel rebar and it won't fire. They raise their Kalashnikov rifles. He tries to duck back around the corner but the dust has become the thickness of glue and holds him steady. He looks up only to see the muzzle pointed at his face, followed by a bright, terrible flash and…

Max woke up in a sheen of sweat. He glanced at the LED clock on the nightstand. Three AM. His mouth was dry and felt like an old sock. He reached for the scotch, but changed his mind and staggered over to the sink and took a long pull straight from the faucet. Getting around one-legged on a sailboat was not easy, so Max installed stainless steel handgrips strategically throughout the cabin and up on deck. With these in place, it would take a strong swell to knock him off balance. He cupped his hands and splashed some more cold water on his face. He was still feeling a little foggy, but he was awake and becoming more so with every minute.

Wide awake at three am, what else is new?

He slowly climbed out on deck. There was no moon and even less of a breeze. The only light came from the streetlamps a block away. This morning the light was filtered out by the thick mist rolling from the river and up the streets of the town. It was pretty common this time of year, but Max felt that something was "off." He breathed in deeply and he could smell the river, a combination of salt and tannin. The salt came from the Pamlico Sound that opened up downstream and led into the Atlantic. Max could cast off at any time and find himself down as far as the barrier islands in a few hours. There, the dark water of the river swirled out into the deep blue of the ocean in a spiral pattern of mixing currents and flows. The tide would bring the salt water as far as the town, and Max saw dolphins frolicking in the river on more than one occasion.

The tannin came from the river. Trees, mainly cypress, leech tannin into the waters that go by and impart a dark color to the water as well as an earthy, tangy, forest-like smell. Nowhere else in the world has Max ever encountered a place where both smells combined: the sea and the forest that never failed to make him sit up and breathe the air in deep lungfuls, over and over again.

Night made the smell even more intense.

At three in the morning in a town as small as this, everyone was asleep and the downtown area was completely abandoned as a rule. The streets were deserted and little noise broke the calm. Since Max was frequently up during the night, he was used to the empty feeling town. It was usually very magical, peaceful.

He was already dressed, so he just pulled on his leg, walked off the boat, and down the street. When the insomnia really kicked in, Max would wander for hours. The old houses were interesting to look at, and he enjoyed being out on his own with nobody to bother him. The air seemed cleaner at night. He always thought it was because there were no cars on the street, so the smell of the fumes was gone with the commuters.

As he came off the docks and walked up Main he turned right on Front Street and followed the course of the river north. Old Colonial and Victorian era homes lined the street and faced the river. The mist was coming off the river with its unique hybrid smell.

This middle of the night stroll was very different. The night felt heavy, oppressive. The quiet was very much like the quiet just before the huge thunderstorm rolls in. Every person who has spent much time in combat develops a sort of "sixth sense" for trouble. The younger Marines called it their "Spidey Sense," and Max's was on high alert. He was had the same feeling he would get walking through a village just before the insurgents decided to light his guys up.

As he walked down Front Street, he could feel the tension building, like in a spaghetti western just before the climatic showdown. He half expected a tumbleweed to blow across the street.

The ancient oaks that lined the street bowed like old hags with shawls of Spanish moss. The occasional porch light cast long shadows that danced eerily when the mist shifted. Dancers dressed in rags. Something made Max turn left on Queen Street. He felt drawn in that direction. Trouble was brewing, Max had a nose for it, and he wanted to get in on the fun.

Just a few blocks up Queen Street was the old Cedar Grove cemetery. Max jogged by it frequently. It was unique in that the archway at the main entrance and the long, low wall that surrounded it were made from tabby bricks. Tabby was a concrete made from lime, sand and oyster shells, and Max thought it gave the place a hybrid look that matched the earth and sea smell of the river. Walls full of shells. Cool. He couldn't remember just how old the place was, but he thought it must date back to the late seventeen hundreds at least.

He knew that the front gate would be locked at night, so Max, after quickly glancing around, slid over the low tabby wall and into the cemetery. He briefly wondered what sort of charges he would get if he was caught here, but the area seemed deserted. The police station was only a few blocks up from the cemetery, but there seemed to be no activity there either. Crouching low, he slid along the wall toward the grove of live oak that marked the oldest section.

The paths were paved with oyster shells, and they crunched lightly underfoot. The white of the shell reflected the ambient light and seemed to glow softly with dim phosphorescence. Max came to the main path that started at the front gate and delved straight into the center of the cemetery. He dodged from monument to gravestone, keeping his head down, as he neared the memorial to Confederate dead that stood at the center of the graveyard. It was a wide, circular mound at the crossing of the major paths crowned with an obelisk topped by a statue of a Confederate soldier resting on his rifle.

Max did not notice the architecture; his focus was dominated by the figures struggling next to it. Two figures were fighting a third. As he crept forward, he could distinguish a woman in the grasp of two men. One held her arms behind her and the other had his hands around her neck. They were saying something to her in low tones that Max couldn't quite make out and she was answering them in a voice that was obviously furious, but slurred. Something was definitely wrong with her. Two on one was a coward's way to fight in Max's mind—especially if the outnumbered person was a woman. Max stepped out of the shadows and strode up the figures. He was well over six foot tall and broad across the shoulders. He always cut an imposing figure before the loss of his leg, but in compensation for his missing limb, he built up his upper body as strong as he could. When he pulled himself up to his full height he could be very intimidating.

"Hey assholes," he said almost conversationally, "didn't your mothers ever tell you it's not nice to beat up on girls?"

The two men spun around, surprised.

"You are awake—no one could possibly be awake." He was a handsome young man, with aquiline features, in his mid-twenties, with his black hair slicked back. Max recognized the leather Gruppa Moda jacket from some leave time he spent in Naples. His boots looked Italian too. Max briefly wondered what some piece of Euro trash with expensive taste in clothing was doing mugging chicks in North Carolina before he replied.

"Yeah, I'm always awake. You wanna let her go, or do you and I have some business to take care of? You might as well give up—the cops are just a block away."

"The police will not be disturbing us, nor will anybody else. I don't know how you managed to escape the fog, but you will regret interrupting us." His eyes blazed with fury, and something else that seemed odd to Max. *What the hell? Was the kid high or something?*

"Ok, douche bag, you want to make this hard, fine. Tell your boyfriend to let the lady go, right now, or I will teach you the meaning of regret."

The kid smiled and so did his buddy. The smiles were unsettling: arrogant, creepy, and somehow perverse all rolled together into the most smarmy look Max had ever seen. The girl looked dazed and completely out of it. Max was beginning to get really angry. *What the fuck? A couple of wealthy assholes slipped some girl a roofie to rape in the park?* The very thought of it made him furious. He was going to enjoy kicking their asses, even if it meant some court-mandated time back on some shrink's couch dealing with his "anger issues." He noticed the first guy glance up, above Max's head.

Instinctively Max stepped aside as a third guy dropped flat on the ground with a sickening thud. He was face down and spread eagle. Max quickly glanced up. There was no tree above him. *Where did this idiot come from?* The prone figure quivered and groaned, snorting with that congested sound that almost always indicates a broken nose. He was not going anywhere soon.

The remaining assailants stopped smiling. Max grinned.

"You can't sneak up on an old dog like me so easily. So what's it gonna be? LET THE LADY GO, NUMB NUTS!" Max commanded in his best Parris Island drill instructor voice. Take charge, assume authority, and demand respect. From years spent in third world shitholes, and some pretty unsavory places in the States, Max learned that he could make people back down just acting like he was in charge and letting them know it. It worked well, especially on the type of cowards who would gang up on a woman, three to one.

The guy holding the woman released her and she sagged down to the grass as he suddenly rushed Max. He came to the lip of the circular mound that marked the monument and tripped on his own feet, his face wide with an expression of utter surprise. He put out his arm to catch himself and Max could hear it break with an audible snap as he fell on top of it. Screaming, he rolled a few feet and then lay still, keening over his broken arm.

Max could not help but laugh: big rolling peals of noise that tore through the silence of the graveyard and rang up the misty streets. So far, two of the three punks were down and he had not even had the chance to raise his hand against them. They were like keystone cops, obviously much more dangerous to themselves than to anyone else.

"I don't know who you think you are," said the remaining one, seething with anger. Froth began to drip from his lips as he spoke. "I don't know what sort of magic protects you, but I swear that I will tear out your throat. I will open you up and strangle you with your own entrails. You will never rise. You will be rot into the earth and the worms will feast upon your festering corpse as you suffer eternal torment."

"Yeah, yeah. You gonna run your mouth or you gonna come

over here to do something about it?"

The man hissed and rushed at Max, both arms stretched out in front of him as if to grab Max's neck. He was quick, but Max met him easily. In one swift, smooth move, Max led with his right, swinging from the waist and putting his whole shoulder behind his punch. As he swung, he stepped forward with his right foot. All two hundred and twenty five pounds of pissed off Marine provided Max's fist with incredible momentum.

Expensive Italian jacket man ran full tilt right into Max's fist. With his face. His head snapped back but his feet continued forward, causing him to flip backwards in an almost complete somersault that left him face down on the sharp oyster shell path.

Broken arm man had taken the opportunity to make a run for it, and Max glimpsed him dart past. He calmly reached down and picked up a fist sized piece of masonry dislodged by the recent struggle. He let fly and nailed the running man square between the shoulder blades. He went down with a cry and disappeared among the gravestones. Max's attention returned to the leader who was just barely able to stand, his hands were both clasped across his face and dark blood seeped between his fingers.

"My teeth! he screamed, although it came out garbled, *Maw teef!* "You broke my teeth!" He coughed and pulled his hands away to spit out shards of enamel onto the ground.

"Well, you insisted." Max felt some pain in his hand and looked down. His knuckles were lacerated and bleeding. *The punk had some sharp teeth, alright. "Had" being the operative word.*

"You will pay for this!" shouted the man in the Italian jacket.

Max noticed that he had lost several front teeth on the left side of his mouth, which was bleeding profusely. His designer shirt was covered in crimson and his lip was split where his teeth had torn through.

"Well, how about a little interest then?" said Max as he hauled off and kicked him in the groin. Max used his left leg this time and his prosthetic shin landed straight in the man's crotch. Because Max was a big man, and very athletic, the prosthetics department at the Naval Hospital had outfitted him with an advanced, heavy-duty, multi-function, artificial leg. For this reason, the prosthesis was heavier than usual, but Max could handle the extra weight. When he kicked the assailant in the groin, his testicles became intimately acquainted with several pounds of high velocity unyielding aluminum, titanium, and plastic. There was the sound of a fist striking a side of beef and he was lifted up on his toes with the impact.

He shrieked like a boiling teakettle and then folded into a fetal position, hands clutching his nether regions. His mouth was still bleeding. He gasped for air and then threw up the most foul mass of black clotted liquid Max had ever seen. It made him smile.

Max turned to the girl, but noticed that the fellow that had fallen on his face was beginning to stir. Max kicked him in the ribs.

"Let me give you a piece of advice," Max said and kicked him again. He thought he could feel a rib cave in.

"You just stay down until me and her leave." Another kick.

"Otherwise, I'll think that you are not listening and that would really, really, make me angry. Deal?" Kick.

The figure slumped back down and did not move again.

"Good," said Max. "I'm glad we could come to this arrangement."

Max walked over to the girl, she was lying on her side, moving slightly with her hands still bound behind her back. He pulled a Spyderco folding knife from his back pocket and cut the rope holding her.

"Hey! You okay?" Max said as he tried to pull her to her feet.

"No, no, I feel...odd," she replied.

"That's okay. The police station is just up the street. Let me get you there and they can call for an ambulance from there." Max cursed himself for not having his cell phone with him. He rarely carried it though, because he really didn't have anyone to call. People who wanted to call him were usually the type of people Max was interested in avoiding in the first place.

"No police, please," she gasped. "I will be alright. I am just feeling a little weak, they threw something in my face and it drained me."

"That cinches it. You have got to see a doctor. Who knows what sort of drug they gave you." In spite of the dim light, Max could tell, to his discomfort, that this woman was beautiful in a very real and take-your-breath-away sort of way. Max would have been hesitant to approach a girl like her when he was a whole person, much less as the cripple he was now.

"No, no, no," she insisted, pulling on Max's arm until she was standing upright. "They won't be any help, and they will make a mess of things. I'm fine, I just need to get back to my boat."

Her eyes were wide. Max felt himself being drawn into them.

A gorgeous babe who does not want any trouble from the cops. It sounded like a recipe for disaster to Max. He had this rule, stemming from seeing several cheap horror flicks, that if any good looking woman were to ever come on to him in an unexpected manner, she would immediately fall into the "up-to-no-good" category. Why else would a beautiful woman show a guy like him interest unless she was acting like bait? Max glanced around, but did not see any lead pipe wielding boyfriend sneaking up from behind.

"Boat?" asked Max. "You on that blue speedster that tied up yesterday?"

"Yes, that's mine."

At least one mystery solved, thought Max. *Good looking and loaded to boot.*

"Just help me to my boat and I'll be alright, okay?" Still a little unsteady on her feet, she leaned into his shoulder. Max could smell the faint scent of cinnamon and cloves. He could also feel himself folding.

"Okay, okay, let's get out of here." Max's hindbrain couldn't help but shout out *sucker*, as he slipped her arm around his neck and gripped her by the waist with the other. She could walk with support and he was able to guide her out of the cemetery and down the street. The fog was less thick than before, (*What did that jerk say about the fog?*) but the streets were still deserted as if everybody in town was still laying low, with their covers pulled up over their heads. It was not until they had wobbled their way back onto Front Street, near the docks, that Max heard a dog bark, for the first time that night. It looked like the town was starting to wake up again.

They said nothing during the walk to the waterfront, but, as they entered the marina, Max spoke. "Those guys that were messing with you, they could come back...with friends maybe. Instead of going where they know to find you, let's go to my boat. It's just a few slips down from you."

"No, I cannot. I need...privacy."

"No problem then. I have a cabin in the bow that has a lockable door and a bed. You will be safe there and I will feel better that you are somewhere I can keep a good eye out. It would really suck if I went to all that trouble to help you out only to have to get you out of trouble again. That would really piss me off."

"So gallant, I think." She smiled in the dim light. "Alright, I will take you up on your kind offer. I still feel weak. Just keep to yourself and we will have no problems."

"Okay. No worries. I wouldn't think of taking advantage of a damsel in distress." He grinned in response to her smile.

He helped her into the boat and then into the main cabin. The fore cabin was very spacious and she said a quick thank you before she slid inside. Max heard the door lock behind her. He settled on the couch in the main cabin after he reached behind it to pull out the twelve gauge. The shotgun was one of those Mossberg Marine models finished in stainless steel to prevent corrosion in the salt air. It was a useful thing to have on a boat, especially if that boat was also your main residence. Five rounds of double-aught buckshot would serve to take care of any unwanted visitors.

Max was tempted briefly to down another oxycontin. Maybe even wash it down with more scotch. He decided to grab some ice water from the fridge. He was on guard duty for the first time in years. It felt good to have a cause and some responsibility. He was not about to mess it up right yet.

He wondered why he was taking in this particular lost puppy, but the answer was obvious to him. The fight at the cemetery made him feel alive for the first time in a long while. It made him feel a whole man again. After all, this old cripple had beaten three assailants all by himself. Granted, they were three of the most inept muggers he had ever heard of, but he felt like he was back on his game. He felt like a Marine again.

With morning a few hours off, Max settled in to keep the watch, a copy of Kipling's *The Man Who Would Be King* to keep him company. No one could get in that cabin unless they went through him first.

Chapter Three

The rest of the night passed uneventfully. Max made sure the doors, windows, and portholes were locked. In front of the cabin door he stacked a pyramid of empty beer cans, certain that their clatter would wake him up if anyone forced the lock. With the defensive perimeter established, he permitted himself to doze, but he cradled the shotgun as he slept.

The sound of the coffee pot's automatic timer woke him up. The rich aroma of Columbian double roast filled the boat. He got up with some difficulty. Sweat covered him and soaked through his shirt. A chill coursed through his body and he rubbed his aching arms. They were covered with goose bumps. He took a few steps and his legs ached with even that little effort. Then the shakes started.

Max had been on narcotic pain pills since he had been wounded and he knew what he was feeling. Withdrawal started with the shakes and the chills. It then progressed to something that was like a full blown case of the flu, including the diarrhea and vomiting. It was miserable. Another busted up vet at the veteran's administration had once told him that no one ever died from coming off of their meds, but they sure wished they had. After once trying to stop cold turkey, Max could certainly agree with that sentiment. At that time the chills and shakes got so bad that he thought he was going into full blown seizures right there in his front cabin. The muscle aches evolved into back-breaking spasms that kept him from getting up to go to the head, so he ended up shitting all over his sheets. He gave detox up pretty quickly. Once he got his meds back into his system, he decided that cold turkey was not the way to go.

Max realized that he had felt so good after the fight the night before, so alive, that he had blown off his usual three A.M. snack of an oxycontin or three. With shaking hands, he rummaged around for his pill bottle and downed two of the little yellow pills dry. Just the act of taking them settled him down a little bit, and he was able to pour himself a cup of the coffee. Mug in hand, he settled back down, closed his eyes, and waited for the familiar warmth to slide through him.

The door to the fore cabin was still closed, so the girl was probably still sacked out. She would probably sleep for awhile given what she had been through and whatever drug the would-be rapists had given her. Max still had a few misgivings about not going straight to the police and he thought it a little bit odd that she, obviously the victim in that situation, would insist they avoid the authorities. He had heard about battered women not wanting to have an asshole boyfriend or husband arrested due to some sort of misplaced loyalty or bizarre ideas of love, but she did not seem to be with those guys at all, so that idea did not fit.

The only reason that he could come up with for her not wanting to go to the cops was that she was probably involved in something illegal or was hiding from somebody. Max thought for a moment about calling the police anyway while she slept and have them send somebody over to at least get her story, but he decided to leave that be for a moment.

The memory of how he felt when he stood over her assailants in victory came back to him. He savored that feeling. It was a feeling he had not had in years, not since he was last a whole man. The loss of the leg was not really bad, in and of itself. He found that he had been able to adapt quite well: he could run, jump, dance, swim, and do pretty much everything he could with his nice, new gizmo on the end of his shin. No, it was much more than the loss of a limb for him; it was a loss of a way of life. Max had always dreamed of being a Marine since he was a little boy. He had watched John Wayne in the *Sands of Iwo Jima* over and over as a kid. The character of John Stryker struck him as a noble man: a rough and tough warrior with a soft spot for small children and ladies out on their luck. That film became the seed of the growing warrior ethos for the young Max. He took that spark and ran with it, seeking to be the best he could at school and the athletic fields so that when he became old enough he could not only join, but thrive, in his beloved Marine Corps.

After a lifetime of striving for perfection, of making himself into the best Marine he could be, losing a leg had devastated him. At first he diverted his energies into healing, and then, once he was out of the hospital, he put the full force of his drive and resolve into become more than "just well." He had regained all of his strength and pushed himself to tear down any barriers his new body presented. Once he had won that battle; once he had beaten the enemy he considered his own limitations, he had nothing left to overcome. Even though he could bench press over three-hundred pounds, something he had not been able to do since he was playing football at Navy; even though he was able to run a marathon on his fake leg, he still found himself on the outside looking in: put out to pasture like an old war horse, discarded. When his medical retirement had come through, in spite of having struggled to come back from his injury, Max felt betrayed. The Marines, the love of his life, having no use for a broken soldier, had tossed him aside. He could not have been more hurt if he had come home to find his wife of twenty years in bed with a younger man. Except he never had a wife; all thoughts of starting a family had been sacrificed for a career in the same organization that now had jilted him.Only thirty three, his life was over.

Without the Marines, he had no goals and nothing to strive toward. The only thing the future seemed to hold for him was a gradual fading away into obscurity as if he never existed at all. He had given in to the fact that never again would he lead men into battle; never again face a man intending to do him harm; never again ride out into that life or death struggle he experienced every day in the streets of Iraq or the mountains of Afghanistan.

Then last night happened. When he found himself thrashing those guys and saving the girl. Even though they were really just some idiot punks, not deadly Mujahedeen fighters, beating them had felt good. Beating them had made him feel whole. Beating them had given him some purpose. This really was why he did not call the police as soon as he had gotten the woman back to his boat. Whatever trouble she was in, helping her had been the first fun he had in a long time and he wanted more of it, regardless of the consequences. A few hours ago his life had been over and he had been a man without a mission. This morning, he had a mission, and she was still asleep in the next cabin.

Light was coming in the portholes full force and, with the oxycontin in his system bringing him back to an even keel, Max pulled himself to the galley section of the main cabin and began to empty out the refrigerator. He had some thickly sliced local bacon, so that went in the frying pan first. While that sizzled, he started slicing and squeezing some fresh oranges. It took awhile to get a decent amount of orange juice, but Max liked his bacon crispy, so he took his time.

With the bacon done, he took the crisp strips out of the pan and laid them in a tarnished frame that he bought at the antique store up on Hancock Street, over by the railroad tracks. The old guy had called it a "bacon rasher." It was a metal frame with vertical slots that Max could put his cooked bacon in. Whatever the old guy called it, it kept his bacon crisp by letting the grease drain off. Max used to just pile it up on a paper towel, but it didn't work very well and before he discovered the rasher, he just put up with soggy bacon. As Max considered bacon one of the essential food groups and certainly a gift from the gods, bacon technology was very important to him.

Most of the grease went into an old coffee mug and then into the fridge for later use. Max always saved the grease as there would be no Southern cooking at all without bacon grease. He then broke some eggs, brown ones, from a local farm into a tall water glass, added some season salt and whisked them until they were frothy. He poured this into the remains of the grease in the pan and stirred the eggs continually until they were a nice, scrambled mess. It didn't dawn on him that his guest might not like bacon *and* eggs scrambled in bacon grease, after all, who didn't like bacon in all of its glorious forms.

He put the food and the juice glasses on the bar that served as a table and added the pot of coffee. He cobbled together a few miss-matched place settings and plates from the dishwasher and arranged them on the bar facing each other. Never before had there been a guest aboard the *Prosthetic Limb* and Max was at least making an effort to provide some sort of hospitality.

The food ready, the table arranged, Max went to the door and knocked softly. No answer. He tried the knob, but it was still locked.

"Hello?" He said softly. Nothing.

"Hello, Miss?" he said, much louder this time, punctuated with a loud bang on the door.

"Are you alright in there?" He listened closely. He thought he might have heard a faint murmur or a rustle of sheets from within, but he could not be sure over the waves lapping against the boat.

He was faced with a dilemma. Max knew that just barging in on the girl was not exactly the right thing to do; after all, he considered himself an officer *and* a gentleman. However, she had been pretty stoned last night; what if she was still out or even deathly ill from whatever she had been given? The last thing he wanted to see was some pretty girl overdosed and dead in his front cabin and if she did need medical attention, she needed it sooner than later. His concern overwhelmed his sense of propriety pretty rapidly.

Interior doors on boats are meant for privacy, not security, so it was a simple matter for Max to snag an all-purpose prying device, otherwise known as a butter knife, off the table, slide it along the latch, and pop open the door.

Light filtered in from between half drawn shades. She was lying there on the bed, still asleep in a cocoon of sheets straight from Target. He slipped to the window and pulled back the sun bleached curtains. Max never got a really good look at her the night before. Here, in the full light of morning, he could see just how stunning she really was. Average height, with a nice figure, at least those parts of her he could see through the bedclothes, and smooth, unblemished, pale skin. She had generous lips, high cheekbones, and a shock of amazingly red hair. Not the pale, washed out, wispy-looking red of the freckled girls with the almost translucent skin, but the vibrant red of a new copper penny. She seemed very young to Max, barely over twenty.

Her eyes, which suddenly snapped open, wide with a combination of fear and rage, were a lovely shade of green.

"Hey," said Max, startled at her sudden awakening. He pulled the shade full open and the sunlight flooded in to cover her and the bed. "I made us some eggs—"

She leaped up like a scalded cat.

"It burns! It burns!" she screamed over and over as she bounced around the room.

Max was stunned. *Was she still high from last night or just batshit crazy?* He stood for a moment watching her as she thrashed about the cabin. Bedclothes flew through the air and she ran into the corner, bouncing off the bulkhead screaming as if in agony all the while.

"It burns! It burns! What have you done to me?" She knocked a dresser over, spilling all of its contents onto the floor. *Should have screwed into the wall when I had a chance*, thought Max, his head turning back and forth to follow her progress all over the cabin like someone trying to follow a game of ping-pong.

Max really was unsure what to do; this was really out of his frame of reference. He tried shouting to her as she ran past, her cries the wail of a passing train.

"Hey, lady! Are you alright? Calm down! Nothing is on fire!" When that didn't work, he returned to his opening line. "I made eggs...," In the old black and white movies, Jimmy Cagney or Humphrey Bogart would have to slap the hysterical dame to get her to calm down. Max wasn't about to do that, although he seriously considered it after the dresser went. He was at a bit of a loss. He grabbed her once, and almost got her wrapped up in a massive bear hug, but she bit his arm, drawing blood, so he decided to let her go.

Max was just about to grab the fire extinguisher and give her a good spray when she tried to dive under the bed. The trouble was, there was no "under the bed." It had a solid frame with pull-out drawers for storage, and she nailed that with an audible thud that made Max wince, followed by silence. He crawled across the bed and looked over the side to where she was lying on the floor, still breathing, thankfully, eyes open and staring right back at Max as he peered down at her.

"Seriously," said Max, "I made some bacon too."

Chapter Four

She stared up at him with her piercing, green eyes.

"Who are you and what did you do to me?" she said, Max thought she looked amazingly calm after the recent display.

"Maximilian Bradley, United States Marine Corps, retired. At your service, ma'am," he replied as he reached down and proffered his hand. She regarded it impassively for a moment and then grasped it in hers. Max sat up and pulled her up next to him.

"You must have been having some wild dreams, but you are alright. Nothing is on fire and nobody is burning."

She gazed at her hands, turning them over and over before her eyes.

"But that...that is impossible," she said.

"Impossible? I think you were still a bit shook up from last night. Do you remember anything?"

"Yes, some." She shook her head, "It is still very cloudy, I think I was drugged or something." She never took her eyes off her hands as she spoke, waving them in and out of the rays of sunshine coming in through the now wide open window. Looking at her palms, then the backs of them, then lifting them straight up, fingers spread, to see the light coming in between. "So beautiful..." she murmured.

"Uh, yeah, okay," replied Max. He dipped his head, trying to make eye contact. She was really starting to give off a sort of weird-dreamland-type-hippy vibe. "Like I said, last night? Remember anything?"

"Hmm?" she glanced up at him, as if suddenly realizing that someone was trying to talk to her. "What? Yes. I remember you. You helped me. So kind."

"Good, good. What were you doing there that time of night, anyway?"

"I was looking for something. Something...historical, I guess you could say. They wanted to steal it from me, but lucky for me, you came along." Her attention turned to the window and she slid off the bed, with almost feline grace, and walked across the room. Tentatively, cautiously, she peered around the curtains and looked out across the water. The window was open, so she could smell the sea air and the sun on the newly cut grass of the park across from the docks. She smiled and breathed in deeply, obviously enjoying the sun on her face and she tilted her head back, taking in the warmth as if she had been cold for a very long time. She reminded Max of a convict, just released from solitary, drinking in the free air for the first time in a long time.

"Incredible and impossible and amazing at the same time," she said. "I have not seen anything like this in a so incredibly long..." She turned to him, grinning, "Can we go outside?"

"Sure, we can breakfast on the deck." Max led her back into the main cabin. He dumped some old beer cans and pill bottles off his only tray and quickly piled on the food and drink. He then led her to the main cabin door and pushed it open with his foot, balancing the now overloaded tray with his hands. She took a few tentative steps, paused for a moment, and then climbed up the ladder to the deck.

Max followed and noticed for the first time that she was clad only in a flimsy tee shirt and panties. His only thought as he followed her was, *nice, very nice*.

On the deck, he put the tray on a fold out table right behind the steering console. Bench seats were built in. He gestured for her to sit and then he slid into the seat across from her. She was leaning back, arms outstretched, soaking in the rays.

"Marvelous," she murmured to herself.

"Sure," replied Max. This girl was definitely a strange one, but he could see her nipples through her tee shirt, so he didn't mind the strangeness so much. "Here, take some eggs. I made the juice fresh this morning."

She took the plate from Max and stared at it briefly before breaking off a tiny piece of one of the several crisp strips that he had placed there. Gingerly, she brought it up to her lips, sniffed at it, and took a tiny nibble off the corner. The response was immediate, and for Max, very gratifying.

"Amazing," she exclaimed as she raised both of her hands to the sky. "I have never tasted anything like this!" Max couldn't help but notice how her breasts moved under the shirt as she did this.

"It's just bacon ma'am. Proof that God loves us and wants us to be happy. How can you not have ever had bacon?"

"I just, I just, haven't had anything, really, not for a long, long time. I don't believe this. Something must be terribly wrong, but it's also terribly right." She had taken up the whole slice of bacon and gestured with it emphatically. "You cannot even begin to imagine how I feel right now."

Wider gestures and much more shifting under the shirt.

"I won't? Try me." Max looked around to see if anyone was up and about to witness this little scene. As expected, the old lady was out with her binoculars and they were trained straight at the *Prosthetic Limb.*

Oh well, thought Max, *maybe the old crow will get a chance to remember what a real set of knockers actually looks like. Might bring back some memories of when the boys came back from San Juan Hill.*

"At least start with your name, I can't just say 'Hey you' all of the time.

"Szabo," she said softly, "Elena Szabo."

"Glad to meet you." Max held out his hand, "Szabo, Irish is it?"

"What?" She looked at Max's hand, but did not reach to shake it. She looked puzzled for a moment.

Max chuckled and withdrew his hand. "Never mind. A stupid attempt at humor my old man used to pull. If someone had an unusual name, he would always ask if it was Irish. He would say something like, 'Chang? Chang? That sounds like a fine Irish name.' When I was a kid, I thought it was pretty embarrassing, and, when I got older, I knew it wasn't a politically correct way to joke around, but, now that he is gone, it just seems, oh I don't know, folksy somehow."

She regarded him for a moment and then said, "It is a name with Hungarian and Yugoslavian origins. I was born near Zagreb."

"That was in Yugoslavia before the split. Croatia now. You speak English very good."

"I speak English very *well*," she replied with a smile. "Better than you, apparently. I have lived in the U.S. a very long time."

"Okay, you got me on that one. So what's with…"

"No, now it's my turn to ask you a question," she interrupted. "The war?" She nodded towards Max's leg. He had been wearing shorts that morning and the prosthetic was very noticeable.

"Oh, this?" Max looked down at it, a little self consciously. "It was from my last tour in Iraq. We were busting in on some bomb makers and they must have decided to go out with a bang because bang they went."

"Does it bother you?"

"The leg or the situation? Of course the leg bothers me. It hurts and it is a hell of a lot clumsier than my original wheel; but it works good enough…well, I mean I haven't let it slow me down much."

"I saw a picture of you back in the cabin; it looked like you were finishing a race of some sort. There were people with two good legs running behind you in that picture. I would say that it did not slow you down at all, not one bit."

"I've worked hard to compensate for it, but all of that work still didn't keep them from retiring me, so, here I am, the captain of this fine vessel you see here." He waved his coffee mug around, the gesture encompassing the entire boat. "I almost called her the *Ennui*, which is French for boring or something like that, because I really have been doing a whole lot of nothing lately. But, I think she did get the right name after all." He took a long sip from his coffee and regarded her closely, as if she was a problem he had to puzzle out.

"Now," said Max, "you can share a little something with me. What is your story and why were a handful of rejects from a Cure concert trying to rough you up? They did not seem a very capable bunch at all. It was surprising they were able to get the jump on you at all."

"I'm not sure about that either, I think I was drugged or something."

"Ya think?" replied Max sarcastically. "You were stoned out of your mind. I almost took you to the hospital, even though you said not to."

"I'm glad you didn't. What made you change your mind?"

"Like I said, I haven't had much excitement lately. I figured I would bring you back here just to see what would happen next."

Elena stood up and looked out over the blue waters where the river met the sound. She did not say anything for a moment, and when she did, she spoke softly, barely above a whisper: "I saw them once."

"Saw who?" Max replied.

"The Cure, I saw them in one of their first gigs. In London."

Max laughed at that. "You aren't old enough, they were big, when? Twenty, thirty years ago?"

She turned to face him, suddenly very grave, "I did see them.

Do you think I'm lying to you?"

"Yeah, right, take it easy, it just does not make any sense." Max poured himself some more coffee. *Shit, why does every good looking chick I meet turn out to be a friggin' nut job?*

"Nothing makes any sense. Not me. Not you. I should not even be here."

"Well, you are. Now what? You need to go to the cops—make a report. Those guys are going to hurt someone else if you let them get away with what they did to you."

"I said no police," Elena replied emphatically. "It would not help and it would just complicate matters. The police will not be able to stop those men. I'm looking for something that their...employer...wants. Or, more precisely, does not want me to get first."

So she is mixed up in something illegal, it could be worse.

"Which is why you should call the cops. You get on the wrong side of this, whatever it is, and you might be the one going to jail." Max gestured at her boat, across the marina. "The feds will take that lovely boat of yours away if they think you bought it with illegal money."

Elena shook her head. "I earned that boat, through the miracle of compounded interest." She leaned back and took in a deep breath. She seemed to savor the salt air for a moment before speaking again. "I am already on the wrong side of things. You do not understand what I am up against. Those who wish to see me fail can't be stopped. They can't be reasoned with. They can't even die."

"What do you mean?" Max asked, perplexed.

"They are the un-dead."

Max spat his coffee out all over himself. He tried to laugh and choke at the same time and so the only thing that came out was a sputtering bark that sounded like a phlegmatic seal with a pack-and-a-half-a-day Lucky Strike habit—non filtered. He had already accepted that this woman was a little off, if not downright crazy, and he was willing to deal with that because she was easy on the eyes. She was definitely a distraction, but this was over the top and she sounded downright delusional. *Undead? As in a bunch of freaking vampires? Biting people on the neck, living in a coffin, turning into a bat, vampires?* Quirky, slightly crazy chicks can be fun. Completely insane chicks cut off your old man while you sleep and throw it out the car window as they speed down the highway with all of your really good albums piled in the trunk... if you are lucky.

She stared at him impassively as he sputtered and spat and could finally pull in enough air to form an understandable response.

"They are what?" Max said and wiped his face with his sleeve, leaving it covered with brown stains. The front of his shirt and his shorts fared no better. At least the coffee had not been *too* hot.

"You heard me, and, if you could compose yourself, you could at least listen to what I have to say."

"I'm sorry," Max could speak again, although he did wish for something a little stronger than coffee at this point in time. *If you are going to slide down that rabbit hole, might as well do it with both feet, Maxy-boy.* "You really took me by surprise with that one, I'd expected some revelation about an-ex boyfriend in some sort of drug cartel you were running from and you stole his boat. Or, speaking of that nice boat of yours, sunken treasure or something.

But this, this is off the deep end, if you don't mind me saying, and I've spent my entire life swimming in the deep end, so I know it when I see it."

"Yes I know it sounds unbelievable. This whole situation is unbelievable to me too. I shouldn't even be here, don't you get it? You have to understand that they don't rest and won't rest until they get what they want or I get to it first and can use it against them."

Max poured himself another cup, black, his head beginning to throb. He took a sip and thought that it really could use a hefty dollop of the old Irish in it. Bushmills in black coffee in the morning was the breakfast of champions in his mind. *Too bad you couldn't get it at the drive through. Gimme a black coffee and Irish-ize it for a buck more.*

"Okay," Max said, still thinking about how he could slip a little something in his drink without her noticing. "Let's just say I accept your point, just for the sake of argument, that you are on some sort of mission against the, well, living dead...or is that a zombie, like *Night of the Living Dead*...yep, I think that's right: living dead: zombie, undead: vampire."

"Now you are just making fun."

"Nope, nope, I am just trying to get my mind around it. I always thought that if I could understand how to file my taxes, I could understand anything. But, the more you explain this, the less I understand. Now, I have seen the movies. In the old movies vampires (I can't believe I am even saying this) are either aristocrats in evening wear who live in castles or, as in the modern movies, vampires are attractive, pale young people dressed like rejects from *The Cure* who are brimming full of the teenage angst they should have outgrown a century or two ago. Those guys were just a bunch of douche bags and not very good ones at that. They tripped all over themselves."

"That is a puzzlement." Pausing, Elena looked around again, taking in the day. "You should not have been able to stop one of them, much less three of them."

"It seemed pretty easy to me. They were weak, clumsy, and obviously not used to fist fighting. Hell, one even fell right at my feet."

"So he couldn't fly either."

Max suppressed a laugh. "Not unless you consider dropping straight down and doing a face plant on the sidewalk flying, no."

"Impossible," Elena continued seriously. "That is not possible."

"You tell me that I roughed up some vampires and you are talking about what is not possible?"

Elena shot him a dirty look. "That's exactly what I am saying. There is something different about you. You did something to them and you are doing something to me."

"Me? I didn't do much except make some breakfast."

"It *is* you. There is something about you that changes things." She picked up a marlinspike that was hanging by the wheel. Max always had the five essential tools of a sailor: a marlinspike for splicing rope, a good knife, a hand bearing compass, needle nose pliers, a good flashlight with a night lens, and a coil of extra line always close at hand. In fact, he was so nervous about being empty handed in a pinch, with his particular disability, that he stashed groups of those five items all over the boat. Just in case.

She pulled the long, steel spike from its leather sheath and took it in both hands. She looked at it, slightly puzzled, and then straining with the effort, tried to bend it. She shrugged and, much to Max's relief, slid the spike back into its sheath and nonchalantly put it back on its hook. A crazy redhead girl was nerve-wracking enough, but a crazy redhead girl with a six inch long steel spike in her hand was downright terrifying.

"You said those men last night were weak, how so?"

"Well, like I said," replied Max, "they were clumsy, awkward, and they sure as hell couldn't take a punch. They acted like they had never fought before...like they didn't realize that a fist in the face could freaking *hurt*."

"It sounds like they were as taken aback by you as I am."

"And the fog, one of them kept going on about the dammed fog."

"Ah," she replied, jumping on this little tidbit of information. "You took them by surprise. They didn't expect to see you."

"That's it, that's what the little son of a bitch said. He said I shouldn't even be awake or some shit like that."

"And you had nothing with you? No holy objects? Nothing blessed?"

"I never was much of a religious person—not that I have a problem with anyone being religious, just that it never did anything for me. I went to church regularly as a kid because it made my mom happy, but I never saw the point. I was ambivalent before the war but Iraq really put the existence of God in doubt for me. If he does exist, he must be a real bastard to let that sort of shit happen to people."

"Oh, He exists. I know this for a fact. He still believes in you even if you don't believe in him. You must have gotten some help if you were able to defeat the undead like that. This means you are special."

Max took this in. It was unbelievable. He couldn't even pull off a simple magic trick, much less muster up some sort of cosmic life saving miracle. It was good old fashioned muscle and years of training and experience that put those punks on their asses and that was all there was to it. No real mystery there. As it was, he was enjoying himself. It was still a nice morning and it certainly was an entertaining fairy tale, as crazy at it sounded. He, never bashful when it came to a good breakfast, continued to eat as she went on and on. His stomach was nicely full at this point and he decided to see just how far her imagination could carry her.

"Okay, about those three dudes. Why were they mugging you in the cemetery in the middle of the night?"

"They attacked me because of what I was doing there, what I am doing in this town, and what I have been seeking in this area for years."

"What's that?"

"Revenge."

"Revenge, huh," Max replied, "now that is something I can understand. Some man did you wrong?"

"Something like that. I have made it my life's work, if you can call it that, to find and destroy the leader of the ones who attacked me."

"And you have chased him all the way to small town USA?"

"No," said Elena, "but something here might give me the edge

I need to take him down. He is too powerful for me to kill on my own. The older ones become more powerful the longer they exist. With every year they exist and every life they take, they become stronger."

"Well, hell. So you are in the monster hunting business. Must pay well." Max glanced again at Elena's boat with more than a little avarice.

"He hurt me once," Elena said solemnly. "He hurt me and many others and I will end him."

Max shifted uncomfortably. Her last comment sounded very much like something a rape victim might say. The very thought of such an obviously sweet and pretty girl being assaulted in that way made Max both sad and angry. He was a man used to violence, but rape was the one thing apart from child abuse that he found very unsettling. This thought also made things very clear to him. Such a trauma explained her odd behavior and the delusions about the vampires. Max was well aware how PTSD can skew a person's perception of reality and if she was this messed up in the head, it must have been a very traumatic event indeed. He suddenly felt very protective of the young girl.

Elena interrupted the awkward silence, "I don't want to talk any more about those things. I want to live just one day like a normal person. I want to go out into town and eat ice cream. I want to walk around with the normal people. I just want to be normal for just one day. Please, come with me. Take me around. Let's do some normal things just this once."

"Well, okay," said Max. Smiling she started walking toward the gangplank. "But I think you should put on some pants first. The people around here might be easygoing, but they might draw the limit on a girl walking about without her britches. Not that I would mind." To Max's delight, she flushed crimson briefly and scampered back into the cabin to retrieve the rest of her clothes. "And some shoes would be a good idea too!" Max called down to her.

While she was gone, Max stood up, collected the plates, and put them aside. He would wash them later. Later is always the best time to wash dishes. She returned just in time to see him slide his favorite .45 caliber pistol into the waist band at the small of his back. He then pulled his Hawaiian shirt over to cover the butt of the automatic.

"What's that for?"

"To cover my pale white self. You got to have a shirt on. You know, 'No shirt, no shoes, no service.' It is the Jungle Bird design, made famous by Magnum PI. It fits my livin' on the sailboat sort of lifestyle. Like it?"

"No, it looks like Salvador Dali got sick all over you. I mean the gun."

"Oh that little thing. It's a Springfield Armory 1911 with all the bells and whistles. Don't worry, I've got a carry permit. With all of those assholes after you, I'm thinking that this old cripple could use a little extra backup if they come after you again. I may not get the drop on them this time."

"They won't be out in the sunlight. I told you."

"So you did, but I'm not one to take chances. The worst thing you can do is underestimate your enemies. Now let's go and have a little fun."

Max led the way down to the dock, only to have his path

blocked by a tall, thin, older man clad only flip-flops and oily, paint-spattered shorts. His face and arms were deeply tanned and the deep wrinkles across his face made him look as if he was constantly squinting. An equally stained ball cap with the words "Cummings Diesel" embroidered on it was perched on top of a dandelion puff of white hair. He took the half smoked cigarette out of his mouth and held it between two nicotine stained fingers as he put both hands on his hips and squared off toward Max.

"Well if it ain't the gimp Marine. How's things in crippleville, Jarhead? "

"Too busy for your bullshit, Chief. Put on a shirt for Christ's sake. You're gonna scare the kids."

"Working on Mr. Habershaw's engine. Too hot down there for a shirt, by God. But you wouldn't know anything about work, especially your pecker. I bet it hasn't seen the nearside of a piece of tail in a month of days." As he said that, he first became aware of Elena just behind Max.

"Oops, sorry ma'am. Beg yer pardon. Didn't see ya back there. It's easy to lose a body if it is behind this big lump."

"Elena," Max said, tilting his head toward the newcomer. "Allow me to present Chief Boson's Mate William C. Whitley, U.S. Navy, retired. A saltier and crustier bastard you never did see. He could have been a cabin boy on the Titanic, except he was too old for the job even back then."

"There seems to be a lot of retired gentlemen around here."

"Oh, missy, this here little burg is a regular Bermuda Triangle for us worn out sea service types. We come here and just disappear."

"You could never disappear Chief," Max interjected, "that white fish belly of yours can be seen miles away; it's positively blinding. And as for your chest, I think you might have a glandular problem. You better see a doctor or start shopping at Victoria's Secret."

"See what I have to put up with ma'am?" He leaned in closer to Elena and winked. "Abuse this is, just plain abuse. I take care of the lad and all he gives me is abuse."

"Don't let him fool ya," Max said, "Chief here runs the marina and will do repairs for cash or whiskey, but not credit. He's been here since he retired. When was that Chief, oh about a hundred years ago?"

"Oh," interjected Elena, "you are the harbormaster then. I hope you got the money I left for you." She gestured behind her, toward her boat. "It was late and I did not want to disturb you, so I put it in an envelope and slid it under your door."

"I got it," Chief replied. "Paid in full with a very nice tip to boot. Thank you. Unlike *some* tightwads around here I could mention." He stared meaningfully at Max, who responded with a simple shrug. "You're all set for the rest of the week and if you would like me to look at your engine, it would be my pleasure."

"No thank you. I get it serviced regularly. You are too kind."

"Ma'am," said Chief, and doffed his hat.

"Yeah, yeah, Chief," said Max, "You are only nice to the pretty girls. Now shove off, we have some sightseeing to do."

"Don't mind me in the least, Jarhead. I'll just be here, slavin' away for the ungrateful."

"Cry me a river, why don't you." Max playfully punched the

old man in the shoulder as they walked past him. Chief gave an exaggerated wince and rubbed his shoulder.

"See what I put up with miss?" he called after them. "You just come to me if you ever need anything; that boy couldn't find his own ass with both hands."

Laughing, Max led Elena off the dock and onto Front Street.

"He's an old coot, sure enough, but his heart is in the right place. It takes a long time for him to warm up to you, but once he does, he'll do anything for you. You, on the other hand. Looks like he took to you right away."

"I guess I have that affect on people," said Elena, smiling up at Max.

"Well, where do you want to go on your day off, as it were."

"I just want to do whatever people do around here," she replied.

"Well, other than watching the grass grow, there are some historical sites pretty close. They have some nice gardens I hear."

"That would be nice. Out in the sunshine, under this marvelous blue sky. Yes, take me to the gardens."

They turned left down Pollock Street and walked the few blocks to the historical district. It was a quiet little town and there was not much traffic, even at the busiest time of day. Stately homes lined the street, each one with a white wooden placard on the front porch explaining the house's historical significance in black calligraphy. The magnolias were in bloom and the scent of them permeated the air. It seemed that each and every house had its own mature magnolia tree right in the middle of a perfectly manicured lawn. It was another part of the town that Max enjoyed. Walking around, breathing in not only the magnolias, but also jasmine, honeysuckle, and azalea. Always a fan of history, especially the Revolutionary and Civil wars, he got a kick out of seeing the "George Washington Slept Here" signs on a few of the houses. *That guy sure as hell got around.* The locals were nice; used to seeing Marines taking in the sights. They would come up to him sometimes, for a handshake and a "thank you for your service." If the weather was hot, and Max was wearing shorts, they would always glance down, trying to get a look at his leg without him noticing. He always noticed. He also noticed the pity that would slip into their voices or dance briefly across their faces. Max hated that.

Today they were not looking at Max but at the girl walking next to him. To Max, she seemed more lovely every time he glanced at her, a grin plastered all over her face. She was exuding this vibe, a feeling of abject joy that he could almost feel coming off her in waves. Almost dancing along the sidewalk, she stopped to peer in a window or to sniff a flower. She seemed to be particularly drawn to the children walking along the tree-lined streets with their parents. At first, she just stared at them with a look that approached awe, and, seeing her smiles returned, she would stop and say hello to each and every one of them. Almost wistfully, she would ask them their ages or if they were having a fun day out. The parents didn't seem to mind. Max supposed they felt the vibe too. As it was, in this town, they just saw a vet out with his lady and felt pretty safe with them. Max could still catch the pitying glances if he happened to watch them instead of Elena. Perhaps they felt she was harmless because they thought he was harmless. Max did not like the idea that people thought he was harmless.

Just before they got to the Palace, she actually bent over a baby carriage and made cooing noises. The mother made a comment about how natural a mother she looked.

"I never could have any," she replied sadly before moving on.

Max was so engrossed in watching Elena, that he was surprised when they reached their destination. Sitting at the corner of Pollock and George Streets, the Palace was a reconstruction of a colonial period mansion, the mansion of the state's first governor in fact, including extensive gardens. Max paid the admission at the visitor's center and they went onto the grounds. Docents, dressed up in period garb, gave tours of the house. As they explained life in the seventeen hundreds, Elena would occasionally correct the guide on one fact or another: how the clothes were not fastened quite correctly or how the colors of the walls were not exactly period. When the docent invited them to try their hand at the authentic harpsichord in the ballroom, she sat right down and played a perfect Minuet in G. The other tourists clapped enthusiastically, but Max stood silent, looking at her as she smiled, the sun's reflection off the candelabra on top of the instrument dancing in her eyes.

"Talk about a ringer," said the guide, coming out of character, "you must have a degree in colonial history or something."

"No, not exactly," she said, "I guess you could say that sometimes I feel like I was there."

Elena really enjoyed the gardens, full of flowers and topiary. She gazed at every blossom and ran her hand through every fountain. Every moment was one of pure happiness and obvious discovery. Almost childlike, she stood still for minutes on end, staring at a hummingbird as it flitted around a honeysuckle patch, sipping from blossom after blossom. She was a beautiful woman to begin with, but the joy and amazement that filled her face made her into the most lovely woman Max had ever seen. Every time she smiled, a thrill coursed up his spine. Watching her revel in the sunshine, Max could not believe the horrible and insane things she was saying just a few hours before.

After the gardens, Max and Elena wandered around downtown for a while. Largely made of red brick, buildings had been standing for a few hundred years and had been used for various purposes through time. Recently, they had been mostly turned into the quaint and artsy shops that attracted tourists. A gallery here, a bric-a-brac store there, and lawyers everywhere. Max had always been amazed at just how many lawyers' offices there were in such a small hamlet. The word "lawyer" definitely sent more chills up his spine than the word "vampire."

Max watched Elena closely as they passed the old Church that stood halfway down Middle Street. Three hundred years old, its yard was full of crumbling colonial era gravestones shaded by ancient live oaks draped with Spanish moss. Max wondered if she, with her fear of being chased by vampires, would either wig out at the sight of so many graves or find herself attracted to the crosses dotting the lawn. She did neither. Ignoring the old church, she headed straight across the street, against the light, and went right into the Pepsi Cola museum on the corner. She sat down and ordered what she said was her first soft drink ever. She drank it with a sparkle in her eye, and declared it "simply amazing." Quickly, they left, off to Elena's next discovery.

Dinner was fun. They sat outdoors on the rooftop of a local restaurant, had a view of the river, and listened to Jazz. Jazz she knew quite well and she hummed along with the songs she knew and tried to hum along with the songs she didn't, tapping her foot in time. Everything that came was "delicious" and she ate her food and most of Max's as well. The chocolate mile-high pie and ice cream at the end was the big hit. Max sat back and let her tackle the whole thing on her own.

They left as the sun was going down, and, walking back to the boat, she slipped her hand in his. This surprised Max, as he hadn't even thought about the day taking *that* sort of turn...he was an amputee after all. Then again, she obviously had issues herself, so things sort of evened out.

When they got to the boat, she kissed him briefly, and with a quick "goodnight," she went into the forward cabin and locked the door. *Well, Maxy-boy, looks like you've had your first date in about four years. Nice girl, good looking, great to take home to meet the family, until she tries to drive a stake through Uncle Mort's heart. It's been a long dry spell for you, you should hang tight and see where this was going.*

With a double shot of scotch and a few oxycontin inside him, Max settled down on the couch and rapidly fell into a rare dreamless sleep.

When he woke up, she was gone.

Chapter Five

Max was not the only person up the night before. Agnes Pritchett had suffered from insomnia for a long time. She did not find the night restful at all. They say that old people don't sleep as much as young ones, but her sleeplessness had nothing to do with her age. No one would guess it to look at her, but she had seen her hundredth birthday come and go not so long ago, and she was as active and alert as she had been when that nice boy, Jack Kennedy got himself shot. She *had* to. She was the self appointed memory of the town and she had to keep alert because no one else *remembered*. She had watched Max go out and she had seen him return with *that woman* in tow. She had spent the rest of the night watching the boat, after making sure that her door was, in fact, triple bolted shut. The crippled man seemed harmless enough, and she had felt sorry for him. He was like so many of the boys that had come home from the Great War or the Second World War without a leg, or an arm, or eyes. She had seen so many over the decades leave home, all hale and healthy, proud to go out and fight for Uncle Sam, only to come back broken shells of their former selves…if they came back at all.

For a time, she had lived in apartments down by the boat works, before they went and tore them down to rebuild that silly Governor's Mansion for the tourists. That was back in forty eight or forty seven, a few years after she finally moved out of her parent's house. There was a fellow downstairs who lost an arm in Okinawa. She could hear him screaming every night from some God awful dream or another. He hanged himself one hot, muggy night. Yes, she did feel some sympathy for the man with the fake leg, but he was going to get himself in all kinds of trouble. *Nothing good comes from consorting with that kind.*

She felt a catch in her chest when the crippled man brought the girl onto his boat. The badness was back in town.

It was long ago: so long ago that Agnes sometimes felt that it would never come again and all of this watching and waiting had been a waste of time. Over eighty years of watching the dark, in case *they* ever came back.

Agnes had been just a slip of a girl back then, not yet twenty. After high school, she took a job as an assistant librarian at the old library, before it moved to its current location on Middle Street. She loved books and she loved the children who would come in. She was delighted every time she could introduce them to Mark Twain or Washington Irving. Prohibition had started a few years before, and things started to change.

Coastal North Carolina had always been a smuggler's paradise. The myriad of sounds, rivers, and inlets were perfect places hiding ships. Pirates had used them to hide their boats and their treasure long before there the United States was a country. Blockade runners used them to get supplies ashore before the Yankees could run them down with their sleek and fast frigates. That was when there had almost been two countries. So, it was no wonder that in her youth bootleggers used this coast to bring in whiskey from Europe and rum from the Islands. With a flat enough boat, a bootlegger could run a load of hooch up the Neuse almost all the way to Raleigh before he had to offload. Once they got past the barrier islands, there were literally thousands of little hidey holes and creeks to slip in and get the deal done before the government men had the slightest clue.

Agnes didn't drink, not back then, not a single drop in all the years since. Drink did not bother her, however, and the whole prohibition seemed a waste of time. What did she care if a body had a drop or two?

The whole town knew about the bootleggers, of course. Many of them were fishermen just trying to make a little extra money. They would go out for a few days and come back with nets full of fish and holds full of fish of another sort. In all, they were not bad folks. Your neighbor might run some at night. The man next to you in church might pick it up from your neighbor in his truck and finish the run. A few extra dollars in the pocket was a good thing and kept the town going even after the market crash. Agnes certainly couldn't blame anyone who had to bend a poorly thought out law if it put clothes on the backs of his children and food in their bellies.

In spite of the bootlegging, New Bern had been a quiet little backwater until the day little Ritchie Adkins came up missing. The whole town turned out to find him, but it was Agnes who finally did. She had a feeling that he was up by the paper mill, and that's where she found him, stuffed in a drain pipe, his throat all tore out. At first they all thought the boy had seen one of the rum runners making a delivery, but that was dismissed offhand. The rum runners were part of the town and they wouldn't do that to one of their own. Besides, his throat had not been cut, but torn apart as if an animal had got at him. The county sheriff decided that it was an alligator that did it; and that was that. Agnes had not been too sure about an alligator. She had never heard of an alligator killing something and not eating it, much less putting it in a drainage pipe. Agnes was there when they put the boy into the ground. As his mother cried and threw herself on the coffin, she promised herself that she would get to the bottom of it as best she could.

She had been a pretty girl, if in a serious way. Glasses from reading too much and hair pulled back in a severe bun gave her a austere and no nonsense appearance that helped keep the children quiet in the library stacks. Her outward appearance really did not reflect the curious idealist that dwelled within. She would pour over Arthur Conan Doyle stories at night, when no one was looking, and she fancied herself a budding detective in her own right. If anything went amiss, it would gnaw at her until she found some way to put it right, whether as innocuous as getting back too much change from the soda fountain, or some perceived injustice concerning the filling of a pothole (or rather lack of filling) on Main Street. When something was wrong, she was going to do something about it.

Richie wasn't the first person to go missing that spring. A Methodist, she went to Centenary United every Sunday and volunteered in the soup kitchen every evening after work. She noticed a few of the familiar faces stopped showing up, one after another. Of course, the tramps in town were a transient lot, given to disappearing for a day or two, off on a drunk or hopping a train for a change of scenery. When one of her regulars did not show up one day, she began to wonder. She had only known him as Mister Bobby, an old toothless gent who could barely walk much less jump on a freight train headed for California. He never, missed his soup. She looked for him by the tracks that night but could not find a trace of him. She did notice that the other tramps seemed nervous, like a herd of deer, huddled together after one of them had been taken down by the hunter. They clustered together, looking uneasily, and refused to answer her when she tried to talk to them. The Hobo code. She would not get any help from them.

A few hobos missing, a sharecropper shack or two found empty...nobody noticed or seemed to care. In late May, however, when the *Anna B*, a fishing boat out of Oriental, came up the river on a wind borne tide without a soul on aboard, people began to lock their doors at night. The boat was owned by two brothers, who had named her after their late mother. They were given to picking up a little extra cargo in the middle of the night before going on to cast their nets in the sound. The deal could have gone bad for them or they could have been pinched by the revenue men, except that their hold full of Bahamas rum was still there, untouched. Not a bullet hole or piece of broken glass anywhere on the boat, which still had a quarter tank of diesel down below. The men were just gone. No one saw them again.

Agnes could feel the tone of the town beginning to turn with the appearance of what was being called "the ghost ship." Locked doors, drawn shades, and children hustled indoors before the sun dipped on the horizon. The spring took an unsettling chill, with nightly mists more suited for late fall than the cusp of summer. She took to staying awake all night, nestled in her chair in front of her window, watching the night pass.

She had fallen asleep one night in spite of herself and woke up with a start. Her lantern had gone out so she was sitting in the dark, but there was some light coming in the window from the electric streetlights that had sprung up all over town in the last few years. Most houses had electricity, but the senior Pritchett insisted on oil lamps as he considered them cheaper and safer. After all, if you left an electric light on all night, it would keep running up a bill until someone came and shut it off. If you left a lamp lit, it would burn up the oil and then go out.

Agnes was awake, but she felt very tired and moved very slowly as she leaned forward to peer out her living room window. *This is what it must feel like to be drunk*, she thought. Slightly dizzy, and still feeling like she was sinking in a pool of molasses, she pressed her nose against the pane. A thick fog swirled through the street, curling up the trees and houses to cover everything in a thick cottony blanket. The electric lights caused the fog to glow with a sickly yellow phosphorescence. All was still, until *he* came.

Out of the darkness and into the light of the street lamps he strolled, casually, as if he had all the time in the world and nowhere particular to go. Very tall and lean, the fog curling around bone thin arms and legs as he walked with a silver tipped cane in one hand. His face was pale, paler than the fog itself, and was framed by long sideburns and goatee of jet black whiskers. He had a bowler hat cocked jauntily on his forehead. A long golden watch chain glimmered as it swung against his suit vest. Agnes thought he looked like he should be whistling as he walked along, without a care in the world. When she thought this, thought about *him*, he started as if he had heard something, stopped in his tracks and slowly turned towards her. Agnes had been struggling to stay awake, but when he looked directly at her, he smiled, and that brought her fully awake in an instant. *Teeth. Oh my sweet Jesus, the teeth.*

He half danced and half floated up the walk, bobbing left and bobbing right, arms swaying in time with music only he could hear. All the time staring straight at Agnes, his eyes two glowing lumps of coal at the bottom of a deep, dark well. He slid right up to the window and only a half inch pane of glass separated them.

"Let me in," he said.

Agnes said nothing, shivering as she stood there, nose to nose.

"Let me in, girl. I just want to give you a little kiss. Just a little kiss and I'll be on my way." He raised his hand and ran his finger across the glass. The fingernail, long and sharp, made a squealing sound as it scratched the window.

Agnes was frozen in place, staring into those coal red eyes. He put his talon-like fingernails under the window pane and began to lever up the window. She watched it slowly rise between them until nothing separated her from him. Her nostrils were filled with the horrific smell of decay, but she still could not move, mesmerized by his gaze. He smiled and his teeth lengthened as he did so, dozens of shiny, white spikes that grew past his lips and glistened in the light. To Agnes, he looked like those horrific fish, more teeth than head, that fishermen sometimes pulled up from the deepest depths. They were also creatures of eternal darkness. She did not move as he leaned in the window and began to reach for her, his hands growing into the talons of a bird of prey. His jaw began to open wider, filled with those horrific teeth, dislocating as a snake does to swallow its prey whole.

Still she did not move, frozen and locked in his gaze. She felt the ice on her arms as his fingers stroked her wrists.

Jarred by the piercing cold of his touch, she suddenly found her paralysis gone. She quickly turned even as he was tugging at her and grabbed the first thing her hands reached: a large, leather-bound book that rested on a shelf nearby. All good Methodists have the Bible close at hand and she swung the book hard against the creatures head and shouted the first thing that came to mind, "THE LIBRARY IS NOW CLOSED!" With a thud the book hit the beast on the side of the head and knocked it against the window sill.

"THE LIBRARY IS NOW CLOSED!" Again, this time an uppercut to its chin that rocked its head back with a snap and sent its silly bowler hat rolling into the night.

Agnes did not know why she said those words, they just felt right to her. She always thought words held power and these were *her* words of power. The library was *hers*. The town was *hers*. She was damned if she was going to let a filthy, stinking caricature of a human being get the best of her. She brought the book down again.

"THE. LIBRARY. IS. NOW. CLOSED. PLEASE. CHECK. YOUR. BOOKS." Each word was punctuated by a blow from the heavy book and blood began to spatter from the thing's torn lips and broken nose onto the white walls, the floor, and the window sill. It began to scream back at her as it struggled to back out of the window, but it lost its grip each time she struck its head.

Finally, it fell backward onto the lawn and scrambled back to its feet. Agnes, disheveled and panting, shouted out the window at it.

"THANK YOU FOR YOUR PATRONAGE, NOW SCRAM!"

It rose to its feet, bleeding from shattered lips and a nose that was now cocked at a serious angle.

"I will tear out your beating heart you bitch!" it growled at her and then turned and leaped across the street, over the house facing hers, and was gone. The mist rapidly followed behind, leaving the street clear and the stars crisp overhead.

Agnes sagged against the wall, clutching her book, crying in soft gasps. She leaned to the side and vomited over and over again until nothing came up and her body was wracked by convulsive heaves. Once she caught her breath, she glanced down at her weapon, the talisman that she used to drive away the beast. She started laughing when she saw what it was. The laughter bubbled up from deep inside her, both of relief and the utter peculiarity of what she held in her hands. In gold letters across the black leather cover, were the words, *The Rise And Fall Of The Roman Empire*. Gibbons' boring volume had been the tool to drive the demon away. Her laughing became louder and more shrill as she looked at the cover. There was never a more serious book for such serious business, indeed, but it still was not the Bible she thought it was. She believed that it had the power to do what it did, and that, she thought, must be what really mattered.

She closed the window, straightened up the curtains, picked everything off the floor, and sat huddled in her father's chair with her book clutched tightly in her arms until the break of dawn.

Agnes stayed up the next night, Gibbon's by her side, and she stayed up the nights that followed. The fog did not return to New Bern, and the spring peacefully slid into a languid summer. The town gave an almost perceptible collective sigh of relief when they could finally feel the events of the past spring fading into memory. She still watched every night, but, by the time summer was turning to autumn, and the children were back to their studies, she once again preoccupied herself with the business of stocking shelves and helping the young find just the right book for whatever report they had been assigned. She could almost convince herself that the encounter with the darkness that night had been just a horrible dream. Almost, because every time she looked at *The Rise And Fall*, kept at the ready on her bedside table, she could see the dark stains the creature's foul blood left on the cover. She hoped that she would never see that thing again, but she knew, just knew, that there was no way she could have harmed it too seriously and that she had only run it off for a time.

The mist returned in the fall. This time, it was a policeman who first went missing.

He picked up his nightstick and his revolver and announced that he was going to walk the docks just to check on things. The last anyone ever saw of him was blue of the back of his uniform jacket fading into the swirling fog. With one of their own missing, the police went into high gear, searching for days along the docks and the river. They came up as empty as a church on Monday morning.

Agnes resumed her nightly vigil when the officer vanished, certain that the Dapper Man would make good his promise and come for her; however, she was not contented to just watch and wait this time. She purchased a town map and pinned it to her bedroom wall. Then, she poured over every book she could find on the subject. She was proud of her little library, but the collection was severely lacking in the occult department. It had Mr. Stoker's novel, of course, but that was fiction and how was she to know how much of that was based on truth and how much was the author's fancy? Obviously, there had to be *some* basis in truth there, because she had seen it with her own two eyes and smelled its rankness with her own nose. Besides *Dracula*, the collection consisted only of Mary Shelly's *Frankenstein* and an anthology titled *Creepy Poems for A Spooky Halloween*. She rolled her eyes but looked in anyway. There was Poe of course, and *The Ghost House* by Robert Frost, but one of the last pieces of verse caught her eye, *Christabel*. It was written over a hundred years before by Samuel Coleridge and ostensibly told the story of a lady vampire in Hungary. The second stanza particularly leapt right off the page.

> *Is the night chilly and dark?*
> *The night is chilly, but not dark.*
> *The thin gray cloud is spread on high,*
> *It covers but not hides the sky.*
> *The moon is behind, and at the full;*
> *And yet she looks both small and dull.*
> *The night is chill, the cloud is gray:*
> *'T is a month before the month of May,*
> *And the Spring comes slowly up this way.*

"A month before the month of May, and the spring comes slowly up this way," she said softly to herself. It was early spring when the badness had come to her town, just like in the poem.

The fogs and the fear made it seem that spring would never come. *And the thin gray cloud that covers the sky without hiding it?* She was aghast. That certainly described the mist that accompanied The Dapper Man, the man with the horribly great fish teeth. It was as if Mr. Coleridge were describing the events of the last spring, as if he knew what was going to happen. *Perhaps that is how they always come.*

She rapidly flipped to the back of the book where there was a small biography of each of the authors. Coleridge's notation mentioned that he had been influenced by the writings of Augustine Calmet, a Dominican Monk who had extensively researched the supernatural across Europe in the seventeenth century.

Now, I really have something to sink my teeth into, she thought. She was on the next train to Raleigh and the University. The library there was bound to have much more she could look through. The trip took a few hours both ways, but if she took the last train home, she would still have several good hours at North Carolina State University. Luckily, there was a station very near the campus. A quick question to a freshman, identified by the silly looking beanie in school colors on his head, and she was in the library soon after.

A quick perusal through the card catalogue told her where to look and she found herself on the third floor, way in the back of the building where the older and more obscure books were kept. As she walked through the stacks, and the smell of old paper, Agnes felt very at ease. Books were her world, and to her, the shelves filled with the wisdom of the ages were more grand than any Roman forum or Greek temple. Any other day, she would spend hours just browsing, picking along the titles on the shelf, looking for something unusual. Today she did not have the time. She scanned the numbers pasted on the books' spines until she came to what she was looking for. She panicked for a moment when she pulled out the book. It was in French: *Dissertations sur les apparitions des anges, des démons et des esprits.* She had taken the language in school of course, but she was afraid that schoolgirl's French would not be up to a volume of such magnitude. She pulled out the next book on the shelf and breathed a sigh of relief. This one was in English, translated in Eighteen Fifty. The translator had also included a biography of Calmet in the preface. Agnes found a carrel in a quiet corner and eagerly opened her book.

Antoine Augustin Calmet was a Benedictine monk, born at the turn of the eighteenth century. He apparently had devoted much of his life to investigating and writing about supernatural happenings throughout Europe. The first chapters were about exorcism and demon possession, so she brushed through those very quickly. It was not until the middle of the book, when a chapter title caught her eye.

DEAD PERSONS IN HUNGARY WHO SUCK THE BLOOD OF THE LIVING

This was more like it! The chapter related a story of a soldier who was billeted in the house of a peasant family:

"They were all sitting down to dinner when the master of the house saw a person he did not know come in and sit down to table also with them. The master of the house was strangely frightened at this, as were the rest of the company. The soldier knew not what to think of it, being ignorant of the matter in question. But the master of the house being dead the very next day, the soldier inquired what it meant. They told him that it was the body of the father of his host, who had been dead and buried for ten years, which had thus come to sit down next to him, and had announced and caused his death.

"The soldier informed the regiment of it in the first place, and the regiment gave notice of it to the general officers, who commissioned the Count de Cabreras, captain of the regiment of Alandetti infantry, to make information concerning this circumstance. Having gone to the place, with some other officers, a surgeon and an auditor, they heard the depositions of all the people belonging to the house, who attested unanimously that the ghost was the father of the master of the house, and that all the soldier had said and reported was the exact truth, which was confirmed by all the inhabitants of the village.

"In consequence of this, the corpse of this specter was exhumed, and found to be like that of a man who has just expired, and his blood like that of a living man. The Count de Cabreras had his head cut off, and caused him to be laid again in his tomb. He also took information concerning other similar ghosts, amongst others, of a man dead more than thirty years, who had come back three times to his house at meal time. The first time he had sucked the blood from the neck of his own brother, the second time from one of his sons, and the third from one of the servants in the house; and all three died of it instantly and on the spot. Upon this deposition the commissary had this man taken out of his grave, and finding that, like the first, his blood was in a fluid state, like that of a living person, he ordered them to run a large nail into his temple, and then to lay him again in the grave.

"He caused a third to be burnt, who had been buried more than sixteen years, and had sucked the blood and caused the death of two of his sons. The commissary having made his report to the general officers, was deputed to the court of the emperor, who commanded that some officers, both of war and justice, some physicians and surgeons, and some learned men, should be sent to examine the causes of these extraordinary events. The person who related these particulars to us had heard them from Monsieur the Count de Cabreras, at Fribourg en Brigau, in 1730.

The other stories were similar and had the same components that Bram Stoker put in his work. She also learnt that these creatures had been a bane for as long as man could remember. The Israelites of the Bible called one *Lilith*, the Greeks called them *lamiae*, and even Ovid was quoted in the book, describing demons he called *strigae* that would fly down upon people and steal their blood. The dapper man had flown. Flown away after Agnes had popped him a good one. It was all there. Vampires, also called revenants, were animated or resurrected corpses that would come to feed on the living. Russia, Greece, Hungary, Rome. All had their vampires and Agnes could see patterns emerging. They could only come out at night, a stake through the heart or head would kill them as would fire. Decapitation. Holy symbols. Not only could they be driven away, they could be destroyed and Agnes was going to be the one to kill that horrid thing with the snappy bowler hat.

One final phrase gave her chills. It was attributed to an old pagan goddess, Ishtar:

I shall raise up the dead and they shall eat the living.
I shall make the dead outnumber the living.

Agnes imagined the missing policeman, his blue uniform stained by the earth mold, face mottled with decay, coming across the street to take her, to feed off her, to make her one of them with Dapper Dan dancing alongside him, his teeth gleaming in the moonlight.

Not in my town. Not while I can do anything about it. I will get them before they get another crack at me.

When she got home, she pulled out the newspaper clippings of every missing person or unsolved murder in three counties since she had started collecting them last spring. She put a push-pin in her map for every incident. A gray one for the place the missing person had last been seen and a red one for every body that had been found. There were quite a few of both cases, but most of the articles proposed more mundane causes of death. Heart attack, suicide, and accident. The ones with the death listed as "unknown" or those where the official cause of death didn't match the way the body was found or what was known about the victim *(twenty year olds don't have heart attacks for gosh sake)* got a second, purple pin pushed next to the original gray or red one.

This thing was like an animal, she thought. *What do I know about animals? I hurt him, that's for sure. What do animals do when they get hurt? The go to their dens, that's what. Straight to their safe place.*

With that thought, she pulled out a ruler and a grease pencil. She found her house on the city map and marked it with an X. She did the same where the house across the street should be. With the ruler, she connected the two marks and extended the line in the direction that the thing had flown.

Straight as a vampire crow flies.

She studied the map for a moment, then, she began circling the pins that represented the earliest incidents last April, *the month before the month of May*, and those that represented the newest ones this fall. Finished, Agnes stood back and studied the results of her efforts. The pattern was obvious as soon as she took that step back. The line cut to the north, straight through the town and went right through a cluster of pins that was just on the other side of the cemetery. It was the poorer side of town. *That's where I would start out if I were him,* she thought. *Take the easy ones, the ones least likely to be missed and build up my strength before venturing farther out. He has to be there somewhere.*

Agnes was not sure if he was intentionally hiding near the Cemetery, or if it was simply coincidental to being in the less affluent area. They were supposed to be drawn to graveyards according to the books, but she could not imagine that it would make a decent hiding place for the undead. There were no large mausoleums, and newly disturbed earth would be a dead giveaway. She decided to follow the line, at the height of the day of course, and see what she could ferret out.

She memorized the path she would have to take to stay as close to the line on her map as possible. It took her through the Cemetery, a place that she had always considered serene because of the ancient tombstones and the large live oak draped with Spanish moss. Now, even in broad daylight it seemed brooding and somehow sinister—as if the infestation in her town was a sickness…a consumption that was spreading decay throughout the spirit of the place.

From the cemetery, she continued north until she reached Craven Street, near the bridge across the Neuse river. It was not far from the drain pipe where poor little Ritchie Adkins was found. The neighborhood was quiet. Agnes stood on the sidewalk and slowly turned around in a circle, trying to take in every detail of the houses that stood on either side of her, looking for something, *anything* out of the ordinary that would lead her to her goal.

Think, Agnes, think. Where would he hide? Where do they make their little lairs?

She began to go over what the books said about the creatures' habits. *They hate sunlight and have to be in their graves before sun-up. They like the dark. They need someplace secure and safe to sleep. There has to be something unique about the place he chooses and something comforting to him. Something to remind him of the crypts and castles of his homeland that the books described.*

The house on the end of the street looked sort of like a castle, with a Queen Anne style turret on the front. It was a little bigger than most and must have looked grand back when it was built and before this side of town fell out of favor with the better off citizens. It was really falling apart and did not look lived in. The yard was unkempt and several of the shutters were hanging askew. Then she saw it.

Basements were very unusual this close to the river as they tended to flood. This house did have one, she could see the small basement windows along the bottom of the house's exterior wall. The odd thing that caught her attention was not the windows, but what they had in them. Curtains. All of the basement windows were covered with thick, canvas, curtains. *Who puts curtains in their basement windows?* The few dry basements she had seen were used for storage and for workshops if they were big enough. In either case, the windows were left uncovered to provide more light in such gloomy spaces. The only reason for such heavy curtains was to keep light out and to keep people from looking in. It fitted what she had learned and she had to get a closer look.

Glancing around and seeing no one watching, she slipped through the neglected and weed choked yard and crouched down against the house. Taking off her wide brimmed hat, she pulled the long hatpin from her hair and used it to dig at the putty that held the pane of glass in its frame. All she wanted was a little look inside. The putty came off in large, chalky chunks and she could just get the tip of the hatpin around the edge of the glass. Slowly and carefully so as not to break it, she gently pried the glass back just enough to get her hatpin past it and onto the canvas. She was able to push the canvas aside a few inches which was enough for her to see in. The first thing she saw was the concrete floor with a drain set in it. The drain would not be unusual at all and the reddish stains on it *could* be just rust, but, just at the edge of her vision, lying on the floor, was a pair of legs. She could make out the black shoes and the cuff of the trousers, but that was about it. The trousers were blue. Blue like the blue of a policeman's uniform. She just had to see more. Pushing the pin as far to the side as she could, she slid the canvas a few more inches aside. She could now see the legs up to the knees, and that the person, or body, was laying on its back. On a concrete floor. In a basement.

A stray ray of sunshine came over her shoulder as she shifted for a better look and penetrated the gloomy interior. It landed on the pair of legs which immediately began to smoke as if a fire suddenly began to smolder inside the cloth. The legs were pulled back into the shadows and out of sight with a horrible sounding hiss of rage and pain. Agnes stood up quickly and began to run. The last thing that she saw before she sprang away frightened, was, perched on a shelf above the pair of legs, a brown bowler hat.

Agnes was certain that the blue clad legs did not belong to the Dapper Man. The missing policeman was down there and he had moved. He had moved when hit by the sunlight. Just like in the books. The beast had made another of his kind.

I shall raise up the dead and they shall eat the living. I shall make the dead outnumber the living.

She had to get away from that place. She had to convince someone to help her. Agnes had convinced herself that she could handle the vampire by herself. After all, she had chased him away that night easily, but more than one monster was another matter.

Just how many are down there, hidden in the darkness?

She began to hurry back the way she had come when she heard the front door slam open and heavy foot falls echoing along the wooden porch. She began to run.

"Girl! What are you doing over there?" a man shouted.

She turned to see a giant of a man, well over six feet tall, with broad shoulders and hands the size of dinner plates. He wore stained overalls and a reddish beard covered most of his angry face.

"Girl! What you doin' messin' round my house?" His boots were loud on the porch as he began to run toward the front steps, keeping his eyes on her, running his hands along the rail.

"My hat, the wind blew it," she called back, clutching her hat to her chest. Hidden underneath it was her hatpin, clutched tightly in her fist.

"Come here, girl! I want to talk to you." He had reached the steps and he bounded down them to the lawn.

Agnes began to sprint as soon as she saw his feet touch the

grass. "I can't! Late!"

"I said, COME HERE!" He picked up his pace as soon as he saw Agnes begin her dash. She went through a gap in the neglected fence and was on the street with him close behind. She could hear the *clomp, clomp* of his boots on the pavement getting closer. She was breathing hard. The life of the librarian had not one prepared her for a foot race. She put her head down and willed her legs to move as fast as they could, but she could hear him gaining on her. Her chest burned and she gasped for breath. Her legs began to feel unsteady underneath her.

"Help!" She gasped. "Somebody help me!"

She could now hear his ragged breathing close behind her and she could almost imagine his hot breath upon her neck. She cut across the sidewalk and ran across the grass, toward a space between two ramshackle houses.

"STOP, YOU LITTLE BITCH!" He was right behind her. Without even thinking she tossed her hat aside and spun around, swinging her arm wide. The hatpin, held like a teacher's wooden pointer in her extended hand, struck the man solidly in the shoulder. His momentum carried him right into her and they both went sprawling around the corner of the nearest house. He was on top of her and his weight was terrible. She thought he would smother with his bulk. Growling, he brought both of his hands to her neck and began to squeeze. Already gasping from the run, Agnes could not breathe at all and her vision began to go gray.

"I'm gonna kill you for that!" the man said as his hands pressed even harder, his fingers digging into her throat. A sound of rushing wind filled her ears and she could feel herself sinking into the whirlwind.

THWAK!

Agnes felt, rather than heard the impact. The man on top of her stiffened and then slumped over. She struggled under his prostrate form for a moment and then felt it being lifted off her. She looked up into the face of an older black man. He was just as big as the man who had been choking her, if not bigger. A snow white beard framed perfectly white teeth. Agnes squirmed backwards on her hands and feet until halted by the wood of the opposite wall.

The black man scowled at the unconscious form he held firmly by the back of his overalls. His other hand held an axe handle, its end covered with blood and a few pieces of red hair.

"Ain't nobody gonna be molestin' gals in my side yard!" He kicked his captive in the small of his back.

"He…he…was going to kill me," Agnes gasped.

"He ain't gonna be hurtin' anybody now," replied the man. "Not if old Lucius Brown has anything to say about it!"

Agnes sat up and put her hands to her neck. She felt bruised where his fingers had been. Lucius gave the man a shake, lifted him up, and dragged him to the curb where he rolled him into the gutter. He then wiped his hand and the end of the axe handle clean on the grass before walking back to Agnes to help her up.

"Are you alright, Miss?" he said.

"Fine. I'll be fine," she replied, even though she did not *feel* fine. "Are you going to just leave him there?"

"Yes, Miss. He'll wake with a hell of a headache and won't mess with you no mo'. I learned him a powerful lesson, I did."

"Should we call the police?"

Lucius laughed. "Police? A black man hits a white man with an axe handle in this town and how you think the police gonna take that? Naw, he'll just crawl back into his little hole and drink hisself silly and won' come out for a month of Sundays. Miss..."

"Agnes, my name is Agnes."

"Well, Miss Agnes, I'm thinkin' this ain't your side of town. Let me see you home. I ain't afraid o' the like o' him. Lucius will see you home and worry about the trash later."

"We can't worry about anything later, we have to do something now!"

"What you wanna do? Ain't nobody aroun' today anyhow."

"What do you mean?"

"Ain't you read the paper, Miss? Everybody, white and colored, done gon' to the football game. This is the fust time this here town has gone to the football championships. Pretty much everybody is gone up to Raleigh to watch the high school play the football for the state title. You'd be lucky to find a policeman even if you needed him."

Football? That was the least of her worries at the best of times, and with her obsession to find the dapper man, she had put all other everyday concerns aside.

"We have to go into that house and finish it now, right now, because they will come for me, and you too, once they learn what we did to their man there."

Lucius glanced at the man snoring in the gutter.

"What do you mean, by that, Miss?"

Agnes told him, the whole story pouring out of her. She told him of the missing people and how it was connected to the fog and the thing that came to her in the night. She told him of the books and what she learned in them. She told him how she connected the dots that no one else could and they led her to the old house at the end of Craven Street. She told him how the man that had chased her and wrapped his hands around her throat must be one of their human servants; familiars to guard the place where they slept. Everything came out in a rush, and when she finished she stood there, breathless, staring up into the old man's wide eyes.

"You tellin' me there some sort of haint in that there house? And it's been makin' people sick and takin' people and killin' them?"

"Yes, Lucius, I know it's hard to believe, but believe me now. Everything depends on you believing me now, at this very moment. If you don't help me stop this now, then I'm afraid I won't survive the night. No one else will catch on and that thing will continue to feed and grow stronger and make more things just like itself until this evil takes over everything. Then there won't *be* any more town."

He thought for a moment, weighing the sincerity of the girl's plea.

"I just knowed that something was going bad. They was blamin' all of the sick folks on the yellow fever and the damp, but my grandmother was a conjure woman and she done tol' me about haints like this one. I thought some of that was jest a bunch of old stories; but, I can see in your eyes that you believe it to be the God's honest truth. That house used to belong to a bootlegger, I reckon, and it sat empty for a spell after he gone out one night and never come back. When that ugly sonofa..., I'm sorry Miss..., that so and so moved in, it didn't feel right at all. No ma'am. It made the hairs stand up on my neck jus' to look at it. Nobody here to help us and the police won't believe you no how. They is likely to lock you up in the loony bin just 'cause you tole that story…help me get that lug indoors before somebody sees him."

He went to the unconscious man, gripped him underneath his arms, and dragged him into the house, the heels digging two narrow furrows in the dirt. They made a hollow thumping noise on every wooden step as he was pulled into Lucius' small house. The place was spartan, but neat. Lucius propped him up in one of the chairs in the room and tied him to it with a length of cord he cut from the curtains.

"My missus would give me what for," he remarked, "if she ever seen me do that to her curtains, rest her soul."

With the brute secured, Lucius turned over the other chair and, with a heave of his large arms, tore the legs free. A few swipes of his large pocketknife, and each of the chair legs had a very sharp looking point. He handed two of the stakes to Agnes, and kept two to himself. He rummaged in a drawer and pulled out two hammers. One he gave to Agnes, and the other he slipped into one of his belt loops. Next he took an oil lantern off the single table in the room, lit it, and retrieved his axe handle.

"We gonna need light in that cellar, and I never go anywhere there might be some trouble without a good piece of wood in ma hand. I hope you are right, 'cause if you ain't I'm gonna have me a heap of trouble explainin' why I gots me a white boy all tied up in my living room. Well, let's go."

They walked out Lucius' house and up the street. The shadows were already beginning to lengthen across the road. *Where has the day gone?* thought Agnes. It was well into fall, and she forgot just how fleeting the sun was at this time of year. Her anxiety grew and almost demanded they turn around and hide somewhere until tomorrow...until they had more time. She realized, walking in the late afternoon, toward what could easily be her end, that they had no more time. Once the dapper man found out what she and the old man had done to his servant he wouldn't stop until he had destroyed them both. Tonight.

Agnes winced as the stairs to the porch creaked under her weight, half expecting the charge of yet another abomination through the front door. It just swung in the growing wind. With its maroon peeling paint from it, the house, resembled the head of a gigantic corpse; empty eye sockets staring from the flesh rotting from its face.

"They's in the basement you say?" whispered Lucius. Agnes nodded. Softly they crept through the front hall and straight back through the house. Dust was everywhere, and the floor was scattered with bits of half eaten food and empty whiskey bottles. The dapper man had certainly chosen a slovenly caretaker for his home, but Agnes surmised that it probably was much easier to control the weak minded. There was no one more weak minded to Agnes than a drunk.

The door to the cellar, just before the kitchen, was latched but not locked. Very gently Lucius lifted the latch, not daring to breathe. It came up smoothly and the door began to glide open, revealing darkness below. Agnes shuddered at the cold that wafted up at her, carrying the sickly sweet smell of decay. Lucius paused, licked his lips nervously, and held the lantern straight out in front of him as he descended the stairs. Agnes followed close behind.

The source of the smell became quite evident as they reached the cellar floor. Sprawled in the corners like discarded rag dolls were several of the missing, their limbs askew and jointless. Decay had taken hold of them in various stages and Agnes could tell that they were obviously long dead. She felt her gorge rise as the lantern light splayed across the corpses. They all had been *gnawed on*. Feeling faint, she stumbled, grabbing Lucius' jacket to keep from falling. She pulled herself against him, burying her face in his back. His rich smell of honest sweat and tobacco overpowered the thick smell of death.

"Do Jesus," hissed Lucius, "we gots to get outta here."

"But you said..."

"Forget what I said, chile. There is no way on earth anybody could not believe this. We get the police and they will believe you, sho' enough. We get them to come, with their guns. They sees this and they believe every word you say."

Lucius backed toward the stairs, taking Agnes with him.

"C'mon girl, c'mon. This here is bigger than both of us."

Agnes permitted herself to be pushed to the steps. She knew that Lucius was right, of course, but she still doubted that they could get the police back here before the sun set. If they couldn't, would the few still left in town be able to fight the thing now sleeping down here or would they all be torn apart and left as so many piles of stinking meat.

Her heels bumped against the first step. She turned to run up them, but a large figure blocked the doorway above them. Blood had run down the side of his face where Lucius had struck him with the axe handle. Blood also dripped from his wrists where they had been tied to the chair. His lips were shredded. *Oh God, did he chew his way free?* He looked straight into Agnes' eyes and grinned madly at her before slamming the door shut. She yelped and bounded up the steps, falling halfway up and scraping her shin. She heard the snick of a lock being closed from the other side just as she reached for the knob. She pulled on it, but the door would not budge. *Locked. Locked in.*

Lucius bellowed when he realized what was going on and reached the door just after Agnes. He pulled her aside and rammed the door with his shoulder again and again, but it didn't budge. They heard wild laughter through the door, and the sound of a large piece of furniture scarping across the floor. There was a dull thud as he pushed the couch, or whatever it was, against the door. The sounds repeated as another heavy object was piled on the first.

"He's barricading us in! The man who attacked me, he got loose and shut us in!" Agnes cried and began to pound the door with her fists.

"Stop that," Lucius said, "that won't do no good no how. He done locked us in, and I'm thinkin' he locked us in with whatever made that awful mess down there. We gots to find us another way out. You said there was windows down there, let's find us a window."

They both ran down the stairs and past the bodies. The cellar was "L" shaped and when they ran around the corner, they were looking at a pair of blue trousers and well shined black shoes. There were no corpses lying on the floor in this part of the cellar, just a long oaken table upon which rested a former member of New Bern's finest. He lay flat on his back, his arms by his side, with his eyes closed. He looked as if he was just sleeping, but his skin was incredibly pale, too pale for him to be simply slumbering. His lips were as blue as a drowned man. Agnes looked up and across the policeman.

"Look, there. There is the window I looked through, you can see where I was prying at the glass."

"I can see how small it is too. No way I can get one shoulder through that, much less the rest of me. You, you might fit if I give you a push."

"I can't leave you here alone with that thing."

"We get you out and you run and get the police. I'll be fine, but you gots to hurry."

He smashed out the rest of the glass with his axe handle, swinging it along the frame to knock out the jagged edges.

"Now git on up there."

Agnes put her hands on the sill and paused. Aside from the table and a pile of bags and tools at the far end, this part of the cellar was empty. No coffin like Mr. Bram Stoker described, no long packing crates filled with graveyard dirt, no large wardrobe, just smooth plastered walls. The policeman looked almost serene and perfect, lying there, with no blemish save two jagged puncture marks on his neck. Of the dapper man, there was no sign.

Lucius grabbed her around the waist and lifted her straight up into the window.

"I said git, now git."

She slid smoothly through and was practically catapulted out onto the lawn. Agnes looked around for the dapper man's caretaker, but she was alone in the yard. Turning to the window, she leaned in and extended her hand.

"Lucius, take my hand. I'll help you."

"Little girl, I said there was no way I could squeeze through that there window. You wanna help me, you go run and fetch the police like I said."

The yard was all shadows. Agnes could see some stirring behind her friend.

"Lucius, look out."

Lucius turned just in time to see the policeman begin to move, his eyes still closed, his hands reaching down and grasping the edge of the table, pushing himself slowly up. His legs swung off the table and planted themselves squarely on the floor.

Agnes looked behind her. The sun was setting, the last rays shining vermillion through the fall sky and bathing everything around her in a deep, red light.

"He's waking up! Kill him before he can get the jump on you."

At the sound of her voice, the policeman's eyes snapped open. They were as red as the failing sun and filled with such cruelty and such scorn, that Agnes' voice failed. She also saw something else in those eyes: a hunger so strong that it broached on pure unadulterated lust. Now sitting upright on the table, the policeman snarled, showing incredibly sharp and long teeth.

Lucius moved quickly for one so large. He raised his trusty axe handle overhead with both hands as he charged, screaming in anger and fear the entire way across the basement. The policeman was just beginning to stand as Lucius brought the axe handle down with every ounce of force his body could muster. It struck him across the face and knocked him back across the table.

Lucius followed, pressing all of his weight onto the policeman, hoping to pin him down.

The light was almost gone.

"In the heart, stab him through the heart before he is fully awake!" Agnes shouted through the window.

The policeman did still seem sluggish, and Lucius was able to hold him with his own bulk as he pulled the sharpened chair leg from his belt. His other arm was across the man's neck, pushing back the head that tried to snap at him with those terrible teeth. Lucius raised the stake high in his free hand and brought it down square into the man's chest just as the teeth sliced into his arm. The stake struck, but with a grinding sensation, it was stopped by the sternum. Lucius pressed down with his whole body, now lying almost fully on top of the policeman whose hands were clawing at his back, creating strips of oozing cuts. With the added weight, the stake penetrated the bone with a pop and tore into the heart just beneath.

The policeman uttered a single, piercing shriek of agony followed by a gout of dark and foul clots of blood from his mouth and nose. The spray caught Lucius full in the face, forcing the vile liquid into his mouth, eyes, and nose. He pushed off the twitching body and crumpled to the floor, trying to wipe the mess off his face. Pinioned, the corpse continued to convulse, its hands and feet beating a tattoo on the long table. Blood continued to bubble out from around the improvised stake. Gagging and spitting, Lucius crawled away from the spreading mess as fast as possible.

The movement slowed quickly and the blood slowed to the trickle. With one last gasp, whatever spark of life that was animating the policeman was extinguished, and the body lay still. Agnes could see a change in the staring eyes. Gone was the fire, now they were just blank and empty. The corpse of the policeman was once again, just a corpse.

"Lucius! Lucius! Are you alright!"

"Prohibition or no prohibition, I need a goddamned drink, pardon my language."

"And I'll buy you that goddamned drink," Agnes laughed, relieved but still shaking from the recent fright. "You need a bath too."

"That I do, let me find something to smash open that door and I'll be right out...After I find that sombitch with a beard and peel the very hide off him."

Agnes quickly looked around.

"It's all quiet out here," she hefted one of her sharpened chair legs, "but I'm ready for him this time."

"Good girl, you keep a watch out. You *always* keep a watch out. I'll be out of here before you can say...well...something a mite longer than *Boo*." He retrieved his lantern, thankfully intact, and walked over to the pile of tools in the corner. "Not much here just some tools and some wall plaster. Here, here is a crowba—"

He was cut off by an explosion of white dust and dried spackle from behind him. A pale form in a well-tailored, brown suit coat leaped out of the wall, landing on Lucius' back, wrapping its arms around him. Agnes' scream echoed Lucius' shout of surprise. He stumbled forward, trying to maintain his balance while punching behind. Agnes recognized the dapper man immediately. She saw the almost perfectly man shaped hole in the plaster he had left.

So that's where he was hiding. They made a hole in the drywall and every morning his servant would take the plaster and cover him up! No one would see the fresh plaster in the gloom of the cellar!

"Lucius!" Agnes started to climb back in the window, but she stopped when she saw the dapper man open his obscenely wide mouth and sink his teeth deeply into Lucius' neck. This time Lucius screamed, high pitched and frantic. He swung his back against the brick of the cellar's outside wall, but still the dapper man hung on.

Lucius felt his life rapidly ebbing away.

"Run girl! Run!" He swung the lantern up and over his head, smashing it on the dapper man's forehead. Kerosene splashed over both of them and, in an instant, they were engulfed in flames, locked together in a macabre dance.

Agnes began to run, the smell of burning flesh and oil too much for her. She only paused at the end of the block to look around. The fire had spread rapidly, and the first floor was already burning as well. She could see no movement at first, but then, in a garret window on the second floor she could see the bearded man, leaning out and laughing hysterically for a moment before he disappeared inside, his laughter echoing above the sounds of the fire. Sparks, picked up by the rising wind, had started the neighboring house smoldering and soon it too burst alight. Agnes stood transfixed as, one by one like a giant set of dominoes, the fire leapt from building to building until the whole street was burning.

Agnes fled the fire, toward the fire station, but she could hear by the bells that the firemen had already been alerted and were on the way. She couldn't imagine how they could stop this burning. As she ran, she met other people coming out of their homes with a few precious possessions. She joined them in the race to the river. Once there, all they could do was wait and watch the orange and crimson glow of the flames as they spread through the town. Agnes watched and cried over Lucius and the dead people in that house. She cried for the town, what it had lost and what it was losing. She cried for herself, having seen the face of evil and knowing that she would be forever touched by it.

The fire raged for the rest of the evening and, despite the best efforts of the citizens and firemen, it consumed almost one third of the little town. A few people died and the charred remains found in the house at the end of Craven street were regarded as just a few more victims of what would come to be known as The Great Fire. In the years since, Agnes thought the fire brought sort of a purification to her hometown. The strange mists never returned and the missing people, victims of the dapper man, were gradually forgotten. By the time the country was sucked into yet another world war, the destroyed homes long rebuilt, the whole terrible spring and fall were nothing but footnotes in local history and lore. Forgotten by everyone except for Agnes.

Even though the years passed without the return of the dapper man or any of his kind, Agnes remembered the last words of her friend, because, even though he was her friend for a few hours, she never forgot him and what he did that fall day. She would always keep a watch out for herself, her town, and her partner in the worst afternoon in her life, Lucius.

She watched and waited for over eighty years and now that the troubles were coming back, she was going to do something. That something was going to involve that young man with the fake leg and that red-headed she devil he had shacked up with in that boat of his. At the sight of the woman, Agnes had felt the same chill she felt when the dapper man had invited her to dance so many years ago. Nothing good could come from consorting with that kind.

Chapter Six

Elena slept fretfully. She could feel Max's presence beyond the cabin door as she drifted off. He seemed trustworthy enough and safe; offering her his cabin without hesitation and not making a single move or comment that indicated he wanted to join her. She locked the door, but she really didn't feel the need because he seemed such an overgrown boy scout—stuck on doing the "right thing" regardless. Old habits die hard and she locked herself in, listening to him putter around, not permitting herself to sleep until all was quiet.

She was exhausted from recent events and, struggle as she might, she could not resist. A poet, Elena could not remember who, once called sleep the "little death." For her, this seemed more than just a metaphor. When she rested, she never dreamed and the time spent was nothing more than a taste of oblivion.

Elena closed her eyes and felt nothingness wash over her.

Her father pausing as he opens the door for her. The look of sadness in his face giving her a moment's hope that he would change his mind. The look vanishes as he takes her hand.

"Come along now, dear. We do not want to keep our betters waiting."

"But father, why can't I stay at home?" she asks as she climbs out to stand beside him.

"We have been over this. Our money can buy us anything we want materially, but the one thing it cannot buy this family is station. You are here to learn about rising above your station and our family will join the nobility if you are lucky. We should be happy that the Lady has offered to take you in and teach you about being a real lady, not some merchant's daughter."

"But—"

"Look sharp, here she comes. Someday you might marry a nobleman if you listen to what she says."

The Lady sweeps down the stairs to greet them, resplendent in ermine. Elena and her father quickly kneel down at her approach. The Lady cups Elena's chin with her hand and raises her head to meet her gaze. Elena finds herself looking into the eyes of madness.

Elena moaned and shifted in her sleep.

The images came at her faster, a jumble of sight and sound. Elena hiding from the Lady. Always hiding while she did horrible things to the other girls. The Lady never found her but he always could.

"You are too good for her little bird," he says, stroking her hair. "She loves the blood, but not like I do. You are special. Your hair looks like blood in the firelight." Elena feels his breath on her neck. "Mine. You will always be mine."

Elena tried to struggle awake. She opened her eyes and saw the cabin around her but she could not move. If only she could make a noise, she would wake up. Elena felt herself sinking back down.

Fire all around her, she was running through the halls, handfuls of jewels clutched to her chest. Out! Out! She had to get out. Shouts all around her. Angry voices and screams. The Lady screaming. Almost to the door. Almos steps in front of her. He is smiling at her.

"Do not fly away, I am here for you. You are mine, for now, for always."

Elena backs up and he follows swiftly. His hands reach out for her like a pair of eagle's talons.

Her final scream ringing in her ears, Elena woke up, sweating. She was incredibly nauseated and she rushed to the nearest porthole and opened it wide, sucking in the night air.

I must tell him, but can I trust him?

She glanced at the cabin door, certain he must of hear her cry out in her sleep, but she is greeted only by silence. The walls closed in on her.

Out, I've got to get out of here.

She crept to the door, unlocked it, and pushed it open a crack. Nothing. Max had left a light on and she could see him clearly, asleep on the couch. Elena noticed the half empty whiskey bottle and some remaining pills on the table next to him.

He didn't hear a thing.

Elena moved past him and out onto the deck. Lighter, the night was giving way to the morning. The nausea gone, her thinking was clearer. She climbed over the rail and onto the dock and then walked off into the pre-dawn.

The first thing Max felt when he woke up was the craving for his morning fix. It did not surprise him that Elena had split during the night. She was one hell of a flaky chick. Easy on the eyes though and actually a fun date when she was off that whole vampire shtick. She had been pretty convincing though, and he did feel himself getting sucked into her fairytale at more than one point. They always say that redheads are wild in the sack, but sure didn't need that level of craziness right now.

He rolled the pill bottle back and forth in his hands. *Who the fuck am I to be calling somebody else crazy? Fucking nightmares. Fucking dope. Talk about hunger; no bloodsucker ever had this sort of monkey on his back.* He could never really figure out if his stump hurt because it was a torn up mess of scar tissue or because it, and he, just needed the pills. They never really took away the pain, just muddled up his brain so he didn't really care. At least, they did at first. Nowadays, Max found that he could actually think clearly with them, if he didn't overdo it. In fact, he never really felt *normal* without them. They calmed him down, they helped him to think about something other than his damn leg. When he did not have them, he craved them. He thought about them and was always checking to make sure that they were still there where they should be. Towards the end of the month, before he could get another prescription filled at the base, he would count them over and over, just making sure that he had enough to get him through without having to miss a dose.

When it was really bad, the phantom limb pains kicked in. In some bizarre twist of neurology, guys like Max who have lost a limb in some sort of trauma, get pains that shoot down their legs, past the stump and into where the foot should have been. At the Naval Hospital some egghead medical student had sat down at the foot of Max's bed and tried to explain the whole thing to him. He seemed pretty excited to share this tidbit of info to Max, never mind that the little turd didn't seem to realize that what to him was a cool aspect of neurophysiology, was Max's day in, day out agonizing chunk of bedridden Hell. Seems people have a map over the entire body imprinted on the brain. Called the homunculus, or little man, it is where the ends of all the nerves on all the parts of the body converge in the brain and tells a person if his big toe is itching, or he hit his thumb with a hammer. When Max got his leg blown off, his brain did not get time to adjust or, as he called it, "remodel". *Remodel, as if your noggin is some frigging Manhattan apartment.* And since Max's brain did not adjust, it thought his foot was still there sometimes. Max could feel his toes burning frequently, and he could swear that if he could reach into empty space where they were, he could grab them with his hand, they felt so real.

The only answer to that is more pain pills. Max stopped taking them because, not only did they not help at all, they made him see things he didn't like. Not only would his damn invisible foot still be killing him, he would be stuck with the Grim Reaper, complete with scythe, hanging out in the corner of his hospital room. It made it really hard to concentrate on the television with a bony finger gesturing for him to come. *Come with me*, it seemed to say, *and I'll make you feel nothing. Nothing is better than this, isn't it?*

There was no way in Hell Max was going to tell the shrinks that one, so he started palming the pills instead of taking them, and tossing them in the trash when nobody was looking. Death stopped lurking, so that helped a little bit.

Tossing the overly earnest medical student out of his room also made him feel better, much better.

When Max finally made his way up on deck, blinking in the sunlight, he could see that Elena's boat was also gone. "Flaky redheads," he mumbled to himself as he started to putter around, clearing the dishes from yesterday's breakfast. *I should get a maid, some sort of boat maid, if there is such a thing.* He then noticed the diminutive figure, standing silently at the end of his gang plank, leaning on a cane and staring at him. His headache ratcheted up a few notches when he saw who it was. Old Miss Pritchett had come a calling.

"What can I do for you ma'am?" said Max, surprised, but remembering to be polite to the old lady. "You lookin' for Bill Whitley? His office is at the end of the next pier over."

"No, I am here to talk to you." Her voice was strong for someone so small and frail looking, and it carried to Max very clearly.

"You can't be, I'm…"

"I know who you are Mr. Bradley, and I know that you *think* you know who I am."

That unbalanced Max for a second. The old lady really did know every body's business.

"Uh, okay." Max walked down the plank to her. His mother had been a very small woman as well, but she, like Miss Pritchett apparently, had an incredible force of will compacted into her little frame. Even as a grown man, Max had been cowed by his mother. When she got angry at him, she would reach up and grab his ear and pull his face down to her level so she could chew him out face to face. That familiar maternal power almost forced Max to go and see what she wanted. Anybody else talking to him in that tone would have gotten flipped the bird as he went back into his cave.

Toe to toe, he looked down at her. Standing together, they really were a contrast in appearance. He, well over six feet tall, towered over her. She probably was not all that tall to begin with, but, through the years she had taken on that diminutive and shrunken appearance of the very old. Max was well muscled and broad shouldered, not the huge muscle mass of a professional weight lifter, but the muscle of someone who had been a Marine his entire adult life, the muscle of the combat trained. Even so, she seemed smaller than one of Max's legs...the good one. His hair was jet black with only a little gray on the sides, while hers had gone the purest spun silver. She seemed incredibly old to Max, and so frail that he was almost afraid that a strong gust of wind would snap her in half. The only thing that did not look aged were her eyes, piecing blue, like the sky after the passing of an afternoon summer thunderstorm. They were not weak or frail at all. They were looking straight into Max's brown ones with a stabbing certainty of purpose, alert and aware, as if she could see right into Max's very core and were very displeased with what they saw there.

"I need to talk to you," she said, poking him in the chest with her cane. "I saw you with that woman, that *thing*. Nothing good comes from consorting with that kind. I saw you with her yesterday. I saw her fly away this morning. "

Oh great, thought Max, *some sort of Bible thumper going to ruin my morning with some sort of lecture about the sins of the flesh and to make matters worse I didn't even get any.*

"Hey, that really is none of your...what...wait...fly?"

"Now don't give me any backtalk, young man." Again with the cane. Poke, poke. "You have no idea with what you are dealing with and how much danger you are in."

"Danger?" *Yep, this was an evils of fornication thing. Why is she picking on me?* "What? For my immortal soul? Please ma'am, my personal..."

"Your soul?" She grinned at him, her teeth were worn and yellow. "Yes, I guess so, but I was thinking more about the tearing-out-your-throat-and-eating-your-still-beating-heart kind of danger."

Max put his hands on his hips in what he called "The Angry Drill Instructor Pose" and squared off at her.

"Now listen, Ma'am, I was taught at an early age to respect the elderly, but you are really pushing it. Eavesdropping? Do you have some sort of parabolic mike up there with your big-assed binoculars? I bet you got them both at the same military surplus store."

"Oh, no," she said with a chuckle, and not a very pleasant one. "I just have my glasses, for looking out. I just know what she is and I think perhaps you do too."

"Okay lady, do you have a point? Because I am very busy."

"Busy with what? Drinking yourself silly? Popping pills so that you pass out on the deck of your little boat for the whole world to see?"

"That's enough." Max turned to leave.

"There is something strange about all of this and you and I

have some place to go. We have to talk to a friend of mine about this."

"I don't need to talk to anybody," Max said over his shoulder. "Go sell crazy somewhere else."

Her next words stopped him dead in his tracks.

"We need to go see the priestess, the Mambos, and talk with her about your undead friend."

"How did you know that she thinks she is wrapped up in some sort of...?"

"I can smell them." Agnes tapped the side of her nose.

"Besides, wouldn't a priest or preacher be more appropriate?"

"No, the Church doesn't believe in that sort of thing anymore. They tend to think of evil as an abstract concept, not in the real rip off your head sort of way. For this, we need the Doctor DeMoliers and you are going to take us to her." Max felt stunned as he walked the old lady to his jeep and helped her and her cane into the passenger seat. Score: old lady, one; Marine, zero.

They did not talk much the whole trip out of town. Agnes spoke only to give directions in a curt, clipped manner, and Max grunted in reply. He had faced up to some very bad and dangerous characters over the years, but he was helpless in front of this old lady. Sure, he could have told her to get lost or simply just skulked back into his boat and waited for her to leave, but once she got her verbal teeth into him, she just did not let go. Big, tough men being cowed by little old ladies was a cliché from the old movies and he certainly folded at her insistence. Of course, his curiosity was piqued to say the least. Either she had been listening in, which seemed pretty unlikely, or she had some sort of inside scoop. As he drove, Max mulled over the latter. It could be some sort of bizarre con job: a good looking damsel in distress lets herself be rescued and then throws this wild story at him before vanishing followed by the Cryptkeeper's mother with almost the same outlandish story. He had some money, but not enough for such a wild and complicated plan. *Was she leading me into an ambush? Roll me for a ten year old Jeep and a fake leg? Laughable.*

Max realized just then, that in the befuddlement caused by the whirlwind that was Agnes Pritchett, he had forgotten to grab his carry piece. Although he was almost certain he could take the old lady in a fair fight, he was not to certain about any friends she might have waiting up the road. A pistol comes in awful handy surrounded by a group of people intending bodily harm...even if they are the blue haired league.

The bridge over the Neuse took them into Pamlico County, and northeast out Route 55, past Ditch Creek and Jones Bay, out where the Sound ran into the salt marshes and ancient cedar swamps. Agnes told him to turn sharply on a dirt road that ran along one of those swamps. Cedar trees, draped in the ever present Spanish moss, with the bare knees of their roots poking out of the water, reminded Max of the dried and decaying skeletons in all of the pirate movies: the moss looked like the remains of clothing and beards, and the knees gave them a crouching appearance as if they were ready to spring into action at any moment, knives gripped in skeletal teeth.

As if reading his thoughts, Agnes piped up,

"Pirates used to hide in these inlets and swamps and, after them, the moonshiners hid here too. No saying what's hiding out here these days." She looked slyly at him. "Yes, sir, no telling what sort of *things* are hiding out here."

Max just grunted. He could think of plenty of better ways to spend his time than going to visit a voodoo lady in the swamps with the town busybody. *At least the zombie movies got the swamp part right.*

The dirt road widened out and ended at a gate which was wide open. A sign on the gate read, "Private Road, Sea Glass Estates Residents and Guests only." On the seaward side, facing the sound, was a row of very nice looking townhouses.

"Well, this sure as hell wasn't what I expected," mumbled Max.

"Pull up here." Agnes gestured with her cane at the end of the row.

"Yes ma'am."

Max pulled the jeep in with a squeal of brakes badly in need of maintenance. He swung out of his seat and walked around to where Agnes was waiting for him. He opened her door and helped her out. She led him to the nearest gate. The townhouse was a new one, but the yard in front was full of mature, tropical plants. Hibiscus flowers, dwarf banana trees, and lime trees dotted the lawn that was bordered by tall, elegant stalks of sugar cane. The walk went over a small, wooden bridge that hopped over a small koi pond before reaching the front door. The fish came to the surface as Max crossed and eyed him as if they knew something he did not.

When they arrived at the front door, Agnes simply opened the door and walked in.

"We are expected," she said.

"Right, she have a premonition about us coming?"

"No, I called ahead. They still have telephones, don't they?" Agnes turned in the doorway and poked at him with her cane again. "Not afraid of things that go bump in the night, are you?"

"Nope," said Max as he followed her in, "If they can bump, I can bump back and I bump back really, really hard."

The foyer and what he could see of the living room was well decorated, albeit in a taste that ran to the very eclectic and esoteric. He recognized African masks, Russian icons, Mayan sculpture, and many other things he could not identify but he was certain belonged in an art gallery or museum or both. One large lithograph did take his attention, it was a black and white drawing of a man, asleep or dead on a bed, he was not sure, with a woman leaning over him, her teeth bared. He could not help but think that the woman in the painting reminded him of someone.

"I see you admire Philip Burne-Jones," came a voice. Max turned and saw the source of the voice. She was tall, and beautiful, lithe and with skin the color of mocha. She walked gracefully, almost a glide, and wore a sarong of brilliant red and orange. She came up to Max and ran her hand down the picture frame.

"He painted it in eighteen ninety seven. He called it *The Vampire*, and although it inspired Kipling's poem of the same name, it really is more of a statement of sexual politics in Victorian England than any sort of supernatural message. See how the woman is the aggressor, and the man but a victim of her unleashed sexuality. They feared the sexual power of women back then." She looked at Max meaningfully, her dark eyes capturing his. "Do *you* fear the sexual power of women?"

"That's kind of a complex question, isn't it? Rife with deeper philosophical and psychological meaning."

She laughed, honest and heartfelt.

"I do like your young man, Miss Agnes. He has some intelligence and a quick wit obviously. Come into the living room the both of you." She led them both deeper into her house. The decor continued to be more of the same. Although Max was not one for lavish decoration, he could appreciate the pieces that she had spread throughout her home, obviously the result of years of dedicated collecting. She slid into a large rattan chair and gestured for them to do the same. A large African drum, about the size of a rain barrel cut in half, with a black and white cowhide skin as the drum face was in the center of the circle of chairs. It was covered by a wide, glass table top and served as her coffee table, a pot of which, by the smell, and three cups on a tray sat on top.

"I was expecting you. Agnes telephoned to tell me everything and it is indeed a fascinating turn of events."

"How so?" said Max.

"Coffee, Miss Agnes?" she said as she poured. "No sugar, cream only, yes?"

"Yes, Doctor, thank you," replied Agnes primly.

"And for you, Mister Bradley?"

"Black."

"Of course," she smiled again. "Of course." She poured herself a cup, also straight black, Max noticed. He always did like a woman who drank her coffee black like himself. It was the drink of a direct person who bore no nonsense or subterfuge. This particular coffee was excellent, much better than the stuff Max punished himself with every morning. Smokey and nutty with a deep rich earthy flavor that curled around his tongue.

"It's Boyo. The coffee that is, grown on an extinct volcano in Cameroon. The volcanic soil and the altitude, above five thousand feet, I believe, gives it a rather unique flavor. It is my favorite."

"And the drum table? Cameroon?"

"The Djun-djuns? No, they are from a little north of that, in Benin, which, by the way is the birthplace of Vudun."

"Ok, I get it, you know the voodoo lady we are supposed to see."

She laughed again.

"No, you dear man, I *am* the voodoo lady you are supposed to see." At this Agnes tittered into her cup.

"You are not..."

"What you expected?" she interrupted. "Expecting a clapboard shack way out in the swamp, covered with ivy and surrounded by alligators? Either some wizened old crone or some morbidly obese caricature off the label on a syrup bottle with her hair wrapped up in a scarf the size of a bed sheet?"

"Well, yes actually."

"Too many movies." She shook her head, smiling all the while. "You are about eighty years and two generations too late for that my dear. My grandmother lived in a place like that because she was dirt poor and because back then odd, old ladies were usually ostracized, especially odd old ladies of color in the south. My mother inherited my grandmother's gifts, just as she had from her mother, and so on past the slave ships, through the old country through the lore and traditions of my people, to when Mawu made the world. I inherited my mother's gifts and am the last in a long line of priestesses in the Vudun tradition as I have no daughters myself," She gave Max that pointed look again, "Yet."

Max suddenly knew what a cat treat felt like at suppertime.

"Well, uh, reverend."

"The title is Doctor. Call me Sharon."

"Doctor? I thought you people were all called Madam or Queen so and so."

"I have a Doctorate in Cultural Anthropology from Brown University with an emphasis in comparative religions. Surprised? Mister Bradley, may I call you Max?" He nodded in reply. "Max, my grandmother and her mother before her did live amongst the alligators, not because they wanted to, but because they had to due to the prejudices of narrow minded and fearful people. My mother fared much better as my father made a decent wage as a longshoreman and I earned my merit scholarships to the Ivy League. I am, shall we say, the modern face of a very old tradition. Much older, might I add, than your Christianity."

"Not mine. I stopped believing in all that, and this, mumbo jumbo a long time ago, if I really believed in the first place. I've seen no miracles and the only thing that ever saved me was my own hard work or the actions of one of my Marines. There is no invisible man in the sky, whatever you call him. There is just metal and machines and a well trained and disciplined warrior. No angel ever comes down to save your ass, you save your own ass or your buddy saves your ass because next time it will be you that saves *his* ass."

"I thought there were no atheists in the foxholes."

"I believe in something alright. I believe in me and mine and a forty five in my hand."

"Hmm." She paused, and glanced at Agnes. "Miss Agnes tells me that the undead have returned to our little backwater. Once you look into the face of that evil, and survive, you are changed forever. Agnes not only looked into the face of evil, she fought it, bloodied it and drove it off. She now has a sense about these things and she says that you have been up close and personal with one of them."

"I'm sorry, but everything seems pretty damn normal to me. If you are talking about my...friend...well, she may be a little weird, but she is no 'creature of the night' or whatever you call them. I saw her in the middle of the day eating ice cream, for Crissakes."

"Yes, that is a quandary, an important one, but let me explain something first." She put her coffee down and went over to a bookshelf near a floor to ceiling window that overlooked the sound. Selecting a volume, she ran a graceful finger over the spine before pulling it out. Max could not help but notice that the full sized author's picture on the back of the jacket was Sharon's. "My master's thesis was on the commonality of certain aspects of folklore. The premise is that, if the thread of a bit of legend has enough in common with other legends in other cultures then that legend must have some basis in historical fact. Take the myth of the Great Flood. Every culture in the world has a story of a great and catastrophic flood. Myths without truth at their core die out over time, yet every culture that is and every culture that was, all have the same, or at least very similar flood story. In order for that to be possible, there must have been some sort of calamity, back in the mists of time, that was so horrible the survivors ensured that the memory would never die."

"The Atlantis thing. I've seen documentaries on it."

"Yes, exactly. You do have some knowledge of it, but it's a pity you got it from television, they rarely get it right."

Max patted his left leg.

"I've spent a lot of time in the hospital. There is not much to do in traction."

"Yes, I noticed. You will have to tell me about it someday."

"Someday."

"Hmm." She walked over to Max and lay the book in his lap. It was titled, *The Shadow World: A Study of The Undead in the Pan-Cultural Narrative* by Sharon DeMoliers, PhD. "I want to give you this...no, I want to lend you this. That way I get to see you again when you return it."

"Thank you, but what does this have to do with the flood."

"Everything! You see, the legend of what the West knows as the vampire is found in every culture on the face of the planet. They are well known in the Vudun tradition. The Ashanti have the *Asanbosam*, which attacks people from above, drinking their blood after opening their necks with iron fangs. The Betsileo have the *ramanga*. The *Rakshasa* in India eat the flesh as well as drink the blood and can only be destroyed by sunlight. They were called *Lamia* in ancient Rome, which had a rather large cultish following by the way, and *Ekiminus* in Assyria. Both must be killed by a stake through the heart. See? Everyone has their vampire, their undead."

"But that is not proof of anything," countered Max, "but that people share common fears. Everybody is afraid of snakes, but that does not mean that there are lizard-men squirming around the local swamp."

DeMoliers continued undisturbed, "Folklore must have some nidus of truth to survive the ages. This truth is, of course, bolstered by experience. I have experienced such things in my travels. One particularly ugly night in the Ukrainian Carpathian Mountains convinced me of the truth underlying all of these legends. Agnes, of course, did not have to travel far to meet her demon, she found it right here at home. Tell him."

Agnes put down her cup, "There really is not much to tell," she started, "I was much younger when he came, and if we had not burned him out, he and his would have done much worse things, I imagine. He was already starting to make more like himself when I...we...found him. It was a terrible thing. Almost the whole town was lost."

"I would agree that it is an aberration," added Sharon, "they are usually selfish, territorial creatures not given to cooperation and intent on existing in the periphery, taking what they need to survive, but not so much as to draw attention to themselves. That is why one rarely encounters them in the country. They largely prefer the anonymity of the big city where a few victims are not missed and, even in the dead of night, they can slip away in the crowds. However, Agnes' experience is not without precedent.

"There is tell of a whole town in New England that was blighted by the creatures around the turn of the century. Gone. Forgotten by all. The only thing left is local folklore. The people in those parts still avoid the wooded valley where the remains of crumbling buildings are said to still exist. I should visit it one day." She looked out the window, pressing her hand against the pane. "And let us not forget a place not too far from here, an entire English colony vanished, leaving behind only one word: Croatoan."

"The lost colony of Roanoke?" said Max. "I am a fan of history, majored in it as a fact. The Marines have always liked having historians in their officer corps and have even encouraged midshipmen, if not to major in it, then to take as many courses as possible. It was disease or Indians that took that colony, not the boogeyman."

Max slid back in his chair, his empty cup dangling from his right hand. His left stabbed the air like a karate chop. It was a gesture he learned in the Marines, used to emphasize a point.

"I think it's pretty obvious that I don't believe in all this stuff. I watch the occasional horror flick, sure, but that is entertainment. You know? The movies. Nobody buys into it, at least, nobody in their right mind. No offense."

"None taken. Trust me, in academia such ideas can be met with just as much incredulity. Speaking of incredulity, I'm sure you are wondering why we are interested in you? An even better question is why are *they* becoming interested in you. Agnes told me you were special, but I did not believe it until I found you standing in my front hall."

"Special?" Max laughed. "I assure you, Doc...I mean Sharon...I rode the long bus to school."

"Not like that," she replied with a slight smile. "Special in that they want something from you or they fear you. I think the latter, given that you thrashed three of them all by yourself, barehanded no less."

"What? How did..."

"I have my ways of finding things out. Agnes is not the only lookout around. Right, Agnes?"

"We must look out for those who are not smart enough to look out for themselves, Miss Sharon," replied Agnes. "I had my eye on our young man ever since he came to us in his retirement. Shame what our country does to our young men. Take them from home, use them up, and then toss them aside when they are no longer useful. I have seen many of them pass through, ever since those insane people blew up the Towers. Half the Marine Corps is stationed within an hour's drive of my town, so I see them coming and going. This one stayed. I kept an eye on him alright, more out of concern than anything, he being one of our boys and all. Until he took her in. One of them she is."

Our man? Our boys? My town? This lady sure is a possessive old biddy.

"I knew you were spying on me and my...friend...I saw you and you saw us. In the daylight. Daylight, get it? That throws your whole creature of the night or undead or whatever theory right out the window."

"No," replied Sharon, "if Agnes says your girl was one of the undead, then I believe she was. As I said, you could not have been through what she has and not have that sense. Much like a soldier, I'm sorry, much like a Marine that has been through battle gets that certain extra sense. Ever feel the hairs on the back of your neck stand up before an ambush? Ever get that feeling that your enemy just had to be out there somewhere and when you go looking for him, there he is? It is the same thing. Experience and trauma hone that innate, indefinable sense in all of us."

Agnes sat there nodding, smiling at Max like a doting grandmother.

"Which brings us back to you." Sharon continued. "As I explained earlier, the more prevalent and impacting a thing, the wider the legend spreads and the longer it lasts. There are legends about men like you, but few. So few in fact, I can recall only they exist and not any of their particulars. You, it seems, are resistant... no...resistant is not the right word...You are anti-magic. It simply does not work around you. I knew you were coming because Agnes telephoned ahead and *only* because she telephoned ahead. I could not feel you coming. The wards I place around my home neither deterred you nor alerted me to your presence. It was only the quick and unexpected change in my dear friend and companion while we were upstairs that told me something was wrong. I have never seen the metamorphosis happen so swiftly."

Max saw a brief movement on the second story landing. Half a female face peered around the corner at him, the single eye in view wide in alarm, her hand gripping the doorjamb. When she saw that Max had noticed her, she was gone in a flash of blonde hair. Max wondered if the good doctor was batting for the other team, or *both* teams for that matter.

"There also is the issue of your aura. You know what those are, Max?"

"Something about energy. All of the so called psychics on daytime television would talk about seeing them." Max shrugged, "Hey, I said being stuck in a hospital bed was boring. I watched a lot of television until the doctors got tired of hacking on me."

"An aura is an energy given off by all living creatures. It is said to be an outward manifestation of that vital spark that animates us, the soul if you will. Only a few people can see them as they are a spiritual rather than physical property. Agnes' for example is yellow, primarily, with shades of green. Even the vampire has one, deep black of course, indicating that they consume rather than give off, light."

"And me?"

"You? You, dear Max, have none."

"So? I never imagined I did. What does it mean to me?"

"Nothing. Absolutely everything. Of course you have one, everything and everyone does, it is just that I cannot see it and I am very, very good at my craft. I have inherited a wisdom built through dozens of generations, and I have honed my abilities through years of study and practice. I am both mystic and academic. You do have an aura, that is for certain. What is equally certain is that I cannot see it. I think that you exist outside the realm of magic, of spirituality, and of what people usually call, the supernatural."

Max grinned. "I could never do card tricks. I got a magic set for Christmas when I was eleven. I couldn't make any of it work so I traded it to a kid in school for his new baseball mitt."

"As I said, it means nothing to you. For someone who never had any sort of spiritual connection, not being in touch with the other face of our world is nothing. How can you miss what you never had?"

She leaned over Max and stroked his cheek. Although Max thoroughly enjoyed female touch, he also was very possessive about his personal space. He was both annoyed and excited at the same time.

"It also means everything to you. Magic and the spiritual does not exist to you and amazingly, when you are around, it does not exist to us either. Let me quote Jesus from the New Testament, the Book of Matthew, as I recall: *For truly I tell you, if you have faith the size of a mustard seed, you will say to this mountain, 'Move from here to there,' and it will move; and nothing will be impossible for you.* Faith can move mountains, but what about the utter absence of faith, or in this context, belief?"

She stood and spread her arms wide, her lithe form taking in the whole room:

"There is balance in nature and in the super-nature. Where there is great belief, there is also great disbelief. If there is power in great belief, then there must also be power in great disbelief. That, dear Max, is why you are important. I do not know *how* this is, but the facts stand plainly before me. If magic does not work, if the supernatural flees, and if the mountains stop moving in your presence, then you are a great threat to the creatures who roam the night to prey upon the human animal. They are now aware of you and they will not stop until you are no longer with the living. Your very existence is a threat to their very existence because they will be forced from the supernatural plane to the natural plane in your presence."

"So, in summary, I have some assholes gunning for me."

"Yes, Max. You do. Some very mean and powerful assholes."

Chapter Seven

As soon as Max's Jeep rolled out the gate, Sharon ran up the stairs to the top floor where she had what she called her studio. She began to pull things out of drawers and shelves: unguents, herbs, candles of various colors.

"Chloe!" she shouted over her shoulder. "Get in here and help me set up the *poto mitan*. We need to set up a powerful working. *He* may not get any benefit from the protection, but the rest of us will need all the gris-gris we can get."

She felt a soft brush against her ankle. She looked down into a pair of clear blue eyes set in a gray, furry face.

"I see you are back to your old self," she said, answered in the affirmative by a curt meow. "At least one of us feels back to normal. Fine. I will set up the ritual by myself."

* * * * *

Max pulled back onto the main road, leaving a plume of dust behind.

"That was the strangest cup of coffee I have ever had," remarked Max.

"She has taken a shine to you, that sure is certain."

"Is sex all you young folks think about?" Max came back, the sarcasm positively palpable.

"Oh, I think about it a lot, especially after the change of life. I'd consider giving you a tumble myself if I was fifty years younger." Agnes grinned back at him, playing along and doing her best to embarrass him. It worked. He mumbled something incomprehensible, feeling the flush creep over his ears. *The old lady was certainly full of it.* He glanced in his rearview mirror.

"Okay buddy, what's your damage."

A larger vehicle, a Suburban, dark blue or black with more window tint than legal, had pulled up behind them as they were teasing each other. It was pretty close to their rear bumper. Even though Max had been back from the war for a few years, he still was very nervous in traffic and drove very defensively, preferring to keep as much space between him and any other vehicles. The first time he drove his old Jeep, when he was fresh out of physical rehabilitation, he had blown through several stop lights purely by instinct. *Over there*, you never stopped for anything: stop signs, wrecked cars, pedestrians. Anything might conceal an ambush or an IED. After a few encounters with a stern, but understanding, local highway patrolman, Max pushed his paranoia down deep and drove like a human being. He never gave up his one cardinal rule, however: never, ever let an unknown vehicle ride up your tailpipe.

"Cool your jets, asshole," Max mumbled.

"What is it?" asked Agnes.

"Some jerk in the hurry to hit the frigging buffet I'm thinking."

"Well, don't make trouble. We have enough of that as it is."

"Thanks, mom." *Now shut up.*

Max put his arm out the window and waved it in a "go around, go around" gesture. The Suburban sped up with a growl of its V-8 engine and slammed into the Jeep's rear bumper. Max and Agnes were jolted by the impact and Max almost lost control.

"Son of a bitch! Son of a bitch!" Max floored the accelerator and the Jeep jumped forward. The Suburban kept on his tail and closed in for another punch. Max swerved left and the larger vehicle just clipped the right rear corner and pulled alongside. The side windows were just as tinted as the front and Max could not see inside at all.

"What the fuck is your problem buddy!" Max shouted across Agnes.

As if in answer, the Suburban turned sharply into the Jeep and, with a crunch, began pushing Max onto the shoulder. Max braked hard just before his tires left the asphalt and the other vehicle shot ahead. He felt the Jeep sway as he pulled it back into the middle of the road, for a brief second he thought it might tip over and squash them both, but it settled out and they were firmly four on the floor and right behind the bastards.

"Get their plate number!" Max yelled, trying to read it himself.

With a squeal of tires, the Suburban braked and Max had to

pull the wheel hard to avoid slamming into the back of them. The Jeep almost tipped again as it scraped by and slipped past. Max was pushing the Jeep to its limit, but the little V-6 was way outmatched on the straightaway. The Suburban was on them again in an instant.

This time the bastards struck the rear corner of the bumper in a move that most cop shows call the PIT maneuver. He was trying to get Max to spin out, but Max was just barely able to keep the Jeep on the road. It was only a matter of time before the heavier, faster vehicle would cause him to crash.

"Hold on, Agnes, time to change the rules of the game!" Max hit the brake, spun a hard right, and the Jeep left the road. Max knew that he had to take advantage of his car's off road nimbleness if he was going to get away from the lunatics in the Suburban. They were jostled as the Jeep ran through holes and ruts in the field. Eastern North Carolina was full of active pine tree farms, a large part of the pulp wood industry. This field had been recently cut, so the stumps and bits of left over white pine and spruce caused the Jeep to bounce and jerk back and forth. The Suburban had lost some ground but was still powering on.

Max heard the crack of a gunshot. Extended out of the passenger window was an arm and the occupant was now holding a black pistol. The black automatic jerked and jounced with every movement of the Suburban. Max could not imagine him being able to aim at all, but if he threw enough bullets their way, he could always get lucky. Max hated when the bad guys got lucky. The spare tire mounted on the back burst with an even louder bang than the gunshots. This was getting too close for comfort. If he had his piece, Max could shoot back, and he would bet that he was better at shooting from a moving vehicle than any redneck or street thug.

They were rapidly running out of clearing and the uncut forest was coming awfully close, awfully fast. He had an idea and gunned it. The pine trees were planted in rows every time they were harvested. The company would wait a decade or two and then cut down those trees, planting new ones in their place. Planting in neat, orderly rows, made the process of harvesting easier. They would just run one of those big John Deere tree harvesters down the line and cut through them like shears through a recruit's, hair leaving logs in neat lines for pickup.

Max hoped he was still as good a judge of distance as he was when he was tearing around Anbar Province in his Marine Corps issue Humvee. He turned toward the rows of uncut trees and sped for the center of the middle row. He was by no means an avid off road hobbyist, but Max had spent some time tooling around in the weeds with his little Jeep. The ideal distance between rows for harvesting the trees was about six feet, or 72 inches. Max's Jeep was 66 inches wide. Something big like a Suburban was about 79 inches wide.

Both side mirrors disappeared in a shower of glass as the Jeep leapt into the corridor of pine boughs. Branches slapped against his windshield and tore away his radio antenna. He kept his foot on the gas and held the wheel as straight as he could. As long as he kept down the center, he should miss the trees and pass through the stand at some point even if he was having a little trouble seeing ahead. A larger limb smacked into his windshield straight on. The glass cracked almost all the way across but held. The wheel was struggling in Max's hands, fighting him as he tried to keep the Jeep running in a straight line. A few inches to either side, and their trip would end real quick and then he would have to face some guns with only his fists and the queen of the geriatrics as his only wingman. A few more moments and he would have his answer: either they came in after them, or they would chicken out and veer off to go around.

With a shriek of tortured metal, the Suburban hit the tree line. Max had guessed right. The wider vehicle could not fit between the trunks as easily as the Jeep, and had torn into the pines until it came to a stop, unable to squeeze farther. He could see the SUV in his rear view, wedged between the trees, their trunks tearing huge gashes on and dents along the sides. Max noted with satisfaction that his pursuer had also lost both his side mirrors.

"Got 'em!" shouted Max in triumph. Agnes was in wild-eyed stunned silence, gripping the dash with both hands. The trees ended shortly, and Max was able to drive back onto the hardtop without any difficulty. With a cracked windshield and both mirrors gone, the little Jeep was worse for wear but still spinning like a top. The hood and roof were covered with bits of pine. One windshield wiper held a broken twig, needles perfectly intact, against the windshield. The other hung straight out, as if someone had been trying to twist it off. The Jeep was filled with the rich, spicy smell of pine.

"I was thinking that the old girl needed some air freshener anyway," gasped Max. "The car, I mean, not you...not that you couldn't use some freshening up yourself."

"Keep your cheek to yourself, young man. Those people were trying to kill us!"

"Yep! Isn't it great! Fucking invigorating baby! Hell yeah!"

"You are insane, positively insane."

"You better believe it!"

The Jeep chugged its way onto the highway and began to pick up speed with twigs, pinecones, pine needles, and bits of mirror flying off in every direction.

"What's next on the weirdness agenda for today, Agnes old buddy? I, for one, am in need of a stiff drink."

"And one or two of your pills."

"Man, do I need to get some better shades. Yes, grandma, one or two of my pills."

"Disgusting habits you have there. How are we going to get rid of those things if you are rolling around in some sort of drunken haze."

"*We* are going to do nothing. *I* am going to drop you off and then *I* am going to file a police report, *I* think *I* can remember a partial plate number to give them, and then *I* am going to have a drink or seven and then crawl into my bunk. Tomorrow *I* am going to go down to the hardware store and get myself some tarps to cover my windows and portholes so *I* can have some doggone privacy. *You* can do whatever you like."

"You still don't believe there is a dark force here. A force that is growing and out to kill you? What do you think that was back there? How much proof do you need?"

"That was either a case of road rage or somebody looking to carjack a cripple and an old lady alone on a country road. That is as dark as you get and it already is plenty evil if you look at it. You will be fine in your condo with the security system and I will be fine in my boat. The police will find those fuckers and I will have a grand old time testifying against them in court. Simple. No ghosts or ghoulies."

"You're a fool. You can't see what is right in front of your face."

"What? See What? Doctor DeMoliers is a very pretty woman and very smart, even though she has a really stupid degree. But she really didn't show me anything. I didn't even get my palm read. No candles, no tea leaves, no real show at all. She was right about the assholes considering my Jeep is all tore up, but that could have been coincidence. Maybe people get rolled all the time in this neck of the woods. Or maybe she hired someone to put the scare into us just to prove that she could tell the future or whatever. Then she'll come calling, telling me that if I give her some cash, she'll make all the evil monsters go away. She looks too classy to be a scam artist, but I guess the best scammers are the ones that don't look like scammers."

Agnes sniffed.

"So untrusting of those trying to help you."

"That's what has kept me above ground all of these years. Paranoia does a body good."

Agnes sulked in silence the rest of the way back to her condo. That suited Max just fine. He was slipping into a post adrenaline dump fatigue and he was not in the mood to chit chat with her any longer. Adrenaline was very familiar to Max, and the high of a life or death struggle always led to one hell of a crash later. By the time he pulled up to her place, he had already convinced himself to get that drink first and worry about the police report tomorrow. Odds were that episode back on the road was a simple attempted carjacking and there was little likelihood that they would follow him all the way back to his place. Agnes primly sat in her seat, waiting. Max rolled his eyes, got out of the Jeep and walked around to open her door for her. She got out and squared off at him again.

"You are a rude and selfish man." She poked him in the chest with her cane yet again. "But, you are important, as the doctor said and I'm not about to give up on you just yet."

She turned and let herself into her complex.

Max stood there thinking about her cane. It looked a little bit masculine for a diminutive lady like Agnes Pritchett. Silver tipped at the end with a matching silver, gnarled knob on the end. It looked like something a turn of the century dandy would have. *She probably has a set of balls too. Brass ones.*

He went back to his boat and climbed into his cave, glad to be alone again. *It would make the world's most bizarre buddy film,* he thought as his favorite drink, whiskey with an oxycontin chaser, began to carry him off, *old lady and cripple fighting the forces of darkness. All we need is a guest appearance from Bruce Campbell.*

Agnes rode up the elevator to her condo alone. "Agnes, old girl," she told herself, "there's a storm a brewing and I think a visit to the Catholic Church is in order."

Chapter Eight

When he awoke, it was fully dark and Elena was standing over him.

"Hey, wake up."

Max groaned and pulled himself up, his head full of cobwebs, "What the fuck do you want? You better have brought a sandwich or something."

"I had a hell of a time waking you," Elena said. She looked at the empty scotch bottle and the pills scattered on the nightstand. "You really need to lay off that stuff. I don't have much use for a drunk, or a pill popper."

"Well nobody asked you." Max rolled over and stuffed his face back into his pillow. He could feel the boat rocking underneath him. "Where the hell are we?"

"I said I couldn't wake you up, so I drove us out a little bit. For some privacy." Elena dangled the keys to the boat, the florescent orange, floating, key fob swinging in the air with every movement. "You left these by the wheel and it was easy to get this tug moving. We are anchored a few miles west of Oriental."

Max did the math. They must have travelled at least thirty miles.

"Why?"

"Because you were out cold and I thought we needed a little distance between us and them."

"Them being the vampire cabal and their minions?"

"Yes, why...?"

"I've had a hell of a day," Max said. "And frigging weird does not half cover it." Max lay back and covered his eyes with the palms of his hands. "Frigging horny old ladies and their voodoo priestess buddies and assholes smashing up my Jeep."

Elena sniffed the air.

"Voodoo. I thought I smelt something like that when I got on the boat. Sort of like ozone. You know, the smell you get after a thunderstorm."

"Yeah, she's gonna make me a zombie or something."

"Don't even joke around. Mambos are bad news, you better watch yourself. She is trouble."

"Funny, she said the same thing about you."

Elena slid on top of him, straddling his chest. She was wearing a short skirt and he could not help but feel the warmth of her across his rib cage.

"Look, I need your help. I thought about it and you are the only one who can help."

"Everybody's wanting a piece of me lately it seems." He slid his hands up her thighs. "What is this you are wanting me to help with?"

She slapped his hands.

"No, look." She opened up a folded piece of parchment and held it wide in front of him. It was brown and stiff with age. It looked like a hand drawn map, but with a huge circle cut out of the very center.

"I don't get it."

"It's a map. You help me get what I want and I can help you get what you want."

"And just what do you think I want?"

"Money. Riches. Gold. What everybody wants."

"I've got all I want right here. I'm comfortable, for the moment, and if you would wiggle a little bit, I would feel even better."

She slapped him.

"Listen! This is important. I think I have found what I am looking for. It must be here." She gestured with the map. "Here is the place where we are going to find the dagger of *Tezcatlipoca*."

"Tezcat who?"

"*Tezcatlipoca, The Smoking Mirror*. Mayan, then Aztec. God of the moon, blood, war, and pretty much anything nasty. He is credited for creating vampires in ancient Meso-America, the Civatateos"

"Jesus Christ." Max sat up and pushed her off. "I need a drink or some coffee at least."

"It's the blood," she said, barely missing a beat as she stood up. "It is always the blood. Blood made me what I am, blood made him his empire, and blood will get me my revenge."

"I'd say you were crazy, but I'm sure I've said that before. Let me make some coffee and then you can try to convince me not to throw you overboard." Max got up and hopped over to the galley side of the cabin. He was too tired to bother putting on his leg. Besides, after yesterday's excitement, his stump was burning awfully and he did not feel like messing with it or the prosthetic. He could get around on one leg in his own boat pretty well anyway and he really did not care how he looked to the crazy redhead.

"Here's the…"

Max shushed her.

"I said, after I have some coffee." She sat silently while he located filter, grounds, and pot, somehow added water to the mix, and started it all to percolating. He leaned against the counter, not saying a word, staring at the machine as it hissed and steamed. Growing impatient, he pulled the half full carafe from off the hot plate, the trickle of fresh liquid hitting it with a sizzle and filling the cabin with the smell of burning coffee. He poured almost all of the contents into what he called his "big-assed mug," and took a swig. It was hot, bitter, and as nasty and brutish as mankind's inner nature. It pulled him kicking and screaming into full wakefulness. Pleased with its potency, he offered the dregs in the carafe to Elena, shaking it and raising one eyebrow. She crossed her arms and shook her head no.

"Fine," said Max, "please go on. You were saying something about blood and I am guessing that you were going to say something more about blood, oh, and yes, I'm betting you might be slipping something about blood in there at some point."

"Don't be a prick."

"I admit, I might be a real jerk if I don't get my full twelve hours of unconsciousness on the best days, but here you are, waking me up in the middle of the night after one hell of a fucked up day. First I was kidnapped by George Burn's grandmother, then I get almost molested by Miss Voodoo, PhD, then I get shot at, and then I nearly total my beloved Jeep, and everything seems to be pointing straight at you. So please forgive me if I am not up to any surprise visits in the middle of the night."

She looked back at him with an expression of abject misery. The beginnings of tears in her eyes, she got up to leave, scooping several antique looking books off the galley table as she did so. Max instantly felt ashamed. He had always been quick to pull out an old fashioned Marine Corps ass chewing, but she was not one of his Lance Corporals, she was just this mixed up kid looking for something to fill in whatever was missing from her life. Fantasy, sure, but for some people fantasy gave their otherwise mundane existences a little more meaning. He had been too harsh and he regretted it.

"Hey," he said softly.

She turned, tears now flowing down her cheeks, "I thought you were special, almost like a gift, an answer to my prayers when you gave me a taste of being human again. You are just a selfish old drunk. I was stupid to think that you would put down that bottle long enough to help me. Sure, you've been hurt, but you are still alive and you are wasting that precious thing, life, smothering it in a haze of pills and alcohol. What a waste! I envy what you can do. I envy that you eat and sleep and can walk around in the sunshine. I envy that you can be in the open and around other normal people. I envy that you can love and grow old and have children and grandchildren. So what if your leg pains you, so what if you think your life is boring now. At least you have a life. You just want to throw it away."

Elena wiped the back of her hand across her eyes.

"I'm sorry, Elena. I was wrong. I shouldn't have snapped. Just a bad day, okay?"

"Bad day, I've been having a bad millennia."

Max paused and pressed his fingers into the bridge of his nose. "Just wait a second. 'Normal people?' 'Millennia?' What is all that about? Are you saying that not only are you being chased by refugees from a grade B horror flick, you are one yourself? Is that what you are saying? As if I have not had enough weird shit happen in the last day, are you sure you want to start with that whole train of thought?"

Elena just looked at him and then moved to leave again. Max surrendered. "No, no, no, don't do that. Everything is weird enough already, that little tidbit is not going to make much of a difference now, Okay? Just sit down and tell me what you want. Here, give me your hand."

She let herself be guided back into the galley. She walked stiffly, obviously uncomfortable, flinching when he tried to touch the small of her back. She sat down just as the cramps hit her and she doubled over, arms crossed over her abdomen.

"You okay?" asked Max.

"No...yes...I don't know. Something is not right." She leaned forward again, rocking on the chair.

"Here, if you're gonna hurl, let me get you into the head." He half carried, half walked her to the bathroom. "You want me to..."

"No, just leave me alone for a minute." Max nodded and closed the door. Elena sat there. It was a nice head for an old sailboat, with a large freshwater shower and a sink in addition to the toilet. The man kept himself clean, at least. She cramped once more and then she smelt it: the rich, coppery smell of newly shed blood. When she was at the height of the hunger, she could smell a drop of it oozing out of a paper cut yards away. There was no mistaking that smell or from where it was coming. She lifted up her skirt and memories centuries old came flooding back.

"Max," she called through the door. "I could use some help."

"What? What's the problem?"

"Ladies' problems."

"What's that?"

Elena rolled her eyes at the door.

"You know, the problem ladies have, *every month*?"

"What? Oh, shit? You mean? Did you bring anything for it?"

"I haven't had a menstrual period in over four hundred years, of course I didn't bring anything for it! It really was not anything I was expecting at this point in time."

"Oh. So I guess you want me to find something."

Elena put her face in her hands and sighed. *Men haven't improved much in four hundred years either.* "Yes."

"Okay. Hold on." Max was amused at this unexpected turn of events. First of all, he could not help the irony in Elena's "predicament" with all of the discussion of her favorite subject, blood. Secondly, in his mind, it explained the tears. It was comforting to Max to be able to dismiss any variability in female behavior and emotions as hormones. This put him on stable, man-world footing again and it gave him an issue he could deal with. He went to the aft of the cabin for his first aid bag. A good warrior always kept a fully stocked and ready first aid kit. He opened a side pocket, and withdrew a zip-lock baggie full of tampons. A combat medic's trick, tampons were perfect for initial treatment and stabilization of gunshot wounds: the applicator made it easy to slip deep inside the hole made by the bullet, the tampon could absorb a lot of blood, it was sterile if the original wrapping was intact, and, as it swelled, it put pressure against the injury and could slow or even stop the bleeding.

Max walked back to the head.

"Here you go, I'm gonna just slip them in." He opened the door a crack and pushed the package inside. There was silence for a second, then Elena called out.

"What the hell are these things?"

"They're for, well, you know..."

"How do they work? They don't make any sense!"

"You don't know how...?"

"Max, the last time I had to worry about this, plastic was not even invented, so no, I don't know how to use one of these."

Max was no longer on familiar comfortable man-ground. This was not the type of conversation he could imagine having with anyone.

"Well," Max said, leaning his head against the door. "You take off the wrapper and then look at the two ends." He paused. "Is the wrapper off? Do you see the two ends?"

"Yes, I can see the two Goddamned ends," Elena snapped back through the door.

"Okay," Max felt like he was trying to talk somebody through disarming a time bomb with ten seconds left on the clock. "Okay.

Okay. You take it, and you turn it…you take one hand and spread your… Okay. Okay." He could feel the sweat dripping down his neck. "Okay. You put the rounded end in…a way…and…you…is it in yet?" *I can't believe I just said that.* "If it is in, then you push the back in while you pull the plastic part out. You leave the string out so you can take it out when you want to change it. I don't know how often you have to do that, so don't ask me."

"You got it?"

"Yes."

"I am going to go up on deck and have a smoke. Let's just put all of the blood stuff aside for a minute. Okay? No more blood drinking, no more blood rituals, and no more about…monthly type stuff. We'll get you cleaned up and then regroup. Might as well go back in to town anyway. I have some spare clothes in the front cabin in the cabinets, you know, the ones you trashed last time you were here? If…you know…you need some clean clothes, you might find some sweats or something you can put on until we get back to your boat."

With that, Max climbed out into the night. He had a box of Maduros stashed in a watertight chest by the wheel. He sat down and propped his foot up on the console. With his remaining great toe, he hit the switch to the anchor windlass and listened with satisfaction at the rattle of the anchor chain being pulled aboard. Buying the windlass was one of the best purchases Max had ever made; pulling up thirty feet of chain by hand was just too much of a pain. With a soft clank, the anchor settled into its fitting. He then punched his toe onto the starter for the engine, it whirred for a bit and then the Cummings diesel roared to life. He pulled down the throttle and the *Prosthetic Limb* slid forward as the screw bit into the water. Max slouched further back in his captain's chair and hooked his foot between the spokes of the wheel. Steering with his foot, his hands were free to pull out a Maduro. He bit off the end and spat it over the side. With a quick flick, he lit his butane lighter and ran the flame over the other end of the cigar until the tobacco started to scorch. Then, and only then, he placed it to his lips and drew in a long breath. Puffing hard, he brought the cigar to a nice bright cherry glow and when the ritual of the lighting was finished, he put the lighter away and leaned back to enjoy his smoke.

The sky was already beginning to lighten, dawn was but an hour, at most, away. This was the calmest part of the day and riding the sound was almost like skating across a sea of glass so smooth was the surface. No chop, no waves, and barely a ripple. With no traffic to speak of, Max had only to keep his boat somewhere between the buoys: red to starboard and green to port.

Elena came up to join him. She looked small and waifish in his much-too-large-for-her sweats, but he was glad that she chose his blue and gold Naval Academy alumni sweatshirt, the one with the hood. She pulled it over her hair and hugged herself."

"It's chilly," she said.

"I guess you don't feel cold when you have your vampire hat on do you?"

"No."

"There you go then. Being human isn't all ice cream and sunny days. You get sick and feel pain and get the runs and all that miserable day by day crap."

"I still would trade you. In an instant."

"No thanks. No way in Hell would I want to live forever. I have enough trouble with living through tomorrow." They stood silently for a moment, looking ahead as the boat made its way out of the sound and up the Neuse.

"I'm sorry," said Max after a little while. "Sorry for being an asshole back there. That was uncalled for."

"No, I'm sorry. I should not have assumed that you would want to help me just because I wanted you to. This all must seem pretty insane to you."

"Truer words were never spoken," Max said. "But I'm all ears. Tell me what's in that red head of yours."

"The dagger is obsidian. Taken from the Temple of the Sun by the conquistadors and lost, it held a power over life and death. I think it will give me the strength to destroy Almos."

"Who?"

"The one who hurt me, who made me into what I am."

Max shifted uncomfortably. *The rape thing. Vampires, sex, rape, isn't that stuff all combined?*

"Oh," he said. "What does obsidian have to do with anything?"

"Obsidian carries energy, even electricity. *Tezcatlipoca* understood that and he also knew that it could carry the life energy."

"I thought you said that this Tez guy was a god."

"He was, eventually. He was an Olmec priest, a sun cultist. Blood sacrifice was the cornerstone of the religion and, as the high priest, he performed the ritual. The victim would be tied to the altar and the priest would cut out the heart and bathe in the blood. What he figured out, was that every time he did so, a small portion of the sacrifice's life energy would transfer to him through the knife, giving him just a fraction more life, more power. I'm not sure how, but he learned how to increase this transfer through his sorcery. As he killed more and more people with that knife, he became more powerful and the more he killed, the longer he lived. He was living off of stolen lives."

"Like the vampires."

"He was not a vampire. He did not drink the blood and he was not turned. He made himself immortal, gradually, over time. By the time the Olmecs fell and the Mayans arose, he was already a demigod. After a thousand years of leading the Mayans in sacrifice, he was a true god, at least to the Aztecs who came after. According to the Florentine Codex, eighty thousand, four hundred people were sacrificed in four days for the re-consecration of the great pyramid of Tenochtitlan. Not *to* Tezcatlipoca, that was a mistranslation, but *by* him. That week alone was a huge transfer of power to him and he was at the height of his power and energy when the Spanish came with a stronger power."

"How so? Christianity?"

"No. Fear. Fear and guns. Tezcatlipoca's power was influence and control by will. The kings of the Aztecs were figureheads. He preferred to keep the guise of a priest, pretending to die or pass the title to an acolyte every generation or so. He had everything he wanted. At least, until Cortez. With their horses, guns, and cannon they made the people fear them more than the old gods. In fact, the people first thought they *were* the old gods."

"So the Spanish spoiled the party. Not surprising if you see how they behave at the World Cup."

"Indeed. So when they eliminated the worship, banned sacrifice, and cast the idols down the sides of the pyramids, Tezcatlipoca was finished. The dagger was gone with the first few shipments of treasure, bound for the vaults of the Spanish king. Tezcatlipoca wasted away along with the belief in the old gods. Catholicism replaced the old ways, which were eventually discarded."

"How do you know this stuff?"

"He told me."

"Who? The Tez guy?"

"Yes. By the turn of nineteenth century, I had amassed a decent fortune, here and there. I became a patron of a French explorer, Marcel Larouche. The French almost took over Mexico during the American Civil War. Did you know that? I sponsored an expedition into the Yucatan and went along. It really did not bother them that I never came out of my tent or covered wagon in the daylight...after all, I was a lady of standing with fair skin too delicate for the tropical sun. I smelled him out, Tezcatlipoca, and found him in a cave in the highlands, barely alive and subsisting on the small sacrifices the superstitious villagers brought him every night."

"Elena, that was what, three hundred years or so after Cortez. He must've been a vampire, ghost, or something by then."

"He was none of those things. He had absorbed so much life energy over the centuries that he still lived on after the dagger was taken. He was just a shell, a withered husk of what he once was. He was as dried up and hollow as an Egyptian mummy, barely able to speak much less move. But speak he did and he told me of his life and his dagger in exchange..."

"For?"

"Some of my blood. To drink and to extend his life just a little bit further. He told me everything for this and, for all I know, he still is lying in that cave: a sentient corpse."

"Morbid. Nasty too. The zombie tells you about the dagger, and what it did for him, but what is it going to do for you? I mean, you don't seem like the human sacrifice type to me."

"The dagger was not just a conduit of energy. Like other forms of quartz, it also stores energy. Like a capacitor, it has the life energy of hundreds of thousands of sacrifices stored away in its crystalline matrix. I should be able to tap into that energy to give me the strength to destroy Almos and bring his petty little empire tumbling down without spilling innocent blood."

"And take his life-force just like Tex took the life force of everyone he killed. You could become the boss vampire yourself with that thing. Is it revenge or power that is pushing you to do all of this?"

She turned at him, angry.

"My life was ruined, taken away from me before it had really begun. I will make Almos pay for that and nothing more."

"You would be surprised at what a little power does to people. Power corrupts, right? Philosophy 101:

"Battle not with monsters, lest you become a monster, and if you gaze into the abyss, the abyss also gazes into you."

"Nietzsche. Smart man, but a little full of himself."

"I don't..."

"He could make a hell of an espresso, though. I couldn't drink any of it of course, but Dostoyevsky raved about it."

"You drank coffee...with Nietzsche *and* Dostoyevsky?"

"I didn't drink it. I listened to *them* while *they* drank it and talked, almost the whole night through."

Max rolled his eyes. "I forgot, you are four hundred years old. I get it. Just don't tell me how Lincoln ate his eggs."

Elena laughed. "So what was the point you were trying to make again?"

"As I was saying," Max continued, "Fredrick Nietzsche warned us about the monster inside us all. Of course, the whole 'monster' thing takes on new meaning in light of current events, but you get the point. Don't fuck up your life for a little payback, it isn't worth it."

She snuggled into his arm.

"I did not have a life at all until you."

"You don't have me," Max chuckled, "at least permanently, and I'm more trouble than I'm worth."

She said nothing, looking out over the water.

"So where is this magical dagger then?"

"I don't know. The last time it appeared was with Edward Teach."

"Blackbeard the pirate?" Max asked, incredulous. "You don't live around here without knowing all about him, but c'mon, pirate treasure? That's laughable and, as delusions go, pretty trite. You might as well say Napoleon had it."

"Nonsense. Pirates preyed on the Spanish gold trade. That is a fact. Did you know that the Inquisition was alive and well in Spain up until the nineteenth century? I was tracked through Spain for years by a Dominican Inquisitor who, it turned out, did not want to destroy me after all. Apparently he had been a *very* naughty boy and he did not want to die and face his eternal judgment. He wanted me to give him what he called the *kiss of immortality*. He was so afraid to face his God that he wanted me to turn him into one of the undead so he would never die. Idiot. I left him slightly anemic and utterly confused but not until after he told me about the dagger and it being taken from the New World. He thought I would trade the information for the gift of immortality. He told me everything the Inquisition knew about the artifact and it being part of Cortez's loot. I don't know where the dagger went after Cortez took it; it might have sat in some chest for years before being put on a ship for Spain, but it re-appears with Teach and he used it. Look."

Elena pulled out one of the old books she had brought. Max had not even noticed her bring it on deck with her. The rising sun gave just enough light for him to see what she was showing him.

"Here, this is a Benjamin Cole lithograph and it was drawn from direct observation of Teach. See, on his left side below the pistols? That leaf like shape in his belt is the dagger. The artist even drew the flake marks along its blade. It fits, Edward was almost indestructible: in his last fight he was stabbed twenty times and shot five times. He wasn't finally finished until his head was cut off and his body thrown into the ocean. It is said that he dabbled in black magic. Part of that magic was very likely the dagger of Tezcatlipoca. If we find his treasure, we find the dagger."

"That's a tall order. Buried treasure is actually something I could get into. Money is good and I could use a new Jeep. The man once lived about an hour north of here, in Bath. Everybody and his brother have been looking all over in these parts for centuries for anything having to do with Blackbeard. If there was a treasure, it would have been found by now."

"We have something they did not: a map."

"Yeah, I saw that. Do you know how many maps have surfaced over the years?"

"This one is real, drawn by Israel Hand and stolen by Ben Worley. I found it in 1920 behind the glass of a mirror once owned by the Worley family. Worley was a fellow pirate and he stole the map during the last fight with the Royal Navy. It took me years to track down the mirror, partly because I did not realize that he, or someone, had hidden it there. I was looking for anything and everything that he may have possessed; looking for some sort of clue. The outline of the coast is recognizably the Outer Banks and, since Teach was destroyed right here, among these islands off Ocracoke, the dagger must be here somewhere. I just did not have all of the pieces until just now."

"So? That map you showed me had a big assed hole in it. I'm thinking that it is a pretty important piece."

"We find Worley, we find the rest of the map."

"And how are we going to do that?"

"Open up his grave. That was what I was trying to do when you first met me. When you helped me out. Worley's grave is back in town and we need to dig him up. His final resting place was a mystery, only recently did I find out where he may have been buried. I was at a historical documents' auction in New York, presented by Sotheby's, when a letter came on the dock. It was a long personal letter written by a friend of the Colonial Governor's wife, Margaret Tryon. I did not purchase the letter, but I did get to examine it before it went up for auction and there was one line that led me here. She mentioned visiting her the grave of her *delightfully scandalous* uncle when she again came calling. It was signed, Sarah Worley. He is here and decades of searching this coast are finally paying off."

"Well, let's go dig him up then!"

Chapter Nine

It took a few hours for the boat to motor all the way up the river and back into town. The sun was high in the sky by the time they got there. They did not mind, as it was a beautiful morning and they enjoyed toasted bagels after only a minor fire in the galley. Elena insisted on cooking for Max, but, cooking apparently was something else she had not done in over four hundred years. With instructions shouted down from Max at the wheel, she did manage to put together an edible, slightly scorched, meal.

As they passed under the huge arc or the Hi-70 bridge, the distinctive clock tower and docks came into view. Closing in on the marina, Max could make out old Bill Whitley perched on the end of a piling, Marlboro in one hand and coffee cup in the other.

"Ahoy, chief!" Max shouted. "Give us a hand will ya? Elena, toss him a line when we pull her up." She did so as they slid up to the dock. Bill, with grace and speed belying his aged appearance, caught it and expertly tied it to a cleat.

"I see the girl done came back. What happen, Marine? You

owe her money?"

"Funny, Chief. We're going in to town. Could you top her off with some diesel while we're gone?"

"Sure, just as soon as you pay me for the last time."

Max fumbled for his wallet and tossed him a credit card. "Here, buy yourself a pretty new dress while you are at it."

Max went below and found his camera bag in the back of a cabinet and emptied out all of his camera equipment. He put two Army issue folding shovels in the big bag along with some zip-lock bags and a first aid kit. Satisfied that the word "Nikon" sewn in big, bright letters on the side made him look more like a tourist than an aspiring grave robber, he slung the bag over his shoulder and went back up on deck after tucking his forty five in his waistband at the small of his back and ensuring that the butt of the pistol was covered by his shirt.

"Chief, we'll be back in a bit."

"Sure, sure."

"Chief?"

"Yeah?"

"You got that old scattergun out in your shack?"

"Yeah. This have something to do with how tore up your Jeep is?"

"Maybe. Maybe not. You just have it ready." With that, Max and Elena walked down the pier. He decided that they should just walk the several blocks to the old Cedar Grove Cemetery. In its current condition, the Jeep would be memorable to anyone who might notice it parked by the gates. Besides, they looked more like a tourist couple if they just strolled along.

Cutting through the historic downtown, past shops and the ubiquitous statues of brightly colored bears, the town's mascot, Max came to a halt. A long, black SUV was parked by the hardware store. Broken side mirrors dangled from their fixtures by a few wires. Dents stretched the length of the Suburban's sides and a single branch, with green pine needles still attached, was wedged under the forward end of the luggage rack.

"Stay here. I'm gonna check this out," Max said as he pushed the camera bag at Elena and began crossing the street.

Nearing the vehicle, two young men came out of the store, one holding several rolls of duct tape in his hands. They were both young, in their early twenties. One was dressed in an expensive looking black suit, over a black shirt and red tie. The other, the one with the tape, was also dressed in black, but the dozens of shiny pins, buckles, and chains on his pants and leather jacket made him look more like an erstwhile punk than his long and over moussed hair seemed to indicate.

"Hey assholes," Max said conversationally, "you owe me a new Jeep."

They both smiled and gave him a feral, predatory look.

"Look here," said the one in the suit. "The sacrifice comes to us. How exquisite. How convenient."

"Yeah," said Max, "I'm just a big smilin' bundle of convenience. Now let's talk about my Jeep and how we're all going to have a chat with the police."

"You are the one who will be coming with us. Our...employers originally wanted you out of our way, but I think they will enjoy talking to you in person." He reached under his jacket and pulled out the black automatic that Max, now that he could see it up close, saw was a standard Glock.

"Not very original. All the bad guys pack Glocks. A Luger would go better with that ugly suit. Throw in a monocle, and you'd be all fashionable and henchman like." Max took a step forward.

"Very well, I'll just bring them your body. Less fun for them, but less trouble for me."

As he raised the gun, Elena came in from the side at a run and swung the camera bag with both hands, nailing the neo-punk full in the face. Two steel shovels add a lot of mass to a nylon and leather case: the man's head snapped back under the impact, blood flying from his nose. Startled, the gunman flinched as he fired. The instant Max saw movement he dodged to his right, reaching behind for his own pistol.

Max's left shoulder was slammed by an impact that felt like he had been hit by a baseball bat, and he fell against the crumpled side of the Suburban. The forty five was in his hand and he thumbed off the safety as he swung it around to cover his assailant. The man in the suit fired a quick shot at Elena, but missed as she threw herself down over the prostrate form of his colleague. He tracked back to Max, but Max was on him first, pulling the trigger twice in rapid succession. The two heavy hollow point slugs punched through his sternum and tore through his heart before exiting his back.

The man in the suit folded onto the ground and lay still.

Max slumped down too, fire beginning to spread through his shoulder. He looked at it and saw bright red streaming from the bullet hole. *If he hit my axillary artery, I'm fucked*, Max thought.

Elena crawled over to him, still clutching the camera bag. Max could see that the punk was still down behind her.

"You're hurt!" Elena cried.

"Yep." Max gestured to his shoulder with his head. "You thirsty, vampire lady? There you go, straight from the tap."

"Awful, you are just awful."

"Gotta laugh to keep from crying, right?"

Elena pressed both her hands against the wound, pushing down into it will all her weight.

"I can't stop the bleeding, Max."

"I am feeling a mite dizzy," he replied. "I don't have a tourniquet handy either. Lift up my arm," he winced as she did so, "and push up into my armpit with your fingers. That'll squeeze the axillary artery. Good, now help me lie down all the way."

"We need to call an ambulance."

"Shit, I'm surprised they aren't here already. The police station is only a few blocks over that way."

Max felt better once his head was lower than the rest of him. He still felt on the verge of passing out, but less so, and he could hear the sirens arriving on the scene. The police came in with weapons drawn and yelled at Elena to lie down on the ground. Max had the presence of mind to re-engage the safety of his pistol before letting it slide from his fingers. Elena refused to let go of Max and shouted back that her friend was hurt and to please let the paramedics in.

The good ol' boys from the hardware store, now on the sidewalk pitched in, yelling that they were messing with the victims and it was the "Eurotrash" who started everything. The police relented and let the paramedics do their job. In moments, they had Max lined up with two large bore IVs, his wound covered with a pressure bandage, and him strapped onto a gurney for the ride to the ER. As they were pushing him into the back of the ambulance, he saw the police handcuffing the unconscious punk and the body of his accomplice. He smiled. The local boys were thorough once they decided who the bad guy was.

"Hey!" Max shouted as the door was closing. "She comes too!" The paramedic followed his pointing finger and shrugged before helping Elena climb in. The doors slammed shut and off they went.

Elena held his hand the entire way there.

"I'm sorry," she said.

"Why? It was really fun. Besides, I got some payback for my Jeep."

"Are you going to go to jail?"

"I doubt it. We have a billion witnesses that will say he pulled his gun first and I've got a permit. We will be fine."

"I don't know. They will be looking for revenge."

"What do you mean?"

Elena glanced at the paramedic, who was carefully studying the ceiling.

"They can't go about in the daylight, so they get those who can."

"And they do this, how?"

Elena glanced at the paramedic, leaned close to Max and whispered. "They used to keep people in thrall by fear and by the power of their blood. Nowadays, there are plenty who would do their bidding out of sheer excitement. Vampires are stylish now."

"You worry too much." Max closed his eyes. "I'm just looking forward to all of the painkillers I'm gonna get now."

The ambulance pulled up to the emergency room. Craven Regional Medical Center served four counties and the staff was no stranger to trauma. They were ready for any member of the gun and knife club. Max was pulled from the ambulance and wheeled inside, Elena holding his hand the entire time.

Max sat up on the gurney as they rolled him in, grinning through his oxygen mask.

"Hi folks! Don't worry about me—it's just a flesh wound!"

Triage nurses are a very matter of fact group of people, and Jennifer Cook was the most matter of fact person in the profession. It served her well when, as an Army nurse back in the First Gulf War, she sorted hundreds of casualties during the liberation of Kuwait. She wore her watch in the inside of her wrist and stuck pencils and pens anywhere they would stay: in her pocket, in her hair, tucked over her ear, on her clipboard, and even under her watchband. Her one nervous habit, although no one would ever admit seeing her nervous at any point in her entire life, was chewing mint gum.

"What do we have here, fellas?"

"GSW to the left shoulder. Through and through," said the paramedic that rode in the back, "I don't think its arterial."

"You don't *think*, do you? Well how about telling me something you *know*."

"Healthy male in his mid thirties, amputee."

Jennifer pulled the sheet off and looked at Max's leg.

"Expensive looking new wheel you got there. Vet?"

Max nodded.

"Iraq?"

Max nodded again.

"That where you lose the leg?"

A third nod.

"Vic or perp?" she asked the paramedic.

"Looks like some punks tried to rob the wrong ex-Marine," replied the paramedic. "The other guy is coming in with the lights and sirens off, if you know what I mean."

"There are no ex-Marines," murmured Max, "once a Marine, always a Marine."

"That's a no shitter right there, Gyrene," said Jennifer.

Having established in her mind that Max was not only the offended party in the shooting, but also a combat wounded veteran, she decided he deserved the red carpet treatment.

"Okay," she called over her shoulder, "we have us a stable GSW to the shoulder. Let's get him to pre-op, get a type and cross, and call radiology to bring their Doppler. If that artery is damaged we'll have to call in the vascular surgeon for a repair, but if it's not, then it will be a routine clean out and sew up." She was already pushing Max down the hall.

"Oh yeah, call X-ray too. We'll need a PA and lateral of his shoulder. Gotta see if there are any broken bones or fragments left in there."

Technicians rushed to fill her shouted orders and, as she came to the next set of doors, she stopped and put her hand on Elena's arm.

"Sorry sweetie, you'll have to wait here. We've got a lot of work to do. It may not look like much now, but these things can go south in a hurry and if that artery is leaking, we'll have to move quick. Go get a coffee or something and I'll come and get you when we know something." With that, she and Max were gone and Elena was standing there, staring at the doors as they swung shut in front of her.

She was stunned for a moment, not knowing exactly what to do. The sun was streaming through the windows of the triage and waiting areas and she began to feel an extreme sense of fear and dread building up deep inside her. With a panicked feeling, she could sense Max going farther and farther down the hall, farther and farther away from *her*.

Sobbing, she glanced around the room, dust motes danced in the brilliant rays of sunshine as they flooded the room. People, each one with his or her own specific problem, were sitting on chairs lining the walls. A television droned on in the corner.

Elena began to get hot, very hot.

She turned and pulled on the doors, but they would not budge. The skin on the back of the neck began feel like she had been scalded there. She began to pound on the door.

"Let me in!" she shouted. "I have to go with him!" She pounded harder. The backs of her hands began to blister and she could just begin to make out the charcoal smell of scorching skin.

In a full blown, hysterical panic, she began to throw herself against the door like a trapped animal, oblivious to the desk clerk's shouts for security. All she could think about was getting away from the burning sun, away from the pain that was beginning to fill her entire being, away from the oblivion that would surely follow the fire.

"Max!" she screamed, thrashing and clawing at the door, "Max! I'm dying! Max!"

Just as the first wisps' of smoke began to curl up from her skin and hair, the one way doors burst open and Max scooped her into his arms.

"I was burning! Burning!" she sobbed as he began to carry her to the exit, dragging his IVs on the floor behind him.

"It's okay baby, we are so out of here."

Jennifer was right behind him.

"Sir! Sir! Get back here this instant, you can't leave until we have cleared you! You might need surgery and you might bleed to death if you open up that shoulder."

"I'm not going anywhere without her, so take your pick: either she comes with me wherever I go, or we leave. Right here, right now." Max noticed that he was surrounded by uniformed security. He also noticed that there was a strong smell of burnt barbeque in the air. Elena was still crying, her face buried in his good shoulder.

"If she is not immediate family, she cannot come back with you and, if you go to surgery, nobody can come back into the OR. Those are the rules and they are the rules for a good Goddamned reason. So Marine, get your Goddamned ass back in that room and on that gurney right now."

"Fuckin' make me," said Max. Jennifer nodded to security and they began to move in. Just as Max was cocking back to try to slug the nearest guard, a voice broke the tension.

"I think that we all have had enough violence for one day. I'm sure that you all would agree."

Max looked over at source of the interruption. Henry "Hank" Beardsley, Chief of Police, stood there with two of his officers flanking him. With a serious buzz cut, stern face, and a crisply pressed, creased, and starched uniform, his demeanor attested to a military background. In fact, Hank was from a long line of soldiers. Ever since the American Revolution, there has been a Beardsley in uniform. Hank's grandfather was in the First World war, his father in the Second, and, after Vietnam, Hank had taken off his Army uniform only to don one of law enforcement. He was a tough, no-nonsense cop who had rapidly risen to Chief of Police and he was fiercely loyal to men in uniform.

"A shooting in a small town like this is big news and, when I heard who was involved, I had to come over in person to size things up. What's the trouble here?"

"We can't help him if he is not going to cooperate," said Jennifer, looking even more annoyed at this latest challenge to her authority. This was her emergency department and she was not used to being told how to run it.

"Well, those Marines sure can be pig-headed, but Major Bradley is a good man, and if he feels strongly on a subject, he must have his reasons."

"Great, so you know each other."

"That we do. My son was a second louie back in the first roll into Iraq under then Captain Bradley. He got the kid back home in one piece. I owe him for that."

"No worries, Mr. Beardsley, that was my job," said Max.

"So, nurse, if Major Bradley insists that his lady friend go with him to hold his hand, then I'd let him. He's done a lot and he's been through a lot and I think we owe him that at least."

The Chief could see that Jennifer was on the verge of relenting, so he pressed on.

"Besides, I'd consider it a personal favor to me if you saw fit to relax the rules just this once."

"Okay, okay. Fine. I know when I'm on the losing end of a proposition. She can come back, but if the surgeons want to take him back to the operating room, we can't have her coming in."

"I won't go into surgery then," said Max.

"All or nothing, eh?" said Hank. "What is she, your good luck charm?"

"Something like that."

Jennifer was just about to object to this when the Chief piped up.

"Those operating rooms have those little viewing windows, she could watch from there if she had to."

Max looked down at Elena. She nodded.

"That sounds alright."

"Great," said Hank. "Then it's settled. Now let's get you squared away and have that shoulder looked at."

Jennifer, feeling defeated, tacitly brought the gurney around and gestured for Max to get back on. She picked up the IV bags that he had been dragging behind him and slapped them on his abdomen. She then began pushing him back to the exam room, this time with Elena in tow.

"I'm just going to come along and have a quick word with the patient, if I may," said Hank.

Jennifer just grunted and shrugged. She was not about to start a fuss all over again.

"About that shooting, Major," said Hank as he walked alongside. "It looks justifiable to me. My guys on the scene say that the people in the hardware store saw the whole thing and it looks like a simple case of self defense. They have some surveillance cameras that look out over the sidewalk and if those show the same thing, well, open and closed."

"Good."

"Unless there is something that you need to add."

Max did not answer.

"Like I said, the people in the store said that it looked like armed robbery. He pulls a gun on you, your little lady causes a ruckus, and you pull your piece and plug him. That's what I told the district attorney when I called him on the way over here. He said that he's not going to pursue charges if that's all it turned out to be. Since you had a legal carry permit and you operated under the law of the use of deadly force in this state, no charges." He paused. "Unless there is something more to the story."

"Like?"

"Well, anything really. Did you know those guys? Did you owe them money? Were they, you know…"

"No, I don't know."

"Listen," he leaned close to Max, barely speaking over a whisper. "Word gets around, you've been on some strong painkillers since you've been hurt. Sometimes a man in your position starts needing something a little *stronger* to keep the pain down, if you know what I mean. If, and I say *if,* those boys had something to do with anything like that. Something to do with keeping you supplied in things you shouldn't be messing with, then it could go very badly for you if something like that came out, you know, later. Self defense in a robbery looks a lot different to the DA than shooting your dealer. So, if there is anything like that going on, you better tell me here and now."

"You gonna read me my rights?" started Max.

"No, no, just a friendly, concerned conversation."

"Well, in that case, the answer is definitely no. I have my issues, but the veteran's administration is all the pusher I need right now. Robbery, plain and simple. Guy wanted my wallet and I would've just given it to him too, except I was afraid they would shoot her when she came out swinging."

"Feisty one, she is; red hair will do it every time." Hank straightened up. "Alright, very well. Looks like you won't be charged with anything and I'll send a man over to get a formal statement when you are back on your feet. I will, of course, have to keep your piece as evidence until this is all sorted out. I imagine a man like you has a couple more like it back at home."

"Something like that."

"Well, looks like this is your stop. I'll leave you be for now. Take care and stay out of trouble."

"Thanks again, Chief."

"Consider it a debt repaid. You are on your own from here on out." With that he turned and walked down the hall.

Chapter Ten

Luckily for Max, he did not have to go to into surgery. He would not have permitted himself to go under anesthesia and risk them trying to kick Elena out again. He had seen just how terrified she had been without him and he felt that he should keep her close for the time being.

Under Nurse Cook's scowling gaze, the parade of consultants came through. When the ultrasound showed no major damage to the axillary artery, the vascular surgeon lost interest and wandered off. The x-ray was clean: no retained bullet fragments, broken bones, or damage to the rotator cuff so the orthopedist happily went back to his golf game. This left an emergency medicine resident to do the little he had to do for such an uncomplicated injury. He irrigated the wound with saline until all of the liquid came back clear, gave Max a tetanus vaccine, and wrote him a script for a week long course of antibiotics. He threw a few stitches on the ragged ends where the bullet exited.

"Keep it clean and dry," he said. "It's gonna ooze a little bit, but only worry if it smells or looks like you have puss coming out. You'll have a big bruise around the hole, but it should start fading in a day or two. If it gets hot or red, come back in. If you see puss, come back in. If you get fevers or chills come back in."

"Shouldn't you sew everything up completely?" Elena asked, looking over his shoulder.

"You don't close up a puncture wound," Max said. "It might cause an abscess formation. Better to let it drain and heal by second intention, right Doc?"

"Right." The resident looked over his glasses at Max. "You've either been shot before or gotten some medical training."

"A little of both, Doc."

"I wouldn't use the term 'little' with being shot at all, but there is no permanent damage done and you will do fine unless you do something stupid. You don't look like a stupid guy to me."

Max glanced over at Elena. "You would be surprised, Doc."

After getting the all clear from the resident, Nurse Cook let them go and, after making sure all of his insurance information was on file, so did the receptionist.

When they finally made it back outside, Max noticed that they had spent most of the day in the ER. It was late in the afternoon, going on evening. Just outside the hospital doors, he hailed a taxi.

"Where are we going?" asked Elena.

"Home, to regroup."

"I know you are hurt, but what about…" He cut her off with a wave of his hand.

"The dead guy will still be there tomorrow, and my shoulder is beginning to kill me. Those Percocet they gave me are worthless. I might as well be swallowing sugar pills for all the good they are doing me. I need to chill out and get something a little stronger in me. Then we can go and dig up your Mister Worley."

"All right, I just would rather not wait too long and have everything slip out of our hands."

"He's been there for almost two hundred years, right? Twenty four hours longer won't make a difference. Besides, I have a feeling that whoever," Max paused, "or whatever is giving us trouble is more interested in watching you, and now me, than making the discovery first. We go home, hole up, regroup and hit the situation fresh and alert. I don't feel like another fight just yet."

Once in the cab, they went back to the pier by way of a fast food joint to pick up some burgers.

"Meat is great for healing," Max said as hefted the warm take out bag.

The Prosthetic Limb was where they left it and the cabin was still locked, so Max felt it was still a secure hideout. Bill Whitley was nowhere to be found, but the fuel gauge indicated a full tank, so Max knew that he had fueled the boat as asked. An early evening thunderstorm was beginning to roll in over the sound and the first patters of raindrops began to fall as Max unlocked the cabin. They settled in with the food and Max, when he thought Elena was not watching, popped a couple of oxycontin and his shoulder started to feel better.

"Got a big squall coming in," said Max as the thunder rolled across the boat. "We usually get really good ones in the afternoon this time of year. Something about really warm water under rapidly cooling skies. Convection. Yep, convection currents and moisture. They usually come in from the sound."

The rain picked up and was coming down in sheets, the sound of a thousand tap dancers across the ceiling blending into one solid crackle of sound. Her face positively glowed with each flash of lightning.

"Very odd of you to use the word 'good' when talking about a thunderstorm."

"How so?" replied Max.

"Well, you are sailor and I would expect that all sailors hated foul weather. You could lose a mast or something. All I have to do is seal myself in and let the engine do all the work."

"It's not like that," said Max after a moment, "I find storms invigorating. Exciting. They make me feel alive and charge me up. I guess it has to do with all of the electricity flying around the sky. And the smell. After the storm, the air smells rich and clean at the same time like everything is renewed and ready to start all over again."

"Careful, someone may mistake you for a poet or a dreamer."

"The only poems I know are obscene limericks and you don't want to know what sort of dreams I have."

"I sincerely doubt that. When you let it out, you are very well read. You would be surprised what I want."

Max walked over to the refrigerator.

"Know what would go good with dinner? Some ice cold beer." He pulled out two bottles, popped off their caps on the edge of the counter, and handed one to Elena. "They have beer back in the middle ages?"

"The middle ages were long before my time and yes, we had beer back then. I never did develop a taste for it. You had to drink it sometimes, especially when the rains were sparse and the water in the wells went bad, but I never did enjoy it."

"Probably because it was made of twigs and berries back then. Try this pilsner, it's an American microbrew at its finest."

She took a sip. It was very cold and tasted of sunshine on wheat fields.

"Good. It's very good. We had this, or much like it, when I was young but it was warm...never this cold. I like it cold. It cools me down to my toes."

"See? Old Max would never steer you wrong, now dig in."

The hamburger was good and the beer did go very well with it. Elena lost herself for a moment in the still novel experience of eating.

"How about some tunes?" asked Max as he got up and clicked on his stereo. He grimaced as he sat back down.

"Does it hurt badly?" Elena asked.

"My shoulder? It only hurts when I laugh. What movie is that line from?"

"I don't remember."

"Hmmm." The MP3 player attached to Max's sound system changed songs and the sound of an expansive tenor filled the cabin. Max closed his eyes and began to hum along.

"What is this" asked Elena.

"I had my player set on random. It's *Facing Future* by Israel Kahakawiwo'ole. I picked it up a while back when I was stationed at K-bay. I mean, Kaneohe Bay. It's in Hawaii. I really got hooked on the local tunes. Imagine a guy weighing over seven hundred pounds with such an incredible voice, playing *Somewhere Over The Rainbow* on a ukulele for that matter. He was a great singer, rest in peace, bro," Max said and raised his beer bottle to the ceiling.

"It's very pretty. Dance with me," said Elena as she got up and tugged on Max's arm.

"Not really a dance tune…" Max started to protest.

"It's pretty. Dance with me," Elena insisted as she pulled him to his feet. He acquiesced and wrapped his arms around her as she snuggled in. Max winced briefly when she rubbed against his bandaged shoulder, but then he settled in. Her hair smelled of cinnamon and Max breathed in deep. They swayed together, barely in time with the music, as the rain streamed down the glass in the windows and portholes, the lightning brightening up the dim room with flashbulb pops. Max could not help but sing along; he knew the words by heart. Hell, everybody in the world knew this song. He found himself singing to her, his baritone voice harmonizing with the tenor coming out of the speakers, singing of hope and dreams and escaping the mundane morass of life.

"I'm sorry," she said eventually, leaning against his chest.

"About what," he replied.

"About burdening you with all of my problems, about getting you involved."

"Don't forget about getting me shot," he added, deadpan.

She looked up.

"Yes, Im sorry about that too."

"I was just kidding. It's okay," he said, looking down at her, into her green eyes.

"I wasn't. You have been literally a miracle for me, a true Godsend…if He exists…and I was so wrapped up in how you made me feel and how you could help me out, I almost forgot that there is a human being beneath your rough and tumble facade."

"It's no facade, what you see is what you get. I'm a very shallow person."

Elena laughed at this. "I don't believe it for an instant. You are kind, and generous, and you helped me and were nice to me even though you think I'm insane."

"I never…"

"You may not have said it, but I'm certain you thought it. I don't blame you, I sometimes think I am insane but reality sets in soon enough. It did today."

"The fuss at the hospital?"

"Yes, I thought I was going to die. Again. The sun was burning me and I had to get to you and I couldn't reach you and there you were."

He took her hand and kissed it gently.

"It's a little red, but not burned or anything."

"The blisters went away just as soon as you showed up. You have an amazing effect on me."

"You are starting to have an effect on me too," he said as he kissed her forehead.

"I'm so very happy I have found you, not just because I am normal when I am with you," Elena said, "but because I feel whole for the first time in a long, long, time. Thank you."

He straightened up and looked at her.

"Elena, don't kick yourself. I've enjoyed you and your 'issues'. It's good to feel needed. It's good to have something to do other than drink myself to sleep or play cards with ol' Bill. The mission is important for someone like me. You get to live and breathe the mission and when one is over, all you can do is think about the next one and the next set of orders. I've been without one for too long. You say that I make you human again, well, you have made me feel *alive* again. I have not felt this alive since I was tearing it up in the war. Fighting is what I do, and stopping the bad guys is what I love. When they cut me up and kicked me out, they took…well…let me put it this way: the leg does not matter at all, it was the life I led that I miss. When that went away, I gave up. In the last few days I have gotten in a fistfight, a car chase, and a gunfight and it was all fucking marvelous."

Chapter Eleven

Elena stretched up on the tips of her toes and kissed him. It was a hard kiss, full of desperation and longing and she held it just as urgently as a drowning man clings to a life ring. Their connection and their mutual need for one another was as palpable and real to her as his lips and the rasping stubble on his chin and across his cheeks. He was solid. He was real. The very concrete nature of his presence was completely unlike the ephemeral world in which she had existed for hundreds of years. She found herself wanting to hold on to this rock of a soul so that her own soul would stay anchored and not dissipate into the mists of time. Her kind might exist forever, but, as year after year passed into oblivion, their humanity would slip away no matter how hard they clung to the vestiges of their past lives.

Some embraced it, throwing off any semblance humanity as fast as they could, becoming more ghoul than sentient being in one tumultuous and horrific metamorphoses. However, even those who struggled with the darkness, who fought it or bargained with it, still lost a tiny piece of themselves with every season. After the passing of millennia they become more and more ethereal and less solid until they are nothing more than wispy wraiths, haunting the lonely places.

When Elena was with Max, she felt her steady and once immutable loss of self halted, slow, and even reverse. She felt steadied and supported and even energized just being near him. Hope was all but forgotten by her kind because once someone receives the dark embrace there is no going back. There is no redemption and there is no reclaiming the birthright of mankind. Only an eternal existence in the shadows and always looking at life that they will never get to live is the curse of the undead caught between life and nothingness. Elena had found her link to the land of the living and she was determined to never let go.

"Whoa," said Max, finally breaking the kiss, "you have to come up for air sometime."

"Come with me," whispered Elena, taking him by the hand.

She led him towards the bow, into the forward cabin where she spent her first night aboard. He began to speak, but she silenced him with her finger tips on his lips and pushed him back until he was sitting on the bed. Then she stepped back and, with a coy smile, began unbuttoning her shirt. One by one the buttons came loose, seemingly unfastening themselves as her fingers gracefully slid over them. The swell of her breasts became visible as the cloth parted and she reached out for Max and guided one of his hands to the soft skin there. When his hand touched her nipple, she felt an electric shock of sensation sweep up from that delicate point, up her neck and under her jaw to linger behind her ear. She closed her eyes and reveled in the sensation for a moment before pushing him back, away from her, and further on the bed.

With a swift motion, she pushed down her jeans and kicked them off to land in the corner in a heap. Smiling, she shrugged of her shirt and stood before him nude, her very pale skin a canvas that the shadows from the raindrops on the window painted a constantly changing chaotic pattern every time the lightning flashed outside. The red of her hair, her lips, and the cleft between her legs made her skin seem even more pale than it had ever been. She slowly glided onto the bed, never taking her green eyes off Max's brown ones.

She straddled him and leaned forward to kiss him and then slowly began to unbutton his shirt, kissing each bit of skin revealed as she worked her way down. She paused and leaned back. Max sat up and struggled to get the shirt over the wounded shoulder but, with a quick "ouch" got his shirt off. Elena then pushed him back down again. She kissed him lightly on his lower abdomen and gently unfastened his shorts.

Max moaned as she took him in her mouth briefly before she went back to slowly teasing him. He was at her mercy and he did not care what was going to happen just as long as it did not stop. She kissed and nibbled and stroked until his arousal was at its peak and then she moved forward on him and slipped over him. As he slid inside her she gasped and closed her eyes tight, biting her lower lip. Max suddenly thought of something she once said.

"Are you sure? I thought—"

"Thought what?" She asked as she began to move against him.

"You said Almos hurt you."

Elena stopped still and looked him straight in the eye. "Not *that* way. This is for you."

"Oh." mumbled Max. "But what about the other night, in the bathroom? Isn't this the wrong time of the—"

"My body seems to...reset...whenever I leave you." Elena leaned forward, took his face in her hands, and drew close, nose to nose. "Listen, if you are going to babble like that the whole time, I will just get up and find something else to do. How you say it? Shut the fuck up and get with the program."

Max relaxed. "Yes, ma'am."

"Good, now be quiet silly man," she said as she arched her back and began to move on top of him once again, slowly at first, but then gradually picking up her momentum as she became used to the feel of him inside her. The little pain that she first felt was fading away, replaced by a new sensation that began to build and build as they moved together. The feelings were like nothing she had ever experienced. There was some of the hunger and anticipation she had felt in the time just before feeding, and the growing excitement that she felt was similar to the peaking of the blood lust, but there was a deeper, more profound experience dawning deep inside her: life affirming and profoundly human.

They worked together, in unison, and for the briefest moments they seemed one being, one mind, and one soul. As he peaked, she rode that wave with him and she felt the energy blossoming in her, starting out in the very center of her, spreading from her middle to the very tips of her fingers and toes. She felt as if pure light must be streaming from every extremity, tearing away the darkness that had surrounded her every moment for centuries, and her and what it meant to *be* her was left shining through.

She collapsed on his chest, not spent, but recharged with every nerve ending tingling and vibrating.

"Life," she breathed, "that felt like life. It was as if all the life not lived over the years came crashing through me all at once."

"Intense," agreed Max. "It's been awhile, I have to admit, but that was the most intense... experience I've ever felt. Amazing. You say you haven't done this in a long time?"

"No."

"Not once in, what, four hundred years?"

She lay her head against his chest, her fingers idly playing along his neck and chest.

"You must understand that my life ended four hundred years ago. I lost my humanity back then and my existence since has been just a shadow: not truly human no matter how we may try to pretend."

"So...your kind...don't..."

"We are dead, after all. The dead cannot procreate. We cannot create life, we can only take it. When we turn, we lose everything that makes us human. No pleasure in food or drink, no pleasure in love; there is just the thirst and the hunger for blood of the living. That is all we really feel. Evil must be behind the change because, even though the good parts of humanity such as love, empathy, and kindness are lost, the worst emotions in mankind, such as hate, cruelty, and greed become magnified. Or perhaps every one of us is just so full of anger and jealousy at being robbed of our humanity that we spend every moment henceforth trying to destroy what we cannot have. Perhaps we are truly damned and possessed by the evil of the hell spawn."

"You don't look very evil to me, and I like you. You are a lovely lady and you really should not wallow in misery like that. There is no predestination, there is no guy in heaven just hanging out behind the clouds waiting to jump out and yell 'gotcha' every time you fuck up. There is just you, and you make your destiny for yourself. The only damnation you will face is when you give up and let circumstances control your life."

He kissed her forehead.

"Besides, you're on my boat and that's the coolest thing ever."

She smiled at him.

"You certainly do not lack in confidence," she whispered.

"Of course I don't, I couldn't get much done as I am without believing in myself and my manifest destiny. If I can strap on a fake leg and run a marathon, I can do anything. You can do anything you want as long as you put yourself in the right frame of mind."

"It's not exactly like that," she said. "Tell me about this manifest destiny."

"I believe it is my destiny to be on top next time. It will come true, oh yes."

She laughed. He liked it when she laughed. Very sincere and very sexy.

"And while we wait for my manifest destiny to...arise once more, fill me in on one thing."

"Yes."

"If vampires can't have sex, what is with all of the seduction and stuff you see in the movies?"

"I did not say that they cannot have sexual relations, I said that they could not experience pleasure like humans do. Some still do. I once read that a castrato, a castrated man, can still have relations if he had been sexually active before losing his manhood. He still has the habit, the ways and means of it, in his brain. It is the same for vampires. The 'how' still exists assuming we had the 'how' before the change, it is the 'why' that changes. Some do it because, even though they feel no pleasure in the act itself, the motions are familiar and a link to their human past. Others find that the dance of seduction itself is a source of mental pleasure. It is about domination and control.

"Still others use their appearance and sexual vibrations as a tool to lure in and pacify a victim. I am ashamed to say that I have used my femininity in this way as well. It is not about the sexual act, but about feeding and is rarely consummated in a sexual manner. The victim may be sexually aroused, they may even orgasm as the vampire feeds and be left with a pleasant, if illusory, memory. But we do not usually have sex with them, and I never have because, frankly, what was the point?

"Of course there are exceptions, but, as I said, it is more about control and domination of another than about giving or receiving pleasure. The only pleasure we feel is in feeding"

"And tonight?"

"Tonight, thanks to you, I felt alive. I have not felt this stirred since I was a young maiden and I never had a chance to act on those urges until you. Being with you made me...no, makes me feel alive. I felt filled with energy, not the energy I take from someone else, not the stolen life energy from the blood, but energy from myself, created deep inside of me and welling out in torrents like the clearest spring. I felt like a life giver, not a life taker in that instant and I felt a oneness with you. I have not felt such a connection with another human being since I was taken from my family and I certainly have never felt as connected with anyone as I was with you. Four hundred years of a solitary existence gone in but a few moments."

"I don't know what to say," said Max, "except that you have made me very happy too. And now..." He rolled over until she was beneath him, face to face and eye to eye.

"And now it seems your manifest destiny has returned," she finished and laughed as she guided him in once more.

Chapter Twelve

They awoke at the crack of noon, curled up together in a protective cocoon of sheets, pillows, arms, and legs. Max was feeling a bit sluggish, as he always did before he got moving. His back was stiff and his leg ached. He had forgotten to take off his prosthetic before falling asleep and it chafed the hell out of him. He felt as if he put his foot in a pot of scalding water. He desperately needed his meds, but he did not want to move and wake her.

Salt air was carried in by the breeze and the gulls were making a ruckus. The first of early morning fishermen were returning to clean their catch. The high pitched shrieks and cries of the seagulls fighting over scraps off the boats caused Elena to stir. Max's arm was right under her neck and he slowly, with the care of a demolition expert defusing a ticking time bomb, began inching his trapped limb from beneath her.

She sighed and mumbled something. Max froze. The sheet had pulled away slightly and Max was treated to the sight of a pink tipped breast. He did not let that distraction deter him from his mission. As she quieted, he resumed the slow yet determined extraction of his arm. With just his hand left to go, she opened her deep, sea green eyes.

"Where are you going?"

"Nowhere," he said, "it is about time to get moving though. I am actually surprised that we did not have any trouble last night."

"I think they can't see us very well. I know that when I am around you, my senses are dulled. I can only see and hear what normal people can. I can't even smell the blood in your veins and you are right here next to me. Perhaps you limit what they can sense as well, at least where you are concerned. With those two gone..."

"The guys from yesterday? What about them?"

"They were in the service of one of the undead. I could tell that much. Human servants allow us to extend our reach into the daylight. They were his eyes and ears as well as his hands. With them gone, he is blind and deaf until he comes searching for us himself."

"We talked about this. You said that it is sort of a spell that the vampire puts on the person. All about the blood and such. If your powers don't work when I'm around, then why did they still come after me?"

"Because some humans want to be in thrall to the undead. It may be a way out of a boring life, or they think it might get them power, or they just think it's cool and stylish. Unfortunately many humans freely serve the darkness in today's society, the power of the blood or no."

She sat up, releasing Max's hand.

"Regardless," she said, "I am grateful for the respite. It is good to move about, day or night, without someone hanging over us, watching us."

She frowned and gently touched Max's still bandaged shoulder. A tiny spot of dried blood shone through, but it was the huge purple bruise, the edges just barely turning yellow, that concerned her.

"Does it hurt still?"

"Not really," Max replied. "It is pretty stiff, but I can move it just fine, and it's not bleeding any more. I am personally acquainted with pain. I can work through this. As odd as it sounds, I've felt worse."

"I'm glad that you are feeling better." She got out of bed and Max watched her shapely nude backside sway itself all the way to the bathroom. After the door closed, he waited until he could hear the shower come on and then he leaned over to the nightstand and ferreted out one of his pill bottles he had stashed there. One after another, he swallowed four of his oxycontin dry and then lay back and waited for the pain in his leg to slowly drain away. He knew how much to take and he made sure that he did not take so much that he would be useless for the rest of the day. Just enough to stay functional and, by the time the shower shut off and the door opened again, his shoulder pain was gone and his stump pain was down enough for him to walk without limping. Over twenty four hours solid in his prosthetic and he was going to head out on it again. It would suck, but it would not slow him down at all. After the Marine Corps Marathon, twenty six miles of hell completed by sheer determination, he had truly known agony. It had been just as bad as when he was in the hospital and the orthopedists cut on him every single day. He got through that, he could get through this, and he could damned well get through anything else that was thrown his way.

Willpower. That was how Max always got things done. Growing up on the farm, and helping with the harvest had been fun, the machines were a treat to run when his father let him. Asparagus was the worst because it had to be harvested by hand. Long rows greeted him in the morning and Max, at nine, insisted on getting the same number of rows to cut as the bigger boys and men. His father said he should start with just one row, but Max, stubborn, kept insisting until his father gave in.

Sharp knife in his right hand, a thick glove on his left, he bent over the plants and took each stalk one after the other. His hands grew bloodier with every nick and scrape of the knife, but he did not slow up. He refused to take any breaks all day long because he did not want to get too far behind and he shrugged off any offers of help. They were his rows and he was going to finish them himself.

Hours after everyone else was done and gone, he was still out there: bend, cut, bag, bend, cut, bag. When it got dark, Max's father walked into the field, and when he approached, Max readied himself to angrily refuse any order to come inside. The old man said nothing, and quietly set up a few lights on tripods so that Max could see what he was doing. Then, without a word, went back in and went to bed. Max finished around midnight, exhausted but satisfied.

Elena finally came out wearing one of his button-down shirts.

"We should get some chow and get started on your treasure hunt, Missy," Max said.

"Yes. Any thoughts?"

"We should wander around, looking like tourists. There is always some history buff walking around in there and they even run tours a couple of times per day. I took a tour of the place a long time ago. Colonial and civil war history abound. We could make a few of those things…what are the things called when you put paper over the gravestone and rub a pencil on it so you get a copy of the inscription? Etchings?"

"Rubbings, actually."

"Huh. Well that makes some sense."

"Go on."

"The old part can get overgrown. Stones broken, worn down and covered with Kudzu, and don't forget the fire ants. There are some big mounds out there. We have to be subtle because if somebody sees us messing around, they'll call the cops and I think I've already used up all my favors for a little while."

"And it was a big favor, that one."

"Well, he thinks he owes me, but nobody owes me anything. I was just doing my job and his son was a good kid. Got out and is studying law somewhere if I remember correctly. So we search the old section," Max continued, " systematically. Start at the far corner and check every stone, every partial stone, and crypt. Nobody will mind if we clear off leaves and junk to read the names, just as long as it looks like we are not going to hurt anything. Once we find it, we are going to have to wait until we are sure we are alone. We might have to wait a long time, until after dusk probably. Does that scare you?"

"No, not really. If the others know where we are, and if they decide to strike, then I believe that they will be just as impotent as they were the first night and just as impotent as I was last night."

Max grinned. "I'm glad I wasn't impotent last night."

She punched him lightly on the chest. "Awful man!"

"Let's hope that they steer clear. If they can't vamp then you can't vamp and that leaves just little ol' me and, if you hadn't noticed, not only am I a cripple, I'm a wounded cripple and I really want to avoid a fight if we can help it."

"Too bad the policeman took your gun away."

"Adapt, improvise, and overcome my dear," said Max as he got up and walked over to the closet door. He opened it, and just beneath the door was another; made of metal with a combination lock in the center.

"It's more like a locker than a real safe. A real gun safe would be too heavy and bulky to set up in a boat like this one. A good thief could pop open this aluminum baby in a few seconds flat," said Max as he worked the combination, "but it will keep out the curious at least."

Max pulled the door.

"That's a shotgun," Elena said. "I can tell because it has two barrels, side by side."

"Yep. Score one for the green-eyed girl."

"I don't know what those others are, but they must be military. I've seen soldiers carrying them on CNN."

"Yep again. AR-15 and AK-47. The good guy gun and the bad guy gun."

Max leaned in and reached down towards the bottom of the closet and pulled out a small black pistol.

"Glock model twenty nine. Similar to the one those assholes were using yesterday, and not by coincidence. These are very popular pistols. Lightweight, easy to use, and tough non-jamming motherfuckers. Called 'Combat Tupperware' because they have a polymer frame. This one is a compact version. I load it up, slip it into the pocket of my shorts, and I've got ten rounds of ten millimeter hollow point goodness ready to go. I won't even pull it unless we are really, really in deep shit because I don't want any more questions from the police. But, it's better for this gimp to have one if he is going to protect his fair lady from the forces of darkness."

"It looks like you are up to the job," Elena said. "Is everything a joke to you?"

"We combat vet types try to find humor in everything. It keeps you from putting your pistol in your own mouth and giving yourself the ultimate personality deconstruction."

"And the rest of those things?"

"These?" Max closed the door. "These are nothing, you should see what I have stashed away in storage. I've been collecting since I was a teenager. Could buy another boat with some of the junk I have tucked away."

"Bullets don't work on some things out there, Max. Don't get too sure of yourself. I'm afraid that we have stirred up too much attention already and if the older ones get personally involved, instead of sending their human servants or the newly turned, your bravado will not help us one bit."

"Swift, silent, and deadly. That's me." Max pocketed the Glock and shouldered the camera bag. "Let's go out and create a little mischief."

Chapter Thirteen

Cedar Grove Cemetery was a sprawling multi-acre piece of land that has been in continuous use for the last three hundred or so years. Predating the American Revolution by several generations, it had gradually expanded year by year as war, disaster, or the simple course of time added to the population tenant by tenant.

Large gnarled live oak with long, sweeping shawls of Spanish moss populated the older southeastern end, and faced the equally ancient and stately waterfront homes. The Northern end was still in active use. Its rolling lawn, punctuated by decorative hardwood and pine, threw the aged and almost forgotten historical side in sharp relief. Every generation that passed added to the ever expanding community of the deceased and, with the exception of those romantics who still harbored a fascination with days gone by, the needs of the newly mourning outweighed the needs of mourners long since dead and gone. The care and maintenance was largely directed away from the areas Max and Elena had to search for the mysterious and absent Mr. Worley.

As is common in many old Southeastern Coastal towns, the remnants of the oyster industry was used in much of the construction and decoration of the old cemetery. The walls and archway, were made from bricks cut from a sort of concrete formed by combining whole oyster shells, lime, and sand. The arch was known to locals as the "Weeping Arch" because moisture condensed at the top of the arc and slowly dripped upon anyone passing below, as if the very stones of the graveyard shared in the passing mourner's grief. The resulting covering of moss and fungus gave the walls an even more aged and decrepit appearance.

The walks were all paved with oyster shells, white and reflective. They crunched loudly underfoot as Max and Elena walked over them—much too loudly to Max's liking. They tried to look as casual as possible. Nothing would bring unwanted questions more than skulking around a grave yard.

Max, as systematic as ever, elected to start at the far corner of the oldest section and slowly work their way back to the center. Worley would have died in the early seventeen hundreds and, by Max's reckoning, that would put him somewhere in the oldest fifth of the graveyard.

Moss, bushes, and that particular Southern annoyance, Kudzu vine, covered many of the graves and headstones, especially those off the main tourist trails. Max found himself fighting with the underbrush to even glimpse the inscriptions. As the afternoon passed, and the lamented Mr. Worley still stubbornly refused to be found, Max began to get frustrated.

"Elena," he said, "we have to change how we are going about this."

"What do you mean?"

"If your guy is here, he is not going to be in a plainly marked grave for one thing," Max growled. "I wished I had thought of this sooner, but if his name was on one of these stones, some egghead historian would have found it a hundred years ago and it would have a huge historical marker next to it just like everything else in this fuckingly quaint town. They would advertise having a genuine pirate buried in their cemetery and they would make some weekend in the slow season John Fucking Worley Day and the boy scouts would decorate the grave with pirate shit so the tourists could have their pictures taken next to it at twenty bucks a pop. Tour guides would take us straight to it. It is not going to be in plain sight and it's not going to be obvious."

"What do you propose to do? This place is all I've to go on. He is here, of that I am positive."

"I don't know." After checking for fire ants, Max, sat down and leaned against a particularly large tombstone. "Whoever put him here did not want him found, at least not by anybody that was not in their little club. If the stiff is the next piece of the puzzle then he was supposed to be found and whoever buried him would have made some sort of way for the right person to find him. Just like when the insurgents would bury their arms caches in Iraq. They would set up clues so that their buddies could come along later and find the stuff. Weeks, months, even years later a mujahedeen in the know could figure out if there was a weapons cache nearby, what was in it, and where it was even if he had never heard of the guy who buried it in the first place. I hope you brought that pirate book of yours along."

Elena nodded and pulled it out of the camera case where it

had been stuffed between the two folding shovels. Max began leafing through it.

"The insurgents had a code, a pattern, that they would use to mark things. They might spray paint a line from the Koran on a wall so it just looked like graffiti. They would write something like the line from Surah four, verse seven: *Allah shall take an account of them.* It looks like a threat to us, at least the few of us who can actually read it, but it tells their buddies that some guns are buried nearby, get it?"

"No, not at all."

"Chapter four, verse seven. Four, seven. Forty seven. The line says, 'AK forty sevens buried here.' Then, across the street, you might find a spent cartridge case from one of their rifles pounded into the trunk of a palm tree. Walk halfway between the two and dig. You'll find something good: their cache or an IED that blows up in your face. I've been lucky on that account, the traps never got me...except for that last one."

"The Mujahedeen learned their craft from three hundred year old pirates?"

"No, green eyed girl. Many groups had ways of communicating and hiding stuff. It is the most natural way to exchange information and materiel if you are the underdog. Hobos during the great depression had a code system to identify homes that were an easy touch for a handout or had a mean guard dog. They would put symbols on the fence posts. American Indians did it too, except they would use symbols to hide weapons caches from the cavalry and food stores from another tribe. Hell, today hackers and anarchist types will draw coded symbols around towns to identify unsecured WI-FI connections for free net surfing. You learn this shit in the counter insurgency game. The way I see it, Teach and his gang were the insurgents with a lot to lose and a lot to gain. They would have hid their loot but made a way for the survivors of their 'cell' to find it again. We just have to think like them."

Max looked around the cemetery. The historical section was anchored at the corner of the old wall and the graves and crypts radiated outward from the corner. Assuming that the target died sometime in the first fifty years of the graveyards existence, then Max had to first find a grave dated around Eighteen Fifty and refine his search inward from there.

He got up and began pacing outward from the corner. He stopped when he got to a likely spot.

"Fredrick James Keene, died eighteen fifty three," he read, "barrister. Figures. Fucking lawyer."

Max then went back to the corner and began pacing in the opposite direction, stopping at a similar marker. He then walked perpendicular from the wall until he reached, roughly, a perpendicular line out from the lawyer's grave. With his search box delineated, he walked back to the center and sat down again. He imagined himself back in Iraq. Back in some shitty small town in some shitty small region in the shitty province of Anbar. He looked slowly around him. Then he closed his eyes.

Patterns.

There are no straight lines in nature.

The human mind wants to create order out of chaos and creates patterns where there are none. Don't be fooled.

Is the garbage bag on the side of the road really just a bag of shit, or does it hide an IED? Choose wrong and die.

What is the mark? What was important to the pirate? In Iraq the symbols important to the insurgent came from the Koran, the AK-47, the date palm, the tribe, and the first born son.

What the fuck motivates a pirate in the late sixteen hundreds?

"Elena, let me see that book again."

She brought it to him and he began to read aloud.

"Edward Teach or Edward Thatch, better known as Blackbeard, was a notorious English pirate who operated around the West Indies and the eastern coast of the American Colonies during the early Seventeen Hundreds. Teach was most likely born in Bristol, England. Little is known about his early life, but in Seventeen Sixteen he joined the crew of Benjamin Horingold, a pirate who operated from the Caribbean island of New Providence. He quickly gained his own ship, Queen Anne's Revenge, and from Seventeen Seventeen to Seventeen Eighteen became a notorious and feared pirate. His cognomen was derived from his thick black beard and fearsome appearance; he was reported to have tied lit fuses under his hat to frighten his enemies."

"Sounds like a crappy Wikipedia entry." He put down the book. "An insurgent loves the Koran, or at least his version of it. What does a pirate love?"

Elena looked at him, "His ship!"

"Of fucking course, darlin'. Those guys loved their ships. More than their wives, more than their kids they loved their ships. The *Queen Anne*. That's what we have to find: something having to do with the *Queen Anne*."

He sat up and scanned the wall. The afternoon was beginning

to pass into early evening and the shadows were becoming long and deep.

"Look at the shells Elena, the shells in the wall."

Elena stared at the section of wall Max pointed out. It seemed like a jumbled mass of mortar and shells and cement to her. Pure chaos.

"That," said Max, "right below the lamppost. Call me batshit crazy, but the shells in the cement look like a capital 'A' to me."

"It still looks like a mess to me, Max."

"Don't just look at it, *look at it*. Imagine you were one of this guy's buddies, sneaking in to mark his grave in the middle of the night, or even burying him in the middle of the night. You have to make a mark quick, so nobody sees you. Dig out a few shells, plaster some more in, and you have your first mark. The shells in the wall are such a jumble, and full of random patterns, nobody is going to notice one that looks slightly like a letter unless he expected that letter to be there. C'mon."

Max led her to the spot, and, now that he pointed it out to her, she *could* see what he was talking about. He then went to the corner and slowly walked along the wall perpendicular to the first, looking intently at the chaos of shells. He paused, backed up while focusing on a spot about midway to the top.

"I think I can convince myself that that right there is a 'Q'," he said.

"Okay," said Elena, "so it's a 'Q.' Now what?"

"Now we triangulate."

She followed him as he walked into the cemetery on a straight line from the letter he had just found, looking aside to the wall with the first letter. He stopped abruptly.

"This is the point where perpendicular lines from both the letters meet. Our boy should be around here somewhere."

They began to look at the markers right around them. There was an ornate obelisk dedicated to a merchant, a whole family: father, mother, and three stones that identified children by first names and, sadly, very young ages. One was broken off, the marble stump jutting out of the loam like the remains of a hockey goalie's last tooth. Many of the inscriptions could only be read after they had brushed off the moss and lichen that covered the old markers.

"Hello?" breathed Max.

"What is it?"

Max stood straight up and gestured down with his head. At his feet was a long, horizontal marker resting on a single layer of bricks a few inches above the ground. It had none of the artistic carvings and long epitaphs seen on the other stones. Max wiped off the green moss to expose a single name: *Anne.*

"That's it, it's got to be it."

"A woman?" Elena dropped to her knees and rubbed off more of the stone's living cover. At the very foot of the stone was the only other inscription: *Ecclesiastes 10:19.*

"The ship is the woman," mused max. "The ship is always a woman, that's a tradition that predates the Navy. What better way to hide the greatest treasure *of* their greatest treasure. Who would think of looking for an old pirate in a woman's grave? I'm certain that's your guy right down there. We just have to get to him." Max looked around. The sun was going down and darkness pooled in the corners and under the trees. There was not another soul in sight.

Max pulled open the camera bag and pulled out a folding shovel. A yank here and a twist there and it was fully extended and ready to go.

"It will take forever to dig with that thing."

"Don't need to dig, darlin'. They used those things to cover a shallow crypt. Dig a small hole, line with bricks, put in the coffin, pop one of these slabs over it and they were done. We don't need to dig. All we have to do is *pry*."

"Max, how do you know?"

Max grinned at her as he started to work the edge of the shovel under the stone slab. "Did I tell you just *how much* television I watched in the hospital?"

With the crunching and crumbling of brick, Max got the blade of the shovel underneath the slab. Pushing it back and forth, he could move the heavy piece of masonry just a few inches, giving him a finger hold to work with.

Max felt something in his shoulder tug and it began to burn again in spite of all of the oxycontin he'd taken.

"Dammit," Max said and let go the shovel.

"What?" Elena reached out for him.

"I got ahead of myself--forgot I still had a hole in me. The wonders of modern pharmaceuticals, I guess. One thing we can't afford is me opening up this wound and bleeding all over the place."

"I don't want to go back to the hospital, Max."

"Me neither. C'mere, Elena. Grab this." She came over and grasped the shovel handle with both hands. Max crouched next to her and wiggled his fingers into the gap between the slab and the brick he had just created. Satisfied with the gap, he looked around until he found a suitable chunk of broken gravestone. With his good hand, he knocked the edge against the crypt until the chunk was roughly wedge shape. This he wiggled into the gap. Then he lay on his back and put both feet against the wedge. The prosthetic was tough. It wouldn't bend, but all the muscle would have to come from his whole leg.

"We are going to slide this puppy off. When I say go, lean your whole body weight into that shovel. It will give you some leverage and help me when I push like a son of a bitch. If we get some momentum going, I should be able to slide it right off in one go. That shovel is hardened aluminum, so it might give a little. If it starts to bend, keep pushing. Elena nodded.

Max counted down and then shoved hard. Elena leaned into the shovel and the stone slab began to move, slowly at first then picking up speed as Max bared down, his teeth grinding in unison with the grinding of the stone. Halfway off, it began to slow again and Elena dropped the now useless shovel and jumped down next to Max. Working together they were able to regain momentum and the gravestone slid off and onto the ground where it promptly cracked in two.

The gunshot crack of it breaking echoed in the quiet of the graveyard and they both crouched low, holding their breaths until silence reclaimed the cemetery. As predicted, in the shallow crypt was the remains of a plain, wooden coffin. It had not weathered well, and they could see fabric and bone through the cracks and holes in the wood.

"That will not buff out," said Max, gesturing to the slab. "We are now felons and if we don't hustle, we will be caught felons." He climbed in to the hole and, ignoring the mounting pain in his shoulder, began to tear apart the coffin lid, the rotten wood coming apart easily in his hands.

As he worked, the mortal remains of John Worley came into view. The flesh had long since rotted away leaving a skeleton with its lower law resting on its chest, it appeared to have the hugest grin in history. Remnants of black hair topped the skull and the planks of ribs showed through a moldered open jacket.

"If that don't beat all," murmured Max.

Resting on the skeleton's chest was a dinner plate of blue and white china. His hands had been folded across the plate and gripped in the boney fingers were a tarnished silver knife and fork.

"The guy must have really loved his chow."

Elena climbed into the hole and looked closer. "This is very odd. I've never heard of eating utensils being included in funeral traditions. Weapons, sure. Coins, jewels, of course. Never a dinner setting."

"Whatever. Just pry them out of his cold, dead gourmand hands and hand 'em up."

"What?"

"We are not archeologists, we are grave robbers and we had better hustle. If someone thought them important enough to leave with the stiff, then they are important enough for us to take. Get his hat too."

Elena gingerly slid the plate out from underneath the dead

man's arms and handed it up to Max who slid it into the camera bag. The knife and fork followed, finger bones falling away as she pulled the silverware from the grip of the dead.

"I don't see anything that looks like a piece of a map," Elena said.

"Who knows what they got it hidden in. They sure as hell weren't going to make this easy. Get his shoes."

"Shoe. He has only one leg."

Max chuckled softly. "Stereotypical. Get his peg leg then. The way medicine was back then, I'm wouldn't be surprised if all of those assholes didn't have some piece missing."

Elena glanced at Max's leg, but said nothing before she got back to the business of prying the fake limb off.

"It's his left leg too. That makes us amputation brothers."

"How about you be quiet and come down here and help."

"Sure, I..." Max heard a sound. A distant whistling floated through the twilight. Max quickly looked for the source and saw, in the distance, a figure standing in the shadows of a tall oak near the center of the cemetery. Max's eyes were a few of the body parts that Iraq had left undamaged and he could see the man quite clearly even at this distance. He was an oddly but well dressed gentleman. Crowned with a bowler hat cocked at a rakish angle, he leaned against the trunk of the tree with his legs crossed. His suit was of an old fashioned cut and from his vest pocket extended a length of watch chain which he held in one hand, twirling the watch at the end in time with his whistling. He was staring right at them.

"Fuck," said Max, turning back to Elena. "We got company."

Max turned back, and the man was gone.

"What? Who?" asked Elena.

"Something weird." Max climbed into the hole with her. "What does your vampire spidey sense tell you?"

"Nothing. With you around, I might as well be deaf as well as blind. When you are around, I am human and humans don't have the senses of the undead."

"Well, we better finish with this all-dead dude because I'm getting a bad feeling like a bunch of screaming fanatics are about to trip their ambush any second and light us up. Here, let me."

Max began to tear the clothes off the skeleton, stuffing each piece into the camera bag. Dust and pieces of disarticulated bone flew everywhere as he uncremoniously dumped the corpse over to get its jacket off. When he was done, the late Mr. Worley was only a jumbled pile of bones at the bottom of his coffin. Everything that was not part of his body was stuffed into Max's bag.

"Get the shovel. Fingerprints." Max climbed out with Elena scrambling close behind. The bag was full, so he carried the shovel in one hand and slung the bag over his shoulder.

He swiftly walked to the edge of the wall, threw the shovel over, gripped the top with both hands, and pulled himself over. His shoulder was throbbing and Max was certain he could feel a trickle of blood down his arm. He leaned back over and grasped both of Elena's hands and pulled her over. He hoped that their exit was covered by the shadows cast by the wall. The twilight giving way to a fuller darkness, and Max felt better now that they had less chance of being seen. Of course, it also meant that they were less likely to see someone following them.

In a matter of seconds, he had the shovel folded down and tucked under his shirt. The last thing he wanted after tearing apart Worley's grave was to have somebody remember him walking away from the cemetery holding the very tool he used to defile a graveyard.

Once they crossed the street and entered the residential neighborhood, they slowed to a walk and Max slid his arm around Elena. They were just another couple out for a moonlight stroll.

Max resisted the urge to crouch down by the hedges and fences. He fought to walk down the sidewalk like a normal man, not one who had struggled to survive in the killing fields of Iraq and Afghanistan. Keeping alive required being on constant alert, wary of every corner and doorway and he, like all vets, had developed a heightened awareness of his surroundings and suspicion of any place that could hide an ambush or an IED. Knowing that someone had been watching them and perhaps was still watching them set his combat instincts in overdrive. Those instincts were screaming at him to get down, to cover his back, and to seek cover, not stroll right in the middle of the open.

He felt the anxiety build. He was too exposed. He did not have anyone on point or bringing up the rear. When he first started venturing out of the hospital during his recovery, these feelings had been so severe that sometimes he could not go around a corner or enter a store without first scanning for someone laying in wait. He would give mailboxes and garbage cans a wide berth, even crossing the street to avoid them. The doctors at the Naval Hospital had diagnosed him with PTSD. More pills were added to the pile he was already taking. He flushed those along with most of the others and learned to deal with it himself. *A little paranoia keeps you breathing.*

His solution had been to push those anxieties down, somewhere deep, and drive on. Drive on they did: down the street, toward the river, and around the corner of the condos overlooking the pier. There they stopped cold. Their path was blocked. They had been expected.

Chapter Fourteen

There were eight of them, standing in a semi circle that went from the edge of the pier to the side of the condos. Max recognized three of them from the incident in the cemetery, but the five in the center were different. The first three were just punks and errand boys. The others were men: square shouldered and self assured, with eyes like raptors. Max knew the look. He knew what they were just as surely they knew what he was. It was the eyes and it was the stance. Max knew he was facing soldiers and warriors. Combat indelibly marks those who survive it. Those who loved it and thrived upon its chaos and brutality carry a special version of that stamp. Max had made easy work of the underlings sent against him thus far, but he knew that those men before him would not make the mistakes their peons had. He inhaled deep and braced himself.

They faced each other, his two to their eight in a standoff direct from a spaghetti western. The tension was palpable. Max's hand itched to grab the pistol in his pocket, but he did not dare pull it in case they already had him covered by a shooter in the shadows. That is how *he* would play it and if these guys were as hardcore as they looked, he did not doubt that at least one of them had a piece ready to go and trained on him.

Elena broke the silence with a whisper. "The Dark Hand, they came in person."

"The who?" Max hissed back.

"The Hand is Almos's five most trusted lieutenants. They were soldiers with him when they were alive and ride with him that they are dead. He knows why I am here."

"Elena," said the tallest of the group. "Our little hummingbird, our pretty flower has finally shown herself once more. Out from the shadows." He spoke with a thick accent Max couldn't identify.

"The Devil take you, Lajos." Elena spat on the ground.

Lajos smiled, showing very sharp and very long teeth. "Such spirit. The dreaming one wants you back, you know. He sent us looking for you so long ago, and we almost had you several times. But your scent grew weaker and weaker until it was gone; he gave up then. You were the only one to ever escape his grasp—until now, that is. When the winds told us where you were, he was not that interested in wasting the effort until those same whispers in the dark brought hints of what you were planning and what you were seeking. Then, he became interested, very interested. You are of no consequence. What he wants is what you have."

"We don't have any spare change, bud," Max countered cheerily. "The Salvation Army is up the road. Go there if you want a handout."

"The American *human*," Lajos spat as if he had something foul tasting stuck in his back teeth. "You have been a problem. Look what you did to my little ones." Lajos grabbed the nearest figure by the hair and pulled his head back. His mouth opened in pain in the larger man's grip. All of his front teeth were missing, likely left in the dirt after his last encounter with Max. "You have ruined him, he can no longer feed himself. I may have to have him destroyed. Pathetic and useless to let a human do this. How you did this to him is another matter. I may let the songbird fly, but you will have to suffer for this affront. You should know your place."

Max made a show of putting his hands on his hips, getting his right hand closer to his Glock. "The only place for me, if you don't take your freak show and leave, is kicking your ass. It's late and I'm tired and I don't feel like fucking with the Backstreet Boys. So back off."

"So full of typical American bravado. The cavalry is not coming and you are going to lose. Did she tell you what she is? She is not one of you; she is one of us and she will use you, take your life, and cast aside your dried husk without a second thought. That is her nature. That is *our* nature."

"Fuck your nature and fuck you…" Max started when suddenly the heavens opened. A flood of water splashed over the two vampires nearest the condo building. It came in a long stream and solidly drenched both men. The end of the stream was punctuated by the hollow *thump* of an empty, bright blue, plastic bucket as it bounced off the head of the nearest one. All eyes snapped up to the balcony where Agnes Pritchett was jumping up and down, punching the air with little blue veined fists and cackling with glee.

"Holy water, you sons of bitches, holy water all over your nasty little heads!" she shouted. She looked over the railing, noticed that all she accomplished was to soak two of the vampires and, at most, ruin their expensive Italian footwear. She gaped, wide eyed, and darted back into the condo.

Everyone had been distracted by the deluge except Max. As soon as he saw the water fall he dodged to the side, simultaneously drawing his Glock with his right hand and pulling the shovel out from under his shirt with the left. He threw the square of aluminum underhand, Frisbee style, as he brought his pistol to bear on the men. He did not expect the shovel to hit anything, just add to the confusion. It impacted square in the tallest man's face just as it was turning back to Max and Elena.

His head rocked back and his nose gave way with a satisfying crunch. He brought both hands to his face. The blood streamed from between his fingers. His eyes were wide with rage, confusion, and unexpected pain.

Max held the Glock in a firm Weaver stance and sighted on the obvious leader: the spokesman with the leaking nose. His right hand gripped the pistol tightly, cradled by his left, with his feet apart, left foot forward. He could not miss at this range, and he was certain that, to the one called Lajos, the ten millimeter opening of the pistol barrel appeared as wide as a train tunnel. He should know, he had looked down gun barrels often enough in his career.

Hissing, the two punks charged him. Less clumsy and more self assured in the presence of their elders, they were quick, but not faster than Max.

Max waited until the last possible moment, he did not want

to be seen shooting two unarmed youths. He fired twice in rapid succession just as the first came within a few yards, and then without pause, fired twice into the second. None of the shots missed. Each vampire took two slugs in the torso, what Marine drill instructors call *center mass*. The high velocity hollow points expanded almost explosively as they breached the walls of their chests, mushrooming as they traveled, tearing tissue and splintering bone.

They were dead before they hit the ground and the momentum of their travel caused their bodies to skid forward, almost to Max's feet.

The remaining undead hesitated. Max could see the confusion and surprise on their faces.

"Fucking run!" he shouted to Elena and took off down the docks. He was running at full sprint and, even with two fully functional legs, Elena was having trouble keeping pace. He was focused on getting some distance between them and the goons. If he could get on his boat and underway, he was certain he could lose them in one of the many inlets along the river…if they could even get a boat themselves.

After he had gone several yards, Max heard a large *whoomp* behind them, as if someone had thrown a match on a propane grill. He turned his head to peer over his shoulder and saw that two of the vampires were fully aflame, writhing and spinning as the fire engulfed them. Their agonized shrieks of pain were horrific to hear. In the frenzied panic of pain they were running into and among their fellows who were in chaos just trying to avoid them. Max and Elena had just been given more time. Max faced forward again and picked up the pace.

"Chief!" Max shouted as he ran. "Cast me off!"

Bill Whitley was at the end of the pier, alerted by the sound of shooting. He heard Max, looked up to see him running toward him, framed by the flicker of flames. He jumped up and went straight to Max's boat, pulling a long diving knife from his belt. With two quick strokes, he cut both the mooring lines and shoved the boat away from the pier. When someone like Max came running from something on fire and yelling for a shove off, something very important was going on and Bill could find time to ask questions later.

"You didn't see us, Chief," Max said as he and Elena jumped into the boat, already begging to move with the current.

"See who?" replied the chief. "If I don't hear from you in two hours, I'm gonna report that boat stolen."

"Good idea Chief!" Max fired up the engine. As the boat pitched forward, he yelled, "You do that. Call it in stolen if I don't get back to you. Now go get your shotgun and hunker down!"

"Who am I shootin'?"

"You'll know when you see them," Max called back, already well away and moving out of earshot.

"Fuck," Bill said to himself as he watched the *Prosthetic Limb* disappear into the night. His shotgun was loaded, which was good, but it was leaning on the desk in his office at the end of a pier over, which was bad. He could hear fire engines coming down Main Street which meant that someone else had seen the fire and called it in. The firemen would be disappointed because Bill could see that whatever was burning had already gone out on its own.

"Fuck," he said again and began hurriedly pulling his gear together. He had just bought a new regulator for his SCUBA set and he did not want to leave it to be trashed or stolen by some punks. "Crazy-assed Gyrene. What he gone and done now? That red haired gal have a husband or something?" Bill dismissed that thought as quickly as it came. Max Bradley was, for all his faults, a boy scout when it came to the dames and he wouldn't be running off with another man's wife.

Bill looked up, the fire engines were not yet in sight, but he did see several figures striding down the pier toward him. They walked with a purpose and that purpose did not look like a social call. *Here they come*, he thought.

To his amazement, as they reached the center of the pier, they levitated and then flew through the air straight toward him. He dropped his SCUBA gear, the precious regulator falling over the side with a splash. Chief Boson's Mate William C. Whitley had been around the world more times than he could count on his fingers and toes. He had been in ports of call from Angel Island to Vladivostok and had been in scrapes too numerable to mention. He had seen amazing things while on watch in the Sargasso Sea in the middle of the night and equally amazing things in Subic Bay whorehouses after a three-day bender. He was as salty and experienced as they come, but he never, ever, had seen anything like this. And yet, just because he had never seen anything like a handful of angry men flying at him like a flight of hungry ospreys looking to grab a fish, does not mean he was frightened, or startled. He never got to be a Chief Boson's Mate by letting unusual situations ruffle him.

Disarmed, with his beloved shotgun yards away, he reached down and snatched up the one thing that might help in such a situation. Bill had been an avid SCUBA diver ever since his first dive off the China Beach R&R facility in Da Nang, Vietnam, and he had taken every chance to dive ever since. The thing he loved to do most while diving was spear fishing and that day had been no exception. With a smooth motion, he brought the JBL Magnum spear gun up to his side, sighted down the bore, and fired at the nearest flying freak. The eight inch long, stainless steel shaft lept forward at three hundred feet per second. It hit his target square in the chest, the razor sharp broad head tip punching through the sternum and heart before lodging in one of the thoracic vertebrae.

The capture line was still attached to the spear and the gun was nearly torn from Bill's hands but he hung on. It was just like spearing a bull shark off Lighthouse Point. When the line went taunt, it did so with the full weight of Bill's two hundred pounds behind it and it yanked the spear back, out of the vertebra and back through the heart. Upon reversal, the sharp, four inch long barbs of the spear head were pulled open and spun. Like the blades of a food processor, the spinning barbs chopped the center of the vampire's heart into multiple, unrecognizable pieces before locking tight against the inside of his ribcage. With his heart now a pool of mush, the vampire dropped from the sky like a stone. He bounced once on the pier before erupting into flames that charred and turned him into a cloud of ash that then settled upon the water, sizzling as the sparks were doused.

Lajos and his remaining two lieutenants shrieked in anger at their comrade's demise, but they kept focused on their goal. The time to avenge their fallen comrade would come later, but first they must fulfill their master's wishes. They flew over Bill, past the end of the pier, and on into the night.

Bill stood, silent and slack jawed, the spear gun sliding from his limp fingers. It clattered on the pier. A few stray motes of dead vampire ash swirled about him as he stared into the night where the remaining flying men had gone as.

"Well if that don't beat all," he said to no one in particular. "Fucking vampires in North Fucking Carolina."

Chapter Fifteen

The *Prosthetic Limb* sliced through the water, the engine at full throttle. Fast for a sailboat's engine, the retrofitted Cummins was pushing the boat at twenty knots and he had put the docks far behind him. He was not getting speedboat type speed, but he was glad he had the new engine put in. At the time it was just for convenience, letting him get in and out of the river quickly before hoisting sails in the sound or the ocean. Now the extra horses were coming in handy and he was glad for every mile he was putting behind them.

"What the hell was that all about?" he asked Elena, sitting beside him.

"It is as he said. Almos has learned of my plans and he sent some of his soldiers to stop me. When we won against his foot soldiers, he sent his lieutenants."

"Those five guys?"

"Yes, the Hand. They were his officers when he was a general. When he became a vampire, he turned them as well so they could serve him for eternity. He is either very angry or very worried to send them so far."

"From Hungary?"

"From Hungary," Elena agreed.

"Now what?"

"We keep running and hope they lose the trail." Elena glanced back over her shoulder. "If my senses are dulled when you are around, then theirs must be as well. Then we hide out and figure out our next step."

"I'm sure you guessed by now that I'm not much of a hider and more into what I like to call 'direct action.'"

"And you must have also used stealth and surprise when it was to your advantage as well. All good soldiers do."

"Marines, not soldiers."

"Whatever. You sound like a little boy sometimes. How about this: It is tactically sound to withdraw and regroup in our current situation."

Max chuckled. "That sounds more like it, but I got to ask where you came up with that?"

"Movies."

"Figures."

Max paused, thinking that he might have heard a splash or splashes in their wake. It was difficult to make out over the sound of the wind and the water. He listened intently for a minute, but did not hear the noise again.

"What is it?"

"Nothing. Maybe a fish jumping or a porpoise, they come this far in you know. Feeding on the little guys we are stirring up."

They sat silently, looking forward. Max thought he noticed something out of the corner of his eye, off to port—a brief shadow flitted across the sky, the stars winking out as it passed.

The hairs on the back of Max's neck were beginning to stand at attention.

He heard the splashes again, this time from off the bow and much clearer than before. There was definitely more than one. Max motored on, keeping the throttle as high as he could at night. He wished he had his night vision goggles, but the one pair he "borrowed" from the Marines before he was let go was stashed off the boat with a few other items of questionable lineage. Some things were better kept away from home.

"Elena, there is a Surefire flashlight in that cubby to my left. Get it out and shine it off the bow. I don't want to hit anything."

She rummaged in the compartment and pulled out a small, black cylinder.

"You turn it on by pushing the button in the back with your thumb. The light will come off if you release it. Don't shine it in your own face or you'll be seeing nothing for a little while."

"Okay." Elena pointed the flashlight toward the front of the boat and turned it on. One hundred and sixty lumens of intense, pure white light streamed from the LED bulbs and turned a circular piece of the deck into daylight. "You weren't kidding about the light," she said.

"Always do things full-assed, never half-assed, if you get my drift."

"What? That you like to say 'ass'? Wait here, ass-man, and I'll let you know if you have to start panicking." Elena began to cautiously walk forward, holding onto the rail cable with one hand and the light with the other. She almost tripped over a cleat, but she still kept her eyes forward. Since the sail was packed away, there was no cat's cradle of lines to negotiate and no boom to dodge. A cleaned up boat presented much fewer hiding places.

The jib was also packed away and she was able to walk smoothly across the foredeck, playing her light to the right and to the left until she reached the pulpit. Once there she leaned over the rail and shone the light directly off the bow. She saw nothing but the water. That far down the river, the banks were a mile away on either side. As the light hit the water off the bow, a large fish jumped through the beam, chasing an evening snack, and fell back with a resounding splash. "The fish of the undead?" Elena said to herself, "I doubt it." She turned aft and shouted, "Max! Nothing over here but some fish jumping!"

"Probably Wahoo. Eating the little guys that hang out in our bow wave. I think we are good to go. C'mon back and let's rustle up some grub."

"I think it's your turn to cook!"

"Well, come on and take the wheel, then. I may be perfect, but I can't be in two places at once!"

She came back and slid into the helmsman's seat, pushing Max off with her hip. "Go make me a sandwich, man!"

"Yes ma'am. You would think you hadn't eaten in half a millennia or something. Coming up." He popped into the cabin and began to throw a few things together. As he worked, he was running the possible scenarios through his mind. With two guys shot and two more burned back in town, the police would have a lot of questions for him. He could have Bill call in the boat stolen, and then he and Elena could ditch it somewhere and hoof it back into town. They could say they were camping or something, he had the gear on board, and they could be 'surprised' to return from their trip to find the boat stolen. He'd have to toss the Glock overboard, no one would find it in the sound. No pistol to test would mean no material connection to the shooting. He would also have to ditch the ammo he used in the gun. They would match the brass casings left on the ground and the bullets inside the dirt bags.

He went to his cabin and found the box of hollow points. He pushed open a porthole and dumped the ammunition into the water, the brass cylinders scattering as he shook the cardboard box. The magazine followed. He then took the slide off the frame and freed the barrel which he tossed out by itself. Frame and slide were last into the drink.

Satisfied that a major piece of incriminating evidence was gone for good, he stripped to the waist and took a look at his shoulder. He'd bled through his shirt and down his side but the bleeding had stopped for now. In the cabinet above the galley sink, Max found his first aid kit. He hadn't been in a firefight in years, but he still kept everything a combat medic would need. Max zipped open the kit and pulled out a stick of Dermabond. Medical grade superglue, the stuff did wonders in keeping wounds closed. He poured it over the hole in his shoulder and waited a minute for it to dry before he put on a new tee shirt. Another oxycontin and the throbbing eased off to a dull ache.

Max took a deep breath, snatched the food off the counter,

and headed back on deck. As he walked through the door, the whisker pole smashed into his midsection. Normally used to secure the jib sail to the mainmast, the pole was a firm cylinder of hardwood about four feet long. Because it had enough weight and strength to secure a sail to the mast, it made an excellent weapon when swung. Max caught its full impact in his solar plexus and it drove all breath from him. The plates dropped with a clatter and he fell back against the cabin door. Frantically, he tried to draw a breath, but all he could find was pain as his stunned diaphragm struggled to work.

Max recognized the tall man in front of him by his broken nose. Lajos the vampire looked quite pleased that he had gotten the drop on the American. He swung the pole again, hitting Max in the side of his good leg, dropping him to his knees. Kneeling and gasping for breath, Max looked up at his assailant. Elena was behind him, struggling in the grip Almos' two remaining "lieutenants." One smiled with a twisted grin caused by a tooth that jutted awkwardly against his upper lip and the other stared at him from a single red eye, the other gone—destroyed in an ancient battle, the socket covered with a puckered scar. *Stupid*, he thought. *Let my guard down. How the fuck did they catch up to us anyway?* He pawed at the right side pocket of his shorts. It was empty. *Fuck! Why did I dump the gun?* He thought he was safe and wanted to get rid of the evidence, violating one of his own cardinal rules: *never get rid of a weapon unless you have another one right at hand.*

"So rude to end our conversation like that," said Lajos with a grin, "we were not quite finished with you yet. I am now more than slightly put out." He brought the pole down hard, right at the junction where Max's neck connected to his shoulder. Fire shot down Max's arm and caused his hand to go numb and drop uselessly to his side. The blow had landed right on the brachial nerve plexus. Max realized through his agony that this asshole really knew how to inflict pain.

"Fuck you," growled Max through clenched teeth.

"No, I'm sorry. It looks like you are the one fucked right now. You could have given me what I wanted and I may have spared your life or, at least, made your death a quick and permanent one. Now, I am going to make you pay for my associates. I am going to make your death a long, lingering one and then I will turn you. Once I do that, I will chain you down and pull every tooth out of your head and let you starve. The hunger will eat at you until you go insane and beg me to expose you to the sun and end your misery. I will keep you though…keep you as a pet and hang you on my wall." Lajos struck Max on the other shoulder and he cried out in pain as his other arm went numb. The two holding Elena laughed at his pain. Her cries were muffled by the rough hands over her mouth.

Lajos leaned in closer to Max, "Tell me how you did it. Tell me how you could destroy two vampires with a mundane human weapon. What makes you so damned special? Are you a wizard? Opus Dei? A Templar perhaps? What is the source of your power? You even knocked us out of the sky."

His breath was disgusting, like a hot wind blowing from a charnel house. Max was still in a great deal of pain and the man was talking nonsense, but he could feel his leg coming back to life. Shifting his weight back onto his feet, Max intoned, "I'm a fucking U.S. Marine, and mister, you have fucked with the wrong fucking jarhead." Max pushed off with his legs and he slammed into Lajos with as much force as he could muster from his semi seated position. Like a medieval battering ram, the top of Max's head smashed into Lajos already injured nose tumbling the vampire over backwards. Max's momentum carried him on top of Lajos and, as they landed together on the deck, he drove his knee into the vampire's midsection.

Lajos may have been an expert on administering pain, but several centuries of near invulnerability and immunity to such mundane things as physical pain made what he now felt an exquisitely unbearable sensation. He vomited all over himself.

Max rolled to a crouch just as snaggletooth aimed a kick at him. His arms were less numb, but they still had not fully recovered. However, he managed to twist just enough that the blow glanced off his ribs and slid along his side. Max caught the vampire's leg in his armpit and held it there. He tried to bring him down by pulling back, but the vampire managed to keep his balance, hopping on his other leg. Max locked eyes with Elena. She smiled back. Slumped in the arms of her captor, she drove her hand into scarface's groin. Pulling and twisting with strong fingers tipped by sharp fingernails, she dropped to the deck to get her full weight behind the emasculation effort. The vampire gave off a high pitched shriek as one of his testicles gave way. Like Lajos, centuries of being immune to pain had made him forget just how vulnerable his nether regions could be. Elena, understanding this, put everything she had into ensuring his eligibility for the choir *ad castrato*.

Her opponent down and clutching himself, Elena sprang up and rushed snaggletooth, who was still hopping around Max as Max weaved right and left, trying to trip the creature. She checked him hard with her shoulder and the already unbalanced man flipped off his feet and over the rail. Max let him go as soon as Elena hit him and they were rewarded by a splash as the vampire hit the water.

With one gone and two down, Max and Elena had a few seconds to regroup. They could not go into the cabin and retrieve another gun without going past the two remaining vampires so Max backed along the deck toward the bow. Max pulled a gaff off its hooks. Six feet long with a wicked steel hook at the end, Max kept it onboard to pull in any large fish when he was out trolling for tuna. It was not perfect, but it extended his reach and he intended to tear up any thing that came at him. His shoulder was burning again but the adrenaline let him push through the pain.

"Elena, I've got a storage box near the anchor windlass. Find anything that might make a good weapon."

She nodded and ran forward.

Lajos and the remaining vampire had recovered somewhat and were coming toward him across the teakwood deck, stalking him like two birds of prey.

"Back off!" Max swung the gaff, the hook whistling through the air. They stepped back, staying out of reach, and Max let the point pass by, he did not want to overextend his swing.

"Look at me," said Lajos, his voice made high and nasal by the swelling that completely blocked his broken nose. "Look into my eyes."

"What is this, a date?" Max jabbed at him with his gaff. "If you want a kiss, you'll have to come closer, sweetie."

"Look at me. See in my eyes what I can grant you. Obey me and, I will promise you paradise. If you do not obey, I can promise you the tortures of the damned." He looked deep into Max's eyes but found only hard-headed Marine resolve there.

Not for the first time, Lajos looked stunned. This American upstart was not wavering at all. Max returned his gaze with an air of defiance.

"What are you?" Lajos stammered.

"I'm the guy whose boat you are on. This is my boat, now get the fuck off." Max lunged forward like an Olympic fencer, snagged one of Lajos' feet with the gaff hook and pulled. Lajos tumbled backward once again, his head striking the deck with a resounding thud. Max reversed the pole on the backswing and shoved the butt end into the stomach of the Lajos' lieutenant. He grunted and folded, gripping his abdomen with both hands.

"Not so tough when you don't have a drop on a guy, are you? C'mon! Come and get me! I'm just an old cripple. Get up and fight like men."

"Fight like men?" snarled Lajos, rolling into a crouch. "Men are but cattle, good only for our nourishment."

"Moo!" yelled Max, bringing the gaff down on the top of his head, the point tearing a long gash in his scalp. Blood gushed from the wound as Max pulled the pole back, taking with it a very large hunk of Lajos' dark, black hair. "Moo!"

"I will have your guts for garters!" Lajos' threat came out sounding like a whine. He wiped the dark blood out of his eyes. His breath came in short gasps. To Max he seemed suddenly vulnerable, as if struggling with newly found weakness.

"Once more. Get the fuck off my boat." Max advanced, poking at Lajos' face with the hook.

"I...," started Lajos just as Max was tackled from behind.

Snaggletooth must have circled around and boarded the *Prosthetic Limb* from the bow. He impacted Max in the small of the back, wrapping his arms around his shoulders. Max threw the gaff forward as they went down in a heap and the end struck scarface in the throat.He fell back, choking and wheezing through a destroyed larynx.

Max was on his belly and the vampire astride him pummeled him with both hands.

Lajos continued to cower, rocking back and forth.

Just then, Elena came around the corner, a bright orange flare gun clutched in both hands. She stopped, took in the scene for a second, and aimed the gun at the vampire on top of Max. She took a breath and squeezed the trigger.

The flare spat out of the gun with a whistle and struck the vampire in the forehead, bounced off, and skittered across the wooden deck into the five gallon gasoline can Max kept to feed the motor of his inflatable dingy. The blow knocked snaggletooth off Max. Now free, Max pushed off like a runner off the starter's block, and ran straight at Elena. Max made sure that the strap of the camera bag was tight on his shoulder with one hand as he scooped her up with the other arm. His momentum carried them both over the side just as the port half of the boat erupted in bright orange flame.

They hit the water as the fireball rolled over them. The gas can had been half full and the flare had explosively ignited the flare vapors. As quickly as it had come, the fireball was spent, but the remaining liquid in the can had been scattered and ignited by the blast. When he surfaced for a breath, Max was greeted by flames rapidly consuming his boat. Runnels of flaming fuel poured out of the downspouts and spread over the river. Max kicked hard to get them both away from the patches of fire and watched as his home was consumed. He did get some morbid satisfaction at the glimpse of a writhing, flame covered figure struggling to climb over the rail and over the side. *Burn baby, burn!* The other two were nowhere to be seen.

"Well," said Max resignedly, "nothing to do now but swim."

"I don't swim very well."

"Yeah, yeah, you haven't swum for a thousand years 'cause you could fly over the water just like Tinkerbell. Well float then, and I'll pull you."

Chapter Sixteen

Watertight, the camera case had enough air in it to make a decent float and Elena held on to it as Max sculled toward the nearest bank, about a mile distant. To graduate from the Naval Academy he had to swim a mile in under forty five minutes in a khaki uniform. He certainly had improved as a swimmer later, competing in the all service triathlons. He was no SEAL, but he had held his own. This was before losing the leg, though, and he was glad to have the buoyant case on his shoulder—which was starting to throb again. Since he didn't have to worry about keeping them both afloat, Max could give his injured arm a rest and simply kick away.

In spite of the improvised float, he was still winded when he finally felt his foot brush against the bottom. The prosthetic was pure drag and really struggled the last few hundred yards.

"Wade." Max stood up in the river, the water coming only to his chest. "We can wade the rest of the way in."

The sand under their feet made slow going, but at least they did not get caught in any mud. They were sitting and panting on the bank in no time. Max propped himself on his elbows and looked back across the water. The *Prosthetic Limb* was fully engulfed and Max could hear the distant pops as the heat cooked off ammunition in his locker. The boat was seriously listing and he expected that it would sink long before the Coast Guard arrived on the scene. Someone had to have seen the fire and called it in. It was hard not to notice the flames lighting up the entire river. Almost on cue, Max heard the sound of an approaching helicopter. Its running lights soon swept into view and it came to a hover near the boat. It played a searchlight over the burning vessel and the water around it, but if they saw any sign of Lajos and his friends, there was no indication. The searchlight moved in a staccato circle around the boat and then expanded out in a widening pattern as the Coast Guard helicopter searched for survivors.

"We got to get under better cover, green eyes," Max whispered as he crawled into the underbrush. "The last thing I want to do is get picked up and spend the next who-knows-how-many-hours down at Elizabeth City station."

"Will they find us?"

"No, in this sort of situation, they are looking for people who want to be found, unless they are already dead, of course. Dead people don't try to hide up the bank. We get away from the water and hunker down and we'll be fine."

They crawled deeper into the woods. Luckily they had not made land in somebody's back yard. The banks of the Neuse were dotted with homes and developments, but the area was still not as crowded as would have been up north. Ensuring that there were enough trees overhead to block searchlights, they settled down to wait.

"What next?" Elena shivered and snuggled into Max for warmth. They both were still soaked.

"Try to figure out plan B...or are we up to plan C yet?"

"We still have the items from Worley's grave, yes?"

"Yes."

"Then we stick to the first plan: we rest and then we get my boat and go wherever the map leads us."

"That sounds easier said than done." Elena did not reply.

"The thing I can't figure out," said Max, breaking the silence, "is that Lajos dude. He was one bad ass dude, but right there, when his buddy had me and I thought I was thoroughly fucked, he just froze."

"Froze?"

"Yeah. I tore him up pretty good, mind you, but by no means had I incapacitated him, especially a warrior like you say he is. I thought he was going to start crying before I got hit. He had his chance at payback, but he just calls it quits and acts like the bottom just dropped out of his world."

"Maybe it did."

"What did?"

"The bottom. His world falling apart. Maybe he came to the same realization I did."

"I'm not following."

"When I am around you, I become fully and completely human. I hunger, I go to the bathroom, and I even get cold." She clung to him tighter. "Perhaps it dawned on him that the reason suffered defeat at your hands was that, he too, was human in your presence."

"That's a bad thing? I thought you liked me."

"I do." She kissed his cheek, his stubble rough on her lips. "I find it joyous but, remember, I hate being a vampire. I have hated it since the first second I realized what they had done to me. Every hour of my existence was full of despair and agony. I even considered, many times, finding a lonely field somewhere and waiting for the sunrise. That would certainly end my monstrous existence. When I found you, I was overjoyed. I have thrilled in every moment near you."

"Must be my aftershave."

Elena smiled in the darkness. "Sense of humor too. You realize that, when Lajos fought you, he must have felt the pain you inflicted. Pain he had not felt in centuries. When he finally realized the meaning of that pain; the pain of being human, the shock must have been unbearable to him."

"How so?"

"Vampires like Lajos are cruel. They delight in the power over mortal men that being undead gives them. Lajos was but a minor foot soldier before he was turned. Undead, he was almost like a god. No human could face him without fear. He relished the taste of that fear. He was invincible to nearly everything save the sun. Just as I reveled in being human once more, he must have been frightened to his very core. You robbed him of his power and, most importantly, you did not bow in fear before him. He fears weakness and impotence even more than death. He always has. If he still exists, he will never forget that. He will find a way to destroy the only thing in the world that could make him so weak. That thing is you."

"I know all about guys with grudges, I've been fighting them for years. Ever walk down a market in Haditha? Washir? You can feel the hate rolling off you like the heat of the sun. Even when they are laughing with you, smiling at you over the cost of a rug, or thanking you for the delivery of some aid, you can see the hate deep in their eyes. They hold grudges for a long time, especially in the mountains around the Khyber Pass. Those guys bear blood grudges for generations. I can handle one dude with a broken nose."

"You didn't merely surprise him; you brought his own screaming nightmare to life. He cannot continue knowing you still live. He will hound you until the day you die, your children, and your grandchildren. Until your seed is wiped away and your name is dead he will continue on and on."

"Guess that means I gotta kill him first, now doesn't it? Where the hell do you get this stuff?"

"Meaning?"

"The psychoanalysis."

"When you have been around as long as I have, learn a great deal. When I was young, I could only see vampires as cruel and heartless. Over the years I have come to understand their deeper anxieties, and, it seems, the more effectively they cause humans to fear them, the more fear gnaws at their insides. I do not know what is inside him exactly. Mind reading is not one of the powers that comes with the transformation, but when you watch and feel as I have, you tend to make very good educated guesses."

"Well, don't try to shrink my head, sister. You won't like what you find at all."

"Is it so terrible over there? There have been wars upon wars throughout time. This one cannot be any different or more terrible than any of those others. Men do things, things they regret... or even things they enjoy, but know they *should* regret. The biggest regret for them is that they do not feel the sorrow or guilt even when they know they should. Do you think your country should be fighting this war?"

"I can guess what you will say next."

"Really?"

"Yes. Whatever I answer, yes or no, you are going to say that is how soldiers have felt in all previous wars. That is the very nature of being called by your homeland to fight. Am I right? Either answer is a valid one?"

"You must be the mind reader, not me, because that is exactly my answer. Every soldier in every war has his doubts as well as his justifications. That is how it is with humans. Vampires love war, well, not all of us, but many do because in the chaos and death of war, we can feed so very easily. I have spent my time near battlefields. I have heard men scream with the joy of battle, I have heard them shudder and weep with fear. I have seen them sacrifice themselves for their comrades, rising to heights of nobility scarcely possible in peacetime; and I have seen them descend into depravity—committing acts that made even my cold flesh crawl. And, most horrible of all, I have seen men who have renounced their humanity as thoroughly as the most hardened undead—transformed by battle into living vampires."

"The one thing you missed, honey, the one thing that motivates all of us, is the very strong desire to make it through without getting your ass shot off and your balls intact. I've got both. Sometimes the only way to make it back is to finish the mission, whatever the cost."

Max shifted and looked around. "Now, how the hell are we going to get your boat. We need to regroup."

"We are not doing anything." Elena stood up. "I am going to get it and bring it right back to you."

"How are you going to do that, fly?"

"Precisely. I am going to walk as far as I need to loose myself from whatever it is about you that keeps me earthbound, and then I am going to fly low through the sky, keeping in the shadows, and, how would you say it, accomplish the mission."

"You are out of your mind if I'm going to let you go it alone. If you don't get lost or picked up, it will still take you forever to walk all that way."

"I know you do not believe me when I say I can do this, but you must trust me on this. I can do this. Lajos and the others, if they survived the fire, will be in too much pain and be too confused to do anything tonight. They will hide wherever they have established a lair, feed to recover their strength, and be after us by tomorrow night at the earliest. We need to make certain that we are not stuck here when they regain strength or add to their numbers."

Max looked at her, sizing her up. He's heard this line before, usually from some young Lance Corporal looking for a chance to prove himself. Max had to give the young guys in his unit a chance to prove themselves, of course. That is how inexperienced Marines became veterans who can do the job and still bring themselves and their buddies home. The trick was to give them that chance without letting them get themselves killed doing it. If the plan was right and the kid had his shit together, Max would let him be first in the door or to flank a sniper. If the kid did not have it in him, Max would send somebody with more experience under his belt, someone with more of an edge into whatever hell was waiting. If Max didn't think that someone was up to the task, he usually put his own ass on the line rather than let some kid buy it. He would rather get himself shot than have to give somebody's mom or wife a folded flag and a "thanks from a grateful nation." This is probably why he was no longer Major Bradley, USMC, but Max the one legged wonder.

Edge. Some had it, and some did not. Elena had it in spades and he could tell she could take care of herself just fine.

"Alright. You go," said Max. "Do you have any glow sticks? No? Okay, steal some from the chief's shack if you can. When you return, come in abeam of that point over there and tie a few of the glow sticks on your anchor chain after you have let it out. It will let me know it's okay to swim in and it will give me something to swim to. Don't have anything else lit except for your running lights until I get aboard."

The decision now made, Max settled back and watched Elena walk off into the darkness. As the brush swallowed her, he felt a momentary need to go after her, to pull her off the task and take the mission himself, but he stopped himself. He had to show his trust in her as well as confidence in her abilities. If they were going to be in this together for the long haul, he needed a troop that was up to the job and *knew* she was up to the job herself. She was very self confident, of this there was no doubt in his mind. He just had to show her that he thought so too. As she slid away, he was certain that she would come back successfully. Max was reminded of an old saying that Trojan women would say to their men on the eve of battle: "Either come back carrying your shield or carried on top of it." Elena was the type of woman who would not only be carrying her shield, but she would also be dragging a couple of sorry bastards behind her by their ankles.

Obeying one of the cardinal rules of the infantry: don't run when you can walk, don't walk when you can sit, don't sit when you can lie down and catch some sleep, Max curled up at the base of a large oak, and using the camera bag as a pillow, tried to catch a quick catnap. Sleep did not come, but he did manage to rest just the same. He had been into martial arts since he was a boy, and throughout his training, meditation and focused relaxation had been some of the most helpful disciplines he had learned. He would calm his thoughts, relax his body, and try to open his mind. Often, he would feel more refreshed than a brief bout of REM sleep and, very frequently, he would find such a clarity of thinking that the answer to whatever problem was bothering him at the time would suddenly become clear. Max credited this process with keeping him mostly sane in the hospital, especially helping him deal with the long hours and days of monotony. He felt himself sliding into a deep meditative state.

"So Max, nice piece of ass you got there." Max looked over and saw himself, save for the fact that the other him had both feet intact, bare feet digging their toes into the dirt.

"She is nice, but more than a piece of ass. I like her," Max said to himself.

"That's pretty obvious. Why? She's probably nuttier than shithouse squirrel."

"That didn't make any sense at all, you idiot."

"So I suck at aphorisms."

"What?"

"Pithy sayings, you do remember English 111—plebe English back at the Academy?"

"Now you've lost me."

"Forget it. The real question is what are you going to do?"

"With her?"

"No, with the millions of dollars in stock options you don't have... of course with her."

"Hang on for the ride, I guess."

"You like her. Why?"

"She's like a red haired Don Quixote, with tits. She has a cause, some windmills to fight, except these windmills fight back."

"So if you take on her cause, you have a cause. You get new bad guys to fight."

"Sounds about right."

"And after? After whatever this turns out to be runs its course, what then? Dump her? Find another chick with a cause?"

"Well, hell. I don't know. You tell me."

"I don't know either, okay, but you had better get it sorted out real quick. You need to figure out if this is something real for you—something long term—or if it is just about the thrill ride. If it is all just shits and giggles, then you might very well have a pissed off girl who can kick your ass on your hands and you really don't need a psycho on your case."

"I'm not really too sane either. I'm sitting here talking to myself for fuck's sake."

"No, you are not, you are dreaming or something. Perfectly reasonable and the mark of a sane mind, if I recall correctly."

"Crazy people never think that they are crazy. Only sane people question their sanity."

"Touché. At least some of that psychobabble the headshrinkers were pushing on you back at the hospital rubbed off." He paused and looked up, "Speaking of someone rubbing you, your ride's here."

Max opened his eyes. His other self was gone and the dirt where he was sitting was untouched. Out on the river, he could barely make out the smooth, aquiline lines of a Sea Ray cabin cruiser. Just off the bow, at the right spot for a deployed anchor, came the emerald green glow of a pair of glowsticks. It was her alright.

"How fucking long was I out?" Max asked himself as he began to creep to the water's edge. There was a Coast Guard boat out in the middle of the river right where the *Prosthetic Limb* went down. Max had not even noticed its arrival. It was displaying the red over white over red sequence of lights over its bridge to indicate that there was a hazard to navigation nearby. Two green lights on its port side indicated that traffic was to pass on that side of the ship, and she was letting boats get by. Good. They should not bother them when Elena and Max cast off.

He slid into the water and, letting the buoyant case keep him afloat, leisurely swam out to Elena's boat. When he reached the hull, he swam aft to the swimming platform and crawled aboard.

"Where have you been, Max? I was worried. I anchored over an hour ago!"

"Let a guy catch his breath!" Max looked up at her, blinking the water from his eyes. "An hour?" *I really was out for a long time.* "How fast did it take you to get there?"

"A couple of minutes. I said I was going to fly. Nobody saw me and Chief Bill was not around, so I took the lights like you said."

"Well, ok then." Max was at a loss for words. He could not believe it, but here she was and dry to boot.

"You wouldn't happen to have any clothes for me stashed away."

"Men's clothing? What sort of girl you take me for, young man? Come into my lair and I will get you a robe. It will be dry at least. I'm sorry, but there is no food, I..."

"I know, you survive on the blood of young virgin boys and, as such, have nothing in your pantry."

She winked, "They don't *have* to be virgins."

Chapter Seventeen

Hank Beardsley was beat; utterly. He felt like he was in his third period of overtime, slogging uphill through rain and mud kind of beat. Elbows on his desk, he rested his head in the palms of his hands. It had been a helluva night and he still had a couple of hours to go before morning. Hopefully the sunrise would bring some sanity to his town. Up until a couple of days ago, the worst that he had to deal with was Marines getting a bit too rowdy down at Applejacks' or some tourists from New Jersey deciding invite themselves into a very quaint, highly historic, but obviously private, home.

That last one had been a real pisser of a call. In her front parlor, old Miss Langstrom, descendant of one of the first families in town, a member of both the Daughters of the Revolution *and* Daughters of the Confederacy, had those Gucci-clad Yankees wetting themselves while she covered them with an ancient double barreled twelve gauge. The old gal was shouting loudly that very gun had dispatched many a Yankee during the "late unpleasantness" and a few more would not make much a difference anyhow.

Faced with having to arrest either a couple of well-heeled tourists for trespassing or one of the nicer, if not deranged, old ladies in the historic district, Hank did what he usually did in such a situation: he bribed them. The tourists received two coupons valid for dinner at any of the lovely fine dining establishments on the scenic waterfront as well as a very polite explanation that white historical markers on most of the homes in town were *not* an indication that said houses were necessarily open to the public. Hank had long learned to keep a stash of coupons in his cruiser. *Got to keep the tourists happy, my man.*

Dear Miss Langstrom received a bottle of Maker's Mark, for medicinal use only. He also kept a bottle or two stashed in his cruiser as well. The shotgun remained with its owner as it had not been loaded in over a hundred years.

Keeping the tourists happy and the locals happy with the tourists was really about the extent of Hank's job until the broad daylight shootout in front of the hardware store. The incident the other day had gotten the whole town riled up. It was the first fatal shooting under Hank's tenure as Chief of Police and he honestly could not recall when the last one had been. Shots had not been fired downtown since the Civil War as far as he knew.

It did look like an open and shut case of self defense. Major Bradley did have a valid permit, which relieved Hank because he legitimately liked the man. Bad enough that he got his leg shot off in the service of his country just to come home and get robbed at gunpoint by a couple of big city punks...punks who were, as of yet, unidentified.

The shooting was just the tip of the iceberg for Hank. Then came the calls of arson *and* shots fired down by the docks. In a frenzy of confusion, both the entire police force and the fire department had mobilized to the waterfront only to find a whole lot of nothing. There was no fire, not even ashes or the telltale scorch marks of an accelerant. No bodies, no blood, and nothing indicating gunplay save for a few cartridge cases that, although recently fired, were worth nothing in the absence of any other evidence. All of the calls had come from people who were a distance away and could give no better information than that they heard shots or saw the flames from a distance. No one who lived or worked right at the scene saw anything. No one, except for that old lush that ran the piers. He said he saw nothing at all except that he thought some kids might have taken a boat out for a joy ride.

Coincidentally, the boat belonged to the very same Major Maxwell Bradley, and, even more coincidentally, it was just reported by the Coast Guard as having burned to the waterline and sunk with no survivors found. *Once is happenstance, twice is coincidence, but thrice is enemy action.* Hank Beardsley was convinced that something pretty messed up was happening in *his* town and it looked like Bradley was right smack dab in the epicenter. He was one man that Hank was itching to have seated in front of his desk right now. He was kicking himself for not putting him on ice when he had the chance. Weakness and sentimentality had caused him to go easy on the cripple. He would not make the same mistake again.

Hank heard a sound out in the hall. He had let everyone except the duty desk go for the night. The whole department had been on the job since the shooting. After the circus by the piers turned out to be nothing, he had let everyone but essential staff go home and get some rest. A few of his officers had been up thirty six hours or so and he felt that it had been the decent thing to do. Leadership can be tough.

He, however, could not rest, even if he tried. So he stayed at the station and let the sergeant in charge go home too.

He heard the sound again. The door to the second floor offices just opened.

"Hello?"

Nothing.

"Ted? What do you want? Who's watching the front desk?"

He peered into the cubical jungle just outside his office. Three figures slid into view faster than he could imagine and he was simultaneously revolted and startled by their appearance. The one in the center, the tallest, was a torn and disfigured caricature of a man. His scalp had been ripped from its very roots and hung loosely over his forehead. His nose was broken and twisted off to the side at an unbelievable angle. The man to the leader's right did not look too frightening, other than a circular burn just above the eyes. The other, standing just behind and to the left was a thing right out of Hank's most worst nightmares.

Ever since he was a rookie cop Hank had dreams of being trapped in his cruiser after an accident. Each time the car would burst into flames because the gas tank had ruptured on impact. The fire quickly engulfed the back of the vehicle and he struggled with the seatbelt latch, trying to get it to let go before he went up in flames with the rest of the cruiser. The source of the dream was always obvious to Hank: he had been to enough fatal traffic accidents to know intimately what happens to somebody trapped in a burning car. Fearing it seemed perfectly normal for somebody who made his living on the road.

The thing standing behind the man with the broken nose brought to mind every such accident Hank had serviced in his career. Except this "crispy critter" as the EMT guys with their typical black humor called them, was standing there, looking at him. It was not being shoveled into a black vinyl body bag, but standing straight up and swaying slightly.

It was bald, all of the hair had been burnt clean off. So were the ears. This gave its head a torpedo like look. Some of the flesh had given way to char and Hank could see the smooth gray surface of skull peaking through the cheek where flesh had blackened and peeled away. A few unburned scraps of clothing hung on its frame, doing nothing to conceal the blackened ruin that was its body. Fat had bubbled from the heat and burst through the skin in many places, leaving sickly yellow tears in its abdomen and thighs. The smell of burned flesh, familiar to Hank from dozens of scenes of highway carnage, permeated the room with its nauseatingly sweet smell of burned pork and gasoline.

The thing gazed straight at Hank with eyes that had not been ruined by the fire like the rest of its body. They were whole and they were leveled at him with malevolent delight. The burned corpse, for what else could it be but a corpse, smiled at Hank as he sat in stunned silence. The teeth were very, very sharp and gleamed whitely in the black of the burned and ruined face. Hank felt a flood of warmth spread across his lap and down his leg as his bladder let go.

"Look and understand," the tall one said, leaning in to lock eyes with Hank. "Look, understand, and fear me."

His eyes were not human: they looked to Hank like the eyes of a predator—golden irises surrounded gaping, black pupils. Wanting to look away but being unable to, Hank felt as if he was standing on the edge of a cliff, feeling the irresistible urge to tumble off and fall into oblivion.

"Look at me and understand," the tall one repeated, but Hank saw nothing but the yawning darkness that lurked beneath. The golden irises seemed to swirl in a circular motion like flashing whirlpools that pulled him deeper and deeper into them until he felt himself drowning in the blackness. Hank felt nausea sweep over him as the sensation of falling took him.

Hank saw himself at his son's graduation from college. College paid for by the GI bill. Then he fell deeper and he saw himself on the tarmac, awaiting his son's return from his last deployment to Iraq. The instant he saw Kyle step off the plane, he had been proud and relieved at the same time. His son had looked older; finally and truly a man. Hank hugged him and held him to make certain he was intact just as he had done after the many childhood falls and scrapes that seem to follow young boys as certainly as night follows day. *Just checking for broken bones, son.* Standing just off to the side of the cluster of reunited families he noticed Max Bradley, standing off to the side, quiet but with a look of satisfaction on his face. Hank noted that the man had no one to greet him, no young wife running into his arms, no towheaded little boy shouting "daddy" as he sprinted in for a knee high hug. Alone but pleased, he had been.

Hank fell deeper still, past images of Kyle leaving for prom, then his first bike ride, then climbing the oh so tall steps of the bus, on the first day of kindergarten, his lunchbox hitting each step with a clang. Then Kyle was just born, a screaming bundle of arms and legs and the doctor was pulling off his mask, letting it dangle on his blood and meconium stained smock. *Meconium,* Hank always thought that was a pretty stupidly fancy word for something as nasty as baby shit. He reached for his son but was struck by the doctor's eyes: twin, swirling, golden whirlpools to forever. The doctor smiled at Hank with teeth that were sharp and white...and growing. They expanded until all he could see was a forest of razor sharp spikes stretching his mouth wide open. Then he lunged, as swift as a snake, and tore into little Kyle's belly. Hank shrieked helplessly as he watched the doctor rip and rend Kyle into a loose jumble of tissue and twitching organs. The doctor raised his head, bits of flesh still clinging to his teeth and laughed.

"See and understand." The tall one was leaning over Hank's desk and Hank saw and he understood.

"Mine, you are mine now. I own now. You will obey me or those mysteries that I have shown you will come to pass. That which is seen cannot be unseen and that which is understood cannot be forgotten. Do you accept my words of power into your heart? Your soul?"

Hank willed himself to move, to jump out of his chair and run screaming into the night, but he could not. He listened to himself answer, "Yes, lord. I saw. I understand. I am yours."

Lajos straightened up. "Good. Attend. Bring us weapons to kill the mortal man."

Slowly, as if sleep walking, Hank rose from his chair and

walked over to the door that led to the armory. As the chief of police, he had both a key to the armory and a code to the keypad lock. It took both to open the vault door and only the chief and the shift supervisors could access the armory by themselves. Hank punched in the code, inserted the key, and the door unlocked and swung free. He went in and began handing out the first guns that met his eyes. Lajos looked past the pistols in Hank's hands.

"Not these. I want the bigger ones over there." He gestured at the rack of M16 rifles in the back of the vault.

"Give us those and show us how to use them."

Hank pulled one out by its black aluminum carrying handle, gripped it one handed around the plastic hand guard that covered most of the barrel, and pulled the charging handle back with a loud snap. He inserted a thirty round curved magazine into the well right in front of the trigger, and, with a single touch to the release lever, let the bolt slam home. With the first round chambered, the rifle was ready to fire and he handed the rifle to Lajos before repeating the process a second time and then a third until all three vampires stood, locked and loaded.

He then silently handed several more fully loaded magazines to them until each had three in addition to the one already locked into their weapon. Hank picked up one more M16 and loaded it. He then showed them how to take it off safety and raised it to his shoulder and fired off a burst into the nearest desk. Papers flew as the high velocity bullets tore into the wood, sending oak splinters everywhere. Hank fired until the magazine was empty and the rifle's bolt locked itself open. He then showed them how to drop the spent magazine, insert another, and release the bolt before standing dumbly before them.

"Good." said Lajos. "Now there is one last thing before we are finished with you."

Hank said nothing, standing in front of them, gazing into those awful eyes, like a little bird mesmerized by a cobra.

"It will take mortal tools to destroy this horrible mortal, tools that you have given us and for that we are grateful. Fighting this powerful man has hurt us, weakened us, and we need the strength of your body to continue on."

Police Chief Hank Beardsley managed a slight gasp as they fell on him as one and began to feed.

Chapter Eighteen

"How are you feeling, Max?" Elena was driving and they were headed west at a smooth fifteen knots, between Emerald Island and the mainland, toward Camp Lejeune. Max said he had a few things they would need stored near there. He was feeling too tired to take the wheel, so he propped himself in the passenger seat and huddled, wrapped in a wool blanket.

"Like shit, thanks." Max shivered in spite of the noonday sun. He ached all over and he was covered in a cold sweat. Every time he tried to talk, the bile rose in his throat. "I just need to get straight. Lost all of my meds last night."

"You really need to give that stuff up, just look at yourself. They really made you an addict in that hospital."

"*They* did not do anything but give me what I wanted. *I* was the one who wanted the pain to go away or, at least, get myself into a state where I did not give a shit. Besides, who are you calling a junkie, Miss Drink-the-Blood-of-the-Living-lest-I-die?"

Come to think of it, Max did resemble one of the newly

turned, struggling with a hunger that he did not understand and could not control. He was shades of pale and gray with deep, sunken eyes framed by dark lids. He shook as if in pain and the desperation in his voice increased with every passing hour. He had vomited several times already and now had nothing left in his stomach. He could only silently dry heave as the cramps rolled through his abdomen.

Elena responded, "I don't need to anymore. The only hunger I feel when I'm with you is for one of your sandwiches."

"Don't even talk about food." Max leaned back as another wave of nausea hit him. "Thank God the runs haven't hit me yet."

"The runs?"

"Yeah. Oxycontin plugs you up better than a week of C-rations. Gives you bad constipation if you aren't careful. What do you think happens when you withdraw off them?"

Elena wrinkled her nose at the thought. "Then why keep taking the horrible stuff?"

"Why do you...*did* you...drink blood? Because you have to."

"I have to because it keeps me alive and I would be weak and insane if I did not feed regularly."

"Same here. It keeps me straight: normal, functional, and clear of thought."

"Those drugs will kill you someday."

"Don't bet on it. Oxycontin is way at the back of the line of things that are fixing to kill me. Your buddies, for example."

"I'm almost surprised that you are still here with me."

"Ha! After last night, I'm in it for the long haul. Those bastards owe me a new boat and I'm not stopping, now or ever, until

I get one."

"At least you have your priorities."

Max grunted and pulled the blanket tighter. As they motored on, he guided her with terse commands. Under the route 58 bridge, past Swansboro, then north and up Queens Creek. They slowed, then glided to a stop at a wooden dock that was next to a long boat ramp. A large sign over the ramp read in yellow letters on a bright red background, "Bulldog Storage at Great Neck Landing. You got it, we stow it away! Winterization services included with boat storage." Next to the letters was a painting of a cartoonish bulldog, fangs peeking out from between grinning jowls, and a wide brimmed drill instructor hat perched jauntily on its head.

"This is where you hide your valuables?" asked Elena. "I would think you would keep them on the base with all of the security there."

"Although they have a nice yacht basin by the officer's club where we could tie up, and I do rate going onboard, being a retired officer, there are a few things in my trunks that I would not want to be caught with either coming or going. They randomly search cars, no matter who you are, and retired or not, my stash could get me a one way trip to Leavenworth. C'mon. Let's go find the Gunny."

"Let me guess, another crusty old war horse?"

"Something like that. When he retired from the Corps, he bought himself this self storage place. Things like that actually make money around military bases with all of the comings and goings. Why keep up an empty apartment when you are going to be overseas for six months to a year when you can keep all of your stuff in a storage locker for a tenth of the cost?"

Elena pulled up and Max struggled a bit with the bowline, his chills were coming in waves. He nearly shook himself off the deck but he got her boat secured. The woman had spared no expense, and the boat had all of the bells and whistles including stern and bow thrusters. She was able to gently drive the boat into the dock sideways and hold it there until Max could get it tied off.

Elena and Max, still draped in his blanket, walked down the dock and opened the gate at the end. A chain link fence surrounded the property. Near the landing were rows of empty boat trailers waiting for the end of the season, and on the opposite end of the property were rows of short brick buildings used for dry storage. In between, there was the office.

"Gunny?" Max knocked on the door.

"It's open," came a voice made harsh by years of unfiltered Camels.

"Afternoon Devil Dog." Max walked into the office. The man gave a grunt in response to the nickname Marines use with each other. The office was in surprisingly good shape. Although the exterior was made from the same, drab cinderblocks as the storage buildings, the interior was new and in pristine condition. The Formica counter top was polished to a high sheen and the wooden paneling across the front glistened with aromatic wood oil. Every metal fixture in the room also gleamed with polish. The man known as "Gunny" was an older man, completely bald, with a serious set of crow's feet adjacent to each eye. His cabana style shirt was pressed and starched. As he came around the counter, Max noticed that his khaki shorts were also neatly pressed, with sharp creases running down the fronts of the legs.

"What can I do for you, Major?"

"I need to get into my unit, but I lost my key."

"Lost it? How'd you do a damned fool thing like that?"

"Boating accident."

"Huh. That'll be a twenty five dollar charge for a replacement, and you gotta fill out and sign this form." He slid the paper over the counter to Max. "And I gotta make a photocopy of your photo ID to staple to the form."

"Why you got to do that? You know who I am."

"Why? 'Cause if you come bitching to me in a month about how someone got an extra key and stole all of your shit, I can prove in spades that it was you I gave the extra key to."

"Ornery cuss," Max grumbled as he pulled out his wallet and fished for his I.D. It was still soaked from the jump into the Neuse, and Max had to peel a few clinging receipts from his license, but the photo was still recognizable.

"Boating accident, you say," Gunny took the damp I.D. and wiped it off on his shirt before making a copy. "Keep better tabs on your gear and I won't have to give you any shit. That's how it works."

The paperwork done, Gunny slid the new key over to Max.

"You look like shit too. You been on a bender?"

"No, just a bug. There's one going around."

"Well, you better get yourself squared away, pronto. Retired or not, we don't want to make my beloved Corps look bad, do we... Sir?"

"Thanks for the key, Gunny. Don't worry, I'll polish up the lock on the way out."

"Good man."

They walked out of the office and into the rows of storage units.

"That man did not like you very much," Elena said with a smirk.

"Him? He loves me like crazy. Most people won't get more than one or two words out of him. Trust me, if you get on his bad side, you will know it and he won't be all sunshine and roses like he was just now."

"You people are warped, do you realize that?"

"Gung ho, green eyes. You won't understand it unless you have lived it. If you live it long enough, it becomes just like a religion. There's no explaining it, it just is."

Max stopped at a corrugated metal door, painted red like all the rest.

"Here we are!" The key went in the lock and it turned smoothly, releasing the lock with a satisfying click. With one swift jerk, he pulled up the door and walked in. The air was dry and clean with no hint of must or mildew.

"Dehumidifiers in every unit. One of the reasons I picked the place. Gunny cares for your stuff better than you do. The last thing I want on my gear is rust or mold."

"Right..." Elena followed Max into the small, perfectly square room. The floor was bare concrete and the walls, those parts that she could see behind the rows of stacked footlockers, were the plain cinderblock of the exterior. There were several dozen of the footlockers, painted olive drab, each closed with a combination lock. In the back of the room were several oddly shaped boxes, made of heavy plastic. Some were square, but several were long and thin, like guitar cases. Max went to one of these first.

"Since we already committed a few state felonies, with the grave robbing and all, I figured we should commit a few federal felonies, you know, to round out your resume." Max spun the dial and popped the lock, opening the first case. Elena saw a glimpse of a military looking rifle, like the one Max had on his boat, but Max reached in and pulled out a small, amber pill bottle first.

"Popeye needs his spinach before he can start haulin' stuff out." Max fished out an oxycontin and popped it into his mouth. The pills were supposed to be time release and, swallowed whole, would give him a steady dose of the narcotic through the next twelve hours but Max could not wait for the slow acting drug to hit. He chewed the tablet, letting it mix with saliva until it was turned to a mush that he could hold under his tongue. It was a junkie's trick that a shot up Lance Corporal taught him when they were both struggling to walk on their new legs again. Those sessions down on the third floor prosthetic rehabilitation clinic could be brutal. Chewed into paste and held under the tongue, the narcotic was absorbed directly into the surface veins just under the oral mucosa and went directly into the blood stream. It was almost as good as mainlining the stuff.

In a minute, Max felt the familiar rush as the Oxycontin hit his system. The shakes dropped away almost instantly and he began to feel normal again.

"You keep drugs with your illegal guns?"

"I've got 'em stashed all over. You never know when you might find yourself in a sorry state without your regular prescription on hand."

"Like alcoholics hide bottles of booze all over the house."

"No, those guys have no self control."

"You are looking like a paragon of self control yourself right now," Elena said wryly.

"Ouch. Sarcasm does not become you, dear. Here, let me show you some of my toys."

He pulled out a slender black rifle composed of plastic and anodized steel.

"M4 carbine, a handy little guy to have around, especially if you are banging in and out of doors. My personal favorite. It fires the 5.56 NATO cartridge at nearly three thousand feet per second. Three round bursts. That'll put a fucking world of hurt on those assholes."

"What is the need for all the bad language? I thought you were supposed to be an officer and a gentleman or something like that? A little I can understand, but all of the time?"

"Life is not like the movies, my dear." Max put down the rifle and began to tear open another case. "I know that the hero is supposed to come up with a pithy saying or a cool catchphrase when the heat is on and everybody is facing certain death. When you are being shot at, and I've been shot at many times in my career, nothing captures the moment than a good, loud, resounding 'fuck' or 'Goddamn.' You don't think of anything cool to say until long after and it's too late. In real life, 'You feel lucky punk?' wouldn't have come out, 'Oh yeah? Well, fuck you!" Better yet, it would have been a mindless scream as the bullets went flying. I'll get the job done first and my ass home in one piece and worry about what my biographers will write down later."

The next case open, Max pulled out some cardboard cylinders. He popped one open and showed her a rounded object with a ring on the top. "White phosphorous grenade. Burns like hell." He tossed it to her, but she stepped back and let it drop to the concrete floor.

"Careful!"

"Don't worry Elena, they're harmless unless you pull the pin... which I don't recommend at this particular point in time."

"Thanks. I won't"

He kept out four of the grenades and then rummaged in a few more crates, taking a few items out of each and then sealing them again. With each new find, he called out the items to her. He even had several sets of clothing packed away. When he finished, he stashed a pair of khaki pants, a couple of shirts and a brand new pair of boots into a camouflaged backpack, along with the grenades, a Glock pistol, and several loaded magazines. The rifle he slung across his shoulder.

Elena stood with her hands on her hips. "Where did you get all of this stuff and what were you going to use it for, World War Three?"

"Something I like to call 'creative requisitioning.' Things get lost, especially in a war zone. If you are smart about it, things get lost in a locker headed for home. A few bottles of booze can make the lance corporal screening your trunk look the other way and piece by piece, you can get out a rifle to put together on the other side.

"As for the why of it, I'm not sure. The docs told me that paranoia was part of my post traumatic stress disorder, which they have been telling me I've had since I first went over. It didn't stop them from sending me back again and again, so I did not pay it any attention. As long as they let me keep taking Marines out into the field, I did not care what label they slapped on me. It's not like I was expecting the end of the earth or a revolution or even the zombie apocalypse which, given the current situation, seems more and more like a possibility. No, I just felt better knowing that I had a stash of stuff to fall back on. Hoarding behavior, they call it. Boy, if they only knew exactly what it was I was squirreling away."

He looked around thoughtfully.

"I almost forgot this guy." Max opened one last box and pulled out a pair complicated looking lenses attached to an olive drab frame. "Night vision goggles. Best thing to see the bloodsuckers coming at you in the dark."

"So you believe me now?

"Believe what?" He fitted the goggles to his face and began adjusting the settings and fit of the straps.

"About the undead and what I am doing here," Elena answered.

"I don't know what to believe. Yeah, I admit that I thought you were delusional when I first heard your story, but now I think it pretty obvious that you, and me by extension, have gotten messed up with some very bad dudes and, since they want what you want, I want to get it before them. Remember: adapt, improvise, and overcome. That is my mantra and it's a good one to have if you are in the keeping-your-ass-alive-and-in-one-piece business. Fair enough?"

"Fair enough."

"Good, let's lock up and load up. Now that I don't feel like puking up my own spleen, I'm doggone hungry and I know a place with curbside service."

Everything in its place, the door closed and secured, they rapidly made their way back to the boat. Max threw a cursory wave at the office, but no one answered that they could see. At the end of the pier Max stopped abruptly.

"You know, I never did figure out what you named the old girl. Every boat has a name and all who ride in her should use it." He leaned over so he could get a good look at the boat's aft panel. "Boz..boz...what does it say?"

"Bosszú."

"I'm guessing Hungarian, right?"

"Right."

"And...?" Max raised his eyebrows, waiting.

"In English?"

"No, Swedish. Of course English."

Elena smiled thinly, "Vengeance."

Chapter Nineteen

Max's "curbside service" turned out to be a seafood restaurant in Moorhead City that sat right on the Intra Coastal Waterway with a back deck that overlooked the Pamlico Sound. They pulled right up, tied off, and sat on the *Vengeance* as a busty young waitress leaned over the teak railing that lined the deck and took their orders. Elena, still enjoying new experiences every day, was at first taken aback by the food.

"C'mon Elena, frying is the backbone of Southern cuisine."

"But they fry *everything*." She picked at her plate, pushing bits of golden fried fish and shrimp around the plate. She picked up a hushpuppy. "Even the bread is fried."

"That's the way they do it." Max grinned. "Give it a try, they'll take you out behind the barn and shoot you if you don't."

She did try her fish, taking a tentative bite at first, and then larger chunks followed the first as she found that she enjoyed the taste and the texture of the crisp breading over tender flaky flounder. Max made a mental note to pick up some Pepto when they were gassing up at the boater's store down the way. If she really had never indulged in fried food before, the gut-busting, lard-laden, over-breaded and absolutely delicious fish would have her perched on the porcelain throne all night long. He did not want his troop too incapacitated. She did enjoy it though, and with such a childish enthusiasm that Max found himself laughing out loud more than once, especially after she discovered the tartar sauce and spread it all over everything including the hushpuppies.

"How's your arm doing?" she asked once she had finished.

"Better. Just a little stiff." He handed her a napkin. "You've got tartar sauce all over your chin, wipe it off before I have to make a joke about porn movies."

"What do you mean?"

"Never mind. What is the plan? What's next?"

"Go through everything we took from the grave. That will tell us the next step."

Max glanced around, worried, but none of the other diners seemed to have picked up on the phrase, 'took from the grave.' Obviously an unusual thing to say at lunch, it could have gotten them noticed in a very unhelpful way. Even though they were sitting in the back of Elena's boat, the tables lining the deck along the water's edge were barely an arm's length away.

"Ixnay on the ravegay," Max hissed, his elementary school pig Latin coming back yet once again. He had used it in Iraq, to the great amusement of his men and the confusion of the allied Iraqi soldiers. As non-native English speakers, they couldn't fathom the very concept behind what was simply child's play back home. It was a joke at first; but when Max and his team realized that the

Iraqis just did not, nor could ever, get it, they used pig Latin to talk among themselves when they did not want anyone outside their circle to understand. The gunny almost bust a nut laughing when Max was able to convince the Iraqi army liaisons that they were Marine "Code Talkers" like in the film with Christian Slater and that they talked in Lakota to each other to keep in practice.

"Hmm?" Elena had a shrimp halfway in her mouth.

"I mean, not so loud," he whispered. "Rule number one of crime is not to talk about the crime when the Craven Country Junior League is having lunch at the next table over." He gave a wave to the nearest table, "Hi ladies, how're you doing. Great shrimp, nice day," and leaned back in to face Elena. "Outside a parabolic microphone, the most sensitive and precise listening device in the history of the world is the Southern Lady. They can hear how many days you are late for your next period or where your uncle buried the money in the back yard or who your neighbor is having an affair with from a thousand meters away. So watch what you say when they are lurking around."

Elena kicked back and laughed, nearly choking on the remains of her last bite. "That is just horrible. You can't be serious."

"As a heart attack my dear. I should know, I've dated a few."

"No. Really? Seriously?" She glanced over at the Junior League table, but quickly averted her eyes when she saw that they all were looking directly at her.

"Yes, well no…mostly. Just watch it, we are not exactly out of the woods yet on this."

"Right…"

Max waved the waitress over and paid for the meal. She offered to help clear away, but, as the food had come on paper plates, he told her not to worry about it. That taken care of, they untied and got underway. As Max was untying the bow line, and Elena was back in the captain's chair out of earshot, he turned to the prim group of ladies across the rail that had been trying so hard to eavesdrop.

"You know," he said in a musing manner. "The best thing after a good meal is a good, hard screw. I think I'm going to take that little redhead back there down to the cabin and just nail her to the wall." He pumped his hips a few times. "She really digs guys with a stump if you know what I mean. A real amputee fetishist, that one." He kicked out with his prosthetic leg and landed in a martial arts stance. "Oh, yeah."

They sat in shocked silence as the boat pulled away. When Max wandered back aft, Elena asked him what he was telling the old ladies as they were leaving.

"Oh, just that lovely ladies like them were the reason Marines like me were inspired to protect the country. You know, something to give them a thrill."

"See Max, you can be a gentleman."

"I try, my dear, I try."

They pulled out and motored up the waterway for a few hours. Max was looking for a place to settle in and he found a quiet inlet off Rockhole bay, way east of Mesic. No roads nearby and a deep water anchorage gave him some assurance of privacy to work out the next step. Safe and secure at anchor, he spread out every single item they took from the grave of the late, lamented Mr. Worley.

With his razor sharp Benchmade knife, meticulously cut out

every seam in every bit of clothing they had taken off the corpse. Shirt, trousers, jacket: everything was rapidly reduced to a pile of rags. Nothing.

"I got zip. Just a bunch of mold and a few assorted creepie crawlies, what about the dude's hat?" Max's hands were black from the mildew that permeated the cloth. The mess did not smell at all, to his surprise, but had the musty aroma of things long left and forgotten. It was not corpselike at all.

"Felt," Elena said as she finished picking apart the dusty tri-corner. "And nothing here either."

"Well, this is getting a bit serious. The shoe had nothing stashed in it. I even pried apart each layer of the leather sole. Nothing inscribed in the buckle either...not a single cryptic word."

"The buttons, front and back, are clean as well. No messages. What about the peg leg?"

"That," said Max, "is something of interest. Smooth, looks unused. By unused, I mean not used at all—no scuff marks, no wear inside or out, and polished. Whoever made it was a real craftsman, especially with hand tools. The fit on these things has got to be precise or they hurt like hell. I had a fucking awful time with my first prosthetic."

"So they buried him with a new leg. Sounds like they cared about him."

Elena's books were spread all over the floor as well, and Max pushed one with his toe. "Cared about him? Who the hell knows. One thing I know is that none of your books here mention that he even had a peg leg."

"It was common back then, right? Maybe nobody bothered

to write about it."

"Seems like a pretty big detail to miss. Besides, his leg was pretty damned odd too."

"How so?"

"When we pulled off the leg, the bone below the knee was cut clean off."

"Isn't that the whole point of an amputation?"

"Yes, when they first amputate, but it changes when you walk around on it. They cut off everything that is not viable and then cut off a few more inches of bone so they can fold the meat over the end of the bone in what they call a 'flap.' The 'flap' makes a sort of cushion that you can put weight on without hurting. Then they send you to physical therapy to learn how to walk again. The pressure from walking on the stump makes the body want to lay down layers of calcium. If you do it right, new bone growth forms a sort of curved and rounded lump that sits nicely in your prosthetic. If you do it wrong, physical therapy I mean, the new bone forms into sharp edges that cut into whatever skin and muscle they put into the flap and then they have to take you back, open you up, and cut away all the bad bone before they send you back to physical therapy to try again. Some guys I was with got cut half a dozen times before the bone did what the doctors wanted."

"And...?"

"And I've seen almost a dozen x-rays of my own leg. This guy's leg looked nothing like mine."

"All right. I'm still not understanding your point."

"The point is, medicine may have changed in a couple of hundred years, but bone growth is bone growth." Max spun in his chair, the metal and plastic of his prosthetic flashing in the light, "This Worley guy may have had a fake leg, but he never did any walking on the damned thing."

"He died right after he got it?"

"Could be, but, it also could be that he got it right after he died. Someone might have cut off his leg after he died, but before he was buried, just to put the leg in there with him. Like you said, false legs were pretty common back then. So, if some knucklehead comes along and digs him up later, maybe he doesn't notice the thing. I'm convinced the peg leg is important."

"Okay, but how?"

"Beats me. It is clean inside and out and I'm not about to cut it up into little pieces just yet."

"What does that leave us?"

"Just the cutlery and the plate. Odd for a pirate to be buried with a dinner setting. A cutlass or a brace of pistols, sure. Some gold or something nautical like a compass, I can see that. A dish?"

"Something in code on it?"

"Not that I can see. Looks like a standard trade china pattern: white plate, blue geisha looking girl with a lantern standing next to a tree." Max picked up the object in question, spinning it around. If flashed alternating blue and white in his hands. He stopped it abruptly.

"What was written on his stone again?"

"Ecclesiastes 10:19."

"Alright, whip out your Bible and let's look it up!"

"I don't have one. I never had much use for one."

"Figures. Internet?"

"Satellite. It came with the boat. Satellite television, phone, internet...the works."

"Nothing too good for Mrs. Szabo's little girl, eh? Fire it up!"

She kept a small terminal in the forward cabin and it took only a few moments for her to bring up a search page. She typed in the verse and read the results:

" A feast is made for laughter, and wine maketh merry: but money answereth all things, Ecclesiastes 10:19."Elena leaned back. "So?"

"The guy liked his chow? Liked to eat? I like a good debauch as well as the next pirate, but I wouldn't want to buried with a bucket of chicken." He walked back to the table and began to play with the plate again. "Pull up china patterns from around then, did they even have blue china plates in use at the time?"

She sat silently, the keyboard clicking under her fingers. Then came the one word answer. "Yep."

"Blue. Like this one?"

"Yes. Very common, in fact. It says here that a Jesuit by the name of d'Entrecolles stole the Chinese method of making the plates and brought it home to Europe. The Europeans started making dishes in the same pattern and undercut Chinese trade, causing a drop in the imports. Some missionary, eh? Spreading the Gospel of Christ while ripping off their manufacturing techniques. Industrial espionage in the name of the Church."

Max almost had a flashback to Catholic school. "Don't talk to me about Jesuits...or trigger happy nuns with rulers for that matter."

He spun the plate again on top of the table, whirling it like a top. He caught it before it lost momentum and tipped over. He spun it again, but it just did not *feel* right. Instead of spinning smoothly, it wobbled almost immediately, unbalanced somehow. Max picked it up and flipped it over in his hands. It actually felt heavier than he would have expected for a simple porcelain plate. The weight was off and it felt denser than it should.

"You got a camera, green eyed girl?"

"That I do. Brand new."

"Why new?"

"Well, now that I can, I was going to try my hand at taking photos of the sunrise."

"Hmm, you've got to stop obsessing. The sun is not going away anytime soon."

"That's what *you* say." She got up and rummaged for a moment before she found the camera. She brought it to him, still in its original packaging.

"Not kidding about the newness. I can still smell the stock boy's acne cream on the thing." He tore open the box and fiddled with the camera for a moment, inserting batteries and the memory card that came with it.

"Let's try her out." He snapped several pictures of the plate, both front and back, from various distances and angles.

"Why take photographs of the plate?"

"So I don't feel like a complete idiot when I do this." Max lifted the plate, held it briefly above his head, and then let it tumble to the deck.

"Wait!" Elena shouted, but she was too late. The plate struck the floor and shattered, porcelain flying in all directions. "What did you do that for?"

"He who dares, wins, my dear." Max knelt down, being careful to avoid any sharp pieces. The white porcelain had fallen away, leaving a smooth, shiny surface beneath. "And, if I were Irish, I would say that the luck of the Irish was with us on this one. Looks like we score."

"We better have," Elena joined him on the floor. "We can't put that particular Humpty Dumpty together again. What is it?"

"Copper. Like those cooking pots you have there in the galley, but have never used...they come with the boat too?"

"You guessed it, but why copper."

"Because," Max said as he gently brushed the copper disk and held it up to the light, "copper can take heat without deforming and conducts the heat so that whatever you are cooking heats evenly. Just like if you wanted to engrave something on it and then cover it with pottery. Whatever you put on it would not warp or deform when you put the pottery in the kiln to be fired and, it would heat evenly so your pottery would not break." He polished it with his shirt sleeve until all of the tarnish of time gave way to the shine of clean metal...metal that flashed in the lamplight.

He looked closely at the lines and words etched into the copper. "Sort of the type of thing you would do if you wanted to make a map that lasted forever but wanted to cover it up so that only somebody in the know could find it."

"Is it?"

"I think it fucking very well is, baby. Get your map out and let's see if it fits."

Elena fished her map out of the camera case, none the worse for wear given its recent dunking. The brass plate fit the hole in the center perfectly and, after Max turned it right side up, the edges of the lines on the map matched the lines etched into the shiny copper perfectly.

Chapter Twenty

"We got it," said Max, eyeing the now complete map on the table. "Now we need to know where it is telling us to go. Am I too optimistic to think that nautical charts came with this tub as well?"

"Not too optimistic, and the Bosszú is *not* a tub."

"Sorry."

"I could talk about tubs, but I know you are still in mourning. Although your boat is probably the cleanest it has been in many years right now."

"No doubt about that...none at all." Max spread the chart next to Elena's map. "Navigation one-oh-one: first find some fucking thing you recognize." He put his finger down. "Okay, this bit is the bay we are in. Rockhole, then if you follow it up..." Max slid the plate over the navigation chart. "You come onto Worley's map about here, a little south of Roanoke. Fitting in a historical context."

"Which is?"

"The first permanent English settlement in the Americas. They grew tobacco, I think, and the rest is lung cancer history."

"Ah, 'X' marks the spot then?"

"Several spots actually." Max pointed to the lines carved into the copper. "I see a mark here on the southern tip of the island, and another on the northern tip. See here? There is another on the very end of Brock island, they look like little roses."

"Roses? What does that have to do with Teach and what he may have hidden there?"

"Or a visual metaphor."

"For?"

"A compass. See that star like design on the lower right hand corner of our modern chart? That is called a 'compass rose' and it is to show you how the map orients in relation to true north and south. Almost all maps put north at the top."

"We know what end of the plate is at the top already because that is how it fits in the hole in the bigger map."

"Yes, but I think the guy who made the thing is trying to tell us something. Perhaps he wanted us, or whoever would come along and use his map, not to look for a compass at each of these spots, but to *use* a compass at each of these spots."

"To do what, exactly."

"To shoot a line of bearing."

"I'm not following."

"Picture a clock face. The top of the clock is north, and is zero degrees. There are 360 degrees in a circle. As you move around the clock face, to one o'clock, two o'clock, you are increasing in degrees. Three on the clock, if twelve is north, would be due east or ninety degrees. South would be 180 degrees and so on."

"Before they had GPS, sailors had to navigate using lines of bearing." Max rummaged in her desk and found a pen. "I learned how to do this in the seamanship and navigation classes at the Naval Academy. We would run up and down the Chesapeake taking lines of bearing. If you know where certain objects are on a map...a clock tower for instance, or the tip of a peninsula, then you can figure where you are by taking a bearing on that object, do the math to get reciprocal bearing from that object to you and draw a line. You would be somewhere on that line. If a clock tower bears due east, or ninety degrees from you, then you must be due west, or 270 degrees from it."

"I think I follow, partially, but what good does knowing that you are on some sort of line do you if you could be anywhere on that line?"

"Easy. You sight a tower and draw a line, then you sight a channel opening and draw a line, and then you sight a large building... we always would use the spire on top of the chapel dome back during my Academy days. Wherever those three lines intersected on the chart, there you were. Here we have three points, now we have to figure out what bearings to use."

"What would they look like?"

"Sets of three numbers."

"Like these?" Elena pointed to the only writing engraved on the copper plate. "They look like Bible verses yet again. Why more Bible verses."

"I'm guessing that the Bible was a bigger deal back then. Everything seemed to be related to a verse somewhere. If they are so ubiquitous, then nobody notices when they pop up."

"Genesis 1:70," Elena read, "Isaiah 1:95, and Luke 2:87."

"Pretty weird verses, huh? I don't know for sure, but ninety five verses seems awfully big for the first chapter of Isaiah." Max brought his pen down on the chart. "Everything with maps and charts starts with north and north is always at the top, so let's start with the first verse which, is also from the first book in the Bible, and plot that from the top point."

"Brock Island," Elena said."

"Yep." Max sat back for a moment and closed his eyes, remembering. "True virgins make dull companions at weddings," he muttered.

"Excuse me?"

"Another thing they taught me back when I was a midshipman. It is mnemonic to help you remember how to convert the compass heading to a true heading on a map. If you want a middy to remember anything, you have to tie it in with sex somehow."

"Really?"

"If you spent your college years locked up in an institution with very few women, you would be thinking about sex all the time too. If you were a guy that is."

Elena laughed. "Alright, go on."

"Because the earth's magnetic field varies everywhere, the reading on a compass' dial usually does not reflect what the true direction is on the earth. Your compass might *say* it is pointing north, but in reality it is slightly off. You have to add or subtract the variation on the compass due to the magnetic field to get a true line of bearing you can actually plot on the map, otherwise you will be off. Every chart has the variance written on it and ours is…about ten degrees west. We take off ten degrees from the first line, and we get 160 degrees and draw it on the chart." Max drew a line running just a little bit east of south from the tip of Brock Island.

"And then a line one hundred and eighty five degrees from the north tip of Roanoke and then one two hundred and seventy seven degrees from the south tip and voila! There you have it."

The three straight lines intersected on the chart, forming a lopsided triangle at the center.

"Not perfect. All of the lines should intersect at a point, but, given the lack of precision in the tools of the day and the fact that the bearings were taken on maps that were current three hundred years ago, I'm actually impressed we got this much."

"It is somewhere in the middle of the triangle? That has to be at least a quarter mile across the longest side." Elena leaned in close to look the chart. Max could smell her hair. Cinnamon.

"I've got a great idea where it is, see those small lines on the shore that kind of curve? Those are topographical lines. They show you what the elevation is and how quick it changes as you move along the map. It looks to me that there is a bluff or hill right in the center of our triangle. If I was going to be burying some loot along the coast, I would want to bury it high up, above the water table, so it does not flood and drown whatever it was I buried."

"That makes sense."

"Yeah. There is still a lot of 'ifs' though. If some farmer did not run over it by accident while planting his tobacco, if some other member of the crew did not come back for it hundreds of years ago, if there was anything there in the first place, if, if, if..."

Elena looked at him confidently. "Not only was Teach one of the undead, he dabbled in the black arts, he would have cast spells of warding to keep his hiding place hidden."

"About that..."

"Is it so unbelievable? He was cruel and nearly indestructible, delighting in the torture of innocent people."

"What does that prove? There were plenty of asshole sadists throughout history."

"Yes, and many of them were the undead, or servants of the undead. He was one of them alright, he survived many gunshots and stabbings. He did not stop until his head was removed from his body and thrown into the sea. That is proof enough. The power of the dagger enabled him to walk in the daylight like a normal man, while retaining all of his powers. He all but tells of it in his flag: the horned skeleton is himself, as death incarnate, and the spear he holds sheds the blood of his victims that sustained his life after death. This he represents by the blood red heart above the drops of blood. He gave clues to what he really was just as he gave clues how to find his riches if he was ever destroyed. He was taunting those around him with that flag and sending a warning to the Church and others who may have wished to seek him out and destroy him."

"And this is why this Almos guy wants the dagger? His buddies back there made that pretty clear."

"Yes, of course. It would make him even more powerful and let him walk off his mountain in safety. The only thing he fears is the sun, and once he is protected from it, he would be unstoppable by man. As it is now, he would rather send others off to do his will and lay the risk of being caught upon them."

"Caught? By whom?"

"The undead have been around since the dawn of mankind. I do not know anything about the origins of our kind...well, that is not exactly true...there are rumors...whispers in the darkness, but we do not dwell on that much. The young ones do not at any rate. Who knows what the old ones ponder as they sit in their long forgotten crypts? As it has always been, when man is threatened, man responds by hunting that threat. There have been vampire hunters as long as there have been vampires and they still exist, working in the background as individuals or groups. Major religions have their own specialized hunters. Every major government does as well, behind the scenes and never talked about or even known by the legitimate, mundane side. Of course, some of my kind have infiltrated the halls of power as well, it is a continuous struggle between the dead and the living."

"That's some heavy X-Files type shit."

"Look at history."

"Oh, I get that history is pretty bloody, but it is bloody because of sadistic, power hungry assholes. You take your Pol Pot or your Hitler: brutal, cruel, power hungry, and definitely sociopathic, but undead?"

"Don't be so sure. 'There are more things in heaven and earth Horatio, than either you nor I have dreamed of in our philosophies'."

"Shakespeare was not a vampire. Too much happy fluff in his comedies, Francis Bacon on the other hand..."Elena shrugged.

"Forget the past, we have to worry about the here and now. Focus on the mission, green eyes, focus on the mission. I want to show you a few things before we go any further."

Max walked over to the bulkhead and brought over several of the things he had retrieved from the storage locker. He was mostly interested in teaching Elena how to use the rifle and pistol. He took her on deck and gave her a quick rundown on how they worked. Sighting the weapons, lining up the front and rear sights with a target, was easy for her. After all, a girl could not have spent the last four hundred years flying around every night without developing a sense for three dimensional spatial relationships. The mechanics of loading and unloading were also essential, and Max drilled her over and over again on how to eject the magazine, insert a new one, and chamber a round.

He taught her about the safety on the rifle: the switch pointing forward for safe, straight up for semiautomatic, and straight back for bursts. In the last position, every pull of the trigger would fire three bullets in fully automatic. Max cautioned her that she was to only use this function if she was confronted by several opponents and she needed to put as many bullets downrange as possible, otherwise she should stick to aimed, individual shots. *One shot one kill, that's the Marine Corps motto for a rifleman.*

The Glock has no safety. Max demonstrated how he could load the pistol and drop it without it going off. The reason for this, is that instead of a safety it has small plastic switch on the front of the trigger. If that switch is not pushed in, the weapon cannot fire no matter what she does with it.

Satisfied that she had a good grasp on the basics, he had her shoot off a full magazine from each of the guns, directing her to shoot at various bits of debris floating by. Max first checked to make sure that no other boats were around before letting her fire the first shot. He was not concerned, however, as gunshots were not unusual for this part of rural North Carolina. Rednecks were always shooting at things in the water: snakes, floating beer cans, driftwood…whatever struck their fancy as being something worth plinking. He was certain that a few shots would not arouse any sort of suspicion and he was right. No one bothered them as she got in some target practice. Max was pleased to see that she was actually very good; a natural.

"It is going to get dark soon, we should pack it in for the day," said Max as he picked up the last spent shell off the deck. "I truly feel sorry for any dumb son of a bitch that decides to cross you. Beautiful and deadly is a hell of a combination."

"That actually was fun…very empowering." Elena dropped the magazine from the rifle and looked into the chamber to make sure it was empty, just as he had taught her. "I can see why people find these things so attractive, I can reach out and kill someone before they get anywhere near me."

"That's the whole point. Just don't be too eager to shoot anyone. I'd rather we finish this whole evolution without having to fire a single shot. If we have to shoot somebody, then we have royally fucked up. Stealth, not brute force, is what we really need right now."

"That is good to know."

"Know what else is good to know?"

"What?"

"How to tear 'em down and clean 'em. A dirty gun will jam

when you really, really need it to work. You have to take care of it just like any other piece of precision machinery."

With that, Max showed her how to disassemble both the carbine and the handgun. He showed her how to scrub the chamber clean so that the cartridge would fully seat when pushed in by the bolt. He showed her how to polish the feed ramp, so the bullets would not hang up when they were stripped from the magazine. He showed her how to scrape the carbon from around the extractor so the empty shells would be pulled out smoothly from the chamber and thrown away from the gun so that fresh cartridges could feed freely. Then he showed her how to put it all back together again and do a function check: working the bolt and pressing the trigger to hear the sharp "click" as the hammer fell on the empty chamber.

"Before long, I will have you doing that blindfolded," said Max with satisfaction, pleased at how quickly his pupil took to his lessons. "I'll make a Marine of you yet."

Elena smiled. "No thanks. I find earth tones very unflattering."

Max laughed. "Well, let's settle in then. Tomorrow is going to be a busy day."

They put everything back into the cabin and locked the door behind them. Anchored for the night, they were indistinguishable from hundreds of boats in little coves up and down the coast, pausing to rest before continuing whatever journey that lay ahead.

Chapter Twenty-One

When Elena came to Max that night, her love making was not as insistent, not as desperate as the first time. Then, she had been reaching out, desperate to get a firm grasp on what to her may have been her only chance to feel like a whole, normal, human woman. Like a drowning person, clutching for a life ring, she had reached out to him and held on to him and what he represented to her as if her very life depended on that one, single, solitary moment. She had concentrated on every single movement, every taste, every sound and moan and gasp of passion as if she only had that one chance to finally be the person she had always longed to be and that it all could be gone in an instant. For so many years, all she had of the sunshine and her humanity were slowly fading memories. If all of this was to be taken away from her again, she wanted to experience it all to its fullest level and have memories so crisp and precise she would not forget for a thousand years the smell of him, the taste of him, and how he had made her feel.

This time, more certain that he, she, and what they had between them was real, Elena relaxed and, rather than forcing events along, let them flow. She started with a nuzzle on the neck, then a playful tickle, laughing as he growled at her, pretending to be annoyed. She let him chase her across the cabin, permitting herself to be caught only after she had shed her clothing, piece by piece. Max was not in a hurry to catch her anyway…at least until she had accomplished that task and the last flimsy piece of underclothing slid off. Her panties struck Max square in the face with a soft slap as she used the elastic waistband to slingshot the brief bit of silky cloth off the tip of her index finger. He covered the panties with both hands and buried his face into them, breathing in the scent of her. *Game on!*

It was more her jumping into his arms than him actually catching her, but the game had to be played to its end, and, regardless how, catch her he did. They tumbled onto the bed and she kissed him gently, lightly. He returned the kiss much more firmly and slid his tongue along her teeth. Elena put both arms around his neck and nuzzled him underneath his jaw.

"Now, now, no biting there, Vampirella."

"Afraid?" Her nuzzling continued down his throat to his chest.

"Not afraid, just not that that kind of boy."

"I'm sure I will find out exactly what sort of boy you are." She grasped him and then unbuttoned his shorts.

Relaxed, almost lazily, she gradually eased him out of his clothes, kissing every bit of exposed skin. His ticklish laughter changed to sighs as she exposed more and more of him. When she finally let him slide inside her, she was more than ready and she was amazed at just how *real* he felt inside her and how well he fit.

It was as if they were made to fit together, like pieces of the same precision watch, crafted by a genius Swiss jeweler. Elena was in no hurry and she slowly moved with him, in time with his breathing. She had all the time in the world and she felt that she could do this forever. This was real, Max was real, and she was real. Solid, perfect, and whole.

Max was as happy, if not happier than, Elena. He felt very comfortable with her. It was not anything she did or said, it was more what she *didn't* do. She did not look on his artificial leg with a look of disgust or pity as Max had seen so many other people do. She did not say anything about how sorry she was that he was not a whole man nor did she ask stupid questions like *does it hurt?* Elena did not overcompensate by making a fuss over the leg either. She did not kiss the stump that ended mid shin or stroke it or tell him that it *almost looked normal.* None of those things. Elena acted like there was nothing wrong with Max at all and that everything on, or in, him was natural and perfect to her. He was not *disabled* (Max hated that word). Elena made Max feel he was a whole man and this made him glad he was with her. He felt whole when she was around and he worried that she may not want to stick around after the mission, whatever it may be, was over.

They finished together just as softly as they had begun and nestled together in the afterglow.

Max did not move until Elena's steady, even breathing told him that she was asleep. He slipped out of bed, pulled on his shorts, went to his pack to retrieve something, and went out on deck. He could see on the depth gauge up on the control consol that there were only a few feet of water under the keel. He stepped off the boat, hands held high to keep what he held in them from getting wet and waded, chest deep, to shore.

At the water's edge Max found a log, the trunk of a tree blown over in some hurricane long past, and sat down. His shoulder hurt, his leg hurt, and the oxycontin was not working as well as it usually did. At least he had something else that would help. Max had taken a few cigars from his storage locker and he had come out to enjoy one without filling Elena's boat with smoke. *What use is it to stash things away for the end of the world if you don't throw a few victory stogies in with the rest of the mess?*

He bit into the end of the Ashton VSG with the maduro wrapper and spat out the resulting plug of tobacco. With a flick, he lit his cigar lighter and ran the flame around the cigar's end, warming up the tobacco before lighting it with great puffs. Lit, it drew smoothly and Max inhaled deeply. *Pure bliss: a nice roll in the hay with a beautiful girl followed by a nice cigar.*

"Didn't you know that those things will kill you?" came a female voice from the shadows, right next to him.

Max jumped, pulling the Glock from his waistband.

"Easy there cowboy, put down the gun. I'm not here to hurt you."

"Never thought you could," said Max, putting his pistol away. Sharon DeMoliers stepped out of the darkness. He saw her perfect white teeth flash as she smiled at him.

"What the Hell is it with everybody sneaking up on me all the time?" Max sat back down on his log and took another long drag from his cigar. "I must be losing my edge."

"Tobacco is sacred to Papa Legba and no Vudun ceremony can start without an offering of it to him. Not only does it please him, but the smoke also guides our prayers to him"

"And all of that means what, exactly."

She slid onto the log next to him. "It means, 'can I have a toke?'"

Max handed her the Ashton and she drew in deeply, held the smoke for a second, then exhaled in an aromatic fog. *Black coffee, cigars, this is one tough lady.*

"You're hurt," Sharon said. She handed Max back his cigar and reached for his shoulder.

"Yeah, got into a little disagreement with a couple grabasstic idiots."

"You got shot."

"How do you know that? Magic?"

"Even better—gossip. Word gets around very fast in a small town."

"Tell me about it."

Sharon pulled his sleeve up over his wound. "Don't worry, I came prepared. This will help." She reached into her cleavage and pulled out a small leather pouch. Max's eyes watered as soon as she opened it.

"Damn, that smells bad."

"It means it's good for you." Sharon dipped her fingers into the pouch and scooped out a large dollop of grayish goop.

"Yuck. What the Hell are you going to do with that stuff?"

"This," said Sharon as she slapped her hand against the hole in Max's shoulder. Instantly he felt searing pain shoot straight through his shoulder. He felt as if it was tearing apart.

"Shit!" Max tried to rub it off but Sharon pulled his hand away.

"Wait for it," she said.

Trembling, Max struggled not to move. After a few seconds the burning faded and an almost pleasant numbness spread all through his shoulder.

"Goddamn," Max said as he wiped tears from his eyes. "What sort of voodoo shit is that?"

"Not voodoo at all," Sharon replied. "Just simple backwoods doctoring. Magic is not all about spells and supernatural powers, mostly it is about knowing things--the right things. My people have lived off the land for a thousand generations. We have learned and passed down all of the gifts that mother earth has given us in her wisdom. One herb stops bleeding, another promotes healing, and yet another is a most excellent local anesthetic. With all of its test tubes and microscopes, modern medicine often misses what is growing in its own back yard. You leave that poultice on until it falls off of its own accord and it will be like you were never hurt in the first place."

"Well, just warn a guy first next time. I almost dropped my cigar."

"You didn't though."

"Nope."

"Well give it back then, I rather liked the flavor." Sharon didn't wait for a reply, she simply took the cigar from Max's hand. She puffed on it for a moment, silently regarding him.

Max sighed. "You know, this begs the question: what the fuck are you doing out here and how the fuck did you find me in the middle of nowhere?" She regarded him silently with dark eyes. "Oh yeah, and just what the fuck do you want, lady?"

"Finding you was complicated, but surprisingly not difficult either. No spell of scrying can see you. You exist outside of magic. None of my arts could follow you or even give me a hint of where you are. Until that is, I decided to look where I could not see at all. I made the most powerful workings I knew how and sent my mind on its flight out into the ether. I could see the smallest insect, I could feel the heartbeat of a squirrel hiding from the hawk, but I could not see you. What I could see was a big, black, empty spot where my vision would not carry. Logically, you would be in the middle of that blind spot, so I hopped in my pickup and drove around until I made my way to that spot and, well, here I am."

"There you are." Max took back his cigar. The end was dry. *At least she is not a drooler.*

"Here I am."

"I'm guessing you did not come all this way for a smoke. So, fess up, what sort of weirdness are you going to lay on me now? I've been pretty popular lately, if you haven't noticed."

"Yes, very popular. People, and some...how to phrase this... not-people, have noticed you as well. Which brings me to my purpose. You are very unique in the world and I fear that your uniqueness is in dire danger of being snuffed out. Some powerful forces are in the process of realizing what you are and the danger you pose to them. Once they understand your power, they will stop at nothing to kill you."

"So you came here to cheer me up, is that it?" Max grinned at her. "Well, thanks. Thanks a lot, you really are a bundle of joy."

"I came here for you or, more specifically, for your seed."

Max choked, the cigar smoke coming out of his mouth and nose in a staccato of coughs like an old steam engine getting started. "Did you say what I think you said?"

"Indeed."

"Man-oh-man. I was in a several-year-long dry spell and now everybody wants a piece of me…literally."

"I don't want to take you away from your little girl. I could go on for hours how that relationship is destined to fail. You have no understanding of what she is, of what her nature is, and what that will mean to you decades from now when you are old and she is still young. I just want to preserve a small bit of you when you are gone."

"I'm not an artifact in a museum to be preserved."

"You are very special. I have done a great deal of research since we last talked. Only once in a thousand years, or even longer, does someone like you come along. Someone who lives outside the realm of magic, of the supernatural, and devoid of any spark of the unseen world. The last one that I can ascertain was Thomas Aquinas, over eight hundred years before."

"A Catholic saint who does not believe in the supernatural? Sorry, but saints are known for their faith. I don't buy that."

"Oh, he did not believe, and it galled him. He is unique in the panel of saints because nowhere is it written that he saw visions or performed miracles. All he did was write long tomes on the subject of faith and the lack thereof. He could not come to grips intellectually with his lack of the divine spark, so he tried to use his intellect to explain what he was missing. Have you ever read his work, *The Dark Night of the Soul*? It is a powerful book. The reader can feel his struggle with his lack of faith."

"Very philosophical and a little too deep for a tree trunk by a river in the middle of the night."

"You are like Aquinas and like him you are different than those around you."

"People who don't believe? There are plenty…in fact I would wager that most people don't believe in this stuff."

"And you would lose that bet. All the great non-believers: the atheists, the agnostics, even some of most religious people who decry the unseen world as folklore or the work of the Devil, believe deep down. Carl Sagan, Einstein, Madeline Murray O'Hare…all of them, even as they proclaim their intellect and state that reason has banished the darkness, are, deep in the recesses of their primitive hindbrains, no more than cave men, clad in animal skins and clustered about the fire sending fearful glances into the darkness and praying that the fire will keep the night and what prowls there at bay. All humans are like that. All except you."

She got up and stood over him.

"You are the rarest of humans because you cannot believe and your unbelief is so strong that it even transforms the world around you. It is a powerful thing that you possess and it is that power I want to preserve and take with me."

She dropped her dress, barely a light shift, bearing two chocolate tipped breasts.

"I want to have your child because I want a child that will have my innate abilities, gifts from the women that came before me and your innate defense against the magical world. Such a child would grow into a great mage, a great practitioner of the arts."

Max felt a lump in his throat as he struggled to keep his eyes on her face. He was losing that struggle.

"Wouldn't they cancel each other out?"

"Maybe, but it is a matter of odds and genetics. A child may get none of her parent's gifts. Perhaps she would receive gifts from one or the other but not both. However, she may very well receive gifts from both parents. Such a child would work wonders."

"And if you don't get your *wunderkind*, what then? Ship her off to boarding school? An orphanage?"

"No, no. Motherhood is very important to me. It is an integral part of my beliefs. I would love her and raise her in the tradition regardless. If I fail to conceive the child that could change the world, then I will simply come for you again, if you live, and ask you again to give me this little thing." She let the shift fall all the way to the ground. Max followed its fall, from the breasts, along a firm and flat stomach, to the tight curls at the junction of her legs. He was feeling very distracted and he could feel the temptation growing in him: an almost palpable presence in his abdomen. She was indeed a beautiful woman and he could tell that she wanted him badly. He felt an overwhelming urge to get up and cup those very inviting and ripe looking breasts and to run his hands along those chocolate drop nipples. *Discretion, however, is the better part of valor.*

"Mrs. Robinson, you're trying to seduce me." *That's it Max, diffuse the situation with an old movie quote to take your attention from your hard on.*

"Yes, I am. Well?"

"I feel like you are trying to put a hoodoo or something on me."

"No, what you feel is just your hormones. What a man feels when he sees a woman who desires him. A love spell would not work. You are immune."

"Good. So the old boy is working on his own then."

"Excuse me?"

"Never mind."

"Do you not desire me? It would be good for you…for both of us. I will not bind you to me or expect any fatherly duties. I can take care of our child myself. No child support if that was on your mind."

"It did cross it once or twice and I really don't want to find myself on some sort of daytime talk show in a few years. *I am a voodoo priestess' baby's daddy.*" Having enough of the cigar, Max flicked it into the water. It hissed as it struck. "You are a very, very lovely lady. Everything I would love to be with: smart, beautiful, a hell of a conversationalist, and you really seem to dig me, but I can't."

Sharon nodded to the boat. "Because of her?"

"Well yes…and no. Of course because of her. She and I have a really good thing going. She is the first person who has made me feel like a whole man since I lost my leg. She does not pity me, she does not feel sorry for me, she just accepts me. This is good. This is *right* somehow. I haven't given much thought to any sort of future, I admit, but in the here and now she is what I need and I will not fuck that up. Also, loyalty matters to me. I never was much for playing around. One woman at a time has always been my way of doing things. It would hurt her."

"She never has to know."

"So? *I* would know and I know that it would make me a totally disloyal asshole to give in to your very tempting offer. That just is not part of the code, my code. Without a sense of honor, I am nothing more than any other jackoff out there and I won't bend even if that means letting such a tremendous woman as yourself slip through my fingers."

"Also," Max continued, "if, and I say if, I ever have a child, I could not imagine not being an integral part of that child's life. I would have to raise him and be a father to him and teach him everything my father taught me. So you see, I cannot, even though I may want to very much, take you up on this request. I have to say no."

She frowned and pulled up her dress. "You are a man of honor and you have your reasons. It actually makes me want to have your child even more. I doubt that any other man would have turned me down."

"As you said, I'm a right unique bastard."

"Quite. I am growing fond of you and I am not angry with you at all. I will continue to watch over you the best I can and perhaps someday you will change your mind."

"Perhaps," said Max.

She walked off into the shadows and he sat alone, in silence, until he could hear the sound of a car engine starting in the distance and the crunch of tires on gravel fade away. Max then got up and waded back to the boat, pulling himself onboard with the diving ladder.

Chapter Twenty-Two

The next day the trip along the length of Pamlico Sound took only a few hours. At over eighty miles from the southern end to the northern end and some forty miles across, Max had plenty of room to open up the throttle and play. The twin, 420 horsepower, Magnum Mercruiser engines roared when he pushed the throttle up and purred like a contented feline when he backed off. Elena's Sundancer was thirty nine feet of well tuned and highly responsive joy: a power boater's wet dream.

After getting his discharge from the Marines, Max had envisioned himself becoming a laid-back sailboat bum living the Jimmy Buffet lifestyle of Hawaiian shirts and drinking booze out of coconuts. After the intensity of the war and the struggles to get back on his feet...foot... the idea of letting the wind and current take him where they may had a certain appeal: the life of a sailboat captain suited him just fine. Just fine, that is, until he got his hands on this fine-tuned piece of machinery. A sailor lives with the ocean, heeding her moods and idiosyncrasies, finessing it like a woman and careful not to get on her wrong side. When all is sunny, and the breeze is firm and steady and the chop light, then all is well and she treats you like a well satisfied and contented lady. If, however, she gets her period and throws thunderstorms and gales and opposing currents at you, you best stay in bed according to Max. Go with the flow, don't fight it, and stay in and have a beer instead of going out into a blow.

Elena's boat, The Vengeance, on the other hand, grabbed hold of the ocean with one hand, smacked her across the behind with the other, and told her to make it a sandwich. When Maz stove the throttle forward, his body pressed back in his seat and his hair and his shirttail fluttered in the breeze. Elena laughed at him and said he looked just like a little boy with a new toy.

As he drove, he made small talk with Elena, but he was still thinking about last night and what Sharon said. The sex thing was bizarre enough, but the mumbo-jumbo about "powers" she thought he had was even more strange. Max had never thought about any sort of supernatural realm. He went through the motions at church, went to Sunday school and Confirmation class, and did everything that a good Catholic kid is supposed to do. He had never felt any sort of inspiration or calling or *spark* that everyone else seemed to talk about. It is not that he disliked any of it, it is just that he did not get any of it. In the Marines he learned to have faith in himself and his fellow Marines: their training and discipline, their dedication and sense of duty. That is where his belief lay and that is where he made his "church." *The Church of General Chesty Puller and the lean, mean, green machine.*

Things had been pretty fucking odd for him lately and he really did not know how to take it but, for now, he was content to bust a few heads, pop an oxycontin here and there, and spend time with this lovely redhead on a kick ass boat. She made him feel good, almost *too* good because he knew, deep down, that the main reason he had turned down the good doctor's offer was because he was actually falling for her. This scared him more than going belly to belly with an insurgent hell-bent on giving him an AK-47 sponsored trip to Arlington National Cemetery. At least he could shoot back at the bad guy with the gun. He had not the faintest clue how to defend himself from a pair of deep green eyes. He knew he was along for the ride and what bothered him was where that ride was taking him and what would happen when he got there. Violence and danger were exciting and he missed facing an enemy on the battlefield. Elena's little quest for payback had enabled him to finally scratch an itch long neglected. Having put on his spurs again, he was not about to hang them back up after this party was over, green-eyed girl or no. Would she go along with that or expect him to put on an apron and settle down, fat and happy, back into a boring retirement?

Elena sat next to him, reveling in Max's obvious delight at taking the *Bosszú* through her paces. She had, of course, spent many hours in the captain's chair herself, but she had always been certain to drive the boat with meticulous regard for the rules of the road. She always drove well within the established speed limits for whatever waterway she was traversing and she, on the other hand, gave all markers and hazards to navigation a wide berth. She did everything she could to escape the authorities' notice, a trait that had helped her survive in the human world for many long years. Max was throwing all caution to the wind, almost daring the Coast Guard to stop them and give them both sobriety tests. It made her nervous as well as excited.

What also made her nervous was what she saw last night. With Max around, she had none of her usual senses and foresight and so she had awakened by chance, noticing that he was gone. When she looked out into the night, she saw the glow of his cigar and she knew why he had left the boat. She was pleased at his consideration to take his rather filthy habit over to the shore rather than smoking on the *Bosszú*. Then she had seen the woman. It took no special vampire power to know what she was after. No woman would expose herself so brazenly in front of a man unless she wanted him. The first long unused feeling to arise in her was jealousy, something she had not felt since she had been turned into one of the undead. Of course she had developed close associations with mortals in the hundreds of years since her transformation, but those associations had been mercenary only. She just used the mortal to gain what she needed at the time, casting them off without a second's consideration. All she could feel when she saw the woman with Max was *mine. He's mine, you bitch.*

Max was different; she realized that Max was now more than just a means to an end for her and more than what he could give her: the humanity that had been stolen from her. Max had become part of her world and this scared her. How could she embrace the feelings that were growing inside of her knowing that she would then have to watch him grow old and die while she stayed young? That is, of course, assuming that he would even decide to stay with her once, as he always put it, the *mission* was accomplished. Then again, she reasoned, he must feel for her too. Why else would he send the woman away and make her cover her nakedness? That comforted her.

But the fear she felt was even more visceral. She did not sense the woman's presence, she could not hear the beat of her heart nor smell the blood that ran through her veins. That night was the first night that she realized that she was truly human around Max. Yes, she knew that she could walk in the daylight and eat and make love when he was around, but she had not really considered that the whole experience came with a price: the loss of the strength and abilities of the undead. She knew this on an intellectual level early on, but seeing him out there with that woman without any way of sensing her drove the point home. It was mere happenstance that she saw them together. In her mind, part of being human was being helpless. For centuries all of her strength and her entire survival had been because of what she had become, not what she had been. Returning to her human state included every and all human frailties that she had forgotten over the years. She wondered if she could get sick now, or even die, or even grow old. If she stayed with Max would she grow old? She did not know and that uncertainty was chilling.

For the first time since she started looking for a way to avenge herself on Almos, she began to doubt that she could destroy him, even with the dagger.

"What is that noise?" Shouted Elena over the music that began to flood from the Bose speakers that lined the control cabin.

"Drowning Pool, *Let the Bodies Hit the Floor*. It's a great hardcore song. We used to play it all the time overseas to get pumped up before going outside the wire." When Elena said she had bought the boat with all of the bells and whistles, she was not kidding. Max was enthralled with the entertainment setup that had been part of whatever package she had negotiated with the dealer. She had both a hard drive full of thousands of MP3 tracks and access to both satellite radio systems in addition to her internet, navigation, phone, and movie setups, all controllable from a touchpad screen right to the left of the wheel. It had taken Max a while to figure out how to work it but once he did, he was thoroughly involved with trying to expand Elena's exposure to what he considered good music.

Flicking through the touch screen menus with his left hand while steering with his right, he picked through the selections, playing song after song that he thought Elena needed to hear.

"It's all about motivation. You have to pump your guys up, get 'em ready to kick some ass. Fear is as contagious as it is ubiquitous and if you psyche your guys up for a fight beforehand, the less likely they are to fold when the shit hits the fan. The hardest thing in the leader's job is keeping that one guy, the first guy, from losing it. Once one guy loses it and lets his fear take over, then the next guy might catch it, then the next, and the next. If you want to keep your platoon in the fight, you got to keep that one guy in the fight. Music is a great motivator, like Robert Duvall playing Wagner from his helicopters in *Apocalypse Now*. It stokes your guys up and maybe unnerves your opponent...especially if they hate thrash metal.

"Hadji don't like Dope, and he sure as hell thinks Rammstein is the spawn of Satan. Me, I prefer a little AC/DC myself. Nothing says I'm coming to fuck you up better than a little *Back in Black* or *Highway to Hell*, but the young guys like the newer stuff and it kicks ass just the same."

"Motivate with music? It sounds like a psychological trick to me." Elena leaned in to look at the tracks displayed on the monitor.

"Psychological, yes. Trick, no. Leaders have been using things like that since the dawn of time to motivate their men. You have Patton's famous blood and guts speech, the cavalry still yells 'Garry Owen,' and even William Fucking Shakespeare got into the act."

Max stood up, both hands still on the wheel and loudly quoted over the sound of the wind, the engine, and *Dope*:

> *Once more unto the breach, dear friends, once more;*
> *Or close the wall up with our English dead.*
> *In peace there's nothing so becomes a man*
> *As modest stillness and humility:*
> *But when the blast of war blows in our ears,*
> *Then imitate the action of the tiger.*

"Henry fucking The Fifth, Act three, Scene one by William Shakespeare the man and the legend, himself. It inspired a lot of troops back in the day, but here in the modern era, nothing gets the guys going like *Die Motherfucker Die* and *America, Fuck Yeah!* Apparently the more times the word fuck appears in a song, the better the guys like it."

"Apparently," she replied. "Does it bother you that you had to resort to mind games to get young men to go out and get killed?"

Max yanked the throttle all the way off. They both lurched forward as the boat rapidly slowed. He turned on her suddenly. "Every single kid that got killed over there tore me up just as if I had lost my own son. I personally wrote letters to every single one of my Marines' families and visited then when I got back to tell them face to face how sorry I was. Every one that I lost was because I fucked up and failed as a leader. I will carry that burden as long as I live."

"I'm sorry. I didn't mean to..."

"Fucking forget about it..." Max slammed the throttle back on. "Everyone else has."

They rode on in silence for awhile, any semblance of a cordial mood gone. Max considered apologizing for his outburst but decided against it. A quick temper was one of the signs of PTSD that the docs back at the Naval Hospital kept harping about and he did not want to even think about giving that bit of bullshit any credence. *Some people just don't get it and never will.*

After a while, the GPS indicated they were getting close to the point Max had triangulated on the chart. He had programmed the latitude and longitude into the navigation system before they set out and the computer had taken them straight there. Max wondered if there was some sort of autopilot that would have navigated the Vengeance all by itself because the doggone boat seemed to have every other amenity. *Just how much does she have squirreled away in her accounts anyway?* The miracles of compound interest and hundreds of years to invest did have advantages.

"Looks like we're here." Max pulled back on the throttle, the boat slowing much more gradually this time. He looked over to where the lines had intersected on the chart and immediately recognized the bluff that followed the shape of the topographic lines he had pointed out to Elena. A hill overlooked the sound, swelling from the farmlands to the west and peaking thirty feet above the waterline. Gray and red clay showed through the earth where the water had cut into the seaward side, making that part of the hill into a shear drop that faced the barrier islands. Max hoped that erosion over the years had not cut so far in as to make this whole endeavor worthless.

"I can pull us in pretty far. You only draft about three feet and I only need a foot or two under the keel to keep the props off any crap that might be on the bottom. I couldn't do this on the *Limb*. Sailboat keels go down a long way to balance out the mast. We would have had to swim in." Max shut down the main engines and used the small bow and stern docking thrusters to gently guide the boat as close as possible. He watched as the depth slowly ticked down on his display and simultaneously cut thrust and hit the anchor release when the gauge showed one foot under the keel. Max was cutting it close, but he wanted to wade as little as possible. People are very vulnerable when they are wallowing through water above their chests.

Max made sure his backpack was full of anything he might need, including the items taken from Worley's grave, and strapped his carbine onto it. Holding both over his head, he stepped into the cool salt water of Pamlico Sound. Elena was close behind. They waded to the shore and then walked along it until the grade leveled off and they could walk inland and up the bluff on its more gradually sloping backside. It did not take them long to crest the bluff and look out over the water and the barrier islands beyond.

Sea oats covered the hill dotted with a few squat Yaupon trees, twisted by the ocean winds. Down slope, the oats gave way to a stand of hardwood and pine that were only broken here and there in the distance by farmers' fields. The remains of an ancient oak, blown over in some long past hurricane, topped the hill. Branches and roots both fallen away long ago so that only the large trunk remained.

"This is the likely spot." Max took out a compass from his shirt where it was hanging by a lanyard around his neck. He looked at its face as he slowly turned his body. "Over there is Roanoke, right where it should be." He turned again. "And over there is Brock Island, right on the money. I think we have a winner. It has to be somewhere right here on top of the bluff. Makes sense: it is a recognizable feature and it is above the flood line. I'm surprised someone has not come along and built a house up here by now. It would have a kickass view."

"We should start in the center." Elena moved toward the fallen oak. Vines had grown sparsely across it, but thick enough in patches to obscure some of the surrounding ground. She could just make out the dim outline of an object shadowed by the large and weathered trunk. A few tugs on the greenery brought into view the long hidden stone.

"I found another grave, Max," she said softly.

"They were partial to those, weren't they?" Max came up next to her, bent down and cleared the remaining vines with several long tugs. The grave was topped by a large, horizontal cap stone much like the one that had housed the much abused Mr. Worley. Lichen covered the weathered surface and it was ringed by the remains of a picket fence, the sharpened ends of the posts no longer pointing to the sky, but in whatever random direction the fall of each individual piece of wood directed. He was not surprised in the least to see a solitary grave on top of the hill as small graveyards seemed to dot the landscape around here. Small family plots right next to occupied homes were common as were tiny cemeteries and even single graves in the middle of nowhere. Max thought it a peculiar Southern tradition, but it was so common in the rural south that no one seemed to pay any attention to them at all.

The fence around the grave was just as common as the out of the way graves themselves, so Max could not give its presence any special significance. What did have some special significance, was the name, still dimly visible on the worn stone: *Anne*.

"Well, we definitely have a pattern. Here, Green Eyes, give me a hand." Both Max and Elena leaned into the capstone, dug their feet into the sandy soil, and pushed. The stone slid off with a grinding sound. No corpse or coffin greeted them, just a wooden stairway dropping into the darkness.

"This is too easy," said Max. "This can't be it. All someone would have to do is come up here and pull the stone off. Some bored teenagers could have found the Teach's hiding place just by coming up here to fuck around."

"He was also a practitioner of magic, Max, and he would have protected this place with wards and spells…"

"That don't work now because I'm around," Max dryly finished for her. "I've been hearing that a lot lately."

He fished around in his pack. "Here, take this." Max handed her a Surefire flashlight, turning on the one he kept for himself. "Let's go find us some mischief, shall we?"

Max put his foot on the first step. They were thick and obviously made from a hardwood of some sort. A thick coating of tar had protected it from the elements and, even though it creaked under his weight, it held firm and did not give at all. He took another tentative step and when he had the same reaction, he beckoned Elena to follow. Slowly, they both made their way down to the bottom stair when Max stopped. They had come down twenty steps, so Max estimated that they were at least ten to fifteen feet under the earth. Roots hung from the ceiling braced by stanchions and crossbeams also made from heavily tarred hardwood.

The bright, white LED light from the flashlights cut through the darkness and Max could see a room with a wooden floor opening up from the base of the stairs. It was small, about ten feet square, but it made Max uneasy still the same. If he was going to lay a trap, this would be the spot. The landings of stairwells were an insurgent's favorite spot to lay an IED or an ambush indoors and Max had learned the hard way to be very careful of them. He motioned Elena to be quiet as he played his light all over the room; back, forth, over floor, ceiling, and walls. He was looking for some sort of tell: a trigger mechanism such as a tripwire, or a discolored spot on the ceiling, or holes in the wall. Meticulously he studied the room until something odd caught his eye.

On the floor, about a foot from the last stair, was a small hole about two inches across. As he slowly ran his light along the floor and across the hole there was another, about two feet distant. Max could see a straight line of these holes running across the room and disappearing into what he now realized was the opening into another tunnel. He leaned forward and peered into the first hole. It was empty and was only a few inches deep as if it was bored into, but not through, the planks that made up the floor.

As they descended the last stairs, their steps disturbed a trickle of sand which slid off the last stair and onto the floor. Max focused on the sand and felt the walls closing in. *What the hell are we doing?* Sand on wooden steps, just like his last day in Iraq...just like his last day as a whole man. The shakes started deep inside him and spread throughout his entire body.

"Max, what's wrong?"

"Trapped, this is all wrong," he panted. "We are walking into the kill zone." Stair landings were deadly and for a second, Max could see the hand grenade, as clear as day, moving down the steps at him. It rolled the full width each wooden step before dropping to the next. It moved almost leisurely, as if stalking him.

He shook his head and the vision vanished. There was nothing there but gloom and dirt. He felt his throat tighten and the panic begin to rise, tugging at him with an irresistible urge to run. This was so much like every nightmare, every flashback, that had pulled him screaming awake every night, soaked with his own sweat and shaking uncontrollably. Ambush. Behind every door, at the top of every landing: ambush. Go into the wrong room and you get shot, kick in the wrong door and you lose your leg. Max was certain he could see movement in the shadows, just waiting for him to step into the room before *they* shot him down. Every nerve in him was screaming *get out, get out now!*

"No good," whispered Max, trying to steady his voice. "Back up the stairs."

"What?"

"No good. No good," Max heard his own voice crack with barely controlled panic. He turned and pushed Elena up the stairs as fast as he could.

Breaking into the daylight, Max slid to his knees, sucking in great lungfuls of the clean, salty air.

"What is it, Max?"

"The place is wired. Booby trapped. I'm certain of it."

"It was like you were somewhere else down there for a second."

"Iraq. Things didn't feel right. Like I was back there and things were just about to go to shit."

"But Max, you are not there. We are here, in the here and now, and so close to getting what we want."

"Gimme a second. Let me think." Max glanced over at the top of the stairs, leading off into the dark, and he felt a sudden nausea come over him. *When did I last take my meds?*

"Give me the gun."

"Elena, it's no good..." Max looked up at her and she stared back at him, face set. Determined.

"Give me the gun. I did not spend the last two hundred years looking for this damned thing just to stop now. Just a few feet more, Max, that is all we need to go."

"Elena, we can come back with some help...dig around..."

"No." Elena calmly reached down and yanked the Glock from Max's hand. "This is my cause and I am going to finish it with or without you."

"Wait," started Max, but she was already stepping down into the tunnel.

PTSD is for pussies, Max.

"Screw you," Max said aloud.

You wimped out. The doctors were right, you are damaged goods.

"It doesn't feel right, I couldn't..."

But she could. She went back down without a second's thought. Never, ever, make one of your Marines do something that you don't have the balls to do yourself.

Max pulled an oxycontin out of his pocket and swallowed it dry. "I just need a minute to get straight."

A minute might be too late, Maxey-boy.

Elena slowly went back down the stairs half furious *with* and half concerned *for* Max. She had heard about this illness that affects soldiers: shell shock, battle fatigue, and now post traumatic stress disorder. Veterans would freeze, panic, or fight at the slightest provocation. Thus far, he had seemed like a rock, imperturbable in the most trying situations. When would he lose it next time? Would he leave her vulnerable? Would he run? Just sit paralyzed, perhaps, at the worst possible moment? She could not depend on him if he was going to go into fits.

At the last step, Elena stopped. This is where Max had panicked but, try as she might, she could not see what it was that frightened him. It would be easy enough for her to fly across the room, gliding a few inches above the floor, but Max was still too close to permit use of her powers. She was still human, and she would have to continue on as a human would: on her own two feet.

She took a breath and slowly raised her right foot from the step and extended it toward the floor. She extended her toe and lowered it as slowly as she could. Max had seemed certain that if something was going to happen, it would happen on that floor.

Despite herself, Elena braced herself as her toe touched the rough wood.

She was suddenly jerked back by a rough hand clutching the back of her shirt.

Swinging wildly, Elena's elbow connected a set of ribs.

"Hey! It's me," grunted Max. "I think I figured it out." He motioned for her to follow him outside.

"Feeling better?" She asked as she regained her footing and followed him back up.

"Yeah. Sorry. I haven't felt that messed up since the hospital. Remind me to tell you about skin grafts sometime and how badly they suck."

"If you are feeling better, then let's go."

"I said I was feeling better, I didn't say I thought the place was safe. The place is still trapped."

"Curses or spell won't work on you."

"So everybody keeps telling me, but I'm talking about a real trap, a mechanical one of some sort."

"What makes you so sure?"

"You don't survive years of deployments without getting a feel for these things. It gets to be sort of a sixth sense." Max noticed Elena's wry smirk. "Not in a supernatural sense, but as an instinct learned from that hard mistress known as experience. That particular bitch is telling me that the place is rigged."

"Rigged? How?"

"I'm guessing that it's pressure activated, something in the floor. There are holes drilled in the floorboards about every two, two and a half feet. You put your weight on one of those boards and a pit will open under you or the ceiling will collapse or shit will shoot out of the walls at you like in frigging *Indiana Jones*. Whatever the surprise, it's bound to be nasty."

"So what now?"

"Something we overlooked. We have all of the pieces; we just need to figure out how they work together. Worley provided us with the rest of the map, the answer had to have been with him as well. What else did we pull off the stiff? Something that looked like a key? I didn't see anything that looked like a keyhole. A cipher of some sort?"

Elena reached into the pack and pulled out the bundle that was Mr. Worley's last earthly remains. She spread them over the ground. "Buttons look normal to me, they have just plain loops on the back for the thread. His clothes are scraps, we cut them apart thoroughly. Same with his hat. That leaves…"

"That leaves his peg leg, although I'm sure it never really was *his*." Max scooped it off the ground and held it close, going over every detail. It was well made, carved out of a single block of wood, and polished smooth. Max could not see or feel any cracks or ridges that might suggest a hidden compartment and, tug as he might, it did not break apart either.

He held it up and stared down its length, as if gauging the warp of a pool cue. He looked at its end, roughly two inches in diameter.

Max began…"Worley did not use a peg leg as far as we know. Somebody cut off his leg so that no one would wonder why there was a wooden leg in the coffin with him. That same person probably hid the map in the china. That map led us here and, surprise, surprise, the place on the map has a floor with holes that fit the end of this peg leg perfectly. Whoever set the whole thing up put the leg in the same coffin as the map because he knew that the man who used the map would need the leg. That person is me."

The peg leg had no straps to secure to the stump, only a wide wooden cup designed to fit over the end of the leg. It was a tight fit, and Max had to work to squeeze what remained of his shin and calf into the hollow cup on top, twisting the wooden object back and forth to get his leg all of the way in. Satisfied that he was as secure as he could be, he waggled it in the air at Elena a few times before standing up and taking a few tentative steps.

"Well?" asked Elena.

"Hurts like a sonofabitch. Tighter than a nun's sphincter. The average guy back then was much smaller, so if whoever carved the thing had the average man in mind, he would have made it many sizes too small for me. I'll be sore as hell tomorrow, but I think I can manage long enough to take a look around."

"I'll be right with you if it gets too much."

"No you won't. I'm even more certain that whatever surprise awaits is pressure activated. Those holes down there are the perfect fit for the end of this peg leg and my guess is that when I step into each hole, it deactivates some sort of switch. There is no telling if your weight would set it off and get us both caught in the same trap. I think this was intended to be a one man evolution and I'm gonna have to take point on this one."

"What if you panic again? What if you freeze up down there?"

"I won't. I'm over it. Sometimes you have to push all that shit down deep inside and drive on. Focus on the mission. That's what I'm gonna do."

Elena remembered the dread and horror she felt and how her skin began to burn and blister when Max was taken away from her in the hospital. "You can't leave me up here alone."

"Why not? I'll leave you the M4. A rifle is no good for exploring a tunnel. I'll take the Glock."

"No," replied Elena, exasperated, "if you leave me out in the sun, I will die."

Max knew better than to laugh. "No you won't. Okay? You will be fine out here, I promise."

"You do not understand Max. If you go down there, I will go with you."

"Well shit. That is a no-go. Like I said, we both can't go through that tunnel together."

"And I'm not staying up here in the sun without you."

"Okay. Fine. We'll just have to wait here until nightfall. Then I will go down and you can stand watch by your own vampire self." Max popped off the peg leg and lay back in the sea oats.

"Since we are going to have some downtime, I'm gonna take a nap. Holler if any of your pasty white friends show up."

"Now?"

"Why the hell not? It's broad daylight, we have good visual coverage of all the angles of approach, and I have a feeling I'm going to be up all night. You have to rest when you can because you never know when you are going to get another chance. Learned that back in boot camp. Take the first watch."

With that Max closed his eyes. Elena watched him a minute, until his breathing became steady, and then she sat on the trunk of the fallen tree and looked around. Max was right, she could see far in all directions from this point and would see someone approaching long before they could see her. She felt relieved. For a moment she was certain he would go down the stairs in spite of her objections and that she would have to go rushing after him lest the sun burn her to a cinder. As it was, the sun did not have long to set and she did get a chance to watch it go down. She sat silently, scanning the fields and woods below them, waiting.

Elena found Max very exasperating at times. He could go from full speed ahead to all stop in a heartbeat. He would worry about matters she considered trivial and then act flippant in the middle of a life or death situation. He could go from boorish lout to sophisticated gentleman of letters in a blink of an eye. Worst of all, he still did not believe her after everything that had happened to them. Was he thick in the head or did he just not care? She hoped he cared. She wanted him to care.

As the sun slipped into the west and shadows overcame their hilltop sanctuary, Elena slid off her log and nudged Max awake.

"Ready? Good." Max pulled on his night vision goggles and forced his stump into Mr. Worley's wooden leg once more. "Take the rifle, remember what I taught you, and stay out of sight. If I run out of there, tearing Hell for leather, don't talk, keep up." With that, he was gone.

Chapter Twenty-Three

Max gingerly made his way down the steps, his light piercing the gloom. With nightfall, even the top of the steps was as black as pitch. Furthermore, he felt unbalanced on the peg leg, so he put his hands against the walls to brace himself. The night vision goggles were worthless below ground as there was no amplifying ambient light beyond the threshold. He would have to stick with the flashlight. At the last step he paused and took a moment to play the light across the room, sizing up the space he was about to traverse. He felt the claustrophobia and panic began to rise again. He pushed the feelings back down. *The mission, concentrate on the mission.*

Nothing had changed since he last looked. All was quiet. Carefully, he extended the end of the wooden leg into the stagnant air and gradually brought it down into the first hole. It slid in smoothly and Max felt a slight give after it had contacted the bottom. He pushed himself forward and brought his right foot down on the floor halfway between the first and second hole. The floor creaked as it gave slightly under his full weight but it held and nothing happened. Putting all of his weight on his right foot, he lifted his left and carefully swung it forward and into the next hole. Still unscathed, he took the next step, and the next step, and the next step, until he was safely across.

The next tunnel was much tighter than the stairwell and, although the roof remained intact, roots pierced the ceiling and hung down like the hair of a drowned woman. He slowly moved forward, counting off twenty paces from the first room. His stump was already beginning to chafe something fierce against the rough wood of the peg leg. Max was certain he would be bleeding by the time he could take the damned thing off.

At the end of the tunnel, the hanging roots had grown so thick that Max had to struggle to push past them and into the room beyond. Slightly larger than the first, its walls and floor were much rougher, comprised only of irregular, bare earth. Beams still held up the ceiling, but chunks of it had fallen over the years leaving mounds of soil here and there. Max pointed his light directly toward the back of the cave like room and was rewarded by a brilliant answering flash. A great deal of very reflective and shiny stuff was placed in alcoves cut into the far wall.

Rather than walking directly across the floor to see what was causing such a golden reflection, Max put his back against the wall and sidled along it, avoiding the center of the room.

Only an idiot would run straight in. Back to the wall.

As he crept closer, he could see that his flashlight was reflecting off a series of large shelves cut deep into the earth. The centerpiece was a large wrought iron chest, its lid open, with hundreds, if not thousands, of golden coins piled high and spilling over onto the shelf and the floor below. Max tried to quickly calculate the pile's street value, but he gave up. Too many zeros. It was obviously a trap: nobody would leave a chest wide open like that and whoever did wanted someone to rush right up and start stuffing their pockets. He was not about to fall for that sort of cheap trick. Thinking about how he might be able to use some sort of grappling hook to snag the chest from a distance, he slowly began to creep back to the entrance.

With a rumble and a growl, the wall behind him burst open and he was pinned by two arms wrapped around his chest. Max pitched forward, rolling in the dirt. The arms around him felt like iron bands and he kicked wildly trying to regain his footing. He could smell fetid breath on his neck, ripe with the sickly sweet smell of decay.

Max got his feet under himself and pushed, bearing the whole weight of his assailant on his back. Just then, he felt a sharp, stabbing pain lance through his left shoulder, right in the center of his trapezius.

"Oh, hell no!" he shouted. "Fucking biting me?" Max threw himself backward, both legs pistoning into the soft earth. He heard a grunt of pain behind him as they slammed into the wall. The stench of its breath thickened as the impact forced it to exhale. Max felt its grip on him loosen for a second, and then tighten up once more. He could feel blood tricking down his shoulder as he leaned forward and then threw himself back against the wall again and again. His flashlight had been knocked from his hand at the first blow, but it dangled from the lanyard looped around his wrist and the light flashed randomly throughout the room as they struggled. The place lit up in strobe flashes as if the struggling figures were not locked in a life or death fight, but were simply thrashing dancers in the nastiest of mosh pits. Max kept smashing into the wall until he felt the grip around his arms loosen.

He felt more pain in his shoulder, this time right at the nape of his neck. Max put his head down and ran full tilt at the opposite wall, planning to turn sideways at the last moment, hoping that smashing into the wall at an angle might push the thing off his back. Almost all the way across, he was pulled backward with a sudden jerk that rattled his teeth. The arms were yanked away from around him and his legs flew out from under him as he did an involuntary back flip and landed face down in the sand. He spat out a mouthful of sand and raised his head to see just what in Hell had been tearing him up.

His attacker was struggling to his feet, hunched over and breathing hard. On his hands and knees, Max backed up quickly, scrambling to bring his flashlight to bear. Whatever clothing the man had once worn, only a few decayed scraps now remained, the rest long lost to rot and mold. The man's pale face was framed by tangled hair that draped across his shoulders like a shawl. His long beard was matted across his chest. Utterly insane yellow eyes gleamed with a feral light and fixed Max with a gaze of pure unadulterated rage and hatred. Seeking to tear out the intruding human's throat, claw like hands reached for Max as he lunged forward, only to be jerked back again.

In the beam of crisp LED light, Max could see what was keeping the ragged man at bay. A long chain trailed from a steel collar welded around his neck to a coffin shaped depression in the wall. It must have been covered by a thin layer of earth just waiting for someone to walk by. The man lunged at Max over and over, hungrily growling as he reached for him, but each time, the chain snapped taut and he was jerked back. Max was reminded of the mean-assed old Rottweiler that lived on the farm down the road when he was a kid. The dog was kept chained to a tree by the driveway and every time Max would ride by on his bike, the dog would try to get him. It lunged after Max over and over, each time stopped short by his tether. The dog did not bark, but gave a low growl that was full of intense purpose. Frustrated after a few attempts, the growl would increase in pitch and the dog would begin to drool as he charged and snapped at the boy on his bicycle. This guy had the same look of anger and frustration, but he also had a madness in his eyes: one of sheer starvation, as if he had eaten in centuries.

"Jesus Christ," Max said in amazement as he looked at the man, keeping just out of his reach. He snarled and snapped his jaws, the saliva running down his chin. "Somebody lock you up down here? Chain you to keep you from running away so you could stay and guard the loot? That's fuckin' sick, man."

The man growled and snapped, the chain humming with every lunge. Max put a hand up to the top of his shoulder. It came back wet with blood. "Shit!" Max thought his tetanus shots were up to date. Hell, the Marines had him vaccinated with every possible vaccine over the years...several times. Antibiotics. He would have to get some of those for sure. Max once read that the human mouth was the dirtiest of all the mammals and this particular specimen did not look very hygienic at all.

Max pulled the Glock from his waistband and pointed it at the writhing figure. "I don't want to kill you, OK? I don't shoot people in cold blood. Just relax and let me get what I came here for and I will call the emergency services and they will come and get you. You look like you need a hospital. I will help you, just let me by."

The chests were well within reach of the chain and Max would have to go through the insane man's territory to get to them.

Max tried again, slowly. "You are in need of medical attention. Relax and sit down and I will get you out of here. I will get you the help you need."

The man lunged again and somewhere behind him a single rusted link gave way, parting the chain. Straight at Max he flew, arms outstretched and hands grasping for Max's neck. His open mouth showed yellowed but very sharp looking teeth, an excited keening emanated from deep within his throat.

The roar of the Glock sounded like a thunderclap in the enclosed space, deafening Max for an instant. He had hesitated only briefly, afraid of killing what obviously was an abused and neglected mental patient, but his instinct for self preservation won out and he had pulled the trigger. The bullet entered the man's chest, dead center, and his lifeless form slammed into Max, carried by the momentum of his charge. Max pushed the body off. He was covered with the dead man's blood. He had a moment of fright that the blood may have gotten into the open wounds in his neck and shoulder. *Shit! What sort of germs did this fucking homeless looking guy carry? Aids? Hepatitis?* Luckily, the blood of the dead man had just soiled the front of his shirt. Max would still need his wounds cleaned.

Max slumped into a sitting position for a moment.

"You crazy son of a bitch!" Max shouted at the lifeless form, "Why did you make me shoot you! I was going to help you, man!

This is fucking insane!"

He could feel the shakes coming on again, so he pulled his pill bottle out of his shirt pocket and palmed two oxycontin into his mouth and chewed them before swallowing them dry. The drug hit his bloodstream about the same time the adrenaline wore off so he experienced a few minutes of dizziness before the shakes subsided. More relaxed, but still pissed that some asshole had locked the pitiful creature in a hole and made him into a human guard dog, Max slowly got up. He had done many things in Iraq and Afghanistan that he was not proud of, but he had never killed someone who was chained down and he was determined to find out who had put the man down there and make them pay. It never crossed his mind that when he and Elena first arrived, the entrance to the tunnels looked as if it had been sealed for centuries.

A few pokes in the ribs with the toe of his boot ensured that the man was truly dead and Max went back to the task at hand. The chest piled high with gold was still very inviting, but, as his father always said, *if something looks too good to be true, it's because it probably is.*

It was too obvious a temptation to risk messing with it. Insurgents delighted in hiding an IED under something tempting whether it be a cache of weapons or a suitcase full of important looking papers. If it looked like something an American might want to grab without thinking, it usually had a nasty surprise hidden somewhere close. *Focus on the mission. What is the mission? The dagger. Get the dagger and fuck anything else.*

From Elena's description, the dagger was not covered with gold or jewels, but was more of a tool. Teach had this tool on him at all times…had to, just to make the "magic" work—if he understood Elena's explanation correctly. The real question was, did whoever buried it down here regard it as something special, or just another knife. If it was placed in the crypt after Teach died, the person may not even have known that it was something special, just that it was prized possession of the boss man.

Max slowly worked along the wall, out from the alcove with the chest and toward the corners of the room, digging into the soft earth with the toe of his boot. He kept his flashlight focused on the dirt in front of him, watching for tripwires or pressure switches. The second time across the room, he unearthed a tuft of fabric. He stopped and knelt down to look closely. It looked like the sleeve of a heavy jacket or coat. From his hip pocket he pulled a long coil of five-fifty cord, so named because of its five hundred and fifty pound tensile strength—paracord was originally used to secure paratroopers to their parachute canopies. As usually the case for anything found to be remotely useful in the military, troops in the field had found a million and one uses for the lightweight but strong and compact nylon cord. Any vet worth his salt does not go out into the field without a coil or two in his rucksack. Max was a firm believer in always having some on hand.

He cut a small hole in the fabric and then looped one end of his paracord through, securing it with a slipknot. Gently shuffling backward, he slowly uncoiled the cord and stopped when he was about ten feet away. Max paused, took a deep breath, and yanked hard. Dust and dirt plumed as the coat came free from the earth. Nothing else happened.

Grinning at his own paranoid-level caution, Max pulled it to him and looked over the coat. Corroded brass buttons were dull in the bright, LED light of his Surefire. The coat was long, it would come down to the ankles of anyone wearing it, and made of canvas or some other thick material. A leather band was draped across the coat, secured to it by loops of material at the shoulder and waist as if it were a sash. Max could see several leather pouches sewn onto the leather sash and from those protruded the decaying wooden butts of several flintlock pistols. In the last pouch, there was something different. He gave it a tug and it slid out into his hand.

The black stone blade had a rough appearance that reminded Max of objects he had seen in museums. The blade was made by a skilled set of hands, working over hours, chipping away tiny flakes of obsidian until a razor sharp edge was fully formed. Sharper than a surgeon's scalpel. Sharp enough to cut out a man's living heart so quickly that the heart still beat as it was offered up to the sun. This was obviously what Max had come to find and he slipped the blade into his boot.

He turned to go when his flashlight caught the pile of gold. It sparkled invitingly.

Fuck. There has to be a way to get a nice payday from all this fucking trouble. But it was rigged, it had to be. No way was someone going to leave it all hanging out there on display like a twenty dollar whore if they did not want someone to just reach out and grab the shit.

Next to the large chest were several smaller ones about the size of a shoebox, with their lids firmly closed. Max thought about that for a second.

Why was the big one left open, but the little ones closed? If they left the pile of gold in the open to tempt some poor idiot into triggering a trap, does that mean then that the smaller ones are booby trapped as well? Do I just grab it and see what happens? Fuck that!

Max's solution came in the form of his five-fifty cord which he gingerly tied through the small brass handle on the nearest of the smaller chests. Yet another use for one of the most useful pieces of a GI's gear: pulling treasure chests out of the wall.

He unwound the cord until he was standing at the room's entrance and gave a little tug.

The box inched toward him.

Nothing. He gave another tug.

It slid another inch or two and still nothing happened.

Emboldened by this, Max pulled on the cord until the chest slid out of the alcove and fell to the dirt floor with a dull thud. He breathed a sigh of relief at the stillness that followed. The big chest was the trap and Max had avoided it with a little Marine Corps know-how.

A metallic clang broke the silence, followed by a low rumble.

"Shit!" Max turned to run as the far wall began to crumble away. He only picked up his pace when he heard several low growling sounds come out of the space where the wall had been. The chest bounced behind him at the end of the cord like and eager dog running along on a leash, bouncing back and forth.

The growls became louder and nearer when Max reached the room with the holes in the floor. He tried to get his peg leg into the first few holes but said, "Fuck it," and dove for the stairs. There was a crash and the whooshing sound of something very heavy and very sharp cutting through the air where Max would have been had he been travelling in the opposite direction. He hit the stairs as the growls behind him were turning into very angry sounding shrieks of rage.

Max popped out of the grave going full throttle.

"Gimme the grenades!" he shouted to a startled Elena.

"What?"

"The bag, gimme the fucking bag!"

Elena tossed him his rucksack. He caught it in midair and dumped the contents onto the ground next to the gravestone. He thought he could see movements down below.

One by one he picked up the white phosphorus grenades and pulled their pins before tossing them down the stairs.

"Max, what?"

Breathing heavily, he held up one hand to silence her as he counted to himself and backed off from the grave.

Four muffled explosions came in rapid succession, each one tossing a plume of white smoke and a shower of sparks up and out of the grave. Max knew that the explosions would do nothing, the grenades did not do damage that way. The only purpose of the small amount of explosive in each olive drab cylinder was to spread chunks of burning white phosphorous as far as possible. Those chunks burn at about five thousand degrees Fahrenheit and put a world of hurt on anybody unfortunate to get too close. Max was satisfied to hear the sounds of agony coming from below. Whatever had been coming after him now had something else to worry about.

Orange flames began to lick out of the opening and cast an orange glow over the top of the hill. Tar was an excellent preservative on wood, but it was flammable as hell. After a few moments, Max could hear crashes as the supporting stanchions and beams began to burn through. He was certain that, by the time the fire had burned itself out, the entire place would collapse, burying everything. He made a mental note to come back there someday with a backhoe and some very large and trustworthy guys.

"Max, what happened." Elena said, looking at Max in shock.

"Just a couple of glitches. I got them sorted out. Now if you could help me get this wooden leg the fuck off. It's really fucking killing me." He took a few steps toward her then suddenly jumped into her, knocking her to the ground beneath him as the first bullets snapped through the air.

Chapter Twenty Four

After years in combat, Max knew intimately the distinct sound of a bullet passing through the air nearby and had Elena down and behind cover before the sound of the muzzle blast even registered on his ears. Travelling at over twice the speed of sound, a rifle bullet passes with a crisp *snap*, pushing its own miniature sonic boom with it. When Max heard it, he knew that a bullet had just passed by, damned close too, and his reflexes simply took over.

"Who the fuck is shooting at us?" Max pulled the rifle out of Elena's hands. More incoming rounds were impacting on the fallen oak, showering them with splinters.

"Almos' men I think."

Max lifted his carbine over the trunk and fired a burst in the general direction of the shooter.

"When the hell did vampires start using M-16s?" More pieces of the tree flew up as they fired back in answer.

"I don't know!" Elena screamed back at him, holding her

fingers in her ears. "Probably when you showed up and broke all the fucking rules."

Max grinned at that. "That's me, baby. I love to shake things up!" He pulled his night vision goggles down over his eyes and squirmed through the grass to the bottom of the uprooted tree and peered down the grassy slope. The roots gave him some cover from which to check out the situation. There was plenty of ambient light now that he was above ground and the scene revealed in his goggles was a two-toned world of green and gray. The view through night vision never looked real to Max and he always felt like he was playing a video game with them on. Games like this were all too real though and he focused on the muzzle flashes coming from the tree line. He counted one shooter and one weapon.

Max fired a burst, aiming just under the flashes that marked the end of their attacker's M-16. An M-4 carbine like his pulled high and to the right on automatic fire and Max was trying to walk his bullets into his target. He rolled away just before another burst from down the hill shredded the roots and let Max know that he had missed again.

"How the fuck did Almos' guys find us all of the way out here?"

"When you went underground, I felt myself turning back into one of them, they must have sensed me."

"I thought they couldn't. Wasn't that what all that bloodletting crap was about?"

"They could not sense me as me. They could sense another vampire in the area and they must have assumed it was me. It would have taken only a matter of moments to fly here."

"Well that's just fucking dandy. How about you sense them first next time, okay."

"Everything is so muddled when you are around, I must have missed their arrival."

More bullets snapped into the tree. The guys chasing after Elena may have been warriors once, but they sure were not used to modern weapons. Most of the shooter's bullets were going high and Max hoped that maybe he would run out of ammo before he actually figured out to use the assault rifle properly.

"I got one guy in the trees. Any idea if there are any more?"

"I don't know. I can't see in the dark and I don't feel a thing. I might as well be blind and deaf right now."

"Just try to watch my back." Max passed her the Glock. "Just point and shoot."

Max popped up and let off a few rounds before popping back down again. The goggles were throwing off his aim and he was certain that the optics had been damaged in his tussle down below with the chained man.

He suddenly heard a cry of alarm from Elena rapidly followed by the loud report of her pistol. Turning, he was momentarily blinded by the fire, the light overwhelming the intensifier for a second before internal sensors automatically turned down the gain. His vision returned just in time to see the shadow rushing toward him a heartbeat before it plowed into him.

Max was pushed aside by the force of the blow, the peg leg falling off as he rolled with the impact. Almos' men may not have been used to using the modern rifles, but they were still warriors of ages past and the remaining two had flanked Elena and Max while the first had them pinned down behind the fallen tree, using the smoke and flames emanating from the grave to conceal their advance.

"Fuck!" Max tried to bring his rifle to bear, but someone was on top of him, raining blows down on his head. He struck back with the butt of the carbine and felt it impact. He shoved hard and felt the weight topple off him. Pulling off his goggles, he found himself staring right in to the leering face of Lajos, broken nose and all. He barely had time to register the sight of the black corregated butt end of an M-16 rifle speeding toward him. Light flashed painfully bright behind his eyes before he fell into darkness.

Elena screamed as Lajos' blow knocked Max's body limp. She pointed the Glock at Lajos and pulled the trigger. The shot went wild and he was on her before she could take another. The disfigured vampire slapped the gun from her hands and then knocked her to the ground with a backhand to the face. She struggled as best she could, but she was still seeing stars as the burned creature pinioned her arms behind her. Certain that the rifle butt to Max's face had ended his life, she could not help but cry out in pain and anguish. Lajos laughed, "See how we beat the living man with his own tools."

"Kill them?" slurred the other vampire, with lips burned almost completely away.

"Him? No." Lajos gestured for his friend down the hill to join them. "Almos wants him alive. As for her, he no longer cares for her. He will have the human, but she is mine."

Alive, Elena thought, *Max is alive!*

Lajos strode over to where Elena was being held and without

warning or ceremony, punched her full force in the stomach. The air was forced from her lungs and she collapsed. Only the strong grip of her captor kept her from falling to the ground.

"I cannot imagine how you can take any pleasure in being with this man. Look how weak he has made you." Lajos punched her again before she could fully breathe again. "Let her go. She is not going to be any trouble." At this command, she was released to tumble to the ground.

"Vida. Orbon. Take the man away now. I will soon follow."

"How do we do that, Lajos? We cannot fly with him," said Vida as he stepped into the circle of light, the barrel of his M-16 still smoking.

Lajos grabbed the rifle out of Vida's hands. "Drag him down the hill and to the road beyond the trees. Act as if there was an accident and wave for the next passing motorist to stop. Kill the motorist and take the car to the airport at Wilmington. Almos has a cargo plane chartered for us there and we will leave before sunrise. I will join you there."

"Yes Lajos." Subdued, the two vampires each grabbed one of Max's arms and pulled his limp body through the sea oats and down the hill. His head lolled from side to side with every bounce and bump, blood still trickling from his nose.

Lajos returned his attention to Elena with a kick to the ribs that made her see stars.

"Almos does not care about you any more, little run away girl. He has a new toy to play with."

Elena rolled over and tried to get up on her hands and knees. Lajos kicked her hard in the back of the thigh, right in the sciatic nerve. Searing electrical pain shot down her thigh, across her calf, and exploded in her foot with such a white hot fire that she collapsed onto her belly. One of Lajos' favorite games was to gradually take apart a living victim piece by piece, and, over the years, he had learned all of the places in the human body where the slightest pressure or pinprick could cause extreme pain. His next kick landed at the angle of her jaw right where the facial nerve popped around the angle of the mandible. Another searing hot jolt of pain shot through Elena's skull.

"You could have stayed with us and joined our happy family, you little wretch. You could have enjoyed all of those years of prey and the wealth we took from them. Oh, the times you missed, little bird. Good feasting during war. Our homeland has seen so much war that we never had to go thirsty."

He circled her and then kicked her in the ribs again, leaving her shocked diaphragm spasming and unable to draw breath. Elena's vision was beginning to gray out. Panicking, she scrabbled in the dirt as if she would find her next breath hidden there and her skittering fingers came across one of the wooden fence posts that once surrounded the grave, now long since fallen and forgotten. She gripped it tightly in both hands as if the solid piece of wood could anchor her to consciousness.

"Almos will certainly destroy your love once he has extracted his secret from him. What he will do to him, however, will pale in comparison to what I am going do to you." He kicked her again and she gripped the post tighter, willing herself to stay awake.

"I will bite through your hamstrings so you cannot run or kick. Then I will break both your arms so you cannot struggle so I can feast on your body. Shall I chew off your breasts first perhaps?

Tear out your cold and forgotten womb?"

As Lajos rambled, Elena's vision swam back into focus, and then brightened. The darkness of night seemed to blossom into the crisp clear colors of the day. Her pain was rapidly subsiding, the ache in her chest and lungs dwindling away to nothing. She ventured a glance down the hill and saw that the vampires dragging Max off had made significant progress. With every step they took farther away, her pain became less and less.

Elena remembered the hospital. When they were wheeling Max deeper into the building away from her, her humanity went with him and she slowly felt her inhumanity return. Unlike then, she was not at the mercy of the sun. Unlike then, she did not fear her return to the undead world. This time she was in her element and every passing second she felt her old strength filling her once more. Lajos was not used to passing back and forth from one plane of existence to another like Elena. She had felt this change so many times with Max that she recognized it easily. Distracted by his own lust for cruelty and the anticipation of what he was planning to inflict on Elena, he did not notice the changes in and around him.

Elena gripped the post even tighter, waiting for him to circle around to her head again.

"Please..." she whimpered. "Please..."

"It is too late for mercy now, after all these years," said Lajos as he raised his foot for another kick.

Twisting and pushing off the ground with both renewed and powerful legs, she thrust the sharpened end of the post at him. The tip caught him under the ribcage and penetrated deeply before sliding up toward his heart. Elena shoved with both hands and felt the give as it slid into its goal.

Lajos started and bucked backward, clawing at the wooden fence post. He could not cry out past the foul blood streaming from his mouth and nose. Barely audible gurgles escaped his lips with a spray of crimson.

"In the words of my beloved Max: fuck you, asshole!" Elena twisted the post and felt something give as Lajos, eyes rolled back into his head, collapsed into himself and was no more. His body was already an amorphous cloud of dust and ash by the time Elena scooped up Max's carbine.

They were all the way down the hill and halfway to the tree line by then. Elena felt invigorated and vibrating with energy. The answer was clear: she was on the hill, away from Max and in full possession of her powers. The vampires were very much under the influence of whatever it was that could make Elena human again. They were with Max so they were as good as human and humans were killed very easily by bullets. Elena put the rifle to her shoulder as she had been taught and looked through the sights. She aligned the front site with the center of the back of the taller figure, relaxed as much as she could, and pulled the trigger.

Three bullets roared away and flew down the slope. The first struck in the small of his back, the second between the shoulder blades, and the last one neatly took off the top of his head. He pitched forward, still holding Max's arm, pulling him from the grasp of the other vampire.

Incredibly slowly, the other vampire began to turn to face Elena. He was moving with a human's muscles and a human's reflexes. Elena watched him leisurely as he tried to bring his gun to bear with glacial slowness. *Sometimes it sucks to be human.*

She played with him, shooting out his knees first so that he had to fall down and kneel before her. Elena let him sit like that for a moment, on his knees and gazing up the hill at her as if he was praying in supplication to his goddess of the night, his Hecate. She shot him in both shoulders when he tried to shoot up at her and she delighted in watching his bullets float by high over her head.

Tired of her game, Elena shot him in the face with her last burst, the bolt locking open over an empty magazine. His head was gone in a flash of gore, so she was certain he was dead. She ran down the slope to Max, becoming more and more human with every step until she was fully whole again when she took him in her arms.

"Wake up Max!" She kissed him deeply and with every fiber of her being. She kept kissing his slack lips until she felt him kissing her back. She opened her green eyes to see his brown ones looking back into hers.

He broke the kiss. "Did you get 'em?"

"Yes, Max."

"All of them?"

"Of course, Max."

"That's my girl." Max closed his eyes and swallowed. "Okay, now I'm really pissed. What say you and I hop on a plane and take care of business once and for all."

"Yes, Max. We will do that very soon."

"Groovy," said Max as he passed out again.

Chapter Twenty-Five

"How do you plan to carry that gun through airport security?" Elena stood over Max as he sat at the galley table in the *Vengeance*.

"The same way I always do."

"You've done it before?"

"Of course I have. I always travel with heat. No telling when some wild-eyed radical is going to decide to bring down the plane."

"But how?"

Max held up the pistol, completely black and all business. "This is a Glock automatic. The Brainchild of Herr Gaston Glock and a fine example of engineering. The movies get it all wrong. It is not ceramic. It will set off a metal detector. It will be seen on an x-ray. What it does have is a plastic frame."

He depressed the disassembly switch on the side and pulled the rectangular steel slide off the polymer frame. Then, he popped the barrel and recoil spring out of the slide.

"See? The part with the handgrip and trigger is almost all plastic. The part that goes boom is steel, but there is not a lot of it." Max reached down and popped off his prosthetic leg, laying it on the table.

"Once I take the few metal pieces out of the plastic frame, I can carry it anywhere and it won't set off any alarms unless they actually pat me down. All I have to do is hide the metal parts. My leg here, a wonder of modern technology, has many metal parts in it. It *will* set off a metal detector. If I know I am going to set one off anyway, all I have to do is make sure that when they wand me, the only things that light up are the things they expect to light up."

"The leg," said Elena.

"Exactly." Max began pulling strips of foam rubber padding out of the cup that held his leg in the prosthetic. "My first prosthetist was a paranoid bastard just like me. He showed me that if I pulled out an inner layer of padding, shoved in the slide and barrel and a few other metal parts of a compact pistol like a Glock, I could cover them up and slip in my leg and no one would be the wiser.

"The metal detector will go off, but what do they do when it goes off? They wand you and if the only thing that reads positive is your fake leg, then they just think that your leg is the problem. They can see I'm not faking." Max put his leg on the table, it ended mid-shin in a rounded lump of puckered pink scar. "See? I'm a poor, harmless, old cripple. Even if some jerk makes me pull off the leg, they still won't be able to see the gun parts unless they start tearing the thing apart. Who wants to be the guy who tears apart a cripple's fake leg? Foolproof."

"The sympathy angle as well, then?"

"Of course. All's fair in love, war, and smuggling, babe. If it works, it works. Hurts like hell though. Without the padding, the metal digs into my stump something fierce. I only have to walk around with the pain for a little while. I usually go to the bathroom right after going through security and pull out the parts and put them in my pocket."

Elena watched as Max finished taking apart the pistol and stowed it away. She balanced the stone dagger in her hand, flipping it end over end and spun it around, playing with it as if she were some sort of seasoned knife wielding desperado.

"It feels wonderful Max."

"What does?"

"The dagger. When I hold it, it feels like electricity flowing up my arm and into my heart. I feel vibrant and powerful. This morning, while you were still asleep, I walked into the sunlight and I did not feel the sun's bite at all. It was not like when I am with you, I didn't feel human at all and the sun was not a warm pleasant thing. I could still feel the fire building up all around me, but it was as if the power of a thousand life forces were surrounding me, penetrating me, and pushing back the rays of the sun."

"No need for sunscreen then." Max grinned across the table at her.

"I also felt stronger," Elena went on, ignoring his sarcasm, "faster, and my senses are so much more keen than ever before. It is as if it amplifies my powers a hundredfold."

"Power is addictive, Elena. After you kill Almos and take his powers into you as well…that's how it works, right…that's a hell of a lot of power for just one person. What if all of a sudden you decide you like being the most powerful vampire in the entire world and you decide to take over? What then? Not that it would be a bad idea, you being the queen of darkness and me being in charge of the harem."

"Harem? What? No. You're just teasing me. I couldn't...I wouldn't...that would make me just as bad as he who I wish to destroy."

"Exactly. What is that line from Nietzsche? *Be careful when you fight the monsters, lest you become one.* Be careful Elena. Half a millennia obsessing about taking this guy out. How many years did you put into just finding that thing?" He gestured to the obsidian blade in her hand. "Over a hundred? Be sure that you don't lose yourself and find out that you have ultimately lost in winning."

"Nietzsche would say that I am already a monster."

"I don't think you are a monster. I think you are quite a lovely girl with a real shitload of pretty fucking horrible baggage. I watched you in the park that one day. Playing with the kids, walking through the gardens. That is the real you. Inside that bloodsucking exterior is a normal human girl who likes ice cream and puppies and smelling the fucking flowers. That's the real you and that is the part I don't want to see go away when you finally do this thing. Take it from me, if you wrap your whole existence around something like this, you are going to feel completely lost when it is all over, and you will ask yourself, 'why bother getting up in the morning?' I'm afraid that you might fill that void with something really crappy like taking that little toy of yours and making yourself up as the royal fucking queen of the undead. It would be a hell of a temptation."

"I would never let that happen. I would destroy it, throw it into the ocean or something."

"Or something. If you start to let that thing change you, make you lose the humanity that you say you have been chasing for centuries, I will personally kick your ass and get rid of that thing myself."

"Thank you, Max. I sincerely mean that."

"I sincerely intend to kick your ass too. Don't forget it."

"I won't."

"Fine. Now we have to get your knife past security too."

"Don't worry about that."

"Why not?"

"I said it amplifies my powers. I will get by, leave it to me."

"You've pulled through so far...fine, I'll leave that to you. As for the new funds, I think we should stash most of them in a good old fashioned safety deposit box and take a bunch with us in case we run into some expenses we don't want traced to your accounts."

The *new funds*, as Max had taken to calling the contents of the small chest taken from Teach's trove, was a not insignificant pile of precious stones. Diamonds, of course, but also rubies, emeralds, sapphires, and opals. Neither Max nor Elena could guess how much the find was worth, but it was bound to be into the millions if, and this was a very important if, they could move the stuff without attracting the attention of the Internal Revenue Service. Elena had amassed some very decent sized bank accounts over the years, but if they were going overseas to look for trouble, an untraceable source of funding was essential. Max was certain that he could get a decent price for some of the stones under the table in Eastern Europe.

"How do you think you are going to get those things past customs Max? Put them in your leg as well?"

Max got up and poured himself a large glass of water from the faucet over the galley sink.

"You don't want to know," he said with a grin. "You really do not want to know." Then he popped the first one in his mouth.

She did not wait to see him finish *that* particular task, but busied herself gathering a few things for the trip. Max was waiting for her on the pier when the cab pulled up to take them to Raleigh for the flight. For Max, the advantage of living on the coast was the water and relative isolation. Isolation, however, came with a price and today the price was an over two hour drive to the nearest airport with direct flights to Europe. Elena had a passport, of course. She updated it along with all of her other documents every time she took on a new identity. It was getting much harder. When she first fled Hungary, all it took was to move to another place and give the people there another name. Now easily accessible computerized records, photographic identification, and even fingerprinting had replaced things that were done on a simple handshake less than a hundred years ago. When governments finally find a way to tie a person's DNA profile to an identification, Elena's days of slipping in and out of society will be over. Perhaps by then she would fall under some sort of non-discrimination law or at least, the endangered species act.

That Max had a second passport was not surprising to Elena in the least. He had already demonstrated his unique form of paranoia. What she did find interesting was that the passport he pulled from the rucksack was not blue, but the reddish brown of an official government passport. "They made sure that I turned everything including my left testicle back in when I was retired, but nobody asked for this, believe it or not. I knew it would come in handy someday."

Passport in hand, they rode the two hours to the airport in silence, not speaking until they cleared the ticket counter and put a hefty charge on Elena's credit card.

Max walked toward the security line, not looking at Elena, but straight ahead. The TSA functionaries methodically checked every person entering and Max was watching them to see if he could see if any were particularly busy or tired. A guy was at the end of his shift, thinking about going home to a brewski and a good steak, he might be less likely to tear Max and his leg apart looking for contraband. "OK, green eyes. Try to go into a different line than me and..." He glanced back. Elena was gone.

Max shrugged it off. She said that she was going to get herself and her new toy through security without risking either of them, but Max could not think of any way she could get *around* the checkpoint.

He stopped in front of the first station, pulled off his one shoe and dropped it as well as his wallet into a plastic bin that he then put on the conveyor belt to go through the x-ray machine. Then, holding his ticket and passport, he stepped through the metal detector; that magic portal between the clean and the unclean, the chosen few and the unwashed masses not allowed onto the concourse. It alarmed shrilly.

The TSA agent waved him over and to the side. He hesitated when Max pulled up his pant leg, pointed, and said, "Must be this little old thing. It can be a pain in the ass sometimes, but the ladies dig it."

Max could see the cogs turning in the man's head. Good. He was youngish, certainly not older than Max, and it was very likely that Max was the first amputee the guy had seen come through his line. Max could tell that he was both unnerved and embarrassed by the prosthetic.

"I'm still going to have to wand you, sir."

"Wand away," Max said cheerfully.

The agent ran the loop of the hand held metal detecting wand across Max's arms, up and down his legs, and along his body. It only chimed when he ran it across the prosthetic.

The man had knelt down to examine Max's leg, and now he looked up at Max, flushing with embarrassment. "I'm sorry sir, but I am going to have to look at your...leg a little more closely."

"Gotta do what you gotta do, kid." Max pulled his leg out of the prosthetic, making sure that the TSA agent got a good view of the end of his stump. The chafing of the Glock parts tucked under the padding had made the scar tissue on the very end of the leg red and swollen, giving it an even more painful look.

Swallowing hard, the young TSA man gazed right into the angry looking, puckered flesh. "I think I'm supposed to run it through the x-ray machine."

Max stood on one leg like a muscular flamingo, intentionally wobbling precariously close to falling. He glanced around and noticed that they had gained quite an audience. Not only had this line ground to a halt, but the ones on either side had as well, everyone looking at the one legged man standing with arms outstretched as if he was performing a curbside sobriety test.

"Foster!" came a very irritated sounding voice, "What the heck is the hold up?" Agent Foster popped up from kneeling in front of Max, still holding his leg in both hands. An older man in a TSA uniform strode up. He was much older than Max and his white hair was crew-cut and stiffly waxed. Two steel blue eyes, bordered by deep crows' feet flashed with annoyance over a handle bar moustache, also white, that framed clenched teeth.

"Just what in the hell are you doing?"

"I was just gonna check out this passenger's leg," Foster replied nervously, waving the offending limb.

"Gimme that!" The senior agent snatched Max's leg out of Foster's hands. Max still tottered.

"Whatever you two guys decide to do, do it quick, 'cause I'm getting really tired standing on one leg."

The older man held the prosthetic out to Max who took it and slid it back on. He turned on the young man who looked as if he was desperately trying not to cringe. "Listen, you stupid-assed greenhorn. Where the hell are your brains? If you feel that you have to inspect something as sensitive and personal as a fake leg, you don't do it on the side of the Goddamned line like it was a Goddamned laptop. You take him into the side room and give him a little dignity for Christ's sake. What the hell were you thinking? I come over here and I see this guy standing on one leg in front of the whole world like a doggone scarecrow while you are dicking around like an idiot! Were you seriously going to make him balance like that while you ran his leg through the x-ray machine? Seriously? Are you retarded or something?"

Foster looked like he was going to break out in tears any second but kept quiet.

"Sir, I'm sorry about this. If you want to make a complaint, there is a form you need to fill out. We can go over to my office."

"No, that won't be necessary. I've got plenty of time before my flight and I've learned not to sweat the small stuff."

The man looked down at Max's prosthetic. "Iraq?"

"Yep."

"Figured as much. I was in Vietnam. Seventh Calvary."

"I figured as much too. *Gary Owen*."

"Yeah. Gary Fuckin' Owen." He glanced down at Max's leg again as if reconsidering the need to X-ray the limb. He paused, and then looked Max straight in the eyes, one old war horse to another, and made his decision.

"Yeah, well. Sorry for embarrassment. You better get going."

"Thanks."

"You're welcome. Take care of yourself."

"Will do."

Max headed down the concourse, looking for his gate. The metal parts hidden under the padding had shifted slightly when the TSA guy was fucking around with his leg and now they really were digging into his stump like the mother of all rocks in his shoe. He could not wait until he could find a bathroom stall to hide in while he fixed the damned thing. Trying not to limp, he walked until he reached his gate.

"Hold it right there and keep your hands where I can see them!"

Max spun around to see Elena, standing with her arms crossed and a self satisfied smirk on her face.

"Not funny," Max said. "Especially not after what I just went through."

"Almost get pinched, mister Don't-Worry-I-have-a-Cunning-Plan?"

"Yeah, pretty much. Need I ask how you got by the goons?"

"The dagger gives me all of my powers even in the daylight... except around you."

"Flew in then? Mind control? Puff of smoke?"

She smiled. "Something like that."

"Ah. Well, let me hit the can so I can un-fuck my leg and then we'll board."

It took Max a few seconds to pop off his leg and pull out the parts of his Glock that went bang and stuff them in his pants pocket. He would have to put them back in the leg sometime before they landed and went through customs, but for now, he felt a hell of a lot better. The flight went without a hitch and, given that Elena had sprung for first class, very comfortable.

"Fly much?" asked Max as soon as he was able to secure a double Laphroaig, neat, from the flight attendant.

"Yes."

"No, I mean in an airplane."

"So do I. I tried to do things as normally as possible to blend in with society. Sure, I could only take the red-eye flights and had to make sure that I left after sundown and arrived wherever I was going before sunup, but I tried to act like a human as much as I could."

Max took a big gulp of his scotch. "Red-eyes, huh. I guess you never had a view like this one, then." He pointed out the window with his glass.

Elena looked out. "Oh, my God…"

The seven fifty seven had broken out of patchy cloud cover to cruise at thirty thousand feet. Clouds were spread out below them like a thick cotton-ball blanket, shining brilliant white in the sun. The sky above was a perfect cobalt blue, brilliant and pristine, with a slight darker tinge way above the horizon that gave just a hint of the edge of space. Breaks in the clouds gave Elena glimpses of a green-blue ocean full of a thousand sparkles as the sunlight flashed off the waves.

"It is so beautiful," Elena breathed, face pressed against the glass.

"I thought you would like it. Would you like to trade seats? Not that I would mind you leaning over me the entire flight. That might be kind of nice, actually."

"Yes, please. Let's switch."

After they traded seats, Elena was right back at the window.

"Never in my wildest dreams could I imagine such a sight, thank you."

"It's no big deal. I prefer the aisle anyway."

"No." I mean thank you for my life. Thank you for making me human. I never would have seen this otherwise."

"I didn't do anything."

"But you did. You don't understand it…I don't understand it…but whatever it is that makes you who you are has made you wonderfully special and I am grateful for every day that I spend with you."

"Well, when you put it that way, you are welcome indeed." He raised his glass to her in toast.

"If I am to die in the old country, I will be able to die happy, having been human for one last time."

"Whoa there, young lady. I don't want to hear any of that maudlin tear jerker crap. If you go into a fight, you go in thinking about how you are going to kill the other guy and take all of his stuff, not about what sort of shit people are going to say at your funeral. You go in to win and you don't think about anything else. We're the good guys. The guys with the white hats and we always win in the end. No doubt about it."

"You don't lack in confidence."

"I believe in thinking positively. If you psych yourself out, you fail before you even get started. Besides..."

"Besides?"

"Your homeboy owes me a boat and I'm not stopping until the son of a bitch pays up."

Chapter Twenty-Six

Customs in Budapest was cursory at best. Elena's inane chatter about bringing her American boyfriend home to meet her old and saintly *nagyanya*, or grandmother, seemed to dull any interest they had in the pair. At one point one of the customs officials clicked his tongue at the sight of Max's prosthetic, but then, with a *shit happens* shrug, let them through.

Max was surprised that they were able to hire a late model Mercedes at the airport. He was not really sure what he expected. Certainly not an oxcart, but one of those ugly, boxy Soviet era Lada sedans, leaking oil and blowing smoke, not some leather upholstered S-class. It made the four hour drive into the mountains much more pleasant.

Max's enjoyment of the scenery was marred only by Elena's extremely fast and aggressive driving style. He had been certain on more than one occasion that she was going to plow into the back of a slowly moving truck only to swerve and pass at the last instant. A couple of times, they cleared the truck only to stare directly into the headlights of oncoming traffic, before scraping back into their lane just in time to avoid a head on collision. Iraq had been less nerve-racking…at least there he could shoot back.

"I guess at some point should ask you exactly where this guy is hiding out," said Max to distract himself from sudden death.

"Hungary's northeast corner is ringed by the Carpathian mountains. With Slovakia to the North, the Ukraine to the East, and Romania to the South. These mountains have been used by thieves and warlords for millennia. It was in the Romanian Carpathians that Vlad Tepes made his stand against the Turkish invasions and gave Bram Stoker the inspiration for his poorly written fairy tale. Romanians actually regard him as a national hero, did you know that?"

"No, I did not. I actually believed that he was all made up for the book. Well, not all the way made up; I heard that there was a bloodthirsty prince who liked to impale his enemies, but not anything I would consider hero like."

"But he was. Brutal times call for brutal actions, but his was one of the first principalities to actually stop the Turkish advances. He saved Romania from the Turks and there actually are statues to him to this day."

"Truth is stranger than fiction, I guess." Max's knuckles tightened as she took an S-curve way too fast. They were in the mountains by this time, and a steep drop off was only a thin guardrail away.

"In the First World War, the Russians and the Austro-Hungarian Empire fought over those mountains for three bloody years, leaving a million soldiers dead in the valleys and on the ridges. All for nothing.

"The Carpathians do form a barrier against invasion from modern armies, though. Tanks and trucks don't cross them very well. The Nazis preferred to invade the Ukraine through Poland, so there were no huge invasions through the mountains during World War Two. Yes, they fought each other in Romania and Serbia, but the real slaughter came from the camps. Bukovina in Romania, Novaky in Slovakia, and," Elena paused, sadness crossing her face, "satellites of the Mauthausen camp in Austria. So much death, so much fear, so much misery. Almos must have reveled in it."

"Sounds like a real asshole." Max leaned over and took Elena's hand in his, gently squeezing it.

"Yes Max, he is. He fought the Turks in these mountains and so much blood came to him here. All he had to do was sit and wait like a spider while the arrogance and hubris of kings and presidents brought him all the victims he needed. He did not have to go out to hunt man because the hate-filled hearts of mankind brought him everything he needed. In wars where people die by the thousands, who notices extra bodies here and there. When people are being killed by the trainload, who notices if they had been feasted upon before they were put into the crematorium. No, the Carpathians have been very good to him. He will never leave."

"There hasn't been much bloodshed lately, why does he stay? Why not the Middle East or Africa?"

"There hasn't? Forget about the Balkan wars. The Mafia runs these mountains now. East meets West. The point where four countries come together. Instead of armies, drugs and guns cross over. People too. With the fall of the Iron Curtain, the slave trade has become one of the most profitable ventures in the criminal world. Young Ukrainian girls, destined for brothels from England to Saudi Arabia, New York to Bangkok, are first smuggled over these mountains in the trunks of Citrons to be sold all over Europe. That is how he now keeps himself in blood and money. Buying and selling girls...girls like me, Max." A single tear ran down her cheek. "Girls who are so much like who I was before he took me. Young. Pretty. Most he sells but some he keeps so he can feed. How many other young girls has he ruined? I must destroy him, once and for all."

"Fuck, Elena. Makes me want to cut his throat just hearing about him. Don't worry. We won't leave until he is nothing but a stinking, rotting carcass and just food for the crows."

"We have had a good start. Your experience in war and your powers have been a Godsend. I could not have gotten this far without you!"

"Powers? The only powers I have are sheer bullheadedness and a powerful desire to win. Where did you get the intel, I mean intelligence? It sounds like you have been keeping very good tabs on him."

"Once I diluted the taint of his blood and severed the psychic link, he could not follow me. Over the years I traveled to the old country to check up on him, to see if he was still there. These mountains have many of our kind, most solitary and existing on the fringes. I am certain that he could feel me come and go, but he never fully realized who he was sensing. In Spain, in the early nineties, I was prowling the allies of Madrid one night and came across a prostitute being beaten by her...customer. Apparently she did not please him to his satisfaction. After I tore out his throat and calmed her down, she told me how she came through Slovakia from the Ukraine by way of Almos' villa in the Carpathians. She was very frightened of me, even after I bought her some food and put her on a bus back home. So she told me everything she knew."

"And the guy? I thought you never killed a human."

Elena looked at him and gave him a predatory smile. "Men who prey on women are not human."

"Ah." *I sure as hell never want to get on her bad side.*

Mercifully, Elena slowed slightly as they drove higher up the mountains that poked into the low lying cloud cover. The road was enveloped with mist that covered the asphalt with slick moisture. At first the scenery was very bucolic, reminding Max of Alpine meadows and dotted with sheep laden farms, but the further they went from civilization the more rundown the houses and the darker the mountains. Even the trees appeared stunted and twisted to Max as if the whole land was suffering under some sort of malaise. Not despair exactly, but more of a surrender to the inevitable. Whatever that inevitability was, he could not guess.

"We are going to Josvafo, a small village in the mountains right along the border. That is where his villa is. Limestone caves riddle the hills and mountains there and the valleys are deep and twisted. It is a good place for him to smuggle and hunt. No one will follow him into one of the caves if he decides to retreat. I really doubt if retreat is anywhere in his personality anymore."

"Once a warlord, always a warlord. Sometimes you just have to bring the war to the lord, that's all."

"Indeed."

"Well boss-lady, it's your turf. What is the plan of attack?"

"We pull into the village and wait until dawn. Since you are here with me, Almos will not know that anything has changed, so we should be able to spend the night peacefully. Then we leave at first light. His villa is several kilometers to the north and I want us to get there at full daylight when he is asleep and his powers are at his weakest."

"Bust down the door and then start staking right and left!"

"Not quite. Vampires usually sleep during the day, but they can be woken and can fight during the day just like you can at night. They must stay out of direct sunlight, but an angry vampire under cover can be just as deadly during the day as at midnight. Also, remember, he now works with the Russian Mafia, if not directly, then as an intermediate. He is bound to have some humans to protect him when the sun is high. We will have to dispatch them first before we can enter."

Max grunted. "I've only got one pistol and ten rounds of ammunition for it. We are going to need more in the way of firepower if we are looking at storming what may be a well guarded and highly secure objective."

"No we don't. Leave the guards to me. I have full powers in the daylight as long as I have the dagger and as long as *you* are far away from me."

"What is it, my aftershave?"

"Your ability to make the supernatural very, very natural. Once we get in, your bullets will work just fine on Almos. He will die like any other human."

"Don't you want me to save him for you to off? Isn't that what a blood vendetta is all about?"

Elena's predatory grin returned. "It is all about destroying him. I don't care who does it, just as long as I can see his corpse disintegrate and scatter into the winds."

"Fair enough. Just remember, the first casualty of war is the plan. Be adaptable."

"Very wise. Who said it?"

"General George Patton. The old bastard was right more often than not."

Josvafo turned out to be much more quaint than Max expected. Steep roofs on the cottages gave a hint of the volume of snowfall expected every winter and their whitewashed walls were clean and well kept. Crossing a covered bridge made of stone and oaken beams brought them to the Tengerszem Hotel. It was four stories tall and all white save for the polished chestnut of the peaked roof. Red shutters, ornately carved, adorned every window. Max half expected a lederhosen clad mountaineer to pop around the corner and yodel at them. As soon as the Mercedes pulled up to the front door Max jumped out and retrieved the luggage from the trunk. He had assembled the pistol as soon as he could after clearing customs and he now appreciated the feel of it against the small of his back.

They settled in for the night and, even though Max locked the door and pulled the dresser across it as well as closing and locking the shutters, the evening passed without incident. He slept with his pistol in hand and Elena curled up next to him. They did not make love that night, but were content enough just to lie together. She was warm next to him and, as she lay across his chest, he could feel her heartbeat. She still smelled of cinnamon, something Max could never figure out, but just having her arms and legs wrapped around him made him feel whole. He liked that. Adversity brings people together and he was feeling closer and closer to her with every passing moment. They were a lot alike in his mind. She shared his sense of justice and an almost chivalrous attitude toward those who cannot help themselves.

He remembered the boy he saved during his last fight in Iraq and saw the similarity in Elena's story about saving the prostitute from her "John" in a place and time where most people would have certainly just walked on by. Max was beginning to think he had found the perfect woman: intelligent, well off, beautiful, and a red headed bundle of kick ass on two legs.

(unmarked page break here)

They awoke together to the light pouring in past the gaps in the shutters. Dressing quickly, they made certain that they lost no time getting to the trailhead where they started their hike after pulling the Mercedes off to the side, concealing it with loose brush. Hopefully, they would be back before the leaves on the braches piled all over the car began to wilt and gave away its position.

Travelling north, the kept to the gullies and valleys as they made their climb. Max made certain that they kept to the military crest, that area about two thirds up any terrain feature where one still has the high ground but is not silhouetted against the sky. As they climbed, oak trees gave way to birch, and birch to fir. Elder and raspberry bushes made their progress slow at first, tangling around their legs or blocking their path with thorns, forcing them to go around. Elena led the way, a bloodhound in REI boots and a wool sweater. Other than pushing her toward routes with better concealment, Max followed her lead. She obviously knew where she was going and they arrived shortly after noon.

Almos' villa was a large country manor that must have been built long before the turn of the century, perhaps even well before the century or two before that. Square turrets flanked the large rectangular main house and gave whomever was in them expansive views of the surrounding countryside. Max and Elena had come along a ridgeline that rose above the plateau which the complex rested, so they could look down into the yard through a cheap pair of binoculars they picked up at the hotel for a few bucks. Apparently some of the surrounding mountains were actually nature preserves and birdwatchers frequented the hotel.

There were a few outbuildings in the perimeter formed by a twelve foot high stone wall, one of which was obviously a garage as they could easily see the vehicles through the wide open doorway. Red peaked roofs covered every building and the walls were white stucco over stone.

"Hell. If I only had a silenced sniper rifle, like one of those Russian SVDs, I could take out all of the guards from here. I bet we could buy one on the black market anywhere around here."

"And the mafia brotherhood would stab you in the back as soon as you walked away." Elena replied as she peered down. "What guards, where?"

"I'm sure you see the two guys wandering along the inside of the wall, but that guy in mechanics overalls by the garage is definitely packing, he keeps checking under his shoulder to see if his gun is still there," Max chuckled. "That's a new guy's mistake. Somebody who is not used to carrying a piece is always going to be fucking with it. It is a sure giveaway."

"So three."

"Five. One in each tower as well. I don't see much more activity and the grass around the wall is not very worn down, so they really don't walk the perimeter much. They are not really guarding as much as just hanging out. Given what you told me about just how dangerous Almos and his gang is, I'm not surprised by lackadaisical daytime security. All they really need is some human types to watch the perimeter during the daylight hours. If some unlucky son of a bitch actually makes it past those clowns and into the mansion, then whatever is inside there will take care of business just fine. Am I reading this right?"

"Yes. If Almos is awakened by someone invading his own home, he will have the home advantage and he will be very dangerous. You are my secret weapon. You will nullify any power and advantage he has in his own house. When I get *you* in, *he* shuts down like a child's toy when the battery is all used up."

"It's your move, green eyes. What're your orders?"

"Hah, orders. I'm not your captain or anything."

"I'm a major. I outrank captains."

"Whatever. Just hold up here and wait. I am going to go back along the ridge until I am out of your...force field or whatever we should call it...and then I am going to move very fast and take down all of those men. When things begin to happen, move quickly to that side gate over there," said Elena, pointing, "and I will let you in. When you come near, my powers will wane, so have your gun ready."

"Yeah. No kidding."

"Very well. Watch closely, Max." Elena sidled away from their hiding place and began to creep along the ridge, keeping in the cover of the trees.

"Elena..." Max whispered after her.

"Yes?"

Max grinned. "Have fun storming the castle."

Chapter Twenty Seven

Elena kept low, hiding in the underbrush as she crawled away from Max. After a few moments, she noticed the familiar sensation of her old strength rushing back into her. Her eyesight sharpened: crisp and clear, every detail sprang forward into her vision as if she had been nearsighted all her life and someone suddenly gave her a pair of glasses. Now she could truly see and the face of the guard nearest her became as plain as if he were right next to her. He had cut himself shaving that morning.

The beating of his heart came next, regular and slow, singing in her ears with its healthy and strong rhythm of life. When she could hear the whoosh of the blood being pushed through his arteries and she could smell the rich coppery scent of it, she knew she was ready.

Faster than the human eye could follow, she flung herself down the ridge. The obsidian dagger in her right hand, she flew just above the undergrowth, dodging trees, their branches whipped by the wind of her passage. She reached the wall and leaped up and over it.

Eyes growing wide at her sudden appearance, the guard tried to bring his AK-47 to bear on her. He was too slow. Not even pausing, Elena lashed out with the dagger as she flew by. The razor sharp edge caught him in the throat, severing the larynx so he could not even gasp out a single word of alarm. Elena was already halfway across the compound before his body hit the ground.

When the dagger struck, delivering its killing blow, Elena felt a jolt of electricity run up her arm and into her chest. It was a delicious sensation and as Elena sped across the grass, she felt herself grow even stronger and she felt her nerves sing as the man's vital energies filled her and flowed through her. More intense than feeding, more electrifying than taking the life blood of a human, the dagger's cut delivered to Elena the very essence of whatever had made that man a living, breathing human being. It was as if she could steal the man's very soul. All of his thoughts and desires and memories were hers now.

The mechanic was not even looking in her direction and he died completely unaware of what had happened to him. Elena had swung the dagger much harder than was necessary, and the man's head rolled through the open garage door and came to rest under a Volvo.

Again, the man's life force flowed into her and she felt an urge to sing out loud with the sensation. She kicked her legs down hard, bouncing off the grass and sailing up toward the top of the nearest tower. She put her hands out in front of her and crashed through the nearest window in a shower of glass, the shards flying out from the frame in a deadly sharp fan that twinkled in the sunlight and sliced into the man stationed there even as Elena reached out with her dagger. Blood sprayed out from dozens of cuts as the flying glass splinters sliced into him. A red mist filled the air, swirling as Elena burst out of the opposite window and rocketed across the roof and into the next tower.

She did not even use the dagger on the next man, but grabbed him by the arm as she flew by, letting go on the other side. He fell in an arc that took him over the wall and into the trees on the other side. She could hear his heart stop as his body slammed from trunk to trunk in a pinball ride of momentum to the forest floor.

The last two human guards were together, side by side, finally realizing that their afternoon had gone horribly wrong. They opened up on that lightning streak of movement that had been laying down a trail of death and destruction throughout the formerly peaceful estate. On fully automatic fire, their AK-47 assault rifles could empty an entire thirty round magazine in a little under three seconds. Elena could see the slow steady winking of the muzzle flashes as they fired at her. She was speeding directly toward them and she could see the spent brass cartridge cases seem to float through the air, twirling end over end.

Every thirty caliber bullet that flew at her left a long trail of pulsating air in its wake as it tore through the atmosphere, three times the speed of sound. As the air expanded and then contracted, moisture condensed behind the bullets and made the following shock waves glisten and glimmer, giving Elena the impression that she was running through a summer's rainstorm. With the twist of the shoulder or the lift of a leg, she was able to dodge every one.

Running between the raindrops.

Elena flew between the upraised rifles and the men holding them, arms extended straight out. She felt a sharp *crack* vibrate through her left arm as her outstretched fist caught the man on that side full in the face, jerking his head back with enough force to break his neck instantly. In her right hand, the dagger plunged into the other guard's chest, pinioning him against the wall like a bug in a collection. As he twitched, Elena felt herself devour his life...his soul.

In an instant, Elena realized the dagger's power. The soul. It took the soul from the victim and gave whatever energy that made it what it was to the wielder. Mainlined it into them. This is why the Mayan priest had lived so long, even though he was not one of the undead. He lived off the stolen souls of his victims and when the dagger was taken from him, the life-force went with it. He had been living on stolen time. This was the source of the weapon's incredible power. She pulled it from the now lifeless body in front of her and licked the hot blood off the cold stone blade.

With it in her hand she felt incredibly powerful. She was faster, stronger. Almost invincible. Invincible. As she glided toward the gate in the wall where she had told Max to meet her, she decided she must never let the dagger go. She would never feel helpless or vulnerable again. She could rule the world of the undead with this talisman and, with the strength it gave her, she could force them into stopping the eternal war with mankind. No more young girls would be taken from their families. Lajos was not the real source of evil. He was just one vampire among many. She had to stop them all. She had the power. No more innocent lives need be destroyed. The undead would all be taken kicking and screaming into the twenty first century or she would kill every single one of the those who resisted and add their life force to her own. She would live forever. She would be a god—a benevolent god. Humankind would feed her and she would take their nightmares away.

Suddenly, as she neared the wall, she fell out of the air and onto the ground with an impact that jarred the knife from her hand. She felt human again.

"Elena," hissed Max. "Open up. You ok? I came down as soon as I saw that the shit was hitting the fan. It all happened so fast. What the fuck happened?"

Elena staggered to the gate and opened it. "I just took care of things."

Max came through the gate and stopped.

"Jesus! What the hell happened to you?"

"I'm...I'm fine." Elena was still unbalanced, reeling from the abrupt return to humanity. Gone was the intoxicating power of the dagger and gone was the temptation to keep it forever. She just felt hungry and tired.

"You are fucking covered in blood. You okay?"

Elena looked down at herself. She was drenched in red. Her arms and legs were covered and when she put her hand to her face it came back dripping. Clot covered her hair.

"I'm fine. None of it is mine apparently."

Max walked around her, giving her a wide berth.

"When you say you are going to take care of things, you sure as hell don't do it half-assed. Pick up your little toy and let's finish the job so we can all go the fuck home."

"That sounds like a fine idea." Elena scooped up the dagger and felt no rush, no return of the power. With Max near her, it was nothing more than a sharp piece of rock. Good. Elena hoped it stayed that way. She wanted to live a real life, not some faint imitation. She wanted to live and have children and grow old and die...with Max.

They strode up to the front door walked in like they owned the place. Silence was all that greeted them.

"Well sunshine? Where are the bad guys hiding out?"

Elena paused. "Down?"

"In the ground. Where else?"

Max walked forward to the main staircase opposite the front door. He stopped and looked up before getting any closer. Stairs still made him nervous.

"It looks clear up, we just need to find a way down."

"This is an old house. Any stairs down would be for the servants. They would be near the kitchen."

Elena walked to the left and Max followed. She quickly found the kitchen and the stairs that servants would have used to run down to the cellar where the food and wine were stored. She gestured to the stairs with her head and slipped down them with Max close behind.

The wine cellar was very large, and dozens of wine racks ran down its length. On the far wall were gigantic ancient casks on their sides with dusty wooden spigots facing them. They must have been there since the villa was built, back when wine was stored in huge barrels. Max walked up to the nearest one and began to feel along the edges.

"What are you doing Max?" Elena whispered.

"Feeling for drafts."

"What?"

Max moved to the next enormous cask. "Feeling for drafts. I saw this in a movie once or twice. The end of the cask is a hidden door and…Bingo!"

He squatted down and twisted on the spigot until he felt a slight give somewhere behind it. Bracing his feet on the stones in front of the cask, he gave it a strong pull and the top swung open.

"See?" Max said, dusting off his hands. "All of that television watching did not go to waste after all." He bent down and went in slowly, paying close attention to the round tunnel in front of him. He hoped that whomever was down here did not have the time or forewarning to booby trap the route of entrance. He ran his hand across the rough grained wood. Nothing. No wires or switches. Clear.

He climbed out of the cask tunnel and into the room beyond, his Glock out and at the ready. The cave was much larger than the wine cellar, larger than the entire villa above for that matter, and carved out of the solid granite mountainside. Several passageways lead off into the gloom.

Max turned to look back into the tunnel to see Elena still waiting on the other side. "Come on, Elena. The coast is clear, let's get a move on."

"Alright. I'm coming."

"Hurry up, it's not like we have all day to mess around down here." He saw movement in his peripheral vision and tried to turn to follow it but he only had time to feel the impact of something very large and hard across the back of his head before the lights went out. His last conscious thought was *Fuck, not again.*

Chapter Twenty-Eight

Max woke to searing pain in both shoulders. His blurred vision slowly came into focus. At first he thought he was floating in mid air, but a quick glance told him he was hanging from his arms, a few feet from the stone floor. His hands were tied to two strong ropes that led to hooks in the ceiling and pulled him up and out in an almost cruciform shape. With his arms spread far apart, all of his weight was borne by his shoulders. The burning pain he felt was from the rotator cuff muscles screaming from the strain. His whole body jiggled and began to swing as he whipped his head around to take in the scene before him. New bolts of agony shot through his arms.

His head still throbbed from where he had been struck and, judging by the blood that had dried across his shoulders and chest like a rust colored mantle, whatever struck him of the head had probably left a large gash in his scalp as well. He was missing a few very important things; most notably his clothes and his leg. He really wished he had his gun too.

The gray granite floor was just an achingly few feet below his right foot and he felt very unbalanced with his prosthetic limb gone; as if he was listing to the right. Max tried to remember what happened to him and he could not. The old fashioned crowbar encrusted with hair and clotted blood wielded by the goon grinning at him across the room gave him a bit of a clue as to how he found himself in this rather precarious position.

Max pulled on the ropes, setting himself swinging again. "What the fuck you smiling at, dipshit?"

"I see you are finally awake. I was beginning to fear that Nikko had done more damage than I would have preferred, Unbeliever."

Max turned toward the voice and tried to focus. "The name is Major Maxwell Bradley, United States Marine Corps, but you can just call me Sir, you fuckwit." Max's far vision swam wildly as he spoke, but began to settle down enough for him to see who had spoken. The cavern was much larger than the one on the other side of the wine cask and it was illuminated by several rows of portable tripod lights along one wall. Flaming torches guttered on the opposite wall, giving the light a flickering, orangish hue. They seemed more for some sort of freakish ambiance than any practical light source. The far wall was brick and Max recognized it as part of the villa's foundation. Someone had expanded the cellar out into the mountain long ago.

"Over here, Unbeliever. Please don't pass out again. I've been waiting almost all night for you to wake up."

Max turned his head to the voice again. Some crusted blood kept his left eye shut. With some effort, he forced his lids to open, and he could see his antagonist much better. Tall and aquiline, a mane of midnight black hair flowing across his shoulders, stood

Almos the Night Raider. He wore an expensive Italian leather jacket and blue jeans. Max's leg, gun, wallet and keys lay on a plain table next to him. Elena sat at his feet. Max focused in on her. She sat silently, but Max could tell she had not been crying, she did not look downcast in the slightest. She looked severely and inexorably pissed off.

Good girl. You take that hate. You embrace it. You fucking use it.

"You got my attention, asshole. How about you come on over here and let me kick your ass for you."

Almos smiled unpleasantly. "Pinioned as you are, you are no threat to anyone, but I'll stay over here, thank you. You see, there are limits to your powers." He pointed to the floor and Max saw a curved line in front of Almos that ran around the room before disappearing out of Max's peripheral vision. It was as if someone had chalked a gigantic circle around Max on the floor.

"As long as I stay outside the circle, I have full use of all of my abilities. If I step in, I become weak and human. Watch." Almos nodded to the thug with the crowbar who nodded back and then began to hover a foot or so above the floor like some Las Vegas illusionist. Slowly he floated toward the circle and as he passed the white chalk line, he abruptly fell with a smack of boot soles on the rock. Then, with a look of utter revulsion, he scampered back over the line. Max guessed that it was about twenty five yards distant.

What the hell is this shit? Flying?

Calm down. Magicians in Vegas fly a lot higher than that. He's messing with your mind.

"Just what the fuck is your damage?" Max asked aloud.

"You are the Unbeliever. You are your own force of nature and I am both humbled and horrified to have you as a guest in my home. I lost track of my little songbird many years ago; only catching the briefest of scents over the years. When I gleaned her purpose and the talisman she was seeking, I sent my...compatriots to find her. Little did I know that they would come across the most important find in the last millennia: you."

"Blah, blah, blah. If you are going to fucking kill me, kill me already, just don't make me listen to any more of this crap. I'd rather die than listen to any more pompous, egotistical, narcissistic bullshit."

"Oh, you may die soon enough, but you are much too valuable to kill offhand. You sir, are like an atom bomb to the unseen world. A powerful weapon indeed; not just against the undead, but all fey folk and those who use magic. With such power at my disposal I could command great respect and control over the supernatural and, by extension, over the natural. When such as I am faced with such as you, I have two choices: to destroy you immediately to remove the danger to myself, or try to use you against my enemies. I will try to convince you of the value of the latter, but have no doubt, I will destroy you in an instant if I must."

Max pulled on the ropes holding him and swung forward slightly. "Talking's a hell of a lot easier than doing. Come over here and we will see who destroys who. You want a piece of me, come over here and get it. Let the girl go and maybe I'll let you live."

"She is here because of you. Once I had you, unconscious and at my mercy, she was more than willing to trade herself and the dagger she possessed for your life. Sentimentality is a human weakness, is it not? She should have given up the last vestiges of humanity long ago. She just couldn't let that last little bit of hope go. Now see where it has gotten her: back to where it all began. Full circle."

Almos paced just outside the chalk line. "You see, you are that very rare thing among men: a man who is so utterly devoid of belief that your unbelief creates an irresistible aura in which nothing magical or what you people call supernatural exists. I have heard rumors and stories throughout the ages, but have never met anyone with this power. You are likely the only man alive who has this effect on us. We are in a very unique position. Join with me. We can achieve many things. Elena has promised to join me if I let you live. I will honor that promise if you come into my family."

Fat chance, buddy. That spitfire redhead will stick a knife in your belly first chance she gets.

"You got nothing I want," Max spat out.

"The girl? I'm sure you want her, but she is not what you think she is. In spite of her clinging to foolish emotions, she cannot deny her true essence. You are nothing but meat to her, just as you are to all of our kind. Cattle to be used for our nourishment, nothing more or less. She used you and she will come to realize this. She will cast you off as soon as she finally accepts what she is. Just like she used the little Capuchin monk in Madrid."

He prodded Elena with the toe of his boot. "You did not know that I knew about him? How you seduced him and made him show you the Florentine Codex? You promised him the eternal life that his pitiful religion, that his pitiful God hanging from broken tree, could not. He came to me after you left him, broken and despairing that he was damned for breaking his vows. He promised to tell me everything about the dagger of Tezcatlipoca if I would only spare him the fires of Hell by making sure he would never die. He was too weak. I enjoyed the look in his eyes when, almost drained completely, he realized that I was going to let him die after all."

Almos looked back up at Max. "The dagger also contains great power, more than you two could imagine. The life force of a hundred thousand victims is held within it and once I smash it, all of those souls will come into me all at once and I will be like a god."

Max grinned. "I sure as hell don't believe in you. You're just a lousy two-bit hustler and a fucking laughable movie super villain. I'll worship you all right: with my size ten boot up your ass."

"You have just a moment to choose, Unbeliever. Life or death. Join me and I will give you the girl for your bed."

"No. She was a lousy lay anyway."

"Riches."

"I got me a government pension, what would I need riches for?"

"I could give you your leg back."

"Fu...what?"

"Once I take the power of the dagger into myself, I will have the power to make you whole again. How would you like that? To be a whole man. To stride powerfully again on your own two feet. No more pity from the people that see you on the street. No more pain."

"How did you...?"

"I was a soldier once, just as you. I know how war can break men and I also know how nations throw their broken men away like so much refuse. I can give you what your country never could. I can give you your manhood back. I can make a warrior again. You would lead my foot soldiers in the expansion of our empire."

"Magic does not work on me. You said so."

"It is all about power. Enough power can overcome any obstacle. The talisman you brought me holds that power."

Max thought for a moment, swinging gently in the middle of the room. His whole body ached for another hit of oxycontin.

"Fine. Okay, but I get her too. Cut me down for crying out loud, this really hurts."

"Max, don't!" Elena cried, fear edging into her voice.

"I gotta do what I gotta do, babe. That is the best fucking offer I have had in years."

Almos gestured at Nikko, who walked into the circle and cut the ropes holding up Max. He ran back out as Max crashed to the ground.

Searing pain went through his leg as he landed stump first and toppled over. Max grunted in pain. "Thanks a fucking lot, dipshit."

Nikko smiled cruelly at his discomfort.

Almos smiled and picked up the dagger. "Watch, Unbeliever, watch the birth of a new age." He held the dagger in both hands and thrust the blade deep inside his abdomen with a grunt. Pulling it out, he held it up high and it began to glow with a flickering blue light. The crisp smell of ozone permeated the air. "With my blood, I have connected myself to it. I have added my blood to the blood of untold thousands before me and now it and I share the bond of blood. The souls contained in this vessel call out to me for release. I will give it to them and they will flow into me and I will have the power of the ancients."

We're screwed.

Shut up, I'm trying to think.

Are you a moron or do you just play one on T.V.?

What?

It's real. All of it. Vampires, magic...all of it. Look at the fucking lightshow for Christ's sake.

Almos held the dagger down upon the table with one hand and pulled a large iron mallet from behind the table with another, holding above his head.

Can't be.

Elena took out six guys with guns using only a piece of sharpened rock. You are in denial buddy. So secure in your own myopic view of the world and your place in it that you couldn't see the truth when it was falling from the sky all around you.

Almos laughed and brought the hammer down, the brittle stone shattering at the impact. With a blinding flash of light, shards of obsidian flew out from the table like shrapnel from a bomb, buzzing as they sliced through the air. Streams of brilliantly arching electricity sprang from the broken handle and shot into Almos where he had stabbed himself. His back arched and he threw his arms out wide, his mouth opened in a silent scream as the energy poured out of his mouth, nose, and ears. His body convulsed in orgasmic shudders.

Get out of my head!

You've lost buddy. If you would just fucking listen for once, in-

stead of being a goddamned John Wayne all of the time, you wouldn't be fixing to get killed by creature feature over there.

Max felt panic well up inside him as he realized the truth facing him in all its Technicolor glory. It shook his self-assured foundation to its core. He felt he was drowning and someone had just yanked the life preserver out of his hands. His entire frame of reference had been torn away and he felt his sanity began to go with it. If everything Elena said was the truth, then Max's wall of pragmatism had been a lie. Max felt something shift deep inside him. He felt a shift in his universe.

Nikko felt it too. Tentatively, he stepped into the chalk circle. He smiled when he did not feel anything change and he began to walk toward Max.

We are going to die now.

Max's emotions rolled over him. His doubt. His fear. He began to shake with pent up frustration and tears began to stream down his face. Nikko's smile widened.

You are letting Elena down just like you let your men down because you are stubborn and don't listen for shit.

Shut up. SHUTUP! I'm still a Marine. I'll always still be a Marine.

"Hey Almos!" Max yelled, voice cracking. "Fuck the leg, the one I got works just fine."

Heart breaker. Name taker. Still a Marine. Always.

He pulled himself up on his hands and knees and began to skitter straight at the table.

Gonna finish the mission no matter what.

As fast as he was crawling, Max knew he was not going to get to Almos while he was occupied with whatever the hell was happening to him. Nikko was only a few steps away and laughing as he reached for Max.

"Max!" came a shout. Max looked up. Elena grabbed the Glock off the table and threw it at him. It tumbled end over end as it came at Max like a pop fly on the first game of the season. He reached up and felt the plastic grip smack into his hand.

Max was not sure if he had gotten close enough to move his radius over Almos or even if it still worked, but he knew he had to take the shot before Nikko and his crowbar reached him. Now or never.

Everyone was wrong about Max not believing in anything. He strongly believed in the immutable laws of physics. He believed in his men and that with the right training and a large amount of guts, good Marines could do anything. He also believed in the piece of fine craftsmanship and precise Austrian engineering he now held in his right hand. He brought the Glock up in a two handed grip, knelt with the stump of his left leg bracing him, took a breath, and squeezed.

He pulled the trigger with every ounce of his belief. He had faith that pulling the trigger would send the firing pin into the primer that would send a shower of sparks into the load of gunpowder contained in the cartridge. He believed that the powder would explode with almost forty thousand pounds per square inch pressure, flinging the bullet out of the barrel of the gun at almost fourteen hundred feet per second.

Force equals mass times acceleration.

Max believed with absolute certainty that the bullet would fly spinning along the path of aim and impact at precisely the spot

Max wanted: the bridge of Almos' nose. The ten millimeter bullet, weighing just under a half an ounce, was still travelling over thirteen hundred feet per second when it struck Almos between the eyes.

Max knew that when the bullet punched into Almos' skull, the hollow point would cause the copper coated lead projectile to fail along engineered stress lines and deform and mushroom as it travelled into his body, the copper jacket spreading apart into the gleaming razor sharp petals of a deadly metal flower that tore through the frontal bone of his skull, bringing splinters of bone with it into his brain.

Kinetic energy equals one half mass times velocity squared.

As the bullet entered Almos' brain cavity, the bullet released most of its energy and caused the pressure to rise explosively in his skull, causing the back of it to explode outward in a splash of liquefied brains and shattered bone. The impact kicked Almos' head back and he gave one agonized cry before the lights went out in his eyes and he fell backwards to never move again. Everything that he was and ever will be was splattered all over the stone floor behind his body.

This I believe, forever and ever, Amen.

Chapter Twenty Nine

Max knelt, exhausted and shaking from the release of adrenaline. Smoke curled up from the Glock's barrel, the slide locked open on an empty chamber. Elena came to him.

"Max. Are you alright?" she asked. Concern filled her voice.

"Peachy keen," he replied roughly. "Better if I had my pants. A man is never more vulnerable when his Johnston is hanging out."

"Yes." She moved swiftly back to the table that was Almos' altar. "And your leg?"

"Yes, my leg too. I won't get far without it."

Elena hurried back and helped him on with his trousers. Max lay back against the stone floor. "Just give me a sec to get straight." He fished in his pocket and pulled out his pill bottle, cracked but intact. The oxycontin was in there, calling to him. Max could feel the weight of the pills in his hand.

Just one. Get straight first then get back to work.

Max could feel Elena's eyes on him. "Do you believe me now?" she asked in a whisper.

"What?" Max did not take his eye from the bottle.

"Everything. Do you believe it is true now?

Max looked up. "After all that? Hell yeah. So?"

Elena looked at him, expectantly.

"What? You think I finally admit there is vampires and shit and you think that I'm gonna explode or something. It doesn't work that way, honey. At least, I don't think it works that way. So what if there is doggone monsters? It don't change a thing. I still know who I am and who you are. I believe in me and who I am and what I can do."

"So sure of yourself," Elena said.

"More now than ever. Even more importantly, I am incredibly sure of you. I believe in you and that is more than enough for me." Max looked down at his hand, thought for a second, and then let the pills spill out all over the floor. "I got you, so I don't need these things any more either."

Elena frowned. "Will you be alright without them?"

"No. In fact, by tomorrow, I am going to be a quivering mess. But that is okay. I trust you. You will be there to wipe my brow and wipe my ass and get me through it because that is what people like us do for each other. Nobody fights for a cause or a pretty flag—not the grunts at least. Your regular schmuck fights for the other schmuck next to him. That is what it boils down to in the end. You take care of each other and you pull together and you get through it if you can." Max stroked her cheek. "You are my cause now, you are the schmuck who has to cover my six and I wouldn't have anyone else. You have my back and I have yours. That is how it is."

"Always," she replied.

"I know." Max reached for his prosthetic. "Now, let's pull ourselves together and clean out this shit-hole."

Chapter Thirty

One thing about rum, it mixes well with anything. Not just with coke or juice or even other booze, it mixes well with the sunshine and the sand underfoot and the smell of the sea air.

Max took another sip of his drink. *There's nothing like drinking booze out of a coconut.* Although he could not imagine where the hell they got coconuts on an island in the Adriatic Sea, but Max really did not care just as long as he finally got his drink. The coconuts and other amenities were probably there because the island of Hvar, just off the Croatian coast was the happening place for newly spawned capitalists from the former Soviet republics. Sandy beaches, beautiful deep azure waters, and beautiful people everywhere. That it was also a holiday spot for the Russian mob was not a bad thing either. Max was able to bankroll this nice little vacation on a few of the diamonds from his stash. He had been screwed on the exchange, but he did not care. Cash under the table had its advantages as well.

They needed a break after putting the hammer on that asshole back in Hungary, so what the hell. As soon as they hightailed it back to Budapest and spent a few days holed up getting through narcotic withdrawal together, Max had asked the ticket agent for the next flight to the nearest tropical resort and a few hours later, there he was: digging his toes in the sand and getting nicely buzzed. He had even managed to find himself a brilliant blue Hawaiian shirt and a straw hat to match.

When Almos lost his mind, literally, all hell had broken loose. That smug bastard Nikko took off at a dead run down one of the tunnels, and Max fired a few snap shots after him, but he lost the "vampire" in the gloom and he was not sure if he had hit him or not. No matter. Once he had his leg securely on, he and Elena made it upstairs and secured the cellar door by pushing a heavy kitchen cabinet across it. Then they gathered the spare gas cans from the garage and splashed the gasoline all over the first floor, pouring a little extra along likely avenues of escape.

Max ran through the villa, singing that song by the Talking Heads about burning down houses as he flung the gasoline over every surface he could find. Then they stepped outside.

A nice victory cigar would have come in handy at the time, but he had none and settled instead for a plain wooden match liberated from the kitchen. As the match tumbled into the nearest pile of fuel, Almos' manor house exploded into flame with a very satisfying *WHOOMP*. Max had checked the place for kidnapped girls before dancing around with the gasoline, but the house had been abandoned. Whether there had been no one else in there from the beginning or everyone had split as soon as the head honcho got his ten millimeter lobotomy, he would never know. What he did know was that no criminal, living or dead, would use that place as a base of operations ever again.

Max glanced at Elena in the beach chair next to him. She looked magnificent in an emerald green string bikini. It had taken some time for Max to tease and cajole her into it, as she was not exactly used to sunbathing. He finally succeeded, after much apologizing about the "lousy lay anyway" comment, but he failed to talk her into going completely naked, or at least topless like much of the comely young lasses parading up and down the beach. This did not worry him much either. He would see her without her bathing suit soon enough in their little rental cottage. For now, he was content to work on his sunburn, sipping booze from a coconut, and look at the girls walking by...when he was sure Elena could not catch him.

"So what now, oh partner in crime?" Max said to Elena's breasts.

"My eyes are up here, dear heart." Elena said and then laughed. "Find some more mischief for you to get into, I suspect."

"Maybe later. I was thinking of a backrub after lunch."

"Backrub, eh? I *know* what your 'backrubs' turn into."

"Hey, you can't blame a guy...you are one good looking woman. Where to after this, is what I meant."

"I want to live life to the fullest. I want everything that I was denied all those years. I want to do it with...you."

Max leaned back and pulled his straw hat over his eyes, settling into his chair with a contented sigh, "I'm not going anywhere. You see, I've grown rather attached to you. That would suit me just fine."

Elena gazed out over the water. "In that case, I think I had better tell you something.

"What's that, green-eyed girl."

Elena's strained voice came back at him, cutting through his pleasant alcohol fueled glow.

"I think I'm pregnant."

THE END

Epilogue

New Bern, North Carolina
3 AM

Agnes Pritchett stirred in her sleep. Like most nights, her sleep was fitful and she woke many times throughout the evening to make certain that all was well, as she had done so every night since the night her town had burned. She moaned softly and then awoke to a sound. Very softly, like the sound of moth's wings dancing on the window pane, she heard the gentlest of tapping.

Slowly, she opened her eyes and looked out across her bedroom. Her condo was on one of the upper floors and it was very unlikely that anyone would be on her balcony, trying to get in, but as she looked at the balcony, she could see a figure standing just outside.

With his bowler hat cocked at a rakish angle and still wearing the absurdly ancient vested suit with the gold watch chain twinkling in the porch light, the dapper man lightly tapped his long fingernails across the glass. It was if he was tickling the pane rather than trying to gain anyone's attention. When he noticed that Agnes was looking at him, he smiled broadly, doffed his hat, and resumed tapping on the glass of her balcony door.

"Well, just come in then if you are coming in," Agnes said angrily.

The man in the bowler hat's smile widened and the door slid open all by itself. He stepped in and, in his peculiar mincing gate, started to dance across the room to music only he could hear.

"Hello, Miss Agnes. We have some unfinished business you and I."

"That we have."

"You hurt me. You hurt me very badly, Miss Agnes, so long ago."

"You deserved it, you wretched thing."

"Is that any way to talk to the closest thing you will ever have to a lover, Miss Agnes? Someone whom you invite into your bedroom?"

"I'm too old to fight you."

"You were a good fight, indeed. When you hurt me and burned me, I had to hide myself away, I did. I hid in the ground and ate rats and worms, trying to get my strength back. It took a long, long time, Miss Agnes, to repair the damage you did to me. Then the others came, and I had to hide myself from them because they were stronger than I and they would have cut me down. They are gone now and I can hunt here again."

He walked closer and then noticed the book on her bedside table. He paused, took a step back, looked closer and then laughed as he picked it up. When he did, he brushed a pile of wooden shavings off the table and onto the floor. There was a small knife on the table as well, but he paid it no mind.

The dapper man sniffed the book like a hungry animal, recognizing the smell of his own blood on it, old and faded as it was. "This is what you used to drive me from your father's house? A history book? How delightful. It pained me like a holy book would have."

"A history book is holy to me, mister fancy man, and *The Rise and Fall* is the holy of holies to a librarian like me."

"Indeed." He let the book fall to the floor and slid closer.

"Pity. You were a beautiful girl once, firm and juicy, now you are old. A piece of dried fruit as it were. You should have let me take you all those years ago. You would have been forever young, forever beautiful. Now, because you hurt me so badly, I will take you now and you will be an old crone for all eternity. What will pain you more? The fact you missed your chance at eternal youth or the fact you will now be decrepit and bent and ugly forever."

"I'm tired. I'm old and tired. I can't sleep and I can't eat, so you might as well and do what you are going to do because I really don't care much anymore."

"Very well, Miss Agnes. I aim to please. This will hurt…a lot." With that he removed his hat and sat on the bed next to her thin frame and leaned over her. His jaws expanded and widened and exposed the multiple rows of razor sharp spiked teeth that Agnes remembered from the window at her father's house and saw every night in her dreams ever since. His breath was foul and reminded her of a dead animal left on the side of the road in the July heat. Obviously savoring the moment, the dapper man slowly lowered his teeth to her throat.

With an agility surprising for her age, Agnes pushed up with both hands an object she had hidden on her chest and under her bedclothes. The sheet tented up and into his chest and he grunted as the object penetrated his rib cage. The dapper man tried to push himself away from Agnes, but she rose with him, pushing hard the entire way. Blood began to run from his mouth and he gaped wide-eyed in surprise and fear.

"You left something behind a while back and I've been itching to return it to you." Agnes pushed hard on the silver handle of the dapper man's cane and it's end, whittled into a sharp spear point, punched through him and out his back, tearing a hole in the absurdly out of date brown suit coat.

He stumbled back and bounced against the wall, clawing at the end of the cane that protruded from his chest. He spun and gurgled and tried to scream and then began to fall apart in front of Agnes' eyes. His flesh dried instantly and then crumbled into powder. His bones fell apart and were consumed by a fire the briefly flared from his impaled heart. With a crackling sound, the fire faded and the ash that was all that was left of him blew around in a rush of air and was sucked out of the open door. The dapper man was no more.

Agnes smiled sweetly to herself. "Never underestimate the elderly. We make up in guile and cunning what we lack in physical strength."

She lay back in her bed, pulled the covers up to her chin, and finally drifted off into a deep, restful, and uninterrupted sleep.

Made in the USA
Lexington, KY
25 April 2013